# St. Martin's Paperbacks Titles
# by Susan Squires

*The Companion*

*The Hunger*

# The
# Hunger

## Susan Squires

St. Martin's Paperbacks

THE HUNGER

ISBN: 0-312-99854-6
EAN: 9780312-99854-7

Printed in the United States of America

St. Martin's Paperbacks edition / October 2005

St. Martin's Paperbacks are published by St. Martin's Press, 175 Fifth Avenue, New York, NY 10010.

10 9 8 7 6 5 4 3 2 1

*Simply put, this book belongs to Jennifer Enderlin. I wonder every day how I got lucky enough to have her as an editor.*

*Become a member and get access to special features about the world of the Companion at www.susansquires.com.*

# One

*The man lay naked on the thick Turkey carpet woven in intricate red and gold, sweating with his exertions. His body gleamed in the firelight. Beatrix watched Asharti run fingers through his blond hair and pull his head back. The baring of his throat, corded with muscle, inflamed her partner within. She trembled with its demands.*

*Asharti caught her eye, laughing, beckoning. "Will you sample him?" she asked in that low, throaty voice that spoke of heat and sand. Her nose was long and straight, her eyes dangerous black pools lined with kohl, her lips full and her body lithe and golden. Anyone would call her beautiful. Asharti wore a heavy red velvet robe meant to protect from the damp in this remote outpost left by the Romans, but tonight in front of the fire it hung open to reveal heavy breasts with prominent, dusky nipples peaked with excitement.*

*Beatrix looked down at the muscled male body. An English knight who had wandered into the wrong village. His sex was heavy against his belly. His eyes, which should be sated, were fixed hungrily on Asharti as she stroked his hair. The rich smell of blood hung in the air.*

*Beatrix managed to shake her head, though her veins itched with need.*

*Asharti shrugged, a derisive smile curving her lips. The only woman who understood her dilemma let her kohl-lined eyes go red; red like her velvet robe.*

LONDON, MARCH, 1811

Beatrix shivered, pulse throbbing. Sex and blood, intertwined. These were only memories. She mustn't let them overwhelm her. She shook her head to clear it. So long ago. Those things happened to someone else, surely, not to her. Who was she? She looked around as if the answer lay in the sumptuous room. Men smoked cigarillos openly, talking and drinking an '87 claret from her cellars under Venetian crystal chandeliers and paintings in heavy gilt frames. Her eyes fell upon the rounded lines of Regnault's *Venus*. The figure seemed so sure, so calm. She took a breath, absorbing her certainty.

There. That was better. She blinked. Her name was Beatrix Lisse, Countess of Lente, these days and she was holding court as she did every Tuesday and Thursday in her stylish house in Berkeley Square. Most of influential London society was here, or the male half at least. Not one of them would say anything she had not heard a thousand times before. But never mind that. She pressed down the desperation. Surprising—it *was* desperation, wasn't it?

Several young men gazed up at her, their chairs drawn close to the chaise in which she lounged. Some faces shone with expectation bordering on rapture. Stupid creatures! They believed her reputation as a courtesan. Others frowned in concern. Those were the ones who noticed her distraction. Maybe it was the hunger that left her vulnerable. Better that than madness. She launched into speech as a defense against that thought.

"You promised me the most debauched man in England, Melly," Beatrix accused the fashionable young fribble beside her. Perhaps a legendary rake would distract her from the darkness she felt growing inside her. "Where is he?" She leaned back with all the languid ease and mock annoyance they expected. They had no idea what real debauchery was, of course.

Apprehension fluttered through the circle. Their goddess was annoyed. Dressed in the silliest heights of fashion, they copied the Beau but failed to understand the extremity of his moderation. Their neck cloths were so enormous they could barely turn their heads. Their inexpressibles had ventured into pale yellow and dove gray. Behind the circle of unripe beaux were the prime movers of British society, ministers and lords, leaders of fashion, artists. They came for conversation, to drink champagne, and to be seen at Beatrix's salon. All waited to exchange *bon mots* with the newest intellectual courtesan. Some wanted more. One might get more tonight, though not what he expected.

"He . . . he will be here, Countess," the very rich and very impressionable Lord Melford promised. "He accepted the engagement before he left for his estates."

"I do not think this nonpareil exists." Beatrix let her mouth turn down.

"Oh, but he does," Alvaney protested. "He has rooms at the Albany House. I live in Number Four, myself, and see him frequently."

"And *have* you seen him?" Beatrix drawled. They mustn't sense her anguish.

Alvaney looked stricken. "Damnme! Can't say I have."

Beatrix managed a shrug of displeasure. If it was her need that left her open to the wash of memory, she could take care of that tonight.

"I . . . I could recite verses, Countess, for your amusement." Blendon's cheeks flushed crimson. They were all so absurdly young.

"I have already heard your verses," she said, surprised by her own gentleness.

"Ah, yes," he said, his blush spreading. "Yes, you have."

"They were quite nice." They weren't. But she liked the bashful ones sometimes. He wasn't the body type she preferred, but that was all to the good. His figure was slight. He would be smooth chested, almost without hair. So, perhaps Blendon. Behind him, Castlereagh, the secretary of the Foreign Office, and the chief secretary of Ireland, Wellesley-Pole, brother of Wellington, were talking politics. Beatrix held up one white hand. "Mr. Castlereagh, I beg you, no more about the question of Catholic emancipation. If they are masochistic enough to want to stand for office, why not let them?" Two young men tittered.

"The answer to that question might tear the country apart," Castlereagh protested darkly.

"Oh, I doubt that," Beatrix sighed. "You'd be surprised how much it takes to tear a country apart." Her task was to make it through the evening without another lapse.

"It is the milk shortage which is tearing my household apart," Melford pouted. "The cook blames the housekeeper, who blames the tradesmen for hoarding."

"Lady Wentworth says your complexion is the result of milk baths, Lady Lente," Blendon ventured.

"Now ladies are buying up the entire supply of milk to bathe in it!" Melford cried.

Beatrix sighed. It was really so easy to become all the rage. "Actually, keeping out of the sun is more important." Something interesting needed to happen here, something she had not seen a thousand times before, or she just might lose control again.

Blendon sat on a small footstool, gazing up at her. "Ladies are also pestering the perfumers for copies of your scent."

"Cinnamon," Lord Halmore said, joining the throng around her. "And something else. Will you tell us what?"

"That is my secret, my lord," Beatrix murmured. The real secret? She wore no perfume.

Nights like this stretched ahead. Gaiety alone could not hold the barricade. Art had always been her refuge. She glanced around at the medieval tapestries, paintings, Roman glassware, Chinese ceramics in delicate shades of celadon. How long could art shelter her?

Perhaps Mirso Monastery was the only true refuge for such as she was. The thought depressed her. She had never thought to come to that. But Mirso was better than madness.

Wellesley-Pole opened his mouth. He was going to take the conversation back to politics. She couldn't bear it. "Gentlemen, I have the headache. Do excuse me." She rose, whispered in Symington's ear, and withdrew, leaving shocked glances behind her. It would only fuel their desire to be invited back. The need in her veins ratcheted up a notch.

In the small sitting room that held her favorite paintings, her most treasured books, Beatrix steadied herself. Dawn in two hours. The last guests tottered to their carriages. The knocker rattled as the door closed. She heard it all clearly. Symington announced Blendon.

"Now, dear Blendon, we can be alone." She needed to get on with it. Time grew short.

Blendon blushed to the roots of his hair. "You . . . you honor me."

"Will you come up and help me take down my hair?" To be admitted to her boudoir to watch her toilette was a mark of distinction. To be chosen to undo those preparations was nirvana to the lucky man selected, because he thought his goal was at hand. It wasn't.

Blendon's eyes grew round. He nodded eagerly. He would have heard the legends of her lovemaking abilities.

Those legends gave her power. She trailed toward the great front staircase. Several discreet servants doused lamps. Darkness stalked them as Blendon followed her.

Beatrix felt the hunger ramping up inside her. She had denied her need for too long. That was her only problem. She picked up a branch of candelabra from a rococo side table. Shadows flickered across tapestries of hunting scenes, making fear flutter in the cornered roebuck's eyes and the saliva dripping from the hounds' teeth gleam. She could hear blood pounding in Blendon's throat. His breathing grew uneven in anticipation. He could never guess what would actually happen here tonight. If he did, he would run screaming into the street.

The desperation that hunted her lived in her memories of Asharti's evil and Stephan Sincai's teachings, surely, though she hadn't seen either of them in centuries. She didn't understand. Had she not spent her life fighting against becoming like Asharti? Always, when she fed, Asharti's evil closed in, urging her to let desire intermingle with the blood. But she didn't. She wasn't like Asharti. Not anymore. Still, in spite of her resistance the darkness gathered round her. She held out her candle against it, but the darkness was strong. It had consumed countless others. In the end, it would win out.

Beatrix pulled aside the heavy draperies and peered down into the square, calm now that her need was filled. The dawn turned the edges of the night to luminescent gray. Blendon stood in the street clad only in his shirt, looking bewildered. That would add to her reputation. They were so suggestible. She suggested that they had made ecstatic love. His imagination would fill in the details. They had not. She had not made love to a man in what, six hundred years? To think they all thought her a courtesan! That was rich. The longing for the act itself had become a distant impression, not even a memory. She let the heavy fabric fall, her protection against the coming sun, and turned into the room. At least she was safe from the memories, temporarily. But that thought alone seemed to spring a catch inside her, and memory flooded her . . .

AMSTERDAM, 1087

*The dress was red, not a virginal girl's dress at all. She glowed with pride as she smoothed her hands over the fine wool covering the budding swells on her chest. "Thank you, Mother," she whispered. It was a marvelous gift, a symbol of passage into womanhood.*

*"Yes, well." Her mother glanced at her and away. "Fripperies, no more."*

*Theirs was the biggest house inside the walls of a medieval city clustering around a port where ships from far-flung places unloaded their cargoes and their money. The stone walls were hung with tapestries to keep the cold out. Bea watched her mother as she sat at her toilet. The golden light of the smoking oil lamps made the room seem warm, even if it wasn't. Mothers just looked like mothers and it was hard to tell if they were beautiful. But she had heard many men say her mother was beautiful, so she knew it was true. She wanted to grow up to be just like her.*

*Bea's mother brushed her own lustrous dark hair until it gleamed. "You're growing breasts, Bea." It sounded like an accusation.*

*Bea shrugged to put off guilt. But the facts were hard to deny.*

*"Soon you'll be changing." Her mother's voice was hard.*

*"How, changing?" Bea asked in a small voice.*

*Her mother rose, rustling the heavy fabric of her trailing dress against the rushes on the floor. She looked down at Bea as though transfixed, then suddenly turned away and went to her jewel box. It was made of carved wood from the lands around the sea far away to the south. Her voice trailed back over her shoulder as she said, "It is time for me to move on."*

*Bea cocked her head. "What do you mean, Mother?"*

*"Our kind moves on every twenty or thirty years," her mother said with seeming carelessness. She hooked large, lustrous pendant pearls through her ears.*

*"Why?"*

*"People begin to notice that we never age after we reach maturity."*

*Aging meant nothing to Bea. She was fourteen. "Where will we go?" Bea had never known a place other than Amsterdam. Was it possible to uproot oneself and just . . . move?*

*Her mother looked sharply at her and then away again. "Somewhere else."*

*Bea knew that tone. She dared not press. Her mother's moods frightened her.*

*Her mother glanced up. "Oh, don't look so like a rabbit, Bea," she snapped. Then she continued, muttering, "You will soon find out that is not what you are."*

*"What am I?" Bea whispered, hoping the question made her seem less like a rabbit.*

*Her mother became brisk. "I have kept you to yourself, but surely you've noticed that you are not like other children. Or like Marte?" Bea just looked up, wide-eyed. Her mother threw up her hands. "No scabbed knees? No sickness of any kind? God knows you're such a little ruffian you must have realized you are stronger, you run faster than others? You can hear things they can't hear, see in the dark where they can't."*

*Bea said nothing. She did know she was different. She had been ashamed of it for some time now. Marte called her a boy because she was so strong.*

*Her mother looped a rope of pearls around her neck. It fell over breasts exposed by the deep square neckline of her aubergine velvet dress. She sighed in exasperation. "Well.*

*You'll learn. The way we all learn. I was never made for this sort of thing, you know."*

*What sort of thing did she mean?*

*"Who was to know I'd be saddled with you? None of us has had a child in as long as any can remember. Why me? I can't . . ." She was growing angry. Bea shuffled from foot to foot, anxious. "Oh, never mind. Get to bed. I'm going out." Her mother's throat seemed full.*

*Bea saw not only the familiar anger in her mother's eyes but something else. Shame? Fear? Bea's eyes widened for only an instant before she whirled to obey, her dress shushing through the rushes. She ran for her room. What had she seen in her mother's eyes?*

*She lay down in her fine red dress that night but sleep was far away.*

Beatrix stared at the high bed in Berkeley Square, still tumbled from Blendon's ecstatic experience of giving. That night so many centuries ago was the last time she saw her mother. She came home from church the next morning to find Marte dead, her mother gone. It was not surprising to her now. Her mother was ill equipped to deal with a child, let alone the turbulence puberty brought to their kind. A tiny flash of anger flared in Beatrix's breast. Could her mother not have left Marte as solace for her daughter during the terrible transition that came after? But perhaps Marte was doomed anyway. Better that Marte died at her mother's hands than Beatrix's.

Why did she remember that night with her mother now? Maybe that night was the beginning. She thought it was Stephan and Asharti, and the terrible time that followed. But maybe it had begun with her mother's . . . disinterest. She squeezed her eyes shut. That began the diminishment of her soul. What was left of her? And was whatever left of her worth fighting to preserve against the darkness?

She tried to brush away the thoughts as though they were cobwebs. Dawn always made her melancholy. She clutched her bloodred wrapper around her and crawled into the great bed, hoping slumber would protect her against her memories.

# Two

John Staunton, Earl of Langley, sauntered west on Piccadilly resplendent in breeches, evening slippers, a perfectly starched cravat, and a coat that fit so snugly he would need Withering's help to get it off again. He hoped the bandage on his shoulder was bound tightly enough that it would not create a bulge. He was due at Countess Lente's drawing room tonight.

Shop windows glittered with raindrops in the light of the new gas street lamps. Expensive hotels spread noisy revelry into the street. Green Park on the left was all night-black grass and the dancing silhouettes of trees in the spring wind. Two Frenchmen had paid for his wound with their lives in Calais. Had it already been nine days ago? He threaded his way up Hay Hill Street.

Movement caught his eye to his left and behind him. He spun in time to block the blow of a truncheon with his stick. There were two of them. No, three. Heavyset men. He got the impression of seedy clothing as he struck out at the nearest. His cane landed a blow across the ruffian's ear. He put an elbow into the one on the left's midsection as he took a blow to his good shoulder from a truncheon.

He managed to turn his back to the next strike and protect his wound. They descended on him. A blow landed on his forehead. Someone wrenched his wounded shoulder backward. He brought his heel down against a knee. It cracked. One of the attackers staggered back. The remaining two grappled with him.

He threw them off. Just enough room—he drew the rapier concealed in his cane. That made them think! John circled his point, watching the man with the broken knee try to straighten. "Well, lads," he panted. "Spoiling for a turnup?"

The one clutching his knee growled, "Get 'im, boys. 'E's just a dandy with a stinger."

The two still mobile rushed forward. John thrust his sword into an upper arm, but the other attacker laid a truncheon over his wounded shoulder. John staggered to one knee. Blows rained upon him. But he got his sword point up and found a belly. He knelt there, panting, as the attackers fell back.

"George!" the one holding his own arm yelled. "Ye're pierced!" The other assailant looked at the blood oozing from his belly with surprise. The ringleader turned to the ragged thug who clutched his knee. With two down and the leader's arm bleeding, the game was up.

"You'll pay for this," he hissed to John. They stumbled away, supporting each other.

John hung his head to steady his stomach. The slick night spun around him. Christ, but his shoulder hurt! His head throbbed. The edges of his vision went black and gold. He was losing his touch. Three, true, but hardly more than muscled hulks. It was his shoulder, that's all. After a long minute, he raised his head and tested his vision. The black and gold edges expanded ominously for a moment, then stabilized.

"I say, there, are you all right?"

A young man with long mustachios dressed in a

lieutenant colonel's uniform of the Twelfth Light Dragoons hung over him. John managed a smile. "Damned cutpurses."

"Bold buggers!" The young soldier grabbed John's elbow. "Let me summon aid."

John shook his head, as much to clear it as to decline. "I am steps away from Berkeley Square. I am expected there." That sounded inane. "I shall do, I assure you."

A carriage clattered by and a pair of gentlemen much the worse for wear inside could be heard slurring their intention to check in at White's. "I am going up Berkeley Street myself, if you wouldn't mind the company," the colonel said.

John ran his hand through his locks. "Not necessary, but my thanks to you."

The young dragoon raised his brows. "I was after the fact," he remarked, handing John his hat. "Excellent swordplay. Name's Ponsonby, by the by."

John placed it gingerly over the knot he could feel rising on his forehead. "Langley."

"Langley? No wonder those fellows got the worst of it! Gads, you've a punishing left! Saw you take a round with the Gentleman himself at Jackson's."

John sighed at Ponsonby's eagerness, and resigned himself to company.

"Your duel with Jepson November last? Let him have the first shot, calm as you please, and then knocked the gun from his hand with your shot. We all wondered you did not drill him. It was he who forced the quarrel." They turned up toward the square.

"Ah, but he was in the right." John let his tone be damping. "I had seduced his wife."

The young soldier smiled to himself. "When Sherry hears of this turnup . . . or Blendon!"

John was glad to relinquish Ponsonby to his engagement in Berkeley Street and continue into the square. Number 46 was a beautiful step-backed house of Portland stone, its great first-floor windows casting light and life into the darkness. John could see men lounging against butter-colored walls lined with tapestries and paintings. The sound of a cello and violin duet poured into the street. Boccerini. Before he lifted the knocker he straightened his cravat, pushing down the pain. He had torn his wound. But it was important that he be seen tonight. The word of the attack on him would spread, thanks to Ponsonby. An appearance tonight would minimize the whole affair. The evening would be insufferable, of course. He knocked at the unconventional blue door. An uneasy feeling rippled through him. Footpads in Hay Hill Street? Unusual. He mistrusted the unusual. The footman ushered him in.

Beatrix glanced up. There was a swirl by the door. Alvaney sprang to his feet. "There he is! I knew he wouldn't fail his engagement!"

"The Earl of Langley," Symington announced.

He was tall, but the shoulders were too broad for elegance. They spoke of strength beneath the perfectly cut black coat—understated, probably made by Weston. Her gaze strayed to his thighs. Beatrix required knee breeches in spite of the fact that they were slightly old-fashioned. She liked to be able to see the shape of a man's leg. Langley's were powerful indeed. His hair, nearly black and curling at his nape, was worn in a casual disarray not casual at all. The eyes were, remarkably, green with that black hair. His skin was fair and fine, a girl's complexion almost, but there were hard lines around his eyes and mouth. His lips were sensual, full, hardly manly, yet the overall impression was one of overwhelming masculinity. She watched him nod to his acquaintances. He was nearly negligent in his address. His gaze passed over the room sharply as though recording everything he saw, then his eyes went sleepy and hooded. Hmm . . .

"Two days late," Blendon noted sourly.

"You can't regret he failed us," Beatrix murmured. "He might have cut you out."

Blendon had the grace to flush. Alvaney dashed forward and collected the new arrival. "Beatrix Lisse, Countess of Lente, may I present John Staunton, Earl of Langley?"

The big man came forward with the innate grace of a man who knew the use of his body, whether in sport or in bed. He bowed over the hand she extended. The curl on his forehead concealed a lump just beginning to color and a scrape. The scent of blood came to her, strongly. Not from the scrape. No, the man was bleeding somewhere or . . . or his clothes had been splashed by someone else's blood. She saw no stain on his black coat. That augured for the blood to be his own. The scent made her need awaken and begin to tremble in her veins.

"I have waited for the pleasure of this introduction," Langley murmured over her hand as his lips brushed her knuckles. His voice was a baritone rumble in his chest.

"I did not expect you, so did not instruct my staff to refuse you tonight," Beatrix sighed.

Langley looked up, puzzled. "Lady Lente?" His countenance looked a trifle drawn.

"You were promised for Tuesday night, man," Alvaney exclaimed.

"Truly?" Langley looked about himself in surprise that Beatrix thought was feigned. He sighed. "Well, one can hardly expect an engagement made a month ago to spring to one's mind." He bowed again. "My deepest apologies, Countess."

The man should show more gratitude! Invitations to her drawing room were worth more than coin of the realm. "Your apology will be accepted upon account," she returned. "You may repay my largesse by being interesting." He wouldn't be. Still, she did want to know why he had appeared at her door bleeding.

His eyes flashed a spark of rebellion before they went lazy and the mask descended. "A hard charge," he murmured. "Since my hostess herself must be so interesting as to fill her rooms each night, her expectations would be great indeed."

Beatrix was taken aback. He had put the onus back on her to prove she was interesting. "That would smack of competition, sir. It would not become a hostess, and it would be churlish in a guest, so I am certain your manners would not allow it," she managed.

"They shouldn't, though manners can be unreliable in my case," he said, unrepentant. "A dangerous state, since manners are the only thing between us and our brutish nature."

"Oh, manners can be used as weapons in service of a brutish nature," Beatrix remarked sweetly. There, that would serve him out for challenging her.

He did not look abashed. Quite unexpectedly, he grinned. "Touché. Pique and repique." The grin softened the hard lines of his face.

She liked him for acknowledging that she had won the round. "A swordsman, then?" she asked, letting her voice go husky. She would fascinate him and so take point and match.

"Langley is quite the sportsman," Melly exclaimed. Beatrix had forgotten him. Strangely, she had forgotten all of them. "Bruising rider, crack shot. Strips to advantage at Jackson's too."

"I'll wager he does," Beatrix murmured. Langley feigned indifference, but Beatrix detected a slight flush. The most debauched man in London was used to being the hunter not the hunted. And yet, he was bleeding somewhere. Perhaps he had been hunted tonight.

"You're both uncommonly lucky," Alvaney noted. "You'd make a killing team at whist."

"Are you as insulted as I am, Langley?" Beatrix asked.

"Chance plays only a limited role in life when you have enough experience to be truly aware of your surroundings."

"Even in games like faro," he agreed. Behind his lazy look he was studying her. "But perhaps we should consult Castlereagh. He is an expert. There is nothing so chancy as politics."

He had decided to direct attention away from himself. She did not choose to let him. She sat forward in concern. "Dear me, my lord. Your forehead! Have you had an accident?"

Langley feigned surprise again. It would have fooled anyone but Beatrix. He touched his forehead. "Why, I hadn't noticed."

The other gentlemen crowded round. "By Jove, Langley, you're hurt!" Melly exclaimed.

"Husband come in on you?" Alvaney snorted. "We won't ask who she was."

Langley's countenance darkened before the eyes went languid. "Dashed footpads set upon me in Hay Hill Street. I hadn't realized they marked me, or I would never have presented myself in such a state."

"Footpads in Hay Hill?" the young men chorused. "What's London coming to? Where were the watchmen? Did you report the incident to Bow Street?"

"Sit down, man!" Alvaney charged, standing to give up his own chair.

Beatrix motioned Langley down. He looked mulish for a moment. Then practicality intervened. He must be feeling it. She noticed he sat stiffly. As he moved, she saw a slight bulge at his shoulder. Ahhh. The bleeding wound was in his shoulder and it was bandaged. Not a new wound, then. He definitely looked pale now.

"Symington, a glass of brandy for Lord Langley?" But her ever-discerning majordomo already hovered with a salver laid with brandy.

Southey, the pedestrian poet laureate, pushed to the front of the crowd. "I can hardly credit footpads in Hay Hill." Castlereagh and Chumley hung over Langley as well. Beatrix had lost the attention of the room. She took the opportunity to observe Langley. He gulped the brandy and the color came back into his face. He was deft with their questions, answering but not answering. It was if he *wanted* them to doubt the footpad story. Once he eased his shoulder and she saw the twinge of pain. He *had* been set upon in Hay Hill Street, but his assailants hadn't made the wound in his shoulder, only opened it, she guessed. And footpads? Not likely. Ah, perhaps it would not do for the most debauched man in England to be set upon by mere footpads, and he wanted his listeners to make up other stories more in keeping with his reputation. What a devious way of achieving it! If he wanted to shock them, why didn't he tell them about the wound bleeding even now in his shoulder and what adventure had occasioned it? Beatrix's senses were heightened by the smell. Lord, she would need to feed again tonight at this rate!

She got to her feet almost without knowing she rose, and took the brandy decanter from Symington. The young men parted for her, unconsciously, as people always did. She stood over Langley. He looked up at her. The green eyes were jaded. They had seen much for one of his tender age and were disgusted by it. How old was he? Not yet forty, she wagered. She gestured with the decanter and he held up his glass. She poured, but her gaze kept returning to his face. He had determination. He thought he was implacable. Silly man! Implacable was the onward march of time, the loneliness, the endless repetition of small failures and large ones in people, in the world, in herself. John Staunton, Earl of Langley, was not implacable.

He was . . . What was he?

All she knew was that Langley was not what he seemed.

• • •

John looked up at Countess Lente as she poured him another brandy. She was stunning in a way that was quintessentially un-English. Her skin was almost translucent, like the petals of a flower that bloomed only at night. Her hair was thick and dark auburn in color. It reminded him of fields burning at night. Her features seemed to speak of former ages. Her nose was straight and only two steps away from prominent, her mouth generous. Her cheekbones provided her face with an inner strength. He would not have been surprised to see her in a Roman toga, or chain mail. But it was her eyes that captivated. He had always been fond of cornflower-blue eyes. Both Cecily and Angela had had blue eyes. Brown eyes had always seemed dull, until now. Lady Lente's eyes were so dark as to be mistaken for black at a distance, yet up close they were bottomless pools of expression. Her eyes said this woman knew secrets men would kill to have her tell them.

Some of those men crowded round him. They fell back as she approached, like iron filings from the wrong end of a magnet. The minute he entered he had felt a hum of life in the room. Now it seemed to emanate from her. One would always know where she was, simply because her presence was so powerful. An elusive scent threatened his senses—spicy-sweet.

Her daring dress of strawberry silk revealed a lush figure. Pastels were fashionable, but fashion seemed irrelevant to a woman like the countess. Countess of what? he wondered as he tossed back the brandy. She was rumored to come from Amsterdam, but she did not look Dutch. Her accent seemed layered with several languages. And where was the count? Dead? Or had there ever been a count? A woman like this might have made him up to give herself a veil of respectability and an ability to move independently in the world.

Talk had it she was the most fascinating woman in

Europe. He hardly believed *that*. Still, he saw in her eyes more than the avaricious, self-centered courtesan. He saw that she had nearly lost hope. There was no . . . expectation in her. It was a strange feeling to look into eyes like that. It almost made one shudder.

"Feeling more the thing?" she asked, in that husky contralto that promised a passion her eyes said she was not sure existed anymore.

"Yes." He realized the room was silent, listening. In actual fact, his head throbbed and his shoulder stabbed pain through him whenever he moved. He must extricate himself from this soiree before he embarrassed himself by fainting in the middle of Countess Lente's drawing room. Still, his weakness could be turned to advantage. "An old wound . . ." he murmured. Let them embellish his rakish reputation. They didn't need to know it was only nine days old.

"Langley," Southey said with disapproval, "these husbands will kill you yet." Southey was bland-looking, with a certain smoothness about him.

"You, as a poet, surely must believe in the exigencies of love," John drawled.

"I do." Southey frowned. "But not the kind of love you practice."

"And what kind of love is that?" the countess interrupted. She arrayed her curves across the chaise in an insouciant challenge, and raised her brows.

"The kind where no heart is engaged," Southey said tightly.

"Ah, Mr. Southey, you cut me," John said softly. "You do. My heart is always engaged."

"Then your heart does not know true love."

John kept his countenance impassive. "Your true love, now, what is that? You will say it is transforming, enlarging." He waved a dismissive hand. "But perhaps it takes a narrow understanding to focus so intently upon one person that one sees no faults. I have a wide vision, Mr. Southey. Perhaps I see love more truly than you do."

"You are both right. Love is blind. But it never lasts," the countess agreed. "That only makes one search for it again and again, looking for that brief moment of transformation—an addiction, really. Are you an addict, Langley?"

"No." He should leave it there. What could possibly possess him to elaborate in front of this sad crowd? "That would admit both belief in the power of love to transform and a weakness I do not acknowledge. I seek amusement. My heart craves no more." Did he believe that? Or was it the devastation tossed at him twenty years ago speaking? It created the right sensation, however. A murmur went round the crowd.

"When the conversation turns to true love, it is time for the evening to end," the countess said, rising. She clapped her hands. "Carriages, gentlemen. The servants will see to your needs."

A bustle ensued. Apparently they were used to this kind of curt dismissal. The countess murmured over lips that bent to kiss her hand adieu. Rich young idlers, important politicians, artists, scribblers, an architect and an admiral, all filed by to pay their respects. They were besotted, though some cloaked it in urbanity. He stood to go.

"Shall I take you up in my carriage, Langley?" Melford asked. "You do not look stout."

"Lord Langley should recoup his strength before he goes," Lady Lente said. Her eyes held unmistakable intent. Blendon's face fell with comic intensity.

"As you wish." John nodded, letting her know it was her command that he obeyed, not his desire. Once he would actually have stayed. The countess would be a skillful bedfellow. It would certainly enhance his reputation, and hers, as she probably knew. But he didn't entangle himself these days and he daren't expose his wound. He could get the desired effect simply by lingering a moment. John closed his eyes briefly. What would these fellows think if they knew that it had been months since he had bedded a woman? Hardly an ecominium for his reputation. In truth, it had been getting more and more difficult. Not physically. He had not failed himself or his partners yet. But he could foresee a time when he would. It seemed a larger and larger effort to . . . engage with women, even in so transitory an act. On the Continent, he had bedded everything in sight. Hard, cold, he had his revenge on women everywhere for Cecily and Angela. He was lucky he had not come away with a souvenir of promiscuity. But it had all turned stale. Now he might bed them for king and country, and his needs still got the better of him on occasion, but he had no taste for it. He had no taste for any of it.

He watched the men exit. The countess was shushing Blendon out the door when John rose. He was about to refuse an invitation any man in London would kill for, he was sure. He managed a fair imitation of steady on his feet. "I must be going too, kind hostess."

Her delicate brows drew together. Apparently she was not used to refusal. "As you will," she said, her lovely, throbbing voice almost flat. "Perhaps our paths will cross again."

He smiled. "I do not doubt it. You hold court on Tuesdays and Thursdays."

"By invitation only, of course," she murmured.

"Then perhaps at other events." He would not give her the satisfaction of seeing him disconcerted. "The Duchess of Bessborough's ball on Saturday?" He doubted she had been invited. Countess or no, she was a woman who lived outside society's rules. And he wanted to punish her for making him feel small.

"Undoubtedly," she said smoothly. "Or Lady Hertford's rout?"

"I live for the occasion," he said.

He bowed once and trotted with a fair imitation of insouciance down the stairs to where the servants waited with his hat and cane and cloak.

Impossible man! Now here she was, all agitated by the smell of his blood and no man to satisfy her. He could not have doubted her intent. Had any man ever actually refused her?

Beatrix ran up the stairs to her boudoir, trailing her shawl of black Norwich silk. Perhaps he doubted his ability to perform, since he thought she wanted a sexual encounter. That must be it. He was weakened by loss of blood and the attack. When it came to that, she could not have taken blood in good conscience from one faint from loss of it. What had she wanted?

Betty helped her out of her gown. Beatrix hoped the girl could not see her state of confusion. She shushed her dresser out of her boudoir impatiently. Taking deep breaths, she willed her blood to quiet. It trembled rebelliously in her arteries. She breathed again. Slowly, the one who shared it slid down her veins. The pounding slowed. She sighed, in control again.

But was she truly in control? She felt herself sliding down a slope she had been on for many years. At the bottom was a black pool she recognized but did not understand . . .

*AMSTERDAM, 1088*

*The servants were gone, the house closed up. Beatrix haunted the muddy alleyways and the winding, narrow streets in her ragged red dress. She wanted her mother. She wanted Marte. But they were gone. Marte's neck was broken, and her mother had . . . left her. Just left her.*

*She hadn't been good enough to love. And what would her mother say about her now?*

*The nuns had apprenticed her to a seamstress and told*

*her an orphan was lucky to get such a place. But the woman
sent her out in daylight on errands, and sunlight grew
more and more uncomfortable. Her skin burned and her
head ached until one morning she refused to go outside.
Her rebellion provoked a beating that looked to be the
first of many. Beatrix had slipped out into the comforting
darkness that night, never to return.*

*Now she foraged in the refuse behind taverns and slept
in the livery curled in the hay at the horses' feet, with only
their breath to warm her. But no matter how much she ate
these days, she was hungry. Was it hunger? It was a kind
of itching, unfulfilled feeling and it was growing.*

*Tonight, it was worse than ever. She wanted to scream.
She stole a whole meat pie from a street vendor and tore
through the twisting alleys with all the speed she could
muster to the marshes beyond the walls of the city. When
she was alone, she stuffed great gobs of the pie into her
mouth until she choked and retched.*

*But it didn't stop the aching, itching hunger. On all fours
in the mud by the side of the raised stone road, she gasped
for breath. How could she make the pain and the throbbing
in her head go away? She couldn't think! The smell of fecund rot surrounded her. A horse clopped on the road far
away. Sensations assaulted her. She wanted Marte. She
wanted . . .*

*She wanted the warm cup of blood her mother brought
her sometimes at bedtime.*

*Of course! Blood would stop the hunger. The clop of
the horse's hooves sounded louder. She had tried to get
her favorite treat before. Her mistress-seamstress did not
keep any in the house. The vendors in the marketplace
sold blood for sausages and puddings, but she had tried
that blood and somehow it wasn't the same. Where was
she to get it? Mother . . .*

*Sobs shook her as the last of the pie came up into
the muck among the rushes. She could hear the horse*

*breathing as it came closer, and another breath, the rider's, and the throb of . . . of blood. She stood, the weight of her soaked wool dress comforting. He was a big man, richly dressed. She saw well in the dark. And he throbbed with what she needed.*

*Why was everything so red? Were they burning the fields? Smoke sometimes turned the moon red . . . She breathed out. She was strong. And the man on the horse had what she wanted. Needed. Throbbing there in his throat. The horse drew abreast of her. She closed her mouth and felt a stab of pain in her lip. She could smell her own blood welling there. The redness deepened and with it came certainty entwined with that smell.*

*She sprang up to the road and pulled the man from his horse. He hit the ground with a thud. A whoosh of air escaped his lungs. The horse neighed in fear and wheeled away. But she had eyes only for the throbbing in the fat man's throat. She fell on him, growling, tearing at his neck. He screamed and thrashed, but the scream turned into a gurgle, and there it was, blood, welling in sweet copper-tinged ecstasy into her mouth. She sucked at the ripped flesh and felt . . . alive. Her itching pain subsided. The man's blood stopped pumping.*

*She raised herself from the wreck of a man. Dimly she knew that his throat was ripped and that she had ripped it. His eyes dulled and his thrashing stilled. When someone saw him, they would say he had been killed by a beast, or a monster. Her mother said she was different. Now she knew how. No wonder her mother left her.*

*She turned her face up to the moon, cold, sure, its cycles predictable, once you knew their secret. She had found the secret tonight to the hunger. And she felt strong. Like a strong monster.*

Beatrix ran her hand over her eyes and massaged her temples as though she could rub away the memories. *Couldn't you have told me, Mother, what I was? Couldn't you have showed me that it didn't have to be that way, ripping throats and killing them? I thought I was evil.*

It was Stephan who told her about the Companion in her blood that made her who she was. Her mother deigned to give her human blood sporadically during her childhood, to keep the Companion quiescent. But when the Companion started to manifest itself and its powers at puberty, her mother had abandoned her, not wanting to be burdened with the role of mentor. That fell to Stephan, and worse yet, Asharti. But she wouldn't think about that, or what followed.

Damn these memories! She had put all this aside hundreds of years ago. She was beyond the hurt, and she avoided evil these days. What did it mean that the memories came back so insistently now? Whatever it meant, it wasn't good.

She turned to the huge bed. Tonight she would not even have the distraction of feeding her Companion. She stepped out of her dress. It was Langley's fault. She shouldn't need blood for a week or more after Blendon. But the scent of Langley's blood had sent shivers of life along her veins. The Companion yearned toward life with an intensity nearly impossible to resist. The rush of life when she was feeding was one way she staved off madness, and also the closest she came to losing control. A thin line. But she didn't lose control. She hadn't with Blendon.

Beatrix shrugged out of her chemise, grabbed a silken gown from her dressing room and pulled it over her head. Then why had just the smell of blood begun that throbbing fervor in her veins? She teased the pins from her hair and let the auburn mass hang down her back. Langley. Something about Langley himself. She sorted through her memory of this evening. He was well made, but so were a thousand other men. She was impervious to men's physical charms. An elusive expression around his mouth and eyes said he wasn't as hardened as he pretended. He was hiding something; his wound, but more. That was it! As an expert at hiding, Beatrix recognized secrecy, even when it masqueraded as disdain. What did he hide besides a wound?

She wanted to know more about Langley.

As she pulled the heavy draperies tightly over the window, it occurred to her that she really could not invite Langley for Tuesday's drawing room after she had so pointedly snubbed him. Of course he had snubbed her in return by assuming that she would not have a card for the Duchess of Bessborough's ball on Saturday. Which meant he was likely to be there. She crawled into the great bed and under the duvet. She didn't have a card, of course. But that could be remedied.

At Number Six, Albany House, Withering opened the door, having clearly disobeyed John's order not to wait up. He took one look at his master and gripped his arm.

"Don't be an old woman, Withering," John protested. "Footpads, that's all."

"You've started your wound bleeding, my lord, haven't you?" The man was fiftyish, mouth drawn down in a perpetual frown, his dress simple and impeccable. He had been with John through thick and thin. "I did, if you recall, my lord, indicate that this was a distinct possibility if you insisted on going out this evening."

"I acknowledge your moral superiority without reservation," John muttered as Withering guided him firmly to the bedroom. The room swayed ominously.

Realizing, apparently, that victory over an opponent who was very near to fainting was easy sport, Withering relented. "Let us just examine your wound, my lord."

After the painful process of extricating him from his coat, John lay back on the bed and gave himself over to

Withering's ministrations. To avoid hearing Withering's predictions of permanent disability, John let his mind wander back to the countess. He could see why she had the town in thrall. She was exquisite, of course, but London had her equals in beauty. No, there was something about her . . . a weariness, the subtle air of having seen everything and of knowing the danger in that. He shook himself. Of course a courtesan had seen everything. But there was more. She teetered on some edge and the town held its breath.

He grunted in pain as Withering tightened a fresh bandage about his shoulder.

"You should have the doctor in, my lord." That was a familiar refrain from his valet.

"I can't afford speculation." Or at least more speculation than his reputation provided. Let the *ton* think him bad. Let mothers and their daughters cross the street as he passed. But they must not guess his double life. Only Withering knew about John's other calling, except for Barlow and one or two others in the government. Of course, his valet never knew the particulars of John's missions, or anything about Barlow. Still, it was almost a comfort to have one person aside from Barlow with whom there was no need to dissemble. John was no fool. Barlow cared only for his usefulness. John *was* useful, the best the underdog British had against Napoleon in a war that had grown frighteningly one-sided. When Barlow ordered him to ferret out what was going on in France, he would do it.

Something was going on, that was certain. Four British agents dead, all in the same grisly and unlikely manner. Barlow hardly credited John's report that the bodies were drained of blood. The French intelligence service had grown strangely effective. Rumor had it there was a new head man. But he and Barlow would put a stop to these atrocities. He set his jaw.

That was it! That was what was so intriguing about the countess! She had secrets, just as he did, and he would bet they were pips. Withering poured some laudanum, but John shook his head. He liked to have his wits about him. Wits. What wits? Here he was mooning over a woman who was like all the other women he had known in his life, not a shred of virtue, no honor . . .

The secret that disturbed him most was that he wanted to see the countess again.

# Three

Withering's dire predictions may have been off, but John was definitely not feeling quite the thing on Friday. He stayed in his dressing gown most of the day, and while he refused the man's offer to fetch a doctor, he did submit meekly to Withering's ministrations and drank the familiar concoction of raw eggs and pepper without complaint. He was about to accede to Withering's offer to procure an early supper to eat in his rooms, when a message was sent up by the doorman from downstairs.

The seal was Barlow's. "That will be all, Withering," he said sharply as he tore open the envelope. He glanced over the single line. "Supper at Brooks's upper rooms. Nine. Barlow."

"Withering," John called. "I'm eating at Brooks. Set out some neck cloths." Had Barlow discovered the identity of the spider at the center of the new French web of spies already?

"Yes, my lord," Withering said, sighing.

In fact, it felt good to get out into the brisk March air as John strode down Duke Street. It was not far to Brooks, where Barlow had engaged a small private dining room.

They talked of inconsequential matters through the Dover
sole and the saddle of venison with its accompanying array
of winter vegetables. Barlow was an old man, with beet-
ling brows that inched across his forehead like caterpillars.
He had been sick when John left for France last, so sick
John hesitated to go. But tonight he seemed in the pink of
health. Even his normally gouty foot did not bother him.
John wondered whether he should tell Barlow about the
footpads who might not have been footpads. He wasn't
certain they were anything but what they seemed. As the
trifle was served, John mentioned a hot tip for the spring
meeting at Newmarket. "Gone to Grass," he said, as the
waiter left a decanter of brandy, a tray of cheeses, and a
box of cheroots. "Turvey has got a new training method.
You should see his horses run."

The door closed softly behind the waiter. Both men
lighted their cheroots. The smoke blended with Barlow's
lavender water scent. He was wearing a touch too much.
John drew on his cigar and sat back, watching Barlow ex-
hale and slosh the amber liquid in his cut-crystal glass.
"You did not invite me to dinner for the pleasure of
watching me smoke."

Barlow glanced up, his old eyes sharp. "We may have
acquired a way to the information we need," he said
slowly. "But there is a slight problem."

Did he know already who the new spider was at the
center of the French intelligence web? The man was
amazing. John chuckled. "Nothing you can't handle."

"Don't be so sure, young man," Barlow chuffed, "until
you know the situation."

John took no offense. The situation must be difficult
indeed to make Barlow so touchy.

"A French operative familiar with the highest circles of
French intelligence was on a frigate that escaped the blockade at Brest," Barlow said. "He was among several passengers let off in Spain who made their way to Gibraltar."

"Sounds promising. I'm sure our intrepid compatriots in the navy picked them up."

Barlow's shaggy brows snapped down. "His name is Dupré."

"Your interrogators are very good at getting Frenchmen to 'parler.' " John took a sip of brandy and watched Barlow. The old man was really quite agitated.

"When you question a man rigorously you get false information. It won't do."

John didn't want to think about Barlow's definition of "rigorous" questioning. That was part of the business. The poor French sod would be singing like a canary, naming everyone and anyone. John drew on his cheroot and watched the smoke curl up toward the ceiling. "You want me to gain his confidence and ferret out his secrets."

Barlow nodded. "You'll pose as a fellow prisoner. Your French is perfect."

John's mind clicked ahead. "It can't be anywhere prisoners are kept in separate cells. It would take too long to get close to him. How about a prison hulk in Portsmouth harbor?"

Barlow leaned forward eagerly. "Excellent idea! You'd be housed together under nominal guard. Easy to get him to trust you . . ."

"If I can find out what you want to know, you needn't interrogate the wretch at all. That will conceal that there has been a leak, which will preserve the secrecy of our effort."

Barlow's smile was that of a predator crouched over his prey. "Exactly."

"Where is he now?"

"Somewhere in the Atlantic making his way back to England. I got the news from a navy cutter. The frigate will be a week behind. A week to get the prisoners settled in the hulk . . . Expect to hear from me in a fortnight."

John gulped the last of his brandy and stubbed out his

cheroot. "I'll be ready. Portsmouth in April. Sounds like quite a little vacation."

Barlow stared at the end of his cheroot. He had something else to say. John remained, one leg stretched out before him. "I don't think we have ever had a man in the field who knew quite as much of the overall picture, the positions of various agents, as you do."

John schooled his face to impassivity. "Your agents don't normally last long enough."

Barlow nodded, thoughtful. "You are a precious commodity. Perhaps we shouldn't send you after this particular information."

John held his breath. "So either you think I would become a double agent, or that under torture I would reveal too much." There were two answers to that problem for Barlow. Barlow could retire him or kill him. John didn't like either of them.

Barlow's old eyes rose from the tip of his cheroot to John's face. "It is a danger."

"I've a fair tolerance for pain." He wouldn't answer the question of being a traitor.

"All men break, boy."

"But you have no one better. So shall we save this conversation until after we find the center of this French web?" John sauntered to the door. "I shall expect to hear from you."

"You will," Barlow muttered behind him.

John slid down the back stairs of the club. He was glad he hadn't told Barlow about the footpads. It would have given him another excuse to send someone less capable than John. The truth was, he only felt alive with the adrenaline of a mission pumping through him.

His thoughts glided back ten years, twelve. When had he become what he was? After traipsing around the Continent, fleeing from the world's derision and from Angela, life seemed empty. Then, while drinking an archduke under the table in Vienna, he had come into possession of some very interesting information. When he woke the next afternoon, he realized his country might well have use for that information. John grimaced. Langley, volunteer spy. He had vowed to spend his life loving his country if he could not bring himself to love women. Painful, how romantical he had been even at what, twenty-seven? He thought having sex with women instead of loving them made him callous. What did he know then? That was before the killing, before he realized he was an expendable commodity to his government, before he knew what dragging oneself through the dregs of humanity could do to you.

He wondered what he would do if Barlow ever retired him. He couldn't imagine how flat life would be without even this slender purpose. *If* Barlow left him alive . . .

Beatrix alighted in front of the imposing façade of Bessborough House, escorted by a young colonel of the Twelfth Light Dragoons, Fredrick Ponsonby, who just happened to be the son of the Duke and Duchess of Bessborough. Friday had been positively interesting. Only one night to procure an invitation to an exclusive engagement whose hostess was notoriously picky about the *ton* of her guests. Beatrix always made it into mainstream society in the end, but the duchess and her ilk were the last bastions to fall. A challenge. In fact, her focus on Langley's dare had kept the memories at bay for almost two days.

The only real risk had been the time frame. She had risen at dusk and sent for her dresser. Betty hardly needed prompting to provide more information than Beatrix could ever want about the duchess. When Beatrix found she had a callow if courageous son, the plan was set. A personally worded note to his rooms, an evening of solo attention; so simple really. Men just liked to be appreciated. A sighed disclosure that she was not to be of the party the following night, and . . . the card of invitation had arrived at ten in the morning Saturday.

A courtesan in such a situation had two choices. She could seek to blend into the crowd, looking more demure, more *acceptable* than anyone. Or she could choose to stand out, and damn the eyes of those who thought she shouldn't be there. Beatrix always chose to stand out.

Now as she ascended the stairs to the great stone portico of Bessborough House, Beatrix exuded calm. Her sable cloak and muff were proof against the raw March wind. Underneath, she knew her deep russet gown of heavy satin would be the envy of every woman in the room, no matter how spitefully they whispered that the color was too deep to be fashionable. She did not care for the tiny puffed sleeves in fashion, so she had her dressmaker lengthen them to the elbow, and slash them as was the fashion in the sixteenth century, with creamy lace peeking out at the slashes. The tiny rim of lace at a square neckline so décolleté she looked in danger of spilling from it at any moment echoed the slashes. She wore garnets, rust red and spread in a net of gold over her breast, and in pins winking in her hair and at her ears.

She let the footman take her wrap. *He* might not be here if he had not recovered from his wound. A niggling worm of disappointment wound through her. She pressed it down. She was here because it amused her to accept his challenge. If he happened to see her, he might appreciate the opportunity he had refused the other night, but that was nothing to her. Of course, she could not really hold his refusal against him if he thought himself too weak to do his part. Did that mean she would grant him another chance? She and Ponsonby ascended the staircase.

"May I present Beatrix Lisse, Countess of Lente?" Ponsonby made the introduction to his parents just inside the doorway to the great first-floor ballroom. Beatrix could feel the duchess's disapproval. But Beatrix had been disapproved of by better women than the duchess. She smiled at the woman, once beautiful, an intimate of the Prince Regent, and let her gaze rove over the Pomona green robe and feathered turban. She inclined her head in a curtsy just pronounced enough not to be rude, but hardly obsequious.

"Lady Bessborough," she murmured. "Thank you so much for inviting me."

The duchess looked stunned. Beatrix could feel Ponsonby redden. Of course his mother hadn't known. "Do enjoy yourself," Lady Bessborough said, her mouth a moue of disapproval.

"Thanks to your so dear son, I'm sure I shall," Beatrix murmured and moved on. Let the good duchess worry about that one for a while. From the doorway, she surveyed the crowd while Ponsonby stuttered his excuses to his mother. She did not see the tall form she was looking for.

Wait! There he was. Over in the corner, watching, though most people of dancing age were engaged in the center of the room. His eyes were just as cynical and green as she remembered. She saw him glance toward the entrance without expectation, as though he had been glancing there all evening, and had the satisfaction to see his gaze arrested in recognition. She stared boldly back. Touché. She was here.

Ponsonby stepped to her side, following her gaze. "Langley," Ponsonby cried and raised a hand. He turned excitedly to Beatrix. "I saw him make hash of three bruisers in Hay Hill Street Thursday night. Pluck to the backbone. Might we inquire after his health?"

"Of course," Beatrix murmured. "I am quite interested in his health."

Ponsonby shepherded her across the floor toward Langley. "Langley, I say, did you survive your ordeal? I'll wager you had the devil of a headache!"

"Nothing to speak of." He bowed. "Lady Lente." His

forehead sported a colorful bruise under his careless lock of hair.

"Surprised to see me?" she asked, one brow raised.

"Not at all." He made his mouth quite serious. "I have been expecting you this hour."

But Thursday he thought she wouldn't have a card. Suddenly she realized that if he knew she had procured one just to meet his challenge, it put her at a disadvantage. How maddening that she was predictable!

"I say, Langley, how do you know the countess? You have been out of town for a month!" He looked from one to another. "Berkeley Square . . . You can't mean you were on your way to . . . when you were—"

"I was promised to the countess that night," Langley agreed.

"Actually he was promised Tuesday and was two days late," Beatrix observed.

"I did move heaven and earth to keep the engagement." Were his eyes laughing at her?

"No. You only moved three thugs by Ponsonby's account."

Langley's eyes shifted lazily to the younger man. "So, you are Bessborough's son."

Ponsonby clicked his heels and bowed. "Your servant."

"I hear the Twelfth Light may be leaving for the Peninsula shortly."

"I haven't heard those orders," Ponsonby said, startled. "Not but what I'm eager to see some action. Our boys would love to be in the thick of it with Wellington."

"He shows promise as a general," Langley agreed. "Not that anyone in the government seems to care. They keep him short of specie and supplies, and he gets half the men he needs."

"Not everyone understands the important role of the Peninsula in the overall strategy of the war," Ponsonby exclaimed. "If we show Europe Boney is not invincible, insurrections will bloom across the Continent like May flowers, and the alliance with Russia must surely collapse."

"But if the puppet regimes are brought down, what will replace them? Weak governments in exile or awkward coalitions . . ." Langley shook his head shortly and was about to continue.

Beatrix clapped her hands. "*No* politics." They started. "Politics bore me."

"And is that the measure of a subject's worth?" Langley drawled, recovering.

"Courtesy should prevent your wanting to bore your companions," Beatrix observed.

"Perhaps," Langley said to Ponsonby, "the weather will turn fine tomorrow. Do you expect wind?"

Ponsonby glanced nervously to Beatrix.

"I expect very windy conditions, if tonight is any indication," Beatrix observed dryly. The orchestra struck up a waltz. She could feel Ponsonby gathering himself. Taking the offensive, she turned to Langley. "Is your shoulder sufficiently recovered for a waltz?"

She saw with satisfaction that she had disconcerted him, if not for brazenly asking him to dance, then for the fact that she had ferreted out his secret wound and he wasn't sure how.

"I am always game for a waltz." He extended his good right arm, while Ponsonby gaped.

She laid her hand on his forearm. The fabric of a shirt, her glove, and his coat lay between them. Yet it seemed she could feel his strength, the warmth of his body, the physicality of him, all in forearm laid to forearm. Dear God, but he felt male!

Langley led her to the floor, leaving Ponsonby looking about himself. Langley nodded, amusement lurking in those green eyes, and clasped her waist with his right hand. He held his left out resolutely at the correct angle, though Beatrix noticed the twinge of pain he masked so carefully. Beatrix stared up into his eyes as she laid her left hand on his undamaged shoulder. Couples whirled around them as they stood, a still center to the music. Almost lazily, she placed her right hand in his left. He held her gaze as he stepped into the dance. His carriage was erect but not stiff, as graceful as she knew he would be. What was it she liked about waltzing? Was it that the steps were not predetermined as they were in country dances? One had to feel them. If one was a woman, one had to follow. Perhaps that was what fascinated her. What other time did she give herself over to the direction of another?

But here, whirling in the dance, she followed him, floating on the music. He was a skilled dancer as she knew he would be. He held her rather closer than was usual, but that was not unpleasant. She felt the music lifting them, his hands on her body, more intimate than was ever allowed in public otherwise. She could smell him, that clean, human male smell. He wore no scent other than the soap he had used to wash and shave. His wound was healing again. There was no smell of blood, thank God. Blood would have been too much for her, close as she was. She closed her eyes and felt his body guiding her. He glided between the other couples, and she ceded all her cares to him. The room whirled. The other couples drifted away until it seemed as though the room and the music belonged to them alone.

"Can we not even speak of weather, then?" he whispered, bringing her back to herself.

"There is no weather here." Beatrix was trying just to breathe.

"No," he agreed and held her infinitesimally tighter still. "Perhaps I should engage in gallantry. I admire your scent. Spicy. It is exotic."

"Cinnamon," she said. "And ambergris." There, she had told him a secret. Why? A constriction rippled through her. What was she thinking? They were practically from different species. The Companion changed everything. She pressed down some half-formed longing and gazed up at him. His purpose was to keep the darkness at bay. That was enough.

"I like it," he murmured. The music whirled to a halt. He held her for a moment longer, though he lowered his left arm to ease his shoulder.

His lingering touch said she had hooked him. Good. By the time he dropped the arm clasping her waist and turned into her, taking her other hand and laying it along his arm, she knew he was fascinated. His refusal two nights ago was only because of his health.

They walked toward the great windows, cracked open to let air into the room. She felt flushed. Ponsonby was nowhere to be seen. Beatrix dismissed him without another thought.

"No hazards on the way here tonight?" she asked.

"Ponsonby would have it that they were dragons. Believe me, they were not."

"Ah, the young are overawed by someone of your reputation." She waved a hand.

He reached for glasses from the silver tray of a passing footman. "Champagne is your drink, I believe," he said, handing her a glass. "And what is my reputation?"

"A sportsman. What does one call it here in England? A buck, an out-and-outer. And of course, they say you are the most decadent man in England."

He nodded. "Yes. That."

"What could you possibly have done that someone such as I would consider depraved?"

His countenance darkened. He frowned briefly before he consciously smoothed his brow. He said in a light tone, "I expect it has to do with the affair I had when I was eighteen."

"Affairs," she said with a small snort. "What boy of eighteen does not have affairs? I suppose it was with an older woman. What will these country squires not think decadent?"

"She was older by a few years. But I expect the scandal was that she was my half-sister." He laid it out cold in order to shock. His mouth was hard.

She paused. "Well, country squires *would* consider that decadent." She shrugged.

"I suppose one who bathes in milk, and 'entertains' the cream of London society would not think that out of the ordinary." His voice was bitter.

She examined his eyes. They were hard, but not with cruelty. He had been hurt. He had done things he wasn't proud of. He had been buffeted by his short life. But he had trueness, a center. It was in his eyes. He glanced away. How touching that it still hurt him! She had resolved that nothing would ever hurt her again, not Asharti . . . not Stephan . . . not even her mother. "What I think," she said, "is that young men of eighteen fall madly in love with quite unsuitable partners, and it is up to their parents or a mentor to guide them and protect them from the consequences of being young and highly sexed and romantical into the bargain. It seems someone failed you."

His eyes widened, almost imperceptibly.

She continued. "I'll wager you didn't even know she was your half-sister. From what I know of your aristocracy, the country could be littered with half-siblings. I have heard Lady Jersey's children called "the Miscellany" they have so many different fathers."

He swallowed, apparently not sure how to respond. Then he mastered himself. "You are very critical, for one of your reputation."

"What you mean to say is 'very hypocritical,'" she observed. "And *you* are very critical of yourself. I'll wager you threw yourself into being just as bad as everyone thought you. The Continent? That's the usual refuge for brokenhearted young men." She saw she had hit home.

She could not help the softness she felt creeping into her smile. "Reputations . . . Well, if my reputation is no more deserved than yours, perhaps we should call a truce." His eyes expressed his consternation clearly. She raised a brow.

For a moment she thought he might shoot back some recital of her own reputation, trying to shock her. But apparently he realized that while very rude and satisfying, that would be a losing game. He breathed out, looked at his feet, then up, straight into her face. "Done." He paused, and cleared his throat. "In that case, we should start over—"

At that moment Ponsonby returned with two of his friends. "My apologies, Countess, but I was waylaid by these rogues and held at the champagne fountain at knifepoint." The puppy had never been less welcome. He introduced Lord Sherrington. Melly she already knew. Sherrington looked eager. He was obviously angling for an invitation to her drawing room.

Beatrix was suddenly tired of being all the rage. What were all these young admirers to her? Their adulation was so easily won it had no value. Still, they would prove a willing source to fill her Companion's needs. She sighed. "You must come to see me. I shall send round cards, if you could arrange to be free on Thursday next."

"Ab . . . ab . . . absolutely," Sherrington stuttered. His neck cloth was so high it poked at his cheeks. His blond, waving hair curled around his ears.

"I shall bring him with me," Melly confirmed in a voice he tried to make deep and bluff. His attempt was ludicrous beside Langley's rumble, but he wouldn't recognize that.

"Of course, *you'll* be there, dear Ponsonby." It was almost comical to watch him brighten.

"Lady Lente, your servant." Langley turned on his heel, and moved off to speak to Castlereagh and Perceval, the prime minister. Disappointment pricked Beatrix. Did he regret his confidences? Resent her insights? She had gone too quickly, misjudged his reticence . . .

"What a rude fellow," Sherrington exclaimed. "I wanted to ask him if what Ponsonby here says happened on Thursday is true."

"And why wouldn't it be true?" Ponsonby protested.

Beatrix let their quibbling fade into the background. Couldn't Langley wait through a little flirtation? He must have known she was about to chance making him an unseemly proposition. Had he just refused her a second time? Indignation beat in her breast.

"Really, Countess . . ."

"What? What is it you're saying?" She felt dulled and stupid.

"I . . . we . . . we wanted to invite you to Lady Jersey's picnic on Wednesday. We're all riding to Hampstead Heath. You have to give a hundred quid to her orphans' asylum."

"I never go out in daylight. If you ever plan a picnic at night, I shall be first in line."

Faces fell around the circle. "But the orphans . . ." Sherrington protested weakly.

Beatrix thought she saw Langley still listening to the conversation with half an ear. He started when Perceval asked him a question. "I shall send round my contribution in any case." She had done more for orphans than Lady Jersey dreamed of, but that was not what preoccupied her.

It was Langley. Damnation! If she abandoned these absurd young men and sought Langley out, it would look like she was chasing him. The evening seemed all at once like a stale repetition of a thousand other evenings, or a thousand thousand. And at none of them had there been anything she *wanted* except sometimes the blood. She would always need blood, but even that had grown stale. Art? Her love of the arts had always protected her, but

that seemed such a slender defense. Her stomach felt as
though it was filled with a heavy ball of dough. Music began. A country dance. The puppies would begin clamor-
ing. She wasn't certain she could bear it. Did Stephan feel
the darkness gathering as she did? He was much older.
The darkness ate up feeling. Perhaps he was incapable of
loving her. Perhaps none of them could feel after repetition had banged at their psyches for so long. Wasn't
Asharti's mad cruelty just another attempt to find something to feel? Or was Asharti's insanity what waited for
Beatrix in the dark . . . ?

Beatrix looked around the room, desperate for an anchor. Slowly, the scene began to swirl as people partnered
and moved into the dance. And then the colors whirled together, and the music assaulted her ears in a kaleidoscopic
cacophony almost horrible in the way it warped reality. She
swayed and put her fingers to her temples. The room and
the crowds ran together like watercolors in the rain. She
thought she could hear Asharti's laughter in the music.

"Lady Lente." Her name echoed around her. She
couldn't tell if it was one or many of the faces, stretched
into inhuman caricatures, who spoke. "Are you well?"
What was happening?

"I . . . I must go home." Her own voice came out
sounding like she was in a cave somewhere distant from
herself. "I do not feel quite . . ."

"I'll . . . I'll get your carriage." It was Sherrington. The
colors whirled and the music wailed. Asharti chuckled.
Was it Ponsonby who fluttered at her elbow? She might
faint at any moment like some young schoolgirl. It was
almost as though she hadn't fed for a long time. But that
wasn't true, was it? She couldn't think. Darkness flickered at the edge of her vision. What was wrong? Nothing
was ever wrong with her. The Companion saw to that.

Strong hands gripped her arms above the elbows, under her slashed sleeves. The touch seemed to shatter her,

it was so electric. Langley's green eyes were clear in her streaming vision. "Let me," he said curtly, in that steady rumble.

Slowly, the whirling slowed around the weight of his grip on her arms. He steered her relentlessly toward the door. "Gentlemen, make way." The crowds parted for her, of course. "I am quite able to navigate." It came out petulant, but at least her voice didn't echo in her ears.

"Of course you are," he agreed. But he didn't give over guiding her firmly down the stairs. As a matter of fact, he took most of her weight, so she couldn't fall even if she stumbled. It was annoying. He seemed to think he was entirely in control. She was stronger by ten times. How horrible to display this disgusting weakness! What would Stephan think if he could see her?

But he wouldn't see her. She would never see him again.

Sherrington hurried over after ordering the carriage. The bucks from the ballroom trailed her. She might suffocate if they clamored after her. Langley seemed to know what she was feeling. He brushed them off, saying in a most commanding voice, "Give her air, lads."

A footman presented her sable wrap. Langley draped it over her shoulders and guided her out the door to the waiting carriage. The wheels had spokes picked out in her signature electric blue. The gold crest on the door from her imaginary count looked impressive. Another footman opened the door and Langley pushed her up into the carriage in a most ungentlemanly way. She sank gratefully into the blue velvet squabs.

"Berkeley Square, man," Langley called up to her driver.

To her surprise, he stepped up into the carriage and sat opposite her. She was so exhausted she could not protest. Did she want to protest? Her eyes closed without her permission. Her stomach still felt queasy.

They were more than halfway to the square when she came to herself. Langley was quiet, though she could see him gazing at her in the gloom of the carriage.

"Feeling more the thing?" he said, his baritone husky in the darkness.

"Yes." She cleared her throat and sat up. "I can't think what came over me."

"Perhaps a touch of the influenza," he remarked. "It often comes upon one unawares."

"It's nothing physical, I'm afraid," she said. It couldn't be. The Companion gave her perfect health. Then she realized what she had just admitted and felt sick all over again. What was coming over her? She could not let it get about that she was a madwoman subject to fainting spells. She had always despised the weak. Now she might well be one of them.

"Still . . . May I call you a doctor? I am fairly well connected in Harley Street."

She shot him a glance. The best defense was a thrust direct. "I should think you would be, what with being patched up from wounds like the one in your shoulder. Does that happen often?"

"Do you often become faint in the middle of balls?" he lashed out in return.

This thrusting at each other would get both of them nowhere. "Think of it as a killing preoccupation with the past," she said as lightly as she could. He would think she was joking, or insulting him. Who would guess she was telling the truth? "The past can be deadly, you know."

His eyes narrowed. "You want me to believe you are making up a cause, when most probably you are not." He paused. "Just as you realized I threw doubt on the story of the footpads the other night so everyone would think I was in a duel over a woman. So that means you really think it is a kind of memory sickness. Is that what you're saying?"

Oh, she did not like this. This man was dangerous. "How ungracious," she muttered.

He raised his brows. "I hate to think we have that in common. In your case, I expect the easy repartee and gracious conversation is a ruse for the young bucks who need a goddess and the old fools who want a beautiful and intelligent woman focused on them. But that is not the real you, is it? There is nothing easy about you."

"I do not know who the real me is," she snapped. "And in any case I do not care to discuss it with someone who has quite as many secrets of his own. Do you know who *you* are?"

He clutched the breast of his coat. "Ah, a thrust to the heart!"

Hmph. He hadn't even claimed his cloak at Bessborough House. He was bareheaded, no gloves, no cane. She flushed. She was snapping at him when he had saved her from certain embarrassment. She cleared her throat. "If you are cold, there is a lap rug in the corner."

"Thank you for your solicitous impulse," he said, mocking her.

"I could say the same."

The carriage slowed. They were already in the square. Would he ask to come up? Her dread of meaninglessness and memory had retreated. Her head was clear. Dangerous as he was, with his ability to observe and his intuition, he was at least interesting. A flash of imagination showed his naked body lying across her bed, his eyes on fire. He would be strongly built, with the bulky muscles of full manhood, not like the youngsters she usually took. How long since she had allowed herself to take blood from the kind of body she enjoyed most? She would be so careful with his shoulder. The sweet richness of his blood, the feel of his rising sex against her belly . . .

Fear washed over her. Such thoughts were not for her! Where had that impulse come from after all these years?

Blood must never be mixed with sex. That way, she lost control.

But probably he would not come up. He had walked away from her twice. She looked at his shoulders and remembered the feel of them under her hands as they danced. She could make him come to her, of course . . . A shudder of Asharti shivered through her. No! She definitely did not want him to come to her under compulsion. What was she thinking? She didn't want him to come up at all. Not now. Not when she was vulnerable to . . . to what? The carriage stopped.

"I'll send a boy for your coat and hat," she said, to buy time. She actually did not know what he would do next. What an unusual feeling! "Number Six Albany House, I believe."

"Not necessary," he said lightly, as he opened the door. "I'll be going back tonight."

He *was* just going to walk away. Maddening man! She should be relieved. He was saving her from herself. Lord knows what would have happened if she had gotten him into her boudoir. He reached to hand her out. Again through the glove she felt his warmth. As she stepped down, she glanced up and caught the liquid heat in his eyes. Ha! He felt it, too. He might be walking away, but he wanted her. Perhaps that was the best of both worlds. Winning, but not claiming the prize. "James," she called. "Take Lord Langley back to Bessborough House."

"Very good, my lady," James returned stoically from the box.

The door opened behind her. "Consider use of my carriage a partial payment of my debt."

She half expected him to promise he would claim the whole payment shortly. But he simply nodded, and stepped back into the carriage. It clattered away into the brisk March night.

How vexing! What a relief! How . . . interesting.

# Four

John sat back into the squabs of Lady Lente's well-sprung carriage as it rolled through the streets of London, pulled by her crack team of matched bays. His pulse was racing. He had barely escaped with his sanity tonight. How she looked right through him! She guessed about his wound . . . Not a safe companion for a man with as many secrets as he had. He flushed as he recalled how she passed off the affair with Angela as a child's infatuation. That she guessed he didn't know Angela was his sister was uncanny. His naïveté then made him flush again now.

Everyone in the *ton* had known at the time except him, of course, including Angela. He was only tortured by the fact that she was married. He urged her to seek a divorce from Parliament. What a moon-calf! Angela wanted no divorce. He looked out on Hyde Park, wet and gleaming in the night. And she knew all along his sins were far worse than adultery.

Ah, but he had loved Angela! Even more than Cecily Warburton. Cecily had betrayed him, too. She and John were seventeen and engaged, not only by family arrangement, but, John thought, by more tender emotions. Cecily

was an excellent dissembler. After she cried off in favor
of a dashing officer in the Horse Guards, John's father
was furious. Cecily's portion had been destined to pay
down the family debt. He had failed to do the one thing
that could have redeemed him in his father's eyes.

John lost himself in London and avoided his father. He
was flattered when the sophisticated Angela Dougherty,
Lady Spenton, took an interest in him. Their affair had
been torrid: all-night sessions in the gazebo, illicit after-
noons in her boudoir—all the intensity of which an
eighteen-year-old is capable. When he realized his relationship to Angela from a remark made at some pointless
rout, his world dropped from under him. It took all his
courage to tell Angela. Angela pouted and said it was a
shame he was boring, because he was a very pretty, ar-
dent lover and Spenton didn't care as long as they were
discreet.

He clenched himself closed against the memory. Discreet? God, he had written *poetry* to her! How discreet
was that? That Spenton knew and dismissed the affair as
trivial was still painful. John realized then how heartless
Angela was, how little he meant to her. Women were incapable of constancy.

John threw himself on his parents' mercy and asked to
come home, only to find his parents knew all. "If there's a
brat from the union, Spenton will acknowledge it. I talked
to him," his father said shortly in the stables one morning
as John saddled his horse for a ride. John was stunned at
this fresh possibility of disaster. Those three months were
hell as he waited to hear that Angela was pregnant.

But disaster did not strike. He decamped to the Continent and drowned his pain in becoming just as bad as
everyone thought him, just as the countess had guessed.
She made it seem so . . . green. Well, no one could call
him green now. He did not believe in virtue anymore. He
couldn't even feel virtuous about acting for his country

when his duties included lying, stealing, killing, and using women. He never let himself fall in love with them. He never would.

The horses clopped along streets toward Bessborough House. How had the countess known so much about him? A horrible thought occurred. Was she a spy for France? She apparently came and went across the Channel as she pleased. What better way to ferret out a country's secrets than to sleep with the *crème* of its political and social crop? Damn! He'd let his guard down. Had she smoked his true occupation?

Bessborough House's ornate façade came into view. He took a breath. He hadn't given anything away. He had been lax because he was on his home soil. It would not matter. He was for Portsmouth soon. He would not see her again.

And yet . . . Did he not have a duty to determine if she was a spy—find out who her French contacts were? He would be exposing himself to her scrutiny. But he was forewarned. And she underestimated him. That would be to his advantage. Now, where could he see her next? He put down the little thrill in his loins that accompanied that thought.

Beatrix spent a wakeful day, her nerves all electric irritation. She didn't need blood, but she needed something. Her old friend Shakespeare could not hold her interest. She tried a book by the new woman everyone was talking about. Austen. Her clear and humorous vision of people and society amused Beatrix for almost an hour. She wrote a letter offering to support that artist Constable. He did light like no one else but Turner, and yet could not gain recognition from the damned Royal Society. She no longer believed art could save the world. But some things must be painted, written, danced, or sung, and she could make sure a few gifted individuals were allowed to do that. She tried not to think about what had happened last night at Bessborough House. Out of control. On the edge. In front of everyone.

And she had no idea why. What brought on this feeling that a great darkness was nipping at her heels? Was madness for her kind inevitable? That was the purpose of Mirso Monastery, to stave off madness. Perhaps Mirso was all that was left to her. But she wasn't ready to retreat so fully from the world. And why not? What did the world mean to her? If she could take a few books, a few paintings with her, why not start tomorrow?

Because then Asharti would be right about her.

That was why she struggled with the darkness. She paced from bed to dressing table and back again. She needed something to focus on besides the darkness.

The answer to that had a name. Langley. It was dangerous to seek him out at all, with the feelings he roused in her. But interest in something seemed to quiet her memory flashes. What to do next? If she invited him for Tuesday it would be admitting she craved his company. If she did not, the earliest she might see him was Wednesday at Hartford House, and that not a sure bet.

She called for Symington. She had employed him first in London years ago, and he had accompanied her to Amsterdam and Vienna. He was the only one who knew her secrets. She paid him well for his powers of organization. In return he suppressed his horror at her nature. Now he was old and somehow they had become . . . comfortable. He presented himself and bowed. Was he still horrified?

"I wish to know more about Langley," she said.

The old man paused. She could see him sorting the folders in his mind. He was a deep old file and since he had been in London for a month, he would know everyone and everything. "Known to be poor," he said, unequivocally. "Father gamed away whatever fortune was left from the grandfather's wasteful proclivities. Estate rumored to be mortgaged to the hilt. Mother largely insane after the early deaths of her other children. Now herself dead twenty years. He is the only legitimate child. Succeeded to the title six years ago. Early arranged marriage fell through when the young lady in question eloped with another. Father counted on the dowry—practically disowned him. He went wild. Affair with his half-sister, who—".

"Yes, yes." Beatrix waved her hand impatiently. "After the affair, what?"

Symington drew himself up. "Wandered the Continent. Duels, affairs. They say he was consort for a short time to Pauline, Napoleon's sister."

Pauline had a nearly insane need for sexual gratification. Had Langley been used for his body? That, coupled with the half sister, would explain his attitude about women. "And?"

"Well, the rumors go on from there. It is hard to know where to draw the line."

Beatrix grew thoughtful. "He appears to be received."

"There is a certain cachet in having him attend one's function. He is articulate. He dances well. He holds his liquor. And he does not disgrace his hostess."

"One has all the titillating possibility of misbehavior without the untidy consequences."

"And, if I might say," Symington added, "there is the role of the prodigal son, returned from the gates of hell and therefore to be pitied, if not forgiven."

"You are wise beyond your years, Symington." She made a salute. "Anything else?"

"Well . . ." Here the old man paused, as if unsure he should add something so trivial. "His valet, Withering, is a stiff-backed old moralist. Why would he stay with so dissolute a master?"

Very interesting, indeed.

"And . . ." Symington was truly reluctant now.

"Yes? Go on."

"Well, one viewpoint that does not quite agree with the rest. He is quite frequently gone from London for a month or more. He puts it about that he goes to the estate in the north when he runs out of money. But Clary, your upstairs maid, used to work at Langley Manor. She says he never comes there anymore but the steward is always making improvements."

"So," Beatrix said slowly. "The poverty-stricken young lord must be sending home money. Where does he go if not to his estates?"

"Unknown, my lady. And Withering is very tight-lipped about his master."

Beatrix straightened. *Very* interesting. "Thank you, Symington. You have been most helpful." She peered at her only confidant and saw creases in his forehead. She lifted her brows.

Symington swallowed. "Nothing of consequence, my lady."

Beatrix did not blink. Her brows continued the question.

Symington cleared his throat. "My . . . my sister is in poor health, my lady. Her husband died last year. She will not see a doctor. Says it's just her time. She lives in Harrowgate, but a spa town has so many ill people, I think it contributes to her melancholy . . ." He trailed off, then said briskly, "My concern will not, of course, interfere with performing my duties."

Beatrix frowned. "Why have you not mentioned this?" She rose purposefully. "Of course you will send for her. We shall set her up in rooms near Harley Street with every consideration. The best doctors . . . I'll give her a recommendation to Dr. Derwin . . . and . . . a female companion! Someone cheerful—that's what she needs. And of course, the support of her brother."

"I . . ." Symington seemed for once at a loss for words. "I . . ."

"Draw a draft on Drummond's for whatever you need."

The old man drew himself up. "You are too good, my lady, to bestir yourself like this."

"What nonsense! You are the one who will bestir yourself. And you must run up and accompany her to town. Take the barouche. I shall make do with the phaeton."

Symington turned quickly away. "Thank you, my lady," he murmured with a full throat as he closed the door. How dear that he hesitated to ask for something so easily accomplished. He liked to be depended on, not to be dependent.

Left alone, her thoughts returned to Langley. Now, how to see him? Tonight she was promised to the prime minister. The Prince Regent would be there. They were trying to get on together. If the old king died everyone knew the prince would replace all the ministers posthaste, but they must appear to be on good terms in case the king recovered. She would probably be the only woman there except for Mrs. Fitzherbert. It might be good sport but for the fact that one person would *not* be there.

Beatrix forced herself to lie down. Monday was soon enough to send him a card for her next soiree. He must think he was an afterthought. Where did he go for a month at a time? He was not as bad as he put about. Why did he encourage the world's misconceptions? She had seen his core of steadiness. She did not think she could be mistaken about that.

But she had been mistaken about people before. Stephan for instance. Asharti . . .

*AMSTERDAM, 1101*

*Beatrix pushed the lout off her with a growl that sounded more animal than human. He thought to take advantage of her. They all did, to their cost.* I shall surprise you, bastard whoreson, *she thought. He stumbled back. She plunged into the dark of the alleyway after him, into the mud and the night soil. Her ragged shawl drooped over one arm. The oaf must outweigh her by six stone. Before he could right himself, she shoved him up against the wall, his jowls heaving, codpiece dangling, surprise making his dull eyes widen. His head thunked against the wood covered with wattle. Power surged in her veins as the hunger welled inside her. She pulled his head down. He struggled but it was no use, of course. Her vision dimmed with the familiar red film. The smell of him, acrid with sweat and fear, filled her nostrils as she ripped at his neck. His high-pitched keening sounded over her low growl. The thick life flowed over her lips and tongue from his torn throat, on and on. He went quiet, sagging against her.*

*A strong hand pulled her away. She whirled, growling as the lump of flesh behind her slumped and fell. Who dared to interrupt her feeding?*

*A man grasped her shoulders. A well-made man, clean, tall, dressed in a rich hauberk and the chain mail of a warrior. That was all she noticed. She curled to shrug him off.*

*"Easy," he whispered. His voice echoed in her mind. She struggled, but his arms were steel. No one was stronger than she was! To her surprise, his eyes went red in the darkness.*

*She stilled. "Are you . . . ?" She couldn't say it.*

*He nodded. "I am as you are." He glanced to the carcass behind her. "And you have much to learn, my pretty feral kitten."*

*She searched his face. Cheekbones. Eyes near black now that the red had faded. High forehead, nose straight, jawline strong. Lips. Had she ever seen lips like that? His hair was dark and curling around his shoulders. He was . . . handsome. She knew she would never forget his face. She was afraid. And yet, to find someone like her, someone who knew . . . Her eyes filled.*

*He gathered her into his arms and cradled her head against his chest. He smelled like her mother, spicy, yet different—thoroughly masculine. "My name is Stephan Sincai. I will teach you who you are and how to go on. I will take the pain away," he whispered into her hair.*

*Beatrix knew she had found a refuge.*

Beatrix tossed under her coverlet. He wasn't a refuge, of course. But what did she know at seventeen, homeless, killing for what she needed, wanted by no one? Except Stephan. The admonishment she made to Langley about first, unwise loves came back to her.

Beatrix pulled the covers up, longing for the simplicity of sleep. How she had loved Stephan! He took her in, became her teacher, her mentor, and later, more. Beatrix once thought Stephan was an anchor—someone she could trust to always be there. Instead he had taught her the ultimate lesson of her kind; the lesson of impermanence.

Her mind flitted over the centuries. They came and went, the men. She fought side by side with bloody Henry at Agincourt. Da Vinci taught her about the art that saved her. De Sade was interesting if only because he practiced so freely what she practiced not at all. But he actually hated women, even her, in the end. She had sought companionship but never a sexual connection. That was too dangerous after Asharti. Astronomers, painters, kings, emperors, philosophers, they all ran together. In the end they were not Stephan. So she sought meaning in causes. She had thrown herself into countless movements, at least until the factions rose and the quibbling over doctrine began. They all came to nothing. That left only art. Art organized the chaos and cut through to truth. Art had been her only solace for centuries. Except for the blood.

*The blood is the life.* Stephan said their kind used it like a mantra, a shorthand for who they were. The symbiotic Companion in her blood gave her strength, powers humans thought were unnatural. But the Companion exacted a price—a life that could be eternal. To what end? Stephan was right. The blood was all the life there was, and suddenly that didn't seem enough.

CASTLE SINCAI, TRANSYLVANIAN ALPS, 1102

"I have returned, kitten."

Beatrix leapt to her feet from the huge carved chair in front of the fireplace in the echoing hall of the main keep. Leaping flames sent sparks shooting up the maw of the great chimney. "Stephan!" She threw herself into his arms. "I thought you would never come."

"Now, child," he murmured as he held her away from him. His hauberk was muddy from traveling, his long dark curls disheveled. A week's growth of beard covered his strong jaw. He looked tired, but his dark eyes still burned with energy under his bold black brows. "A lady does not throw herself upon her returning lord. Have I taught you nothing?"

Servants came, bowing, to take his cloak. Beatrix smoothed the rose brocade of her heavy dress over her breasts, and held out her arms to show the drape of the sleeves, tight over the shoulder, with cuffs that widened into points two feet in length. It was lined in the palest silk to match the silk that covered her head and draped under her chin. "See what the seamstresses have wrought, Stephan? Am I not beautiful?"

"You are quite beautiful, my little one. And, I might add, hardly feral anymore." He called to one of the servant women for mead. She hurried to do his bidding.

Beatrix smiled. "I have learned all your lessons about the Rules, Stephan, no matter how boring. You promised when you returned we would learn more exciting things. Shall you teach me how to ride horses and fight with swords?"

"Perhaps," he said. "But first you must meet someone." He turned and motioned toward the dark arch of stone that led to the great entrance hall. "Asharti, come meet your new sister."

From the shadows, a young woman peered, nervous, her eyes taking in the great plank table, the tapestries that lined the stone walls, the sconces that sent the smell of burning oil to join the wood smoke from the fire. She was beautiful in a way Beatrix had never seen. Her eyes were dark, like Beatrix's own, but they were lined with black smudge that made them look exotic. Her skin was too olive but it was fine, and her features were finely drawn. She wore a shapeless striped garment with a hood that covered her from neck to ankle, tied at the waist with a rope net like a girdle. She hesitated at the doorway as though she expected something fearful.

"Come, child," Stephan encouraged her, holding out a hand. "No one will hurt you."

"Who is this?" Beatrix asked, drawing herself up. "I have no sister."

Stephan continued to hold out his hand to the newcomer. "Have I not heard you mourn that there were none like you your own age?"

The girl—she looked a few years older than Beatrix—came forward slowly.

Beatrix felt her breath catch in her throat. "She is like me?"

Stephan smiled. "Just like you. Asharti comes from the city of three religions, Jerusalem. She was made by a Crusader who was one of us."

"Made! You mean she was born human and one of us shared the blood? You said the Rules did not allow that! And only born vampires are allowed to live," Beatrix protested.

Asharti looked at the ground, afraid, then up at Stephan under her lashes.

*"It is not allowed. But what has happened, happened. Is that a reason she should not be given the same chance at life I give to you?" He did not wait for an answer, but shook his head. "You will welcome her, Bea, because that is the only action worthy of a generous soul. I will teach you both, and you will be solace and support to each other on your journey."*

Beatrix's eyes filled, shamed that Stephan had found her wanting. He reached for the girl's hand. The poor creature was so unsure, she was practically trembling. He grabbed Beatrix's hand and joined the two young women.

*"You are both in need of a sister,"* he said, in that wonderful voice Beatrix had grown to love. *"And someday, together, you will make them all believe in the future of our race, as I do."*

Stephan's face, with its strong features and expressive eyes, fairly glowed from within. Beatrix decided she would not mind a friend, someone who understood her. But it was more important still that she not disappoint Stephan.

She squeezed the girl's hand. *"Asharti. That is a pretty name. Do you speak Dutch?"*

*"I speak the French better,"* Asharti said slowly. *"Robert, who make me, he teach me."*

*"Je parle français, un peu. Stephan, can I take Asharti to my rooms? That golden-colored dress would look very well on her, and it does not become me at all."*

Stephan smiled with satisfaction. Beatrix flushed to know she had pleased him. *"I counted on your generous spirit, kitten. I have ordered the servants to draw two hot baths."*

Beatrix covered her eyes, trying to push back the past. Asharti. If Beatrix could have seen the future . . . But she hadn't seen the evil then. No, she had been glad to have a fellow student of Stephan's teachings. Asharti had progressed rapidly. It wasn't long before she lost all shyness. It seemed she had lost all fear. Instead, the anger lurking always in Asharti's heart had surfaced. From the perspective of centuries, Beatrix thought the anger and the fear were intertwined . . .

*Stephan rapped Asharti's fingers with a small pointer as she reached for a handful of walnut meats. "Pay attention, both of you! You must know the history of your kind."*

*Asharti snatched her hand away, pouting. "Boring! What do I care for Rubius and some monastery and a fountain?" Her petulance warned of a tantrum.*

*"You care because one day they may be your salvation. Rubius, the Eldest, and the Council make the Rules that govern us. The fountain is the Source of the Companion. And Mirso Monastery is the last refuge for our kind." Stephan strove to keep his annoyance in check. Both Beatrix and Asharti knew it. It made Beatrix nervous. It made Asharti bold.*

*"What if I don't want salvation?" How did Asharti dare challenge Stephan and why did he allow it? He seemed to indulge Asharti as he would never indulge her.*

*"When you are as old as I am you will begin to value the Vow and Mirso Monastery."*

*"As old as you are," Asharti snorted, lifting her finely arched brows. "You are not old." They sat in the solarium at the top of the castle, the precious glass of its windows no longer used to let in the sun, but to paint the walls with a starscape of shining fragments. Stephan liked to give lessons there, as though the proximity of the universe could enlarge their souls.*

*"More than a thousand years," he said then held up a finger to Asharti's protestation. "I was born when the Carpathian Mountains were called Dacia. We were part of the Roman Empire. The yoke of Rome was hard, yet the Romans dragged us out of tribal warfare and brutality." His eyes glazed as he journeyed to another time, another place. "I thought I would never tire of drinking the blood,*

*feeling the life shoot down my veins. Now I take comfort in the fact that someday I can join the monks who chant and starve their Companion until their needs are small, their powers diminished, their pain and memories gone. It keeps us sane, in a way, to know there is a last protection in taking the Vow."*

Beatrix shuddered, unable to imagine anything more horrible. "How does it protect?"

Stephan stared out at the stars. "Because it cannot be renounced, it protects us from ourselves. Once taken, it is secure. We are secure."

"Of course you can renounce it. All you have to do is leave," Asharti protested. Beatrix could feel her sister's anger. Asharti hated to be checked, even by Elders she did not know.

Stephan suppressed what looked to be a smile. "Only in death, my pet."

"You said it was nearly impossible to commit suicide," Beatrix observed, wary.

"And so it is. The Companion's urge to life is strong, even if one can inflict enough damage to one's own body to die."

Beatrix shuddered. Stephan said actual separation of the head was necessary to kill a vampire—decapitation— something their Companion could not repair. "Then . . ."

"I was talking about homicide," he said, in that calm voice he reserved for the most brutal facts about their life.

"They would kill one of their own?" Asharti asked, outraged. "I would kill them!"

"Yes, they would," he said, ignoring her second comment. "If one can renounce the Vow, then what protection is it?"

"How do you know so much about this Vow if no one who takes it can leave the Monastery?" Asharti asked with narrowed eyes.

"I was born in Mirso, to a refugee who arrived big

with child. I grew up serving Rubius." He took a breath. "One day Rubius told me I must go out into the world to experience life before I could return. He cast me out. I was reluctant to leave my prison, but once the doors were open I did everything, experienced everything; kindness, brutality, intellectual exhilaration, sexual depravity... all of it." His brown eyes stared at the cold stars. "And slowly, everything palled. When you have done it all over and over again until you can predict the failure of your hopes down to the last detail, what is left?"

Beatrix shivered. "You are not like that now. What changed?" she whispered.

He forced a smile. "You two gave me an interest in life again."

Asharti eyed him as though he was lying to her in a way she could not quite comprehend. Beatrix opened her eyes wide as the burden of his statement settled on her shoulders.

"So," Stephan said briskly, "I am invested in your learning. And that brings us to practicum, lovelies." Stephan rose. "Tomorrow night, I shall show you how to translocate. And to take blood without ripping throats, Bea, and without draining your victims, Asharti."

"I like the last drop." Asharti's expression was bold.

"Humans and vampire kind exist in a delicate balance. Disturb that harmony and all suffer. Killing humans every time we feed would mean that humans discover us."

"We are stronger than they are," Asharti said, shrugging.

"True," Stephan soothed. "We take what we require. But we exist in secret, one to a city, feeding and leaving our food source intact to provide sustenance another day."

"I will do what I like, Stephan. Who can stop me?" A challenge direct! Beatrix could not believe her ears. Was Asharti mad? She held her breath, expecting Stephan to flash his eyes red. He didn't. Asharti gave a sly laugh at her triumph and turned, about to flounce from the room.

*"I would be so sorry to leave you home tomorrow, my dear."* Stephan sighed. *"But Beatrix and I will manage on our own, if you can't behave."*

Asharti whirled, her delicate brows drawing together in a frown. *"You wouldn't."*

Stephan smiled.

Beatrix was sweating. The memories would not let her alone. Did that centuries-old lesson come back to haunt her today because Mirso Monastery really *was* the only thing left to her? It was a final step, taking the Vow. But it might be her only defense against the darkness.

She felt her grip loosening. Was the darkness a result of boredom? True, no one said anything she couldn't predict anymore. All disappointments had been experienced a hundred times. She had no passion for life, hadn't for centuries. Art? Even art no longer solaced her as it once had. She would give anything to go back and find a different way through the pain Stephan and Asharti had caused. The scars they left were the only indication of what had been excised, surgically, one night more than six hundred years ago. A small sound escaped her, a cry of pain or protest, she wasn't sure which.

She needn't decide on Mirso and the Vow tonight.

Langley. She would think about how to know more about Langley.

John walked up to Albany House in Albany Court off Piccadilly, returning from Lady Hartford's. The countess was definitely invited for Wednesday. How bold of Lady Hartford, he thought with satisfaction. Now if only her rout weren't two whole days away. The doorman handed him an envelope addressed in a sloping, feminine hand. John traded a shilling for the card with an assumption of nonchalance. He took the stairs two at a time and slipped into Number Six. He ripped open the envelope as Withering appeared.

> *The Countess of Lente requests the presence of*
> *the Earl of Langley at eight P.M. on Tuesday for*
> *a small gathering at Number Forty-six Berkeley*
> *Square. She hopes he will strive to remember the*
> *date.*

That was all. No signature, only the challenge in the last line to tell him it was a personal invitation. His mouth repressed a grin. "Brandy, Withering," he said, exultation in his voice. "I am going to beard the lioness in her den tomorrow. Satin knee breeches. Or she won't let me in."

# Five

*Where is he, the wretch?* He wasn't coming.

Beatrix rose suddenly. It was nearly midnight. She had made the others go half an hour before. They huffed to the street below, stiff with resentment. Now she went to the piano. Perhaps music would soothe her. She flipped through the tablature impatiently until she came to Beethoven's Piano Sonata in C sharp minor. It had always reminded her of moonlight: melancholy and wise. It had the weight of emotion she needed to steady her. She sat, opened the sheet music. *Breathe.* Her hands hovered over the keys. Then she let the music sweep her away.

At that moment, the door opened and Symington stepped into the room. "John Staunton, Earl of Langley," he announced in stentorian tones.

Beatrix looked up in time to see Langley stroll through the door. She took a breath, the realization of her expectation making her flush. *He is no better looking than any other man,* she told herself as she corrected the hesitation and let the music flow on, dramatic, sorrowful. She could not let him know how he affected her. *Yes, the green eyes and black hair are an unusual combination. True, too, the downward slant of the eyes and the full mouth are not in the usual vein.* She normally liked men whose features were chiseled and austere. His weren't. The cleft chin was almost jaunty, belying the serious eyes. Her gaze fell to his massive sloping shoulders, the thickly muscled thighs in those ridiculous knee breeches she required. Yet there were many built like that. She concentrated on the music.

*So what is it about him?*

The last notes hovered in the air. She stared at the keys, longing to look up.

"You are a quite a virtuoso, Countess," Langley drawled, after clearing his throat once.

"Nonsense," she murmured, chancing a glance up under her lashes. "All it takes is practice. I have had lots of time for that." Langley stood, staring at her. She rose.

He inclined his head. She held out her hand. She could feel the emeralds heaving on her breast. He took her fingers lightly and brushed them with his lips. Thank God for the fashion of wearing gloves! The thought of his lips on her bare fingers made her throb. She pushed down other images that rose, unbidden. Damn, the man was dangerous!

"Lady Lente." His baritone sounded half again as male as any other man she knew.

"You're late, Langley." Her voice came out a hoarse whisper. She cleared her throat. "I suppose I should be flattered that you made it in the same week as the invitation."

"My deepest apologies. I was engaged. The notice was so short," he murmured.

The rogue! She would wager a pony he had no other engagement. And he should be flattered he got an invitation for this evening instead of a month hence. As if she could have waited a month to see him. A voice inside her said her interest would be short-lived. She told it to be quiet. Short-lived or not, she would enjoy that sense of expectation. "Symington, brandy."

Symington bowed and retreated.

Beatrix tried to look demure. "Tell me about your engagement." Let the battle begin.

He smiled and shook his head. How that smile changed his face! "I think discretion is in order," he murmured. "How are you feeling tonight?" What cheek! How dare he bring up her indisposition. And wait—discretion implied he visited another woman? How dare he?

"Ah, I see. Well, you are here now. Perhaps you can share some of the conversation that makes you so in demand."

"Conversation is not what makes me in demand." Langley cocked his head, daring her to match him, truth for truth.

"You put a female to the blush." She did feel hot, but it was just the room. She moved away from the fire.

"I think not, my lady," he murmured.

Her eyes could not help but open a little wider. "Then tell me about yourself, Langley. I would know more of such a man. Where do you hale from?"

His face closed. "The north. Poor land, harsh climate, crags and moors mostly."

He didn't want to talk about himself, unlike any other man she had entertained here. "You don't seem poor."

"As Alvaney said, I'm lucky at cards." His voice had an edge. Bitterness?

"Lord Melford says enclosing the commons is a way to get more from the land. Perhaps you could try enclosures." She was talking inanities in order to avoid talking about anything else.

Langley drew himself up. "And what is Melford doing to provide for his poorer tenants who supplemented their income by grazing a few animals or planting a garden on the commons? What will happen to them?"

Was he outraged? Unexpected. "Parliament approves the petitions all the time."

"Just because Parliament approves it, doesn't make it right."

"You must have a seat in your House of Lords. You could speak out for your beliefs most eloquently, I should think."

"Waste of time with the lot in there now," Langley said, downing his brandy.

So, the most debauched man in England had social views. Had no one noticed, or did they just dismiss the fact? He was more complicated than they imagined.

"But back to you and your background." Beatrix felt relentless tonight. "We are bordering on politics, and you know how I feel about that. Siblings, Langley?"

He took a brandy from the tray Symington offered. Symington melted into the background. "None my father acknowledged." His voice was steady.

"No siblings," Beatrix noted. "Father deceased since you hold the title. Mother?" It was unseemly to ask about someone's background. And she knew the answer. But it was part of her public persona to be outrageous. And she wanted to see his expression as he answered.

"Died when I was a child," he said shortly. A flash of pain. Ah. Loved his mother, or regretted that he didn't? Complicated.

"Alone in the world, then." She could see he hoped she would move on. "And yet not alone, for our parents live on in us, do they not?"

"I hope not." He tossed back a gulp of brandy.

"I hear you are the image of your father."

Langley forced a smile. "Unfortunate, but true," he said lightly. "And now, perhaps you will answer similar questions." He lifted his brows. "Your parents' influence?"

Sauce for the goose was the last thing she wanted. "I think early mentors can be more important even then parents." Dangerous direction. How dare he make her slip?

"Then who mentored you?"

She cocked her head. The devil! And she had given him the opening. What would he think if she talked of Stephan? But then, she wanted to shock him. "Ahhhh, that was a man, not my parents. His name was Stephan Sincai. He showed me . . . everything important." Langley poured himself another glass of brandy. She pressed on. "He showed me how the world worked, even when that wasn't pretty." She stared up at Langley, daring him to judge her.

"I wonder why you like to shock people, Lady Lente," he observed, not shocked at all.

"Normally I am the soul of discretion." He must have realized she was hunting him after receiving her invitation. Fine. Men liked to be desired, as long as no one mentioned marriage.

"That would be a requirement for a life such as yours."

There, *there,* he was judging her! "And yours as well, I should think."

He looked startled. Why would he look startled over her accusation of his infidelities? He had acknowledged his reputation. And he couldn't doubt she would retaliate. Interesting.

She came to herself and smiled. "Truce?"

Had she smoked out that he had a secret life? Or did she know because she was a spy? Lord, but she was beautiful when she smiled! But even smiling there was something distant about her, as though she found the world wanting. The courtesans he had encountered, and they had been legion, fueled their success by hanging on every word of men who wanted to talk about themselves. Not Lady Lente. She made the men around her struggle to catch her interest. That kept them coming back. But he would wager they didn't truly interest her.

She was everything he hated in a woman. No virtue, no

loyalty—she was the logical extension of Angela and Celia. She hated men and longed to betray them. A perfect spy.

And yet, there was a sadness about her that he found . . . intriguing. *Don't lose your head, Langley,* he told himself. *Just remember what she is.*

"Let's see . . . truce on the personal, no politics," he mused to bait her, "what is left?"

"I didn't say 'nothing personal,' " she remarked pointedly, that smile still lying somewhere in her eyes. "How about poetry? I always think a man's favorite poet says quite a bit about him." She picked up her own glass of champagne from a side table and sipped delicately. "For instance, our prime minister. Mr. Perceval's favorite is our poet laureate, Mr. Southey. You see how appropriate, do you not?"

He knit his brow. Perceval was not exactly daring. Southey did make sense.

"And Mr. Castlereagh's favorite is Alexander Pope. The young men are, of course, all devotees of Lord Byron."

"You judge them ill for their choices?"

She shrugged. "Southey perhaps counts against Perceval. But Pope is a genius, if a structured one; a realist if you will, like Castlereagh. As for Byron—he is rampantly popular, which should count against him, but his poetry isn't ill made. Byron told me himself his favorite poet was Pope. He needn't have bothered, of course. It's there in his verses."

So, Lady Lente thought she was in control again, did she? John kept his silence, waiting.

She turned those brown eyes that knew everything on John, and put a finger to lips rouged slightly for effect. The rouge was not needed. "And you? Hmm. Should I guess Shelley for his social idealism? You obviously feel strongly about social issues. Or Wordsworth because underneath you still believe in traditional values like virtue?" She paused, thinking.

Her words struck to John's heart. She had guessed his penchant for virtue? But he had never thought himself traditional. He wanted to shock her. "Neither, Lady Lente. Blake."

Her eyes opened, before she cast them down. "'Tiger, Tiger burning bright, in the forest of the Night,'" she murmured. "'What Immortal hand or eye could frame thy fearful symmetry?'"

"You, too, are a force of nature, Countess." He bowed slightly.

"Don't distract me from the issue, Langley," she said sharply. "So you like Blake's traditional view of God, but you love the syncopation of his verse—not traditional at all."

"I would hardly consider Blake's view of God traditional," John protested.

"He believes there is one. That is traditional in itself." She tapped one finger to her lips. "But then there is his leap of faith . . ."

John felt himself blushing. Perhaps one's favorite poet did reveal too much about one. "You refer to 'second innocence'?"

"How else could one believe that one can be transformed into a being with an ability to wonder, even after one has seen all the horror of the world?" Lady Lente's voice sank. "Or perhaps it is only hope, not belief."

John felt his soul had been stripped bare. He was casting about for a distraction when the countess rose suddenly, all insouciance laid aside. He had never seen her so energetic.

"Come," she said. Her green silks rustled. She strode to the far end of the long drawing room and threw open a pair of double doors. John poured himself a brandy from the side table and lounged after her so as not to look too eager. He found himself in a much more intimate room. Magazines were strewn over the floor, papers were scattered across a desk along with a teacup, still half full. This was where the countess lived.

She glanced around. "Well? Are you going to come and look or not?"

John sipped brandy with an assumption of negligence, "I can see quite well from here."

What he saw was two paintings, hung side by side. A glance at the other walls told him her art collection was even more extensive than the paintings in the grand drawing room would indicate. Fragonard, Rubens, a brooding Goya, only the best. The countess was a woman of the world, and apparently a rich one. He returned to the two in question. On the left was a masterful depiction of a river in fading light with clouds piling into a sky that dwarfed figures in front of an old mill. The light was luminous. You felt you were looking into an exact representation of an afternoon in Suffolk. Constable. The Royal Society disdained him, but John had always thought he was a genius. He leaned in and saw the painting was called something about "Flatford Mill."

The painting on the right was a conflagration of wind and light that shone forth on a raging sea. It showed a ship breaking apart before your very eyes. You could feel the power of the waves, the wind tearing the swells into froth, the anguish of the figures cast into the water. The paint was laid on, not in Constable's translucent perfection, but in great swatches of dramatic color. John did not need to peer at the name plate to catch the name of the painter. It was a Turner. But the title of the piece arrested his gaze. *The Wreck of a Hulk, 1810.* He hoped to God the scene was not prophetic.

"You see?" the countess said triumphantly. "It is the same in painting."

John stood, transfixed. Finally he cleared his throat, driven to fill the silence. "Constable is Pope and Wordsworth, but Turner is Blake, of course." He cast about for something else to say. "Of course, if you have seen Constable's sketches, they have much the same power."

"You know him?" The countess sent John an appraising look. Then she turned back to the painting. "Still, he feels a need to refine in a way Turner is beginning to leave behind. Turner is learning to cut to the visceral nature of the light."

John cleared his throat again. "Couldn't one say the same in music? The precision of Haydn contrasts with the passion of Beethoven."

The countess stared at him. "A passion so consuming it survived deafness. He must have believed that passion would triumph . . . His hunger to make music gave his life purpose."

"Hunger . . ." John murmured. Did he want the life he had chosen? Did he want anything? "You haven't said who your favorite poet is."

"Oh, I like both styles. Pope is a master. Wordsworth is—"

"No," John interrupted, his voice almost raw. "Time to step up to the mark, Countess. Name a name." John wanted that name more than he had wanted anything in a long time.

She blinked, her long lashes brushing her cheeks. She swayed on her feet. "Blake," she whispered, her impossibly dark eyes big and riveted on John's face. There were questions there and, if he was not mistaken, a tiny, vulnerable spark of hope.

For a long moment silence reigned.

The countess came to herself with a start. Her countenance snapped shut. "I have had enough of you tonight," she said brusquely. "You must have better things to do." She shushed him through the door. "Symington," she called. "Show Lord Langley to the door."

John did not acknowledge the dismissal. "You've been associating with the wrong men."

"What?"

"You should surround yourself with men you can't bully." He stared into those dark eyes.

"Bully!" They widened in outrage. "Rudeness will get you nowhere, Langley." She turned and made as if to go. He reached for her wrist. The shock of touching her shot through him. A leaping flame of life rose in her eyes as her head jerked toward him. She was more alive than anyone he had ever seen. Their eyes locked and that vitality poured over him. Was this what lay hidden behind the veil of disinterest she usually projected?

"Tell me you don't bully the men in your life," he whispered.

His answer was a faint crinkle of humor around her eyes that rinsed the outrage away.

"Would you care for a ride tomorrow . . . shall we say at four?" He made it a challenge.

She examined his face so intently his soul felt stripped. But part of him felt full and getting fuller, longing to be stripped. She had made no move to take her wrist back. At last she shook her head. "I never rise until late."

Disappointment washed through him. He realized he had been holding his breath and consciously let it go. He managed a shrug and released her arm. "Perhaps another time."

"Shall we say half past seven?"

What? After dark? But he did not want to be the one to cry off, so he voiced the only barrier that might count with her. "What about your salon?"

"I come downstairs at ten."

"I shall call at half past seven, then."

She cocked her head in speculation. "Don't think you've gotten what you want."

"I might say the same," he murmured. He turned and strode toward the door, needing to be the one who left. In moments, he was in the street. Had he seen what he thought he had seen? Was the moment of revelation real, or was it all an act?

He strode off toward the corner of the square, his mind churning with a growing anger. It had been her game in the first place, this silly naming of poets. When called to account, she threw him out. The worst of it was if she had asked him to stay tonight, he might have succumbed to her wiles. What a weakling! Had he not had enough of women who had no constancy, no virtue? And who was less virtuous than the countess? She did not even bother to hide her shoddy morals. She used men like handkerchiefs and tossed them away. And the fools stood in line to give her the opportunity to do so.

It was the damned vulnerability he had seen in her expression as she breathed Blake's name that wouldn't be dismissed. She had bared her soul in that one word and she knew it. No wonder she reacted so violently. But he would not succumb again.

His body reacted to the shot that rang out before his mind could register it. He had ducked up the front stairs of the nearest house, behind a pillar that held up its pediment, before he realized he had heard a thunk in the tree nearest his head.

The bullet was meant for him. He searched the square. Wind moved through the great trees in the center; the elms were still bare and clacking, the oaks creaking. A pair of carriages crossed the other side, oblivious, the horses' shoes ringing on the street. He thought he caught movement in Hill Street from the corner of his eye, but when he looked, there was nothing.

But it wasn't nothing. All doubt was banished now. Those hadn't been footpads in Hay Hill. Someone was trying to kill him. That meant someone knew what he was.

# Six

Beatrix practically ran to her boudoir. She heard a shot ring out in the square, but she did not even ask one of the servants to inquire. Let banditos take up residence in the square and murder passersby. She didn't care. How had she revealed so much to him? Why? Was it the thunderbolt to her heart when he had told her he valued Blake above all others? And when had Blake and Turner become her favorites? Could art transform reality into something even more real and more invested with emotion? Was there second innocence, God forbid?

Ridiculous! Once you had been tarnished by the cruelty and stupidity of the world there was no way back. She did not believe in transformation. She sat at her dressing table. Did she?

Yet she had every edition of Blake's poetry, as well as some of his illustrations. So primitive. So evocative. Had she lied to Langley about Blake being her favorite? Beatrix ran her hand through her hair, pulling the pins out and letting it cascade to her shoulders. She looked into the mirror at a face that would never change. No. Transformation was not possible. Her innocence had been ripped from her centuries ago . . .

COURTYARD OF CASTLE SINCAI, TRANSYLVANIAN ALPS, 1102

*"We hunt tonight, kittens," Stephan said. He swung his cloak around his shoulders. Beatrix had never seen a man look so fine, though she had to admit her experience of men was limited. The leather jerkin he wore over a linen shirt and hose and boots was meant to make him look like any other man. It failed. How could anyone mistake those shoulders, those smoldering eyes, those cheekbones? The excitement of the night coursed through her. She and Asharti would learn how to feed tonight. There would be no more goblets of blood presented by Stephan, safe and unexciting. She glanced at Asharti. Her sister had come to heel fast enough when Stephan threatened to leave her behind.*

*The two girls swirled their cloaks on. It was cold in the mountains. "Will we go to the village?" Beatrix asked. "It is a long way, in the cold."*

*"Never feed close to home, and never in the same place twice." He took their arms. "No, we go far, and we have another way to travel. Tonight I will show you one of the most useful gifts from our Companion."*

*"Translocation!" Beatrix practically squeaked.*

*"How does it work, Stephan? Show us now," Asharti commanded.*

*"First you must understand the process," Stephan said patiently. "You call your Companion and it lends you its power. If you draw enough power, a field is created around you. Light does not escape. Others cannot see you."*

*"You mean we are invisible?" Beatrix asked, shocked.*

*"I have seen it with Robert," Asharti said smugly.*

*"And then, my pets, if you continue to call, the field*

*becomes so dense it pops you out of space. You can learn to direct where you will reappear, with practice."* He saw Asharti start to speak and lifted a finger. *"You must hold to me, so that we end in the same place. It hurts a bit. So be prepared."* He lifted his cloak and they snuggled into his body, one on each side.

*"Now call,"* he ordered.

Beatrix thought a connection to the one who shared her blood. Companion, come to me.

She felt a tingling rush of power down her veins. *"Again,"* she heard Stephan say, from farther away, it seemed. Companion! *The world went dark around them. She couldn't even feel Stephan beside her. The tingling ramped up and up, and she wasn't sure she had control of it. It engulfed her, mastered her. Her Companion cried out for life, and power. Pain engulfed Beatrix. The world disappeared. And then the pain was gone. The world appeared. She felt Stephan clutching her shoulders. But it was a different world than they had left; a dark alleyway that stank of cabbage and piss. A series of buildings, all in some state of disrepair, lined both sides of a narrow dirt passage. Loud, deep voices and shrill laughter came from inside the largest of them* "Voilà!" *Stephan announced.* "The yard of the Rose and Thorn in Sigishoara."

Beatrix looked around, trying to get her bearings. *"We can do this . . . anytime we want?"*

*"It takes much energy. There are limits,"* Stephan warned. *"And it takes practice."*

*"Freedom!"* Asharti hissed. Her eyes glowed.

Stephan nodded, smiling, and pointed. *"The next man that comes out the front door is yours, Bea. Do as I have taught you. Take but a little, and we will practice again tonight."*

Asharti clung to his torso and rubbed herself like a cat against him. *"Stephan, I am hungry. I should go first," she pouted. Beatrix did not like how Asharti had begun to treat Stephan over the last several weeks. This kind of cloying behavior made Beatrix's blood boil. The puzzling thing was that Stephan did not try to stop it.*

*"Your turn will come."* Stephan drew them forward to peer around the corner of the building. He nodded at Beatrix as the door to the tavern swung open. Light and noise spilled out across the narrow dirt track of a street. But the man who stumbled out was gray-haired. His face was marked by an early encounter with the pox.

Beatrix shrank back, shaking her head. *"I don't like that one."*

*"You do not need to like them, Bea. They are food."* Stephan said, exasperated. He had never been exasperated with her in front of Asharti.

*"Can I not take one more comely?"*

*"Bea is going to take forever. Hold me, Stephan, to keep me warm."*

Stephan put his arm around Asharti. Beatrix resolved that the next man out the door would feel her compulsion, no matter if he was a leper. The older man staggered off down the street. It was late. The moon was setting behind the buildings. Surely the men would come out soon to go home. She jerked toward the opening door. A man stumbled out and fell on his hands and knees in the street. *Let him not be vomiting.* Beatrix thought as she glided out of the alleyway. The man picked himself up and swayed, looking around to get his bearings.

*"Good evening,"* Beatrix said softly in the language of Dacia, where Castle Sincai sat. The man was young, though not as young as she or Asharti, and coarsely made. It could have been worse. Stephan had taught her to call her Companion gently so it would not overwhelm her like it did when she was hungry and desperate, but slide up along her veins to do her bidding.

The young man looked at her with his own kind of

*hunger in his eyes. "What is this?" he asked. But Beatrix had let her eyes go red. She had him.*

*"Come with me." She backed toward the shelter of the narrow yard. The young man, now slack-eyed, followed. When they were hidden, she made the man kneel. Why couldn't they feed in a nice dining room like the one at home? This one smelled. Since Stephan made her bathe regularly and followed his own advice, she found the scent of unwashed men repulsive. But her distaste was overwhelmed by the call of her blood. She thought about the man lifting his head, and he did, baring his throat. She could feel the blood pulse in him. It excited her and the one who shared her body.*

*Asharti glided by her. From behind her Stephan said, "Draw your teeth."*

*She ran her tongue over her lips. Her canines were already sharp and long. She was breathing heavily. She imagined blood coursing down her throat.*

*"Feel for the pulse," Stephan instructed. She caressed the strong throat. Yes, there it was, beating at her thumb. Her growl surprised her. "One gentle bite, no tearing, and then you suck. Your saliva will keep the blood flowing."*

*She glanced up as Asharti pulled another young man to kneel beside her own. A shock of gold hair, sleepy blue eyes—she saw no more. She could spare no attention for Asharti. She placed her canines over the throbbing pulse and bit down. Her canines pierced the salty-tasting skin easily. Blood flowed up around them. To suck was natural. She pulled in rhythm to the heartbeat and the thick liquid coursed down her throat. She sucked and sucked. Her Companion sang a familiar song in an ecstasy of fulfillment. Beatrix shared the ecstasy as her reward for providing the blood. It sang in her veins and she was whole, powerful and whole.*

*"Enough," Stephan said above her. He shook her shoulders. "Enough, Bea."*

She raised her head and licked her lips, blinking at him. "Good." He smiled. "You mustn't take enough to kill him. Now button his shirt."

Beatrix reached for the man's collar. Stephan moved to Asharti, who pulled at the neck of her chosen. He watched for a moment then called, "Enough," his hand on her shoulder.

Asharti pushed his hand away and continued sucking. Stephan shook her, but Asharti wouldn't stop. Finally he took her by the neck with one hand, pinched her jaw open with the other, easing her canines from her victim's throat. He drew her up bodily and looked her in the eyes. "Enough," he said sternly.

Beatrix led her young man past Asharti and Stephan. How had Asharti missed hearing Stephan's order? Asharti raised her eyes. Beatrix was shocked to see open rebellion there.

Stephan set her firmly on her feet. "The whole point was to take only a little, Asharti."

"I like the last drop," she said, sulky. Then she raised her eyes to Stephan. "Do you not like to feel the life coursing into you? Have you never taken the last drop?"

"I have." Stephan swallowed. "But that is not how we survive. Do you not listen?"

"I listen." She shrugged.

"Well." Stephan's voice hardened. Raucous singing echoed from the street. "Let us go home for tonight. We will try again another time."

He folded the two girls in his cloak, and just as three men turned into the yard, yelling, "Hey, who goes there?" the darkness whirled up around them and they were gone.

Later that night, Beatrix slipped into Asharti's room, drawn by her need for answers. Asharti was sitting in bed, staring at the fire. At the opening of the door she looked up. Whatever emotion was in her eyes drained away. She smiled. "So, Bea, we graduate."

*Beatrix nodded and sat on the Turkey carpet in front of a dying fire. The room was cold. "How do you dare challenge him?" she asked after a moment.*

*"Oh, that. How can you* not *challenge him? It would be easier for you than for me."*

*"He cares for us. All he asks is that we learn the way."*

*"Men want power over us, Bea." She sounded sad. "I know that better than you do."*

*"Not Stephan. He wants to give us the tools to live in this world. They are a gift."*

*"All men want power, Bea, even Stephan." Asharti said it with finality. Her eyes were hard. She turned to look at Beatrix and softened. "Oh, he has given me a gift, I admit it. He has taught me not to be afraid. I thought I would always be afraid."*

*"Afraid of what?" Beatrix whispered.*

*Asharti's eyes moved back to the fire. "Them." Beatrix didn't know what she meant, but couldn't ask. Not when Asharti's eyes were so angry. Asharti came to herself. "You have to find yourself, Bea, not just be what he wants."*

*It seemed so noble. Asharti seemed so sure. She stared helplessly at Asharti.*

*"Only then will you be worthy of him . . ."*

*Beatrix felt she had been slapped. She blinked at Asharti. Asharti's rebellion made her worthy of Stephan. Beatrix felt only admiration, even awe, for Asharti at that moment. Asharti knew things she had never even considered. She vowed to be worthy of Stephan, and Asharti, as she had not been worthy of her mother. But inside doubt grew a canker. Could she do it?*

*"Come, you are shivering," Asharti beckoned. "Get under the quilts with me."*

Beatrix shook herself. Was that night the beginning of her lost innocence?

True, she had taken life like a feral beast before that

time. But a beast is innocent. It kills to defend itself, and because it needs to feed to live. Before she met Stephan she did not know right from wrong. Stephan's teaching was the beginning of her end. Or maybe it was Asharti. Beatrix let Asharti lead her almost to destruction. For both, the need for blood was entangled with desire. All Beatrix could do was to suppress it, lest she become like Asharti. She had learned, in all those centuries. She had learned to suppress the desire. She squeezed her eyes shut.

All this talk of second innocence brought back Stephan and Asharti. She twitched the draperies closed, then turned and leaned against the window. It was Langley's fault.

He was a match for her. She liked that. Maybe he was right. Maybe she needed a man she couldn't bully.

What was she thinking? What she needed was a string of young men to offer their necks to her. She could risk nothing more than uncomplicated adoration. She couldn't get tangled up with a man like Langley. He would demand more than dalliance. He was the kind of man who wanted to possess a woman, body, heart, and soul.

In spite of her better judgment she was looking forward to riding with him tomorrow night in the darkness. She breathed. In. Out. Of course, she could expect nothing more than a week of interest. She would hope for nothing more. A week without memories or fainting spells, perhaps. She curled in her bed as the March winds outside whispered at her window.

John walked back to Albany House as light first seeped through the brown haze of London. The masts of the ships crowding the Thames to the south rose between the church spires. Already the streets were filled with hawkers and tradesmen beginning the blustery day. He had been walking all night. He hoped the wind calmed today or she might not keep their tryst. Imagine a woman riding out at night! He had no doubt her horse would be highbred and more than just stylish, or that she would come alone, without a groom.

Was he insane? He had no wish to connect himself with a nightmare like Pauline Bonaparte again. The information he had given Pauline last year in Sicily misled her brother about the size and courage of Wellington's force in Portugal, making Masséna slow and overconfident in his attack. That turned the tide. Yet success came at a terrible personal price. The woman's appetite for orgasm was insatiable. Any man with a strong cock and a disposition to use it would have done for her. He felt soiled. He had worried about extricating himself from a liaison with the sister of an emperor. Yet in the end all it took was presenting a dim-witted colonel with equipment of legendary size and Pauline thought the change her own idea.

He pushed down the part of him whispering that Beatrix Lisse was not like Pauline Bonaparte, or any of the others. He did not like the flare of hope that flickered in that corner. He was looking forward to a little dalliance in the week or so before he went down to Portsmouth to engage in some dalliance far less pleasant. No more. And he would find out whether she was a spy, given time. That was his reason for proposing his assignation.

He tipped his high-crowned beaver to the sleepy footman at Albany House as the watchman doused the street lamp in Albany Court. Withering had strict orders not to wait up for him, and for once, as John let himself quietly into Number Six, the wretch seemed to have obeyed him. A card was propped prominently on the table in the foyer.

John recognized Barlow's hand.

He ripped open the missive and scanned it hastily. Damn! So soon? The winds in the Channel had been so contrary that the frigate bearing the French prisoners had put directly into Portsmouth instead of coming up the Thames. The prisoners were being taken on board the hulk *Vengeance* even now. He was ordered away directly.

He watched Barlow's note burn in the grate. It told him only to proceed to Albemarle Street and that he would rendezvous in Drayton. His mind raced. A mill was taking place in Petersfield that would serve as an excuse to tool down that way. Blackstrade was fighting a local man. He strode through to his bedroom.

Withering was just shutting a valise. "I packed a few items only, my lord," he said smoothly. "Shall I step round to the livery and collect the carriage or will you be traveling post?"

Curse the man! The fact that his valet realized that an envelope with that particular handwriting on it would provoke a journey said Withering knew more about John's double life than he intended. "Livery," he said stiffly. "Give me an hour. Let it be known I went to Petersfield for the mill and will be visiting friends in the area."

"And how long do we expect to be absent?"

"Not long."

The old man's face betrayed nothing. "I trust my lord has provided for an exit?"

John recognized the worry. "When have I not, old friend?" He clapped him on the back.

Withering sniffed. "I shall have the usual bandages and disinfectants ready."

John smiled. "I shall endeavor not to need your ministrations. Now off with you."

Withering retreated. John took out his pistols and examined the barrels, checked the shot and loaded them. He was almost to the door when he remembered his engagement tonight.

Damn again! There was nothing for it. He took a sheet of foolscap and dipped his pen.

*An unexpected obligation of the first importance has arisen. I must leave town for a few days. Though it pains me to delay our engagement, I*

*have no choice. If you can forgive me, I shall wait*
*upon you when I return.*

> Yours,
> Langley.

Inadequate. She was proud. Men did not cry off engagements with her. He was weak enough to regret that the ride with her was lost. She would never grant another. He called for a link boy and gave him the address. Then he strode out into the clamor of the early morning.

Mrs. Williams led him up to Barlow's sitting room without even remarking about the hour. Barlow was already there, untidy but alert. "Got my note at last?" he grumbled. "You were out carousing when you should have been home in bed." He peered up at John. "Are you foxed?"

"I am not." He sat, before Barlow could even gesture to the chair. "I'll need money."

Barlow gestured to a leather pouch upon the table and John pocketed it. "Papers?"

Barlow took a heavy envelope from his desk drawer. "You are a merchant, one Jean St. Siens from Dieppe, caught dealing with English smugglers. A load of wool for all those military uniforms Boney needs so many of. Of course, you will let on that that might not be your only game. That will give you something in common with Dupré. An officer of the Transport Authority will pick you up in Drayton and deliver you to the *Vengeance*. His name is Younger. Meet him at the Plow and Angel." Barlow threw a piercing glance at John. "How long do you need until we spring you?"

"As for that," John said lightly. "You can't."

Barlow's caterpillar brows inched together.

"It might cause suspicion if I am paroled so soon."

Barlow pursed his lips. They both knew that keeping their new knowledge secret was essential to the larger goal of cutting out the heart of Bonaparte's network of spies.

"No," John continued calmly. "I must escape, not be rescued."

"Prisoners do not escape from the hulks. You know that."

"Growing squeamish or losing faith?" John asked, his voice casual.

Barlow bit back a retort. "All right. There will be one guard who knows who you are and can vouch for your identity, if things get out of hand. Faraday. He can help you escape."

John grew serious. "Promise me, no matter what happens, you won't parole me."

Barlow looked mulish. Then he sighed. "Very well," he groused. "You have my word. And one more thing."

John raised his brows in inquiry.

"Dupré comes out with you for further questioning, or not at all."

John nodded. Poor wretch. It was death or torture for him in the name of Britain's national security. Dirty business. But John had known that for a long time. He strode out into the sunlight for a breakneck drive to Petersfield, and a possibly uncomfortable few days ahead.

Beatrix rose a little after the sun had set. How luxurious to sleep straight through for nearly eleven hours. No dreams, no memories tormented her. She would call for Andorra to be saddled at seven. Or perhaps a quarter past. A little late would be good for Langley's soul. She sipped champagne mixed with the juice of Spanish oranges and opened the day's messages.

Invitations. A protestation of undying love from Blendon, accompanied by a very bad poem. He would be hurt by her attentions to Langley at the salon this evening. She ripped open the final envelope. She did not recognize the hand, but a glance at the note told her all.

So.

He tossed her aside in favor of . . . what? She glanced at the note. "An unexpected obligation of the first importance." A familiar heaviness swirled around her. She blinked slowly and sat on her dressing table stool like one of those great ascension balloons with the hot air let out of it. She jerked her head to the side, trying to avoid her painful thoughts. Impossible, of course. When she raised her eyes, she found herself gazing at her mirror. The problem with immortality was repetition. Comical, really, that she had tried so hard to avoid rejection. She had transformed herself into a fascinating woman. No man had abandoned her in . . . nearly seven hundred years. Yet repetition would not be denied. Langley discarded her without a thought. She did not cry. She had not cried in centuries. She only stared in the mirror, as though her face was a code for which there was a solution.

There wasn't.

# Seven

A wave washed over the side and drenched John's breeches and boots with the smell of the sea. The *Vengeance* loomed ahead against a sunset sky filled with the heaped clouds that threatened rain. Spray lashed his face. He shifted with the swell to keep his balance. His hands were shackled behind him with heavy iron. He was bound for purgatory in the form of a ship, stripped of masts and sails, lurching in the harbor and crammed with three times the human cargo the designers had intended.

When a frigate was no longer seaworthy the navy either broke her up for scrap or dismasted her and made her into a prison ship, commonly called a hulk. The *Vengeance* heaved sullenly on the swells of the coming storm. The English did not like to think they needed permanent prisons. Most English prisoners were only waiting transport to Botany Bay and the French would be paroled to France as soon as the war was won. Why should England pay to construct prisons just to get them through the present crisis? Crisis followed crisis and the war with France dragged on. So they filled the gap with ships. What better place to stow prisoners than in the middle of freezing water, in a confined area that was easy to guard?

The four guards in the skiff heaved at the oars, drawing the skiff up beside the frigate. All was quiet late at night. The gun ports were locked shut. The decks were empty, except for sentries striding fore to aft. No light shone save under the quarterdeck where the captain of this abomination and the guards would be barricaded behind heavy oak overlaid with beaten iron to protect them from their charges. Below, five hundred prisoners were left to their own devices, living in squalor. The skiff kissed the side of the hulk covered with seaweed and barnacles.

His commitment took on frightening proportions. Thank god Barlow had provided one guard aboard who could vouch for his true identity and watch his back. Prisoners on the hulks died from starvation, disease, or violence by both prisoners and guards. John had begun to think of this faceless Faraday as a lifeline already.

The guards did not unshackle him so he could crawl up the stairs poking from the side of the hulk. One called out sharply to unseen men above. A hook was lowered from a boom. They slipped it under one of his arms at the shoulder and signaled. The rope jerked upward and he was hauled bodily aboard, wrenching his shoulder with the weight of his own body.

Collapsing on his knees upon the deck, he heard a rough voice say, "Well, what 'ave we 'ere? The latest Frenchie, lookin' for a lesson?" He raised his head and looked into a heavy English face that spoke of coarse beginnings. Thick lips, thick brows, dull eyes, and largish ears, all stuffed inside an English naval uniform that looked two sizes too small. The ruffian jerked his knee up and caught John's chin. John went reeling to the deck. Dimly he heard the wastrel say, "Strip off them fine clothes and take 'is boots. They'll bring some shillings in town."

Panicking, John thought of the sticking plaster that held the oil-cloth pouch flat to his chest. Two shapes descended on him. One pulled at his boots, the other unlocked his manacles. When his hands were free, the guard rose and kicked him over his loins. "Get that there coat off, French dog." He squirmed out of his coat and unbuttoned his breeches. The guard crowed at finding the three louis he had left in the pockets. When all that remained was his shirt, he rolled onto his belly on the deck. They pulled it off him, but they couldn't see his oilskin packet pressed against the boards. They tossed him some roughly made togs of yellow canvas as he lay naked and shivering on the deck.

"'Eave him below wif 'is fellows," one of them cried.

He scrambled to his hands and knees, his back toward the ruffians, clutching the canvas uniform to his chest to cover the packet. They shoved him through a hatch. He tumbled down a ladder to the deck below. Lying in a heap, he tried to breathe. The air down here was close and fetid with the odor of bodies and tobacco, tar and that fecund smell of wet wood at sea.

John rolled his bruised body onto his back hoping he hadn't broken anything and saw the square of lighter black disappear. When the echo of the wooden hammer battening the hatch had died, John heard breathing and movement around him. Coughs, soft oaths in French and English and something he thought was Dutch swelled over his returning senses just as rough hands dragged him up. As his eyes adjusted to the greater darkness he could make out dim forms of crouched men and swinging hammocks.

"Ye cain't stay 'ere. Deck is full."

"Get down to the orlop. That's where the new ones goes."

He stumbled and was pushed toward another hatch. He half slid to the deck below, landing on a body crouched at the bottom of the ladder. He fell to his knees.

"A new one, eh? Down! Down below."

"I'll take them clothes." Someone made to snatch the canvas he clutched to his chest. John tore himself away and made for the next hatch. Throwing himself feet first into the blackness, he slid down, breaking the hold of the hands that snatched at his arms and ankles.

The orlop deck was pitch-black and, if possible, the atmosphere was even closer than on the decks above. It was a wonder men didn't faint or even die down here.

*"Français?"* a voice whispered.

"According to my parents." His flawless French had saved his life many times.

"There is room in the corner."

John looked around. It was so black he could not see at all. But hands came out and guided him, more gently than on the decks above. "Did they give you a blanket?"

"They gave me these rags and a kick down the hatch." He stumbled over bodies.

"François—get Linnet's blanket. He can't feel the cold now."

A thin blanket was pressed into his hand he was pushed down into a narrow space under the hammocks. "Merci," he whispered to his benefactor. "Your name?"

"Reynard," came the fading reply.

John settled himself as best he could, feeling his sore ribs and back for damage. He shrugged his wrenched shoulder and decided it was not dislocated. Then he donned the canvas suit and pulled the thin blanket around him, shivering.

"If you live long enough, you may inherit a hammock," the denizen above him said.

"I'll live," John vowed under his breath. *"Pardonnez-moi."* He apologized to his neighbor.

"No apologies needed. He's dead. You have his blanket. At least you'll have more room when they haul him out."

John pushed himself against the tarred bulkhead, away

from his neighbor corpse. His stomach protested against the rise and fall of the ship with the swell of the growing storm. He fouled his sleeping place with vomit. No one seemed to notice except the man above him, who let out a guffaw. "You'd best get used to being belowdecks in a heavy sea," he cackled. "Or you'll end like Linnet there."

For the first time, a thread of doubt wound through John's heart. His plan to find Dupré, convince him to reveal the name of the central figure behind the French intelligence, and then escape seemed a little naïve. And Lord knows naïveté had been his undoing in the past. Well, if he failed, he would just go to Faraday . . .

He wouldn't fail. He wouldn't ask to be taken off the hulks, no matter how bad it got. He couldn't fail Barlow, and he couldn't fail England. If French spies had free rein, how far was it from invasion and defeat? England was the only thing between Bonaparte and all of Europe.

He clutched the blanket round his shoulders and tried to think of anything besides the heaving of his stomach. An image came to him of Beatrix Lisse; her hair like coals glowing faintly red, and her eyes, normally so languid and bored, snapping when provoked . . . He smiled. Oh, she would be angry with him about now. Would she hear that he had missed their engagement for a mill? He did not doubt it. And he could never tell her otherwise. But it would not matter. A woman like that would accept no reason why he should not have kept his engagement. By the time he returned, her obviously capricious interest would have moved on.

It was for the best. A man like him had no business with any but the denizens of Covent Garden. Beatrix Lisse was just the same, of course, a courtesan. She made no attempt to hide it. But she had more intellect, more mystery, more emotional intensity somewhere below her cavalier attitude than any woman he had ever met. Was she a spy? Useless to speculate. She would never let him get close enough to find out, now. He would have to leave that to Barlow. The thought that she would never receive him was depressing, though.

His stomach got the better of him once again. He was in for a long night.

The only way he knew it was day was that the prisoners were rousted to the waist of the ship for counting, deck by deck. He had shivered all night in the dark stench of the orlop deck. By morning there was hardly air to breathe. So the brisk wind blowing across the waist of the *Vengeance* felt like heaven, in spite of the cold that struck to his bones. His fellow prisoners were a ragged bunch. Some yellow canvas suits were so weather-beaten they were almost white. Each bore the initials T.O. for Transport Office. Some prisoners were naked or nearly. These might be taken for madmen with beards and hair in disarray. Whether they had traded their clothes for food or had had them stolen, it was impossible to tell. The prisoners were thin, some spectrally so. He glanced around the deck, packed with silent men. The guards were a sullen lot, sailors judged unfit to go to sea. They were the dregs of the navy. Which one was Faraday?

A little officer, almost as round as he was tall, made his way to the edge of the quarterdeck. His uniform was tricked out with gold braid at every turn, and he wore a huge rosette of gold upon his hat. The effect only served to make his person seem less elegant, not more. He did not wear the epaulettes of a captain, however. A lieutenant his age who hadn't made captain never would. That could turn an ambitious man mean.

"Is this our jailer?" John whispered to the man pressed against him to his right.

"Lieutenant Rose," the Frenchman spat.

John glanced around, recognizing the voice. "Reynard?" The man nodded, his eyes crinkled. He was a large man with a nose that was much too large and a generous mouth that gave his face an open expression.

"Thank you for the blanket. I might have frozen to death."

"Shush," another man hissed. "Do you want punishment?"

A guard jerked his head around. "You there!" He pointed to John. "Step forward."

Now John knew why the deck was silent. He pushed his way to the front of the crowd. A guard approached and ordered him to lace his fingers behind his neck. Then the brute gave him a back-handed blow to the head with his truncheon. John staggered, but he got his feet under himself and stood. This adversary was the one who had hit him the night before.

"Ohh, Lieutenant, we got a live one here," the brute chortled, and raised his truncheon again. John braced himself, but someone behind the guard called out in a reedy voice.

"I was warned about that one. He'll be punished, never fear. But we've more important game afoot just now, Mr. Walden."

"Back to your place," Walden growled, disappointed of his game.

John stood where he was, fingering the blood at his temple, before hands pulled him back into the crowd. He tore his gaze from the guard, who seemed excited by his insolence. What did Rose mean, he had been warned? There was an air of expectancy among the prisoners.

The lieutenant cleared his throat loudly at the edge of the quarterdeck. "I know how you murderous lot fuddled the count yesterday to give your extremely stupid compatriots time to make good their escape." His voice held a natural whine.

John could feel the prisoners hold their collective breath.

"Carpenters are even now sealing the holes you cut between the decks."

Clever, John thought, to send men slipping between decks so that the escapees would not be missed. Still the prisoners held their breath. They cared not if their ruse was found out if it had served its purpose. John did not like the smug smile on the lieutenant's pudgy face.

"Gentlemen." The lieutenant nodded to four guards who pulled on ropes hanging from a boom on the forecastle. The rasp of rope against wood was nearly drowned by a murmur of dread that went through the packed bodies as they began to understand what might be coming.

The bodies that flopped over the rail of the forecastle were naked and gray-white, having been submerged in the nearly freezing water for some time. They were pierced by the same kind of hooks that had raised John last night, but these went through their backs and protruded through their sternums rather than being hooked under their arms. Any blood had washed away. That left them looking more like carcasses than human bodies. A horrified gasp went up around the deck. John went still. Escape was looking more difficult by the moment. He hoped Faraday would have some ideas. He searched among the guards for a face that might be friendlier, but he could see only hardened scowls and self-satisfied grins.

"So you see," the lieutenant continued, "as usual, escape failed. Why do you do it?" he mused. "Sure, it lends interest to my job, but to you? Disappointment and death." He rubbed his hands. "Now to the punishment. Rations to be cut in half for three days."

A groan went up from the prisoners.

"And . . ." The lieutenant's voice rose over the din. "All trade is suspended with the shore. You'll make do with prisoners' rations from now on."

At this the groan turned to an angry growl.

"And all your possessions forfeit."

The prisoners looked around in panic. There was some brouhaha belowdecks. A crane pulled up a net from below filled with bedding, clothing, and a mishmash of what might, in some other world, be trash. The net was swung out over the side and into the bay.

Moans of despair shot through the crowd.

"Get them below. No exercise today." The lieutenant turned on his heel and retreated to the rear of the quarterdeck to confer with his officers. Guards began to herd the men below.

"Each to your decks," they called.

The prisoners shuffled below with sagging shoulders and hanging heads. Taking what few things these men possessed might have broken their spirits. John felt a profound shame that British men could treat their fellow humans so.

The decks with gun ports were open during the day but the orlop deck got light and air only from the periodic hatches to the decks above, so it was dim and dank even in the morning. The prisoners handed up three corpses after stripping them of anything of value. Reynard stopped some quarreling with a sharp word.

John introduced himself to those immediately around him, hoping to find Dupré but having no luck. Reynard and Vidal, the man whose hammock hung above him, soon put John straight about life aboard the hulks. Normally men practiced all sorts of simple crafts: carving, weaving straw hats. They traded with merchants from Portsmouth for raw materials and sold their finished goods for a pittance compared to what they were worth. The shillings they earned were used to buy enough food to avoid slow starvation, or comforts like playing cards or a decent blanket—all gone now. Their supplies were forfeit and the means to trade their finished products cut off by the lieutenant.

John's stomach was shocked at his first meal. The

bread, what little there was of it, was raw and gooey inside, burned outside; the stewed vegetables had been near to rotten going into the soup. There was no meat, meat being served only every other day, but his fellows assured him the meat would be near spoiling or past the point. John's stomach knotted itself in protest.

In the afternoon, making his way around the orlop deck, he found the prisoners from the French frigate *Reliant*. Pressing down his satisfaction, he struck up a conversation about the appalling conditions. Dupré turned out to be sallow-faced, with lank hair and burning brown eyes under heavy brows. "I am glad to meet one whose fame has run before him."

The man's eyes narrowed.

"You are a man of importance to the emperor," John apologized hastily. But he saw with approval that he had planted a seed of curiosity in the man's speculative expression. They talked warily of Dieppe. Dupré had lived there and John knew enough of the town to reminisce.

"Why would a simple merchant end in this hell?" Dupré asked, eyes hooded.

"Some merchants are not so simple." John kept his voice low. "I traded with England."

Dupré had the faintest air of doubt. It would be unremarked by any but John. "Many traders disobey the law without ending in the hulks."

John smiled softly. "I bought wool destined to be made into uniforms for our glorious army." He paused. "And perhaps they thought, mistakenly, I traded in less tangible articles."

"Ahh." Dupré nodded, looked about to ask another question, and shut his mouth.

*Good,* John thought. *Let him wonder.* "I understand money cures many ills on these hulks. We are brothers of Dieppe. Do you fancy the orlop deck, monsieur? Or should we negotiate our way up the ladder?"

Dupré was nothing loath. Reynard helped John negotiate a place on the gun deck. He spent a whole louis to buy a place not only for himself but for Dupré and Reynard. Reynard accepted his gesture but then took him aside. "Never be carried away by generosity, nor by any other feeling here," the man admonished. "Get used to shutting your heart to all pity on the hulks. It is the only way you will survive."

Reynard could not know that Dupré, at least, was not an object of disinterested generosity, and John did not enlighten him. The three men made their way to their new places. On the gun deck, some prisoners had carved a little personal space, where they once kept books, or an upended barrel on which they played with greasy cards. All was gone now, except for an easel set next to a porthole that held an exquisite naval scene painted in oils. The oils themselves still gleamed wetly on a palette and stood in small bottles on a shelf.

"You seem fortunate," John said. "Your possessions alone survived."

The painter snorted. He was a young man of perhaps eight and twenty, and comely. "I get a pound apiece, but the lieutenant gets ten. The brute who sells them in Portsmouth gets twenty. The lieutenant would not cut off the source of his income." He bowed. "Louis Garneray."

"He takes a cut of all our sales. I give his prohibition three days," Reynard observed.

An idea flickered through John's brain, a fragment only, but with possibilities.

"Monsieur Garneray," he said, looking at the very fine painting showing eleven hulks in Portsmouth harbor. It was most precise. "Have you ever made engravings?"

"I did some woodcuts and a little metal work before I joined the navy." The young man drew his prominent brows together, puzzling.

John waved a hand airily. "And if someone bankrolled

you, you could obtain the necessary engraving supplies from your connections? You will need special paper and ink."

Garneray nodded, wary. "It would take a week." Reynard looked speculative.

"Then consider me your banker," John said. "I have some very particular scenes for you to copy. I believe they would be a boon to your fellow prisoners."

"Special scenes?" Garneray asked. "What kind of scenes? Naval?"

"I should rather say . . . commercial. They are devised by the county bank."

"Ah," Reynard breathed, understanding. He nodded at John. "You, sir, are a dangerous man, and a welcome addition to our company."

The prisoners were ninety percent French in the *Vengeance,* and they had formed their own society, with its own rules and its own form of justice. The guards, what few were needed to keep the floating prison secure, stayed abovedecks supervising exercise, or in their quarters, gaming. They did not venture belowdecks. So the rule of law for deeds committed by prisoners on prisoners was left to the prisoners themselves. Disputes were judged by a council of eight, and punishment meted out at their direction. Stealing was punished ruthlessly with lashing, not surprising when the little a man had was all that stood between him and starvation or fever.

That afternoon, they found one of the prisoners had preserved his deck of cards, concealed upon his person. John joined the game with Dupré. They played Macao. John knew he would get no information from his quarry yet, but he wanted to make certain Dupré would seek another meeting. Nothing engenders confidence like winning money from a man at cards. So he brought out a small portion of his sous, determined to lose them to Dupré.

It was hard. At one point, when John had won his third hand in a row despite all he could do to lose, he began to wonder if Dupré was playing poorly on purpose. Dupré's expressions were as hard to read as John expected, but the man still did not win. His lack of skill foiled even the advantage of his opaque nature. He seemed distrustful of John's luck, and a premonition of disaster invaded John's breast. Would he ever get the man to reveal his secret?

# Eight

"You are a man most naturally secretive," John observed to Dupré the next afternoon. "It makes you the devil of an opponent at cards." A lie, of course. He had managed to lose some money to the man, but that had not increased Dupré's trust. Perhaps anyone who traded with the British was suspect. Could Dupré not see that such a man would be perfectly placed to carry messages from French agents in England? John had thought him more imaginative. But he had not asked again about John's trade.

They played whist as they waited their turn to go up on deck for exercise. John now wore a money belt around his waist. Reynard was Dupré's partner. John had some ensign named Philippe. Word had it the bodies of the escaped French prisoners still dangled from the booms. Impotent outrage alternated with depression in the prisoner population. Dupré seemed unaffected. Underneath John's outward calm his spirits were low. He had never been less proud of being English. The fact that he was going to kill Dupré or turn him in for torture did not help. He was as bad as Rose and company in his way.

"I think," Dupré observed, "that you also have a secretive habit."

Was Dupré making his overture at last? "Perhaps we have that in common. Along with a certain . . . familiarity with human evil."

"Ahhh." Dupré played down a card. "You mean that outrage comes hard for us."

Damn him. John peered at his hand. He needed to lose this rubber since he had won the last. But there was nothing for it. If he played a smaller card in the suit, the others would remember when the king he held was revealed later. "To a certain kind of man, outrage seems pointless." He laid the card and collected the trick.

"Don't think I am sanguine." Dupré perused his hand. "I would rather be elsewhere."

"Without doubt. I have extremely urgent business." John made a stupid lead into a suit he knew was Dupré's strong second.

"Merchants always think business is urgent."

"Let us say our cause would think my business urgent, too," He must go so carefully.

Dupré glanced up under his brows as he took the trick. "Easy to say. But *if* what you say is true, what will you do about it?"

John looked from Reynard to Philippe. "What any good Frenchman should do. Escape."

"Shush," Reynard hissed. "Escapes are most often betrayed from belowdecks."

"There are spies for the English among us?" young Philippe asked, appalled.

"Spies are everywhere," Dupré observed. He showed no signs of rising to the bait.

Philippe took the trick in spite of John's best intentions.

"Yes," John said, his voice flat. "So I have heard."

He thought for a moment Dupré might say more, but again he closed his mouth. He clearly thought that whatever

John might know, it was not worth exposing his own position. John's frustration threatened to well from his belly into his eyes, so he stared at his cards.

The guards called the number of their mess and rousted them onto the deck for exercise. They were made to circle round the waist under the bodies of the two dead prisoners. It was cold on deck, but still the bodies were bloated and foul-smelling. The prisoners circled round the small shack built on deck to house the food supplies and the Bentham stove that cooked their miserable rations. The anguish mixed with anger over the treatment of the prisoners' last remains was palpable. John could hardly wait to be herded below.

Lieutenant Rose came to the edge of the quarterdeck to watch them, grinning. "French dogs," he said to his second-in-command. "They have no spirit. One must only be masterful."

John's blood rose. *Cold, be cold,* he warned himself. Ahead, Reynard stiffened.

Laughter echoed behind them. It was a particularly nasal, British sort of laughter John had heard a thousand times in the clubs of St. James's. A barrel of half-rotted potatoes stood at the corner. He saw Reynard lean over. His heart sank.

In the long moment when he knew what would happen, conflicting sentiments rushed through John's breast. He should not endanger himself or his mission. Reynard was right. There was no room for sentiment here. But even Reynard could not hold to his own advice, and what better way to engender some faith in his loyalty to the emperor?

Reynard whirled and hurled the potato straight for the lieutenant. It struck him smack on the chest, bringing him around. The soft fibers burst over the lieutenant's coat with a satisfying squelch. Almost without thinking, John stooped to the barrel, grabbed a huge potato, dunked it in a bucket of tar and flung it like a missile. It struck the

lieutenant at the throat, cascading black, smelly goo over
that braided uniform. And this time the lieutenant was
looking straight at him.

The other prisoners dove for the barrel, dipped their
rotten weapons in the tar and began hurling them at the
officers. Rose shouted for their heads, but the English officers soon had to retreat. Even after the guards began
laying about themselves with their truncheons, the tarred
potatoes continued to fly. Dupré took a blow to his head.
John felt the truncheons on his shoulders. The screeching
triumph in the prisoners' voices gave him strength. He
had thrown six of the gooey missiles when more guards
came charging out the door from the cabin under the
quarterdeck. John saw Dupré go down and dragged him
between himself and Reynard for protection. But the
melee soon petered out. Prisoners groaned, holding their
ribs or their heads. Rose shrieked, a blackened, sticky figure, tar in his hair, on his gold braid, his white stock.

"Get the tall one," he cried. Hands grabbed John. "I
was told he was a troublemaker. Lash him and put him in
the Hole. I don't want to see his face for a week."

Four guards overpowered John. Reynard stared, pain
in his face. Dupré was looking speculative. John grinned
and began to sing "La Marseillaise." Reynard swallowed
and joined in. Others followed, one by one. Soon the deck
was filled with a baritone chorus.

"Bring the rest of the prisoners on deck for punishment." Rose had to shout to be heard.

Dupré joined in the singing last of all. John was
hauled over to a capstan and tied across it. The hulking
guard, Walden, grinned and tore the canvas from John's
back. John looked around without much hope. Where
was Faraday?

Beatrix canceled her salon on Tuesday, claiming illness.
Symington sent messengers all over town with the cards

crying off. In a way, she *was* ill. She just couldn't bear the open adoration, the posturing on their part, the forced gaiety on hers, or worse yet, her forced nonchalance. She would have ended screaming at them. But being left to her own devices was even worse. She had paced herself to exhaustion, locked in the artificial darkness of her boudoir all day, and now as dusk fell the night stretched ahead ominously.

A light knock on the door brought her around. She had let all the servants have the evening off. "Go away."

Instead, the door opened quietly and Symington entered. He bore a tray with a tea service. "The cards have all been delivered, your ladyship. I thought you might like some chamomile tea. It's very soothing."

The last thing she wanted was chamomile tea. But the fact that he sensed her distress and brought her something calming was touching. She sat at her writing table while he poured it out. She took a sip. "When . . . when do you go to your sister?" she asked, trying to gather herself.

"I was thinking of putting that off for a week or two," he said impassively.

She looked up sharply at him. "It was tomorrow," she said. "You were to go tomorrow, and you *will* go tomorrow. You'd never forgive yourself if you put it off and something happened. And . . . and there was something I was to do while you were gone." Her thoughts were so scattered. "Yes. I'm going to hire the house you saw . . . where was it?"

"Wimpole Mews, just off Harley Street. But I'm not sure you're up to that just now, your ladyship." The old man's face was crunched in concern.

"Nonsense," she said briskly. "Just the thing for me. I'll meet the agent at dusk tomorrow: When will you return?" She sipped her tea resolutely.

"A week, ten days at the most, I should think."

Ten days without Symington! "Perfect. You have picked out a companion for her?"

"Miss Cadogan will move into the house to ready it as soon as you have purchased it."

"Oh. Should I . . . ?"

"She will present herself here at the end of the week."

Beatrix sighed. "So organized, Symington. I have come to depend so upon you."

"Frederick will look in to see if there are any messages you wish to have sent. Mrs. Mossop will handle the drawing room gatherings until I return."

She nodded. But she didn't dismiss him. There was something else on his mind. She could see it in his face. "I take it you know why Langley left town. You might as well tell me."

Symington glanced down. "A mill."

She frowned, thinking for a moment only of grinding flour. Then it dawned. "He left town to see a prize fight?" She tried not to let the outrage tinge her voice.

Symington nodded. "He plans to stay with friends in Hampshire afterward, I hear."

She cleared her throat to be sure she could speak. "Well, off to your packing with you."

"Is there . . . anything I can do for you?"

His voice was so solicitous she almost broke. She smiled. "No, my friend. Nothing."

She watched as he let himself quietly out.

And there was nothing, nothing anyone could do. The quiet of the house was eerie. Outside carriages passed in the square. Life at night in London went on. With her more than human hearing, she heard it all. But inside it was nearly silent. Faintly she heard Symington up in his fourth-floor room, packing, and other than that . . . nothing.

She had a dreadful feeling there was more of nothing to come. How stupid of her to be so upset about Langley crying off! He cared for her so little that a prize fight could draw him away.

What did it matter?

Because she wanted to be with him and it was a short leap from that to caring for him. You couldn't care for them. It left you vulnerable. She hadn't cared for one of them since . . . Stephan, really . . .

CASTLE SINCAI, TRANSYLVANIAN ALPS, 1105

*"You did well tonight, Bea," Stephan said. They were alone in front of the fire in Stephan's quarters where they often sat reading and talking until dawn. She was warm now, having huddled in Asharti's bed until her friend fell asleep. Then she had stolen up to the solarium.*

*Beatrix gathered her courage, remembering Asharti's words. "Why did you not punish Asharti for disobeying you, Stephan?"*

*He was drinking wine. He poured her a glass now. It was her first. It took him a long while to answer. "Because she has a harder road than you do, child."*

*"She does not," Beatrix protested. "Why is her way harder?"*

*"Because she is a human made by another vampire, not born to the blood."*

*"And my way was easy?" Beatrix clutched her wine glass with white knuckles. "I was abandoned, left to defend myself and rip throats for my blood because I knew no better."*

*"But you were born to your condition. You know deep inside yourself that what you are is what you were meant to be. There are some among our kind who say any vampire made is doomed to go mad or to tread an evil way. Asharti knows this."*

*"That is why you are not supposed to make another by sharing blood."*

*"Yes. That's why the Rules say that if ever, by accident, you do, you must kill them."*

*"That isn't fair—to kill someone when it is your fault they are what they are."*

*"No, it isn't fair. That's why I protected Asharti when Robert le Blois wanted to kill her."*

The one who made her wanted to kill her? How horrible! *"Will Asharti go mad?"*

*"That is an old wives' tale."* He stared into the fire. *"But I do think that to have the Companion thrust upon you is difficult. We must help Asharti accept the responsibility it brings. And we must realize that her way is hard."* He looked up at Beatrix. *"Can you do that, Bea?"*

Beatrix took a breath and let it out. *"I will try, Stephan."* What she would try to accept was Stephan's lenience with Asharti. But in truth, why shouldn't he admire her? Beatrix did.

He smiled. How she loved it when he smiled. *"I knew I could count on you."* He gestured with his glass. *"Are you not going to join me?"*

She smiled and ducked her head, then sipped her wine. *"It is very good."*

*"How was it to feed on your own, my dear?"* His voice was so kind. She stole a look at him. The firelight played across the planes of his face. His dark hair curled at his broad shoulders, full and lush. His teeth were perfect, like all of their kind. His leather jerkin made him seem more masculine than ever. *"It was good to be in control, was it not?"*

*"Yes. It felt . . . natural. And now my Companion is shouting life down my veins."*

*"It is a marvelous feeling. We are very lucky to be who we are."* He held his wine glass up to the firelight and it glowed bloodred. *"The blood is the life."*

*"The blood is the life,"* she echoed, and sipped. She felt an overwhelming desire to be close to him, so she slipped from her chair and sat on the great white-furred bear rug

*at his feet. She laid her cheek on his thigh and felt her blood thrum inside her, somewhere low.*

*Stephan stroked her hair. Beatrix felt her Companion rise within her. "There is much that I would show you, Bea." His voice was husky. "For a woman to survive in the world, she must use the skills she has. Men are strong . . ."*

*"I am stronger than any man," she protested. But her attention was on his hand, lifting her heavy hair from her back to stroke her neck. It made her shiver.*

*"Yes, and that strength will be useful. But other ways will be useful as well."*

*"What kind of ways?" she asked. The heat of the fire seemed to pool in her center.*

*"Let us call them feminine arts," Stephan said. "One can't always compel what one wants. The subject can feel the compulsion if you are too bold. A man can lead other men or overpower them, but women need a subtler way to prevail."*

*"How do you mean?" She let her head loll against him. He stroked her throat, and his touch spoke of red wine and fire.*

*"I will show you if you will let me. Will you let me?" He slid from the chair to sit by her.*

*She looked up with a little thrill of fear. Was there something she needed to learn that he felt he must ask permission to teach her? "I trust you to teach me whatever I need to know."*

*"Know, then, that I would never hurt you." He set down his wine and began to unlace the leather laces that held the bodice of her gown together. "I will show you something that, over the years ahead, will give you much pleasure, and a way to get men to give you what you want without using the Companion." He smiled wryly. "Two purposes in one? What could be better?"*

*Beatrix felt her breasts swell with breath and something else as he opened her bodice. She was not a babe.*

*She had seen men and women rutting, a coarse and violent act with much grunting and sweating. It was frightening, as though people turned into beasts, alienated from their own humanity. She had been a beast once. She had no desire to return.*

*Stephan must have seen the doubt in her eyes. "I promise you will enjoy yourself," he whispered in her ear. His breath on her neck made her shudder.*

*But not with fear. "I give myself over to your tutelage," she whispered back. After all, it was Stephan who had rescued her from the rutted streets of the slums in Amsterdam, cleaned her and dressed her and taught her, talked to her as an equal. She always strove to please him. He wanted her to learn this. She would please him now.*

*She lifted her chin. He cupped her neck with one large warm hand and slowly brought his lips to hers. Their mouths touched, lightly. His lips were a caress that sent feeling shooting down between her legs. He was gentle. Not like a beast at all. She sighed and relaxed against him. His other hand stole around her waist. She let her lips melt against his. His tongue darted out and he licked her lips. Surprised, she gurgled a laugh into his mouth. He retreated, smiling.*

*She glanced down, almost shy. "My apologies, Stephan. You surprised me."*

*"No apology needed." His expression was tender. "Have you ever been with a man?"*

*She shook her head, then looked up boldly. "But I know how it is. I have seen it done."*

*He nodded. "Ahhh. Of course."*

*She caught his tone and bristled. "I know, for a start, that you must take off your braies."*

*"So I should." His eyes crinkled at the edges as he shrugged off the leather jerkin. He stood. Under the flowing shirt, he plucked at the lacings of his braies. Beatrix felt her eyes go big. He was going to take off his clothes*

*just like that? He slipped his braies down over his hips.
He stepped on the heels of his soft leather boots, pulled
out his foot and kicked them away one by one. His legs—
they were so strong. She could see cords of muscles under
the curling, dark hair on his calves. Her gaze turned up to
the bulge of his thighs. The shirt hid what she wanted to
see—what she was afraid to see. He crouched beside her,
cupping her jaw with his hand.*

*"And you, Bea? What of your clothing?"*

*The skin of his palm was rough against her cheek
and electrifying. Her breath came shallowly. She swallowed. Could she finish what she'd started? She plucked at
the laces of her bodice. The lacing went from her neckline
down in a vee to the lowered waistline of her heavy blue
wool gown. He moved her hands away and pulled the laces
gently free, one by one, until she thought she might faint.
Then he reached into the vee, cupping her breast with his
palm over the fine linen chemise she wore beneath. Her
nipple contracted as though it was a night-blooming flower
touched by the sun. He slid the gown off her shoulder.*

*She looked into his face, seeing the caring, the affec-
tion in his dark eyes. He must love her, to take such care.
Before she realized what was happening, her overdress
was on the floor. The wool was like a blue puddle. She sat
in her underdress, her breasts rising and falling. She had
never been so aware of her body: the breath in her lungs,
the flushed feeling, the liquid between her legs that
seemed to grow more heated by the moment.*

*"Stephan . . ." she whispered. He took that as permis-
sion and leaned in to press his lips to hers. Her arms slid
around his neck and she pushed her breasts against the
hard wall of muscle she could feel under his shirt. His
tongue found its way into her mouth and this time sh*
*wasn't surprised, except by the intimacy of that*
*Moisture shared, body to body. He kissed her d*
*the act promised he would delve deep in m*

*He lifted her out of the crushed wool of her dress, holding her tight to his body. Against her hip she felt a hardness and wondered for a moment before she realized what it was. She smiled into his mouth and snaked her tongue in to lick his lips and teeth.* She *had done that to him. He wanted her. She ran her hands over the supple moving muscles of his shoulders under his shirt. No, this wasn't right. She wanted to feel his naked skin, and see all of him. She squirmed out of her chemise and lifted his shirt over his head. She took a breath. She had seen many men without their shirts. Huge brutes of men and boys like willow wands. But none were like Stephan. The little movements of muscle under his skin seemed calculated to distract her. But she would not be distracted. His chest was lightly dusted with black, curling hair, through which dark, soft nipples peeked. His belly was taut and a vee of hair pointed down toward a nest of hair that framed a very hard rod. It made her suck in her breath.*

*"It is just me," he reassured. His eyes went molten and he touched her shoulder, almost reverent. "You are . . . beautiful." He shook his head and chuckled. "I sound like a lovesick boy."*

*There! He had said it. She dared not smile, or even look into his eyes again, lest he retract it or explain it away. Lovesick. That was how she felt; light-headed, sick with love. She let her nipples brush across the hairs on his chest. He gave a low groan and pulled her to him.*

Beatrix sat shivering in front of her cold chamomile tea. The night was vivid as if it had happened yesterday.
_____ _ n her the joy of making love.
_____ _ ad introduced her to the ways of sex.
_____ was love. And sex with a man led to
_____ ix could not be trusted with sex, so
_____ erself for six hundred years. She
_____ had intercourse, hadn't been hurt.

She fascinated them, took their blood and left them like Blendon, standing naked in the night.

Until Langley. She thought she had put Stephan behind her. He surfaced tonight because Langley had abandoned her to go see two men batter each other senseless, and that mattered to her. "Senseless" was the operative word. It was all so senseless. There was no second innocence. She had seen it all and everything happened over and over again, and you couldn't escape it.

Or perhaps, as Stephan suggested so long ago, the only refuge was Mirso Monastery.

Her path was winding down. Nothing would stop the darkness, whatever caused it. The only lights in the night were the glowing spires of Mirso. She would take the Vow and spend her days in chanting, renouncing the pain of the world forever in return for peace.

But what if peace was another word for numb? Was dull paralysis the only choice? She closed her eyes and prayed, to whom she did not know. She did not pray for redemption, only for escape from the memories that seemed to be driving her to Mirso Monastery.

She must get through tomorrow. She would buy a house for Symington's sister. After tomorrow, she would think what to do.


The Hole was a dank blackness no more than six feet square with six inches of tarry and foul salt water floating in it. He had been there without food or water he could drink for days—he wasn't sure how many. The builders had sealed the room with sheet metal to keep out the rats, just to prevent the occupant getting his own supply of fresh meat. John was naked, freezing, and bloody with twenty strokes of the lash. It could have been worse. Rose was so anxious to get on with general punishment and so sure the Hole would kill John, he didn't take time for the number he might have ordered. John wondered how sailors stood the ever-present threat of flogging. He had heard that fifty and a hundred were not unusual in a flogging captain's ship.

Time dragged. He was in pain. He wasn't hungry anymore, but thirst ate at him. His shoulder ached. It had been only three weeks since he was wounded in Calais. Did he have enough strength to outlast Rose? Maybe Rose had forgotten him. Maybe he would rot in here forever. And what of Faraday? He had heard no guard called by that name. No guard had given him any sign. Perhaps Faraday could not have stopped the lashing, but he might have seen that John got some water. John wouldn't let himself think that there was no Faraday, or that, if there was, he had decided not to help John. That would mean it was him alone against Rose and the hulk. Could he just stand up and say, "I'm really British and I work for the government" if things got too bad? His English was flawless. But so was his French. Would anyone believe him? Would anyone exert themselves to send for Barlow? He couldn't imagine Rose doing either.

It didn't matter. If he stood up and shouted he was British, the mission was a failure. Barlow's best chance to find who was at the center of the French network would be gone. John couldn't let that happen. He wouldn't. He would hang on.

Such thoughts circled in his brain until he fell into half-sleep. Then dreams came to him whether he would or no. Dreams had never been his friends. He had dreamed of Cecily or Angela, his fights with his father, returning from the Continent to see Langley Court in disrepair. He sometimes dreamed of being discovered as an agent, giving up all his country's secrets at the mere threat of torture. But this time his dreams were different.

No, this time it was Beatrix Lisse who haunted him, or saved him. He felt a strange connection to her in the long dark hours in the Hole. He dreamed of the tryst they never kept, riding with her at night, neck and neck, their steeds powerful between their thighs, the scenery flashing past. And she was laughing in that full throaty contralto she had. She was so vital! Sometimes he dreamed of holding her in his arms inside a huge, darkened cathedral. And she would look up at him. Tears would glisten on her dark lashes. Her eyes would go hot with desire. The air would be filled with that elusive cinnamon scent she wore. He would lead her to a pew. Her ripe body yielded to him, and he was strong and alive.

Always, when he came to himself in the pitch-black, sodden wet, he realized how foolish he was. He knew these dreams were born of fever. Yet the drive to life ever-present in those dreams leaked over into his dark hell, and gave him strength.

"I told you not to give in to generosity," Reynard admonished without rancor. He helped John lie upon a thin straw pallet. He propped John on one elbow. The gun deck might be dim in the late afternoon light, but John blinked against it, unused to any light at all. "Didn't I, Dupré?"

"You did." Dupré wiped the sweat from his forehead. "Pelting Rose with all that tar . . ."

John closed his eyes. He was stiff from the lashing, though they said it had been more than a week. His lips were cracked, his mouth like wool. "You started it, Reynard . . ." he croaked.

"You should never have tried to cover my actions," Reynard muttered as he helped John gulp water from a tin cup. "Slow now, brother. You're weak as a kitten. We thought you were dead." He touched John's shoulder where the Calais bullet had left a pink circle of new skin, and surveyed the other scars. There were many of them, twelve years of service writ upon his body.

Dupré loomed over him. "For a merchant, you have seen a fair amount of action."

John was too dull to match wits with him. "I told you how it is with me," he murmured.

"And singing 'The Marseillaise'; that was certainly stupid of you." Dupré shook his head.

A reedy voice came from behind Dupré. "I been a-saving of some salve, if the gentleman could use it." A sallow young man ducked his head and pulled his forelock in the naval salute.

"Thank you," John whispered.

Reynard nodded at the sailor and took the salve. " 'The Marseillaise' *was* stupid," he agreed. "But its spirit might have kept some of us alive through what happened next."

"What did Rose do?" John asked, his throat raw, as he watched the sailor retreat.

Reynard and Dupré together turned him upon his belly. "Kept us all on deck, standing like sardines." Rough hands scraped the salve across his back. John bit his lip to keep from crying out. "He put a pump and a fire hose in the launch, rowed round the hulk and shot freezing water full on us for the rest of the day and most of the night." Reynard's voice dropped ominously. "Some got sick, like Dupré here. We lost six men in the days since."

"I'll be all right," Dupré said irritably. But he couldn't help but cough again, and the cough was wet. "A passing influenza, nothing more."

John saw the look in Reynard's eyes and knew he feared worse.

"You're not so spry yourself," Reynard told John. "The dirty water in that damn hole has got into your welts. You're burning up."

"Excuse please," a soft voice said, deprecating.

John craned around. The cuts on his back shrieked. A diffident middle-aged man who looked like he would be more at home in a bakery than as a prisoner of war held out a wooden bowl to Reynard. "We pooled some meat we got from the Portsmouth thieves today. And we traded with a sailor for some grog. Thought as how it might set you up prettier."

John managed a crooked smile. "I expect I could use prettying. I have nothing to give you for it. They took all my money."

"Oh, no, sir." the man said, horrified. "You mustn't think we wanted payment."

"Thank you," John said, touched that they would share their little. "Thank the others."

Reynard took the bowl. The man bobbed and backed away. Reynard turned to John.

"Rose relented?" John croaked.

Reynard gently touched his lips with the gooey salve. "If you mean did he let the traders back on the ship, yes. He ain't going to cut off his nose to spite his face," Reynard said. "And Garneray has got his supplies and set up a new trade."

"Does Rose collect from us, or from the traders?" John asked. Suddenly that was crucial.

"He likes to make us pay him direct."

"Excellent," John sighed.

Reynard cupped a hand around John's neck and lifted his head while he held first more water and then a cup of grog that was composed of almost undiluted rum to his cracked lips. "Down the hatch. Gulp it now." Then he sat back and pulled a thin blanket up over John's naked body. "Just lie easy here, and rest. We'll save your meat for later."

John felt a lassitude come over him, like he was swimming in warm water. The grog was powerful on a stomach so empty. "Out of curiosity, is there a guard named Faraday on the ship?"

"Not that I know of," Reynard said, puzzled.

"I thought not," John murmured as the grog overtook

him. He closed his eyes. An image of Beatrix floated before him, smiling, full of life. There would be no help.
John had to believe escape was possible. He would get
what Dupré knew and make it out of this hell. And to do
that, he would hang on to that image of Beatrix . . .

# Nine

When John woke he heard a wet cough in the darkness. "Dupré?" he whispered.

"How did you know?" the man said wryly as his coughing fit subsided.

John dragged himself up on his elbows, feeling the scrape of the blanket against his wounded flesh. "God, I need to take a piss."

"That's good news. It means your innards are working. The bucket's in the corner." Dupré pointed away to John's right in the dark. "Can you make it?"

"I'd better, or I'll wet myself right here." He crawled over and between bodies, relieved himself on his knees with a sigh he could not suppress, and made his way laboriously back to his place. Dupré pressed upon him the bowl of meat he had saved. John knew he must eat. He scooped the faintly rancid-smelling stuff into his mouth, hardly chewing.

"Slowly, my friend, or you will bring it up again."

John deliberately put the bowl down and took a breath. Now, when Dupré thought John had a cause for it, was the time to show some vulnerability and earn Dupré's confidence in return. Let him not betray himself when his brain was so fuddled. "Dupré," he whispered. "I have to get off this damned hulk before they kill me. I have information that can help our cause."

"What information?" Dupré hissed.

John smiled in the dark. "Ahh, now that does not seem wise, much as I sense we have in common. Suffice it to say I think it might put the nail in the coffin of these British brutes. It has to do with some ships I've contracted to move troops, and where. I'm only afraid of giving the information to some bureaucrat and never having it reach the person who could act upon it."

"Then you have no choice but to tell me. You see, I know who should get the message."

It would not do to seem too eager. "And of course it would not be wise of you to tell me." He could feel Dupré smile. "We are at a stand, unless we escape together, each with our piece of knowledge." John waited for his adversary to assess the situation.

"We will present the puzzle pieces for our emperor's triumph." The cough came again. A hand found his in the darkness. It was even hotter than his own. They shook on the agreement.

"Let us devise the details, then," John whispered. *And I had better work quickly,* he thought. *Lest one or both of us meet our maker before we can put the smell of tar behind us.*

The enforced gaiety of her nights had been banished. Beatrix had canceled all her evenings. The Prince Regent sent daily notes importuning her to attend some event or other. A lengthy missive in his own hand was waiting for her when she rose this evening, saying he had been cupped of twenty ounces and the doctors feared for his rapid pulse, all for the love of her. She knew Mrs. Fitzherbert, that soft dumpling of a woman, had succumbed to just such tactics. She had heard that bets at White's were two to one against Beatrix holding out. Those bettors would be poorer for their insolence. What did she care for the likes of Prinny?

What did she care for anything? She tossed the prince's letter into the fire. The memories had been unremitting. It was if they were trying to tell her secrets she couldn't hear, even though they had taken to shouting. She did not look into her mirror anymore. Her eyes were haggard. She needed to feed. The Companion itched at her, whispering "The blood is the life," but she did not allow the young men who left her posies to come up, and she couldn't think about disappearing into Whitechapel to look for her blood. It all seemed too much.

Was he back in London? She had no way of knowing.

Symington had not come back. He sent a note saying his sister was too ill to travel at the moment, but he had hopes of starting in another week. She was alone. She was so tired of it all. Perhaps she was tired enough to sleep. Was it day? She didn't know. The heavy drapes might be holding back the sun or just the night life of London. She lay down on the rumpled bed. She had not let in any of the servants to change the bedding in days. Her eyes closed.

It didn't matter if Langley was back in London. It would be the same as with Stephan . . .

CASTLE SINCAI, TRANSYLVANIAN ALPS, 1105

*Beatrix dismounted lightly from her horse in the stable yard of the castle. Two grooms hurried forward, flickering lamps held high, to walk and groom her mare.*

*"Apollonia," she crooned, patting the sweaty neck. "You shall have extra oats tonight for being such a courageous girl." It was not every horse who would brave the forest at night, but she and the mare had a special bond.*

*The animal trusted Beatrix to keep her safe. Beatrix chortled at the thought that a wolf might dare attack them. Its temerity would be short-lived. Beatrix was more fierce a creature than any wolf. She had felt wolves tonight, in the darkness of the trees where no moon could penetrate. But the wolves felt her, too, and slunk away. She was mistress of the night, and both Apollonia and the wolves knew it.*

*She wound her way from the back door up through the kitchens to Stephan's quarters. She glowed inside. It was not just the exhilaration of her nightly ride, taken at ten like clockwork and lasting for an hour or even two. It was not her Companion, who surged within her from a recent feed. Beatrix was drunk on love. The last six months had been heaven. They had hunted together, the three of them. She had learned to savor the thrill of it, yet to deny herself the last drop. Always, as she fed, she thought of Stephan and let her loins boil, no matter who actually bared his neck to her. Stephen said they were just food, but for her, the feeding was tied with her dawning sexuality. Asharti said she felt it, too.*

*Beatrix loved Stephan with an intensity she had never thought possible. Stephan made love to her almost every day, carefully, lovingly. True, he always shushed her when she tried to tell him how much she loved him, but she could see his own love in his eyes. To think that after all the women in his long life, Stephen had chosen her to love forever was . . . was delicious.*

*She had taken special care in the last months to be kind to Asharti. Asharti must not know about her and Stephan. Asharti liked to spend long hours alone, which was very convenient when you thought about it. And Stephan was most careful never to show Beatrix preference when they were all together. Still, Asharti would be hurt if she knew. How could she not? And Beatrix had grown to love Asharti, too. She loved Asharti's feistiness, her determination to get what she wanted from the world.*

*Asharti was a strong person, not just physically, they all were strong that way. Asharti was a survivor who would make the best of where she was. Beatrix was sometimes jealous of her, sometimes just admiring, but in all but loving Stephan, she let Asharti take the lead. Sometimes she thought Asharti must know. How could see not see Beatrix's bliss? But if she knew, Asharti would have confronted her about Stephan. When it happened, as it must, she only hoped she would not lose Asharti's friendship.*

*Beatrix burst into Stephan's quarters, where she had spent so many nights writhing in ecstasy as he showed her new ways to reach bliss and how to help him reach it, too. The bed was neatly made. Fire crackled in the grate. Two goblets of figured glass waited in anticipation of her return. The room smelled like the myrrh he imported because she liked the scent.*

*Her gaze returned to the wine glasses. A tiny circle of wine shivered in the bottom of each. She walked slowly to the little table that held the goblets, not wanting to think But she couldn't help herself. She raised a wine glass to the light.*

*The dregs of wine floated there in red revelation. The goblets supposedly waiting for her had already been used, in this, the most intimate of Stephan's rooms. She stood, transfixed. How amazing that the world could change in a single moment over something like wine. She stood somewhere far away, looking at herself and marveling. Then she smashed the goblet with a shriek against the hearth, raised her heavy wool skirts and took off at a run for Asharti's room.*

*She was crying by the time she pushed open the heavy oaken door. The panting pleasure on the far side told her everything. She stood, shaking, in the entryway. Stephan looked over his shoulder and raised himself on one elbow. His other hand slipped from Asharti's darkly furred mound. Asharti herself shuddered one last time and opened her* eyes. They widened at seeing Beatrix, and then her expression grew sly.

"You . . . you . . . betrayer!" Beatrix hissed, tears coursing down her cheeks. She could not say she thought he loved her only. She was ashamed that she had felt sorry for Asharti. How naïve she had been! How foolish . . . "I . . . I hate you!" She was not sure which of them she meant.

Stephan got deliberately up from the bed, and picked up a robe of oriental silk she knew only too well. He wrapped it around his nakedness, but not before she saw that his erection was subsiding only slowly. The fact that his cock had risen for Asharti made her blush with shame. How had she not realized?

"I am sorry you had to find out this way," Stephan said with maddening calm. "I thought you were almost ready to understand."

"Understand?" Beatrix said, her voice rising, "You thought I would understand?"

He held out a hand. "Let us go to the solarium. There are things I would tell you."

"Nothing you can tell me will make a difference." She practically choked on the words. All she could think about was getting away. She turned on her heel and stumbled from the room and down the stairs, the sobs in her chest growing. She was not quite certain where to take refuge. Stables. She would go to the stables while she thought how to make her escape more permanent. She couldn't stay here. Not when Stephan betrayed her so calmly, so heartlessly.

She was halfway across the cobbled stable yard when a growing darkness, blacker than the night around her, whirled in front her. She turned and ran for the gate into the forest. He was after her in two enormous strides. His hand clamped on her upper arm. She spun, growling, her eyes red with her Companion, her teeth bared. She clawed at him and struggled in his grip.

"Bea, Bea," he cooed. She scratched his face. Blood dripped down his cheek before the wound closed. She struggled, shrieked in anger and frustration. Still his voice never rose above a whisper. "Shush now. I understand. Shuuuussssh."

All at once the fight went out of her. She was not the only one for him. He didn't love her. Her life force drained onto the cobblestones. She would have fallen if he had not held her. Sobs came up from her belly and keened in her throat. She struggled for breath. The blackness at the edge of her vision had nothing to do with her Companion.

Stephan swept her up in his arms. She clung to him as he took her into the greater darkness of the stable, into a vacant stall piled with hay. They sank there while she sobbed and heaved for breath. But you couldn't cry like that forever even if you wanted to. Soon she realized he was kissing her hair and rocking her, his arms around her. She could feel his heart beating in his chest. Animals moved in adjacent stalls. The comforting smells of warm horsehide and musty hay enveloped her. She felt dry, like dust floating away, lost in the wind.

"I know you are hurt. You think I don't care for you. But I do. God above, I do," Stephan whispered in the darkness, his breath warm on her neck. "You are important to me. Far more important than anything else in my life. But you are also part of something important for our kind, a grand experiment if you will, that will set the course of our race for millennia to come."

"I am an experiment." Her voice held no outrage. The time for outrage had passed.

"In some ways. You and Asharti—a treasured and precious experiment."

His words pounded nails into her coffin.

"You know our Elders think that those who are made are not as good as those born with the Companion. They would kill those like Asharti. Understandable in some ways, since those made so often go mad, killing indiscriminately."

"I used to kill," Beatrix said in a small voice.

"Exactly my point. You were born vampire, but you were no better than one made. It made you perfect for my purpose. And so few of us are born now, my choices were limited."

Hardly a flattering description of the reason he chose to rescue her.

"I want to prove," he continued softly, "that with nurturing, with training, born and made are equal. Not that we should make others willy-nilly. But if one is made accidentally, that one must not be killed. You and Asharti are my chance to show that. I will teach you how to go on. I will train you for full and productive lives." He lifted her chin. "You do see, don't you?"

"I see you do not love me." The words were torn from her throat.

"But I do," he said, looking straight into her eyes as though that proved his sincerity. "I love you both. And when you two prove that born and made are equally capable of taking their places in our society, others will be saved, now and in times to come."

She did not care for saving lives in years to come. She wanted Stephan to love her now. But her throat closed around any words she might have said. She rocked there in his arms, dry and hollow. After a while she managed to croak, "How can you love us both?"

"Ahh, that is complex, Bea," he whispered. "You will know yourself someday. It is because I have known love in all its permutations. I have loved so many, in so many ways, that I can select the way I choose to love. I choose to love you both, in different ways, so I do."

"You do not know love at all then," she accused, sitting back. "I do not choose to love you, Stephan. I just do."

He smiled. "For now. I am your first taste of the simplest

*kind of love. There are others, Bea, which you will know in all the countless years ahead, long after you have forgotten me."*

He thought she could forget him? He put a finger to her lips to stop her protest. *"I hope you will remember your love for Asharti. You will be her anchor after you leave my protection."*

Leave. Silence stretched while she gathered her courage. *"Do you want me to leave?"*

*"No,"* he whispered. *"Of course not. But you will."*

She did not reply but simply blinked at him in disbelief.

*"You have so much to experience, so much to offer. Men will worship you. You can shape the world if you will. You will leave me far behind."*

She turned her face up to confront him. It was the first time she had ever done so. *"It is not I who would leave you,"* she said, dry inside. *"You betrayed me. Is that not like leaving?"*

He smiled tenderly and stroked her hair. *"Someday I hope you feel differently."*

*"Don't say that, Stephan."* She did not want to hear this. How could he not see that sleeping with Asharti was a betrayal? And he was not telling Asharti all this about leaving. *"What about Asharti?"*

*"She will go, too."* He sounded so weary. *"Was I right? Have I done you both an injustice?"* In spite of her anger a moment ago, all she suddenly wanted was to comfort him. She leaned in toward his body and took his face in her hands.

*"You took me out of a bestial life, Stephan."*

*"Yet I have hurt you,"* His eyes were infinitely sad. *"It was inevitable. There is so much hurt ahead for you. It is all so inevitable."*

Maybe, maybe she could make it right between them. Perhaps this experiment was the excuse, but he must have loved her all these months. He just needed to remember

*that. Her newly wakened sensuality rose in her. The soft
flesh between her legs swelled in anticipation. She must
put it back the way it was between them. She reached up
to kiss his chin. "I don't hate you Stephan. I love you.
Take joy in that tonight." She let her eyes go wide with
promise. "Asharti is up in her room. And I am here."*

*He slid his hand around her nape, turning her face up,
his strength held carefully in check. "Oh, Bea, Bea." He
examined her, as though he could tease out some truth
that would turn pain into joy. She took the initiative and
brushed her lips against his.*

*She pushed away Asharti, and her anger, and her anxi-
ety. Stephan needed her. The tingle of his lips against hers
sent shocks down to her now-swollen loins. The inevitability of what would happen here overwhelmed her.
Stephan needed her.*

"Leave me alone!" Beatrix shrieked. "Can't you just leave
me alone?" She threw herself out of bed and heaved on
the bell rope again and again. The room was spinning; the
sounds were beginning to resemble an off-kilter carousel.

A startled footman opened the door. "My lady?"

"Is there any laudanum in the house?" she panted, her
night dress clinging to her sweating form as she steadied
herself against the writing desk.

"I . . . I don't know." He was flushing and going pale
in turn.

"Well, ask Mrs. Mossop, and if she doesn't have any
then get out to a chemist, or call a doctor or something. I
need laudanum." She pressed her hand to her forehead.

The footman scurried out the door.

If she couldn't get the memories to leave her alone,
she'd drug herself out of any memory at all. She *wasn't*
going to keep getting dragged back to a time that was so
painful, or to people who had hurt her so much. Let laudanum stop the spinning. And laudanum would keep her

Companion quiet about wanting blood as well. A perfect solution all around.

It was four days before John managed to take his exercise under the derisive jeers of the guards. He could not yet wear the rough canvas shirt of the prison uniform Reynard had so carefully mended, so he was naked to the waist, welts lacing his back. The corpses of the escapees were gone. But John had not forgotten them. There would be no help. Faraday must have been a figment of Barlow's imagination. Or something had gone wrong. It was up to him alone to do the impossible and manage a successful escape for himself and for Dupré.

He watched carefully as barrels of supplies were loaded over the side with the boom the sailors called the cat's-paw. Neither he nor Dupré were in any condition to make the four-mile swim to shore in icy waters. Indeed, Dupré had been unable to take his exercise today.

The prisoners shuffled around the freezing deck. There was a dense and chilling fog in the harbor. "You survived, you bugger." The familiar gargoyle face of Walton, the guard who had lashed him, loomed out of the mist. "Nobody survives a lashing and that long in the Hole."

"Sorry to disappoint you," John muttered. The bell sounded the end of their exercise.

"Talk back like that, and maybe you'll have another go," the guard threatened, grinning. "Someday soon we'll see just how far you'll go to avoid the lash, now you've tasted it."

John wiped away emotion and staggered below. He'd better get off this ship soon if he was going to survive. And if he did, he wanted to plant a little bomb for Rose that would explode after he left. Useless, he knew. If not Rose, then some other would take over the hulk, likely as bad. Nevertheless, he stopped to see if the scheme he had put in play was likely to bear fruit.

Garneray was the richest of the prisoners, since his paintings commanded a pound apiece, and since his belongings had not been tossed overboard. A rough curtain was drawn around his painting space. John called a greeting and was invited inside the luxurious thirty square feet.

Garneray's painting of Portsmouth Harbour filled with hulks still stood on the easel, next to the port, but Garneray was hunched over a barrel. John smelled acid. Garneray had a pound note laid out and was carefully copying it in acid upon a plate of metal. Heavy rag paper was stacked on the floor.

"How goes it, my friend?" John asked. He sank onto a stool, exhausted.

Garneray grinned. "I am learning a trade, against the time I am paroled."

John cleared his throat. "I have need of your new art, since the guards took my money."

"I heard you and Dupré have information which must reach our government."

John raised his brows.

"There are no secrets in a ship like this."

"Should I be alarmed?"

"If yours was an average escape I would say yes." He perused his metal plate. It was half a perfect likeness of a pound note off a Dorchester bank. The other half was blank. "But there is not a man aboard who would not like to poke the British in the eye. I could not answer for any of us under torture, though."

"No man knows if he can withstand torture." He stared at Garneray. "Will you provide?"

Garneray nodded. "You started me in my trade. Was this not in your mind then?"

"No. I thought I had enough money. I had another reason, which I will keep to myself."

Garneray shrugged. "You may have five-pound notes now. Pound notes will take longer."

"A hundred pounds then."

Garneray rose, took a large dark blue glass bottle labeled "linseed oil" from his little shelf. He popped the wide cork from its mouth, slipped out a roll of five-pound notes, counted out twenty to John, and stoppered the bottle again.

John put the roll of soft in his pocket. He nodded.

"How long before you try?" Garneray asked.

"How often do the supplies come on board?"

"Twice a week."

"Then, in a week," he said, and slipped out through the curtain. He hoped he could stay out of the guards' way until then. And he hoped Dupré would last that long.

All was ready. Reynard was the liaison between the prisoners and those who bought their wares. On the pretense of giving a message to Garneray's art dealer, he arranged the whole under the very noses of the guards. It was risky. But John could think of no other way to avoid swimming for it. It would happen in four days. John thought Dupré would make it.

The portholes slapped shut for the night as the prisoners were locked below. Dupré was called up on deck to get their miserable evening meal. Reynard read by the light of a tallow candle. John sat shuffling cards, wondering why they chose Dupré. The guards knew he was ill. A dreadful premonition began to grow in John's belly. Their heads both jerked up as Dupré stumbled down the companionway, scattering food across the prisoners.

John and Reynard rose as one, crouching under the low deck. John fought his way over bodies toward Dupré. He lay facedown, still. John turned him over. The man's eyes bulged in surprise. A dark stain spread over his chest. Dupré craned his neck to see the wound then lay back, realization filling his eyes.

"Who did this?" John asked as he undid the man's waistcoat.

Dupré half chuckled and shook his head. "A shadow."

"Did any of you see?" John accused the others around him.

Murmured denials. The wound was bad. Behind him, Garneray said, "No doctor till tomorrow morning now. I'll go up land tell the guards we need one."

"Help me get him to his place, Reynard," John ordered. His mission was melting away.

They did what they could. They cleaned the wound with grog and bound it. John thought a lung had been pierced. They made him as comfortable as possible. John volunteered to sit up with him. Now, in the small hours, John's spirits sank. Dupré would no more escape than he would fly. He would not even make it to see the doctor in the morning. A candle guttered next to Dupré's pallet. The other prisoners had edged away from the dying man.

Dupré looked at him from eyes too bright. His face was gray and clammy. He seemed to go in and out of his senses. Only a few moments ago he had been raving about bats and blood and immortality. Understandable in one who was about to meet his maker. Now he seemed to have gained focus, though his breathing gurgled with blood. He motioned to John.

"A few more hours," John whispered to him, leaning close. "A doctor . . ."

"Too late," Dupré gasped. Blood dribbled from the corner of his mouth.

"Not too late," John protested without conviction. It was an act. Dupré either told him what he came to this hell to find out now, or he had done it all for nothing.

Dupré rolled his head impatiently. "Think, man! You know in your heart."

John bowed his head. "I know."

He did. "You must bear the burden alone."

John closed his eyes so he would not seem desperate for

the information. Dying men were perceptive. Their illusions had been stripped from them. When he had command of himself, he opened them. Dupré grabbed his neck with one cold, sweating hand and drew him down. John turned his head and put his ear to the barely moving lips.

"Take what you know to Asharti." Dupré gasped for breath that wouldn't come.

John pulled away. What kind of name was that? Dupré was whispering again. John bent.

"The Comtesse de Fanueille. They will say it is Fanueille." His voice was fading now. It was only a breath. John could not even be certain of the words. "But he is . . . her pawn. Do not trust him . . . with what you know. Asharti will . . . understand and act."

A *woman* was the spider in the center of the web? "Where do I find this Asharti?"

"Paris or . . . Chantilly." With his last strength, he clutched John's arm. "Be careful. There is evil. I have seen things . . ." The eyes faded. "Fear her . . ." he whispered.

The lips stopped moving. The gasping breath stilled. John sat up. There was a small smile still hovering around lips almost blue with lack of air. Even as he looked at the bright, fevered eyes, they dulled. The hulks had claimed another prisoner.

John sucked in his breath, feeling dirty. Dupré died thinking he had achieved a final act that helped his country. John could not but admit relief that he hadn't had to kill the man or put him into Barlow's tender hands. But he knew if it had come to that, he would have done it. He was his country's man. He had known that was less than noble for years and yet gone on. Now he must escape, and use the information he had wrenched from Dupré against the French. He did not feel triumphant.

He closed the eyelids over the staring pupils. "Go with God," he murmured and stood up. He turned and found

Reynard standing behind him. How much had he heard? He peered at the bluff man's face in the darkness, expecting duplicity, avarice, some expression of his intent.

He saw only sorrow.

"A miserable way of escape, poor sod. But at least he is away." Reynard heaved a sigh.

John hoped he found a different way off the hulks. He had done what was required. Dupré was dead. And he had a name. Asharti.

# Ten

"Symington, are you back at last?" Beatrix murmured, opening her eyes. The old man was standing over her. And he had a strange young man standing behind him.

"You have not been taking care of yourself, my lady," Symington admonished.

She shook her head, pushing her hair out of her eyes. "It doesn't matter."

Symington picked up the half-empty bottle of laudanum from her night table and pocketed it. "Well, you must pay attention now," he said sharply, in tones remarkably unlike a servant. "Rivers here is applying for a post as a new footman, and you must interview him. Privately." He pushed the fresh-faced young man forward.

"Sorry to come to you so informal, your ladyship, but Symington here said you wouldn't like me wearing a cravat."

Beatrix blinked. He wasn't wearing a cravat. She could see the blood beating in his throat at his open collar. "What I need is more laudanum, Symington," she threatened.

"Later perhaps," he said calmly. "But now it is time to

do your duty." He turned to the door, leaving the nervous applicant shifting from foot to foot. "And be careful, won't you?"

Beatrix sighed. The old man was a termagant. She looked at the boy, for he was no more than a boy. The fog was lifting from her mind. The laudanum must have worn off. She felt her Companion rise along her veins, needing. She sighed. Symington knew she was always careful with them. She hadn't caused one more than passing inconvenience in six hundred years. Wasn't that what Stephan taught her?

"Come here, young man. Sit beside me and tell me your name."

It was today. Reynard and Garneray were set to help. The whole ship might know, including Rose and his thugs. Reynard never let on that he heard John's last exchange with Dupré. John didn't ask. The supply barge thumped alongside. Two bargemen had twenty counterfeit pounds apiece in their pockets. The man who oversaw the quay where the cargo would be unloaded had twenty from Garneray's art dealer, sympathetic as long as Garneray was not the one to go, and the dealer himself got another thirty. Garneray had made up another twenty in pound notes for John, since he would arrive on shore naked, without food or transport.

If he was lucky. John volunteered to get his messmates' rations from the cookhouse on the deck with Reynard and Garneray. The bargemen began arguing with the guard who oversaw supplies. John was about to slip inside the cookhouse, when the hated voice rose behind him.

"You there! Troublemaker! Get over here."

John's stomach turned. He was so close! Slowly, he faced his persecutor. The other prisoners shuffled on toward the cookhouse, but heads turned.

Walden was shorter than he was. As he stepped up to

John, he had to look up. His pinched face squinted in dissatisfaction. "You been misbehaving again, ain't you, troublemaker?" he asked, his breath reeking of grog. "I'll bet we got to flog you."

John kept his face impassive. Here it was, just what he had hoped to avoid. He would not survive another lashing and the Hole. The mission would fail.

"What will you do to avoid a lashing, Frenchie, eh? Say 'please don't lash me, sir'? Would you say that? Come on, say that."

John gritted his teeth. Succumbing might make the brute bolder. Resisting was just what he wanted. He took a breath. "Please don't lash me."

"Sir." The guard raised his truncheon. The prisoners around him muttered.

"Sir." John ground it out.

"Good." The brute grinned. "Good. Now, I don't think you need them clothes. Strip."

He was very glad Reynard had the money this time. The prisoners had stopped where they were. John took off his canvas suit. Next would come the order to the capstan. It was over. The guard walked around him. John felt a truncheon to the backs of his knees. He fell to all fours and struggled to kneel. The prisoners crowded round. The guard looked up, as surprised as John. He raised his truncheon. "Get back there!" But he was only one. John saw two others come tripping down the quarterdeck ladder in their haste. Rose came to the rail.

"What goes on there?" he shouted. "Get those men below!"

Hands pulled John to his feet. He was in the middle of the crowd of prisoners. The hated guard was outside the circle. Hands pushed John down where he couldn't be seen, shoved him through the cookhouse door with Reynard and Garneray.

"Quick, man," Reynard whispered. John crouched inside

an empty barrel. Reynard pressed the little pouch of forged notes into his hands.

"Bravest thing I ever saw," Garneray said softly.

"You jest. I just stripped and begged for mercy," John muttered.

"That's what was brave," Reynard whispered as he pushed John's head down and raised his mallet to tap home the lid. "I would have clocked the bastard, and it would have been over."

"I'll send back for you," he promised.

Garneray laughed. "Do not make promises you cannot keep, friend. We are wed to a devil named Rose, and like to remain so."

"Rose will soon be gone," John said, as the lid closed. He could hear Reynard's bitter chuckle as the barrel rang with the thump of the hammer.

"Go with God," Garneray said as they let themselves out to the deck. John had said the same to Dupré in what he hoped would be different circumstances. He felt for the cork and pushed it out. The bunghole would be his only source of air.

Shouts. The barrel tipped and John rolled over and over, barking his knees and elbows. The bargemen hefted it into a net. God allow that no guard noticed the ropes that sagged with too much weight for an empty barrel. A clunk in the bottom of the boat and then the rocking of the water. His barrel should be the last cargo loaded. Light streamed in through the little bunghole. More shouts. The barge pulled for shore. It was a good half hour until they thunked against the quay. His barrel was jostled, heaved up, rolled along some wooden surface, then hauled upright.

No light came through the bunghole. He waited, cramped, trying to keep his breathing shallow. He expected discovery at any moment. After all, he had disappeared on deck in the middle of a crowd of prisoners, leaving his clothes behind. His only chance was that in Rose's hurry to get the rebellious prisoners below, no one noticed John was not among them.

At last all around him was quiet. Now he would find out whether he was strong enough to push out the barrel top. He pulled numb legs under him, ducked his head, and put his shoulder to it. Nothing happened. His healing welts scraped against the wood and opened. He stopped, chest heaving. He tried again. A shriek of metal against wood and the barrel top popped free. He rose, gasping, and the barrel fell, taking him with it.

He was in a warehouse. Dim stacked barrels like his own rose around him. He crawled out and pushed himself to his knees, swaying.

Now, unless the transport officers were waiting outside the door, it was time to pay some rude fellow for his clothes and put some distance between himself and the horror of the hulks. If only it was not a horror of British making and if only he was not leaving newfound French friends behind in hell.

The image of Beatrix which had come to him so often in the hulks fluttered into his mind now. They were riding at a gallop in the dark along Rotten Row and her cheeks were flushed and alive. She might be the reason he had found the will to survive, to complete his mission and escape. It was as if her image was a guardian angel, urging him toward life. He didn't care anymore that she was a courtesan. His dream of her was constant. How could she not be capable of constancy? Now he had unfinished business with her. There was the matter of a promised ride.

"All right, Symington, you've had your way with me." Beatrix said. "I've fed, I've bathed. You've taken away the laudanum. And you made me come downstairs to find you." The old fox must have planned it, for all the draperies downstairs were closed against the fading light.

Symington was polishing silver, a task anyone else in the house could have done, but which he always reserved to himself. "You're looking much better, if I may say so, my lady."

"You may not." Beatrix felt like a trapped animal, waiting for the memories or the spinning colors to resume now that her protection was gone.

"Then might I thank you for purchasing the house in Wimpole Mews?" He went on polishing a spoon, though it already gleamed. "It is quite suitable, and very generous."

"Oh. Yes." That seemed so long ago. "Is your sister safely there?"

"Yes, my lady. She's better already for the sunny aspect of the house and Mrs. Cadogan's cheery chatter." He cleared his throat and examined the spoon. Apparently finding it wanting, he began rubbing it again. "Your ladyship will want to hear the news of town, of course. Lady Freston is in a family way again. And Lord Langley has returned to town, just this afternoon."

Beatrix's stomach fluttered. She couldn't think. That was bad, wasn't it?

Symington didn't even glance at her. "Strange, that. Lord Devonshire's man says Withering has been agitated, expecting his master home for several weeks. And now he's back and looking thin and drawn, quite under the weather."

Beatrix wasn't listening. Langley would be a reminder of . . . of other times her heart was engaged and she was tossed aside. But she wouldn't have to see him. She didn't go out. She'd had no one to Berkeley Square in . . . however long it had been. But still there was the damnable flutter . . .

John climbed the stairs in Thomas Barlow's house with some effort. It was nearly nine o'clock. He was not yet fit, though he had consumed a huge meal paid for with counterfeit pounds and had had a full night's sleep in Petersfield. He must report to Barlow before he could do the one thing which had kept him at his journey all day, in spite of his fatigue.

Mrs. Williams showed him into Barlow's study and promised him a bite to eat, notwithstanding his protests, or waiting to see if her master invited him to dinner. She was a woman whose kindness was innate. He looked into her weathered face and saw the British character whole. She could be dour and querulous when berating Barlow for disregarding his health in favor of his government service. Yet, like Withering, there was a core of goodness that shone through her eyes. Could she and Withering possibly balance the Roses of England?

Barlow came into the room. He seemed surprised.

"Didn't you think I'd make it?" John asked.

"We had almost given you up after Faraday was transferred to the *Ravenshead*. I was about to send someone in, regardless of the risk to the mission. Did you get the name?"

John nodded.

Barlow peered at him. "God's nose, Langley, you're a pale scarecrow. Are you well?"

"A little knocked about," John acknowledged.

Barlow sat down, leaning forward. He said nothing, waiting.

John gathered himself. "You will scarcely credit it but Dupré named a woman. Asharti."

"A woman! Was he bamming you?"

"I think he was sincere. He knew he was dying. He thought I had vital information to impart to her."

"He's dead, of course, since you didn't bring him with you."

"Yes." John did not tell Barlow that he hadn't killed him.

All talk stopped while Mrs. Williams brought John a cold mutton pie and a largish scoop of plum duff, with apologies that it wasn't something more. John thanked her, saying he was fairly sharp set, and fell to with a will. When finally John paused for breath, he saw Barlow with a finger to his lips, tap-tap-tapping while he thought.

"Asharti? What kind of a name is that?" he mused.

"I have no idea. She is the comtesse of one Fanueille. Do you know him?"

Barlow's eyes flickered. John imagined him sorting his vast store of information. "An impoverished minor aristocrat from Provence . . . the title is a fake . . . has risen in Bonaparte's esteem . . . was given command of a division under Soult. Returned to run the provisioning units—siege engines, salt pork, and the like. He is the minister of foreign trade at the moment."

"Then he is well placed for his wife to act through him."

"So. You will go." Barlow looked up. "You should know the situation has grown more serious." His brows inched together. "The French have broken the blockade at Brest."

"How?" The French had been rebuilding their navy at a feverish pace after their crushing defeat at Trafalgar. All those ships escaping to invade were an island's worst nightmare. So England had been blockading ports up and down the French coastline and the Mediterranean.

Barlow stared into the fire. "One of our ships drifted into its neighbor in the fog. The two tangled and fell off the blockade. The French somehow divined the mishap and slipped through." He did not wait for John's question. "The ship that perpetrated this enormity was found to be unmanned. All aboard were dead."

"How?" John whispered, knowing the answer, not wanting to hear it.

"Drained of blood."

"I will go, of course," John said. "When can you arrange a packet? Tomorrow?"

Barlow nodded. "You must find a way to eliminate this

female mastermind. And find out what plague is causing this loss of blood. They have loosed some weapon against us. If this phenomenon reaches England . . ."

John nodded. Now there was but one more thing to do here, or his soul was not worth the price of the Satan's bargain he had made with Barlow for so many years. "English treatment of prisoners on the hulks casts no favorable light upon our nation," he said, then hesitated. Better just to say it out. "An increase in the allowance for food, removal of the worst officers, even such small improvements would remove a stain on England's honor."

Barlow frowned and offered John a glass of negus. "The Transport Office is notoriously corrupt," he murmured as he poured. "And every competent officer is needed on the high seas."

"Can you not talk to Admiral Strickland?" The admiral was one of the very few outside of Barlow who knew what John was. Unfortunate, but inevitable. His good will had been needed to place John on a ship of the line at the right time on a mission back in '05.

Barlow frowned "He might be enamored of the job you did for the admiralty with that Spanish frigate, but this is beyond his powers. Parliament hardly has the votes for enough tax revenue to supply Wellington. There's no chance of money for French prisoners."

John clutched his drink with both hands. He had known it was so. But he would not give up entirely. "I have never asked for payment for the small exercises I perform."

Barlow looked wary. "We value your services the more because you are a volunteer."

"There are two favors I would beg." The admiral would arrange them, but probably not on John's word alone. Barlow must be the go-between.

Barlow raised his alarming brows. "Besides reforming the entire naval prison system?"

John smiled tightly. "I want parole of two men from the *Vengeance,* Paul Reynard and Louis Garneray. Surely the admiral's influence extends so far?"

"Perhaps," Barlow made no commitments. "And the second request?"

"There is a counterfeit ring operating in Portsmouth. The bills are modeled after those issued by the Dorchester Bank. One Lieutenant Rose has set the prisoners to making them, against their will of course, and is passing them in Portsmouth to buy his personal luxuries."

Barlow's eyes opened wide in his wrinkled old face for a single moment before they regained their habitual closed expression. He straightened in resistance. "The admiral would not take kindly to counterfeiting but one hates to bother him with such trifles."

John rolled the dice. "The man I have known for fifteen years would do this thing for me."

"Then I suppose I must do it." Barlow frowned.

That was John's parting gift to his fellow prisoners.

"Go home and get some sleep, and for God's sake, get your man to feed you."

John had no intention of going home. It was after ten. He'd hire a carriage to take him to his livery, then it was on to Berkeley Square. It was Wednesday. She might be alone. And he had only one night to claim the ride he was promised.

# Eleven

Beatrix heard the pounding on the front door even from the writing desk in her boudoir. She listened to the voices, one in particular. It was him! Symington had strict orders to say she was not at home to any visitors. That would protect her. Did she want that?

The knock on her door was a formality. Symington opened it before she could answer. "Lord Langley to see you, your ladyship." His look was smug, though his mouth was prim.

Damn Symington! What was he about? She tried to still her breathing, and found an unfamiliar feeling pulsing between her legs. It wasn't fair! She wasn't strong enough to face him now. She would lose control if she wasn't careful.

He entered and just stood, hands clasped before him as though he must control them. Symington slid out and shut the door. She stared, silent. He was thinner. His coat and his knee breeches did not fit him as tightly as they had. The lines around his mouth were deeper. He was paler, too, and there were faint, dark smudges under his eyes. The eyes themselves burned with green intensity.

She had seen that look a thousand, thousand times. She hardly expected Langley to display it so nakedly. What did it mean? *He* was the one who had cast her aside to go to a mill!

He started to speak, swallowed once, and began again. "I regret that my business kept me so long away."

God, no! He was going to lie to her. But why lie if he didn't care about her? Maybe . . .

"I had a touch of the influenza." He looked away as though that was the lie. But he *had* been sick, she could see that. It didn't explain the mill.

But she didn't want him to explain. She daren't be around him at all. Even now she was acutely aware of his body inside his clothing. Her unruly blood pooled in her loins. He was dangerous because she cared whether he cared about her and because she dared not indulge her body's reaction, lest she go the way she once had gone, the way Asharti went still.

He was waiting for her to speak, but she couldn't. Her throat was full.

John looked into her brown eyes and saw the pain there. She had heard that he cried off from their engagement to go to the mill in Petersfield. That much was obvious. He couldn't even tell her it wasn't true. But she was not indifferent. He licked his lips. She was not indifferent. Neither had she screamed or thrown him out. No, she sat there, saying nothing, looking up at him with those wonderful brown eyes. That was cause for hope, wasn't it? He cleared his throat.

"I've come . . . I've come to claim the ride you promised me a month ago."

"I . . . I don't think—" Her voice cracked.

"Are you the type to break your word?" If she refused him now, he'd be lost. Worse, she would confirm an opinion of her he wasn't sure he held anymore.

She swallowed. "No," she whispered. "When would you like to claim it?"

He took a breath. "Now."

Beatrix watched silently as Langley saddled Dorrie. His chestnut gelding, Fletcher, stood quietly in the cross-ties, already tacked up. She tried to focus herself by examining Langley's horse. The gelding had a wonderful set to his shoulder. He must have been gelded late, because his neck arched with muscle. If only her head would clear she could get control. What was she doing here at nearly midnight with the one man she swore she would never admit into her thoughts again? She was taking a night ride with him—something precious to her, intimate. Of course, this wouldn't be her usual ride, alone in Hyde Park at a full gallop that would scandalize the *ton* if they knew. The poor caretakers replaced the locks she broke on the northeast gate at Marble Arch routinely. No, this would be a sedate clop around the square.

Well, she would redeem her promise, but she wouldn't put her heart into it. Wasn't her heart the problem? It was thundering in her chest even now.

He led the horses out onto the mews. Their hooves clopped on stones damp with dew. The fog had settled over the city. "My lady?" he invited, holding both horses' reins while he bent and cupped his hands.

She lifted her chin and placed one boot in his palms. He tossed her up easily and she turned to sit in her saddle. She lifted her habit to lock her knee over the horn and pushed her other heel down in the stirrup. Her impulse was to canter off, but she would not give him the satisfaction of being rude. This was his ride, and she would trot behind him in his limited concept of what a ride at night could be. He would be timid, if not for himself, then for her. A turn about the square and her obligation was filled.

He swung himself into the saddle. Her gaze lingered

on his thigh against the leather. He might have lost some weight but he was still finely made. Dorrie pranced and her muscular back moved against Beatrix's most private parts under the saddle. He studied her horsemanship as she settled Dorrie then trotted west along the square, making no remark. Several carriages loomed out of the mist. If there were figures in the shadows, she did not care a whit for them, nor did he.

With a sharp intake of breath she realized he meant to take Mount Street all the way to Hyde Park. At Park Lane, he turned north, past Grosvenor Gate and Brook Gate. At the Marble Arch Gate he hopped down. She chuffed disbelief to herself. He could never gain entrance.

"Unlocked," he announced before he even reached the gate. "The keepers grow careless."

He *knew* it was unlocked. Was it still broken from her last assault upon it? How did he know? Had he . . . prepared for this?

The gate swung open. Fog hugged the grass, weighted by the dregs of the night. He swung up to his saddle and gestured her in. Dorrie sidled and jigged in anticipation. Beatrix kept her under tight rein. This would be only a stroll. The mare must learn to contain herself.

Beatrix was taken by surprise when the big chestnut gelding shot by her, Langley's heels in his side. Damn him! She hardly had to give Dorrie the office to start and the mare was off in pursuit. Dorrie was swift and surefooted with experience of the park at night. Beatrix let her have her head. She thundered up behind the gelding. "Ha!" Beatrix shouted, the animal pleasure of a gallop thundering inside her in rhythm with Dorrie's hooves. They drew abreast of Langley and his mount, but he had been holding the gelding in, and now he let him stretch out.

*It will not be so easy as that, Langley.* She tapped Dorrie's flank with her heel. The mare glided forward again. The two horses were neck and neck, racing on the graveled track. Beatrix was hardly able to see a handbreadth ahead in the fog and the dark. The wet air plastered her hair against her head, soaking her garments. Foolhardy. She looked over and saw Langley grinning like a maniac and realized she was grinning, too. To sit the gallop was frantic sex, opening your hips and thrusting them forward to keep contact with the powerful plunge of the horse's back. She felt invested in her body as never before.

Around the turn, clattering over the Serpentine Bridge, through the flower gardens, she and Langley plunged, their bodies giving with the stretch of the rein at every stride, as they leaned over their horses' necks. First one led and then the other. The animals were evenly matched. Life surged down Beatrix's veins. She had never been so attuned to her horse, or the horse next to her and the man riding that horse, and the night itself. A hard left at Rotten Row and then they were careering down the long straightaway. Another left at Broad Walk. If anyone were walking here, they would have been scattered like fall leaves. Beatrix was panting when the eastern gates loomed out of the fog again. She clucked once to Dorrie, who surged ahead.

Beatrix pulled up the mare, breathless and laughing. Langley slowed to a trot behind her, grinning and shaking his head, chest heaving. They patted their horses' steaming necks.

"What a marvelous piece of horseflesh," he gasped. "If you ever want to sell her . . ."

"Your boy is lovely, too," she returned, stroking Dorrie. Both knew they wouldn't sell.

They walked on in silence through the gates, listening to their horses blow. Beatrix felt . . . quiet inside. Not dull, as she had been of late, not anxious in dread of her memories, but quiet, almost content. She glanced at Langley. "I did not expect you to have the courage for a gallop."

"I know," he said.

"But you expected me to follow you."

"Yes."

"Don't think you know me," she warned.

"I shall take that upon advisement."

Beatrix fell silent. She did not know him, either. That felt . . . interesting, for a change. After so long in the world, it was difficult to find something unexpected.

Either both of them were feeling that quiet contentment or both were afraid to speak for fear of quarreling. They walked back down Mount Street in silence. Carriages passed them. The watchman at the corner of the square argued with some drunken young men under the luminous halo of the street lamp in the fog. It didn't matter. Nothing could touch the peace she felt inside.

As they came to the mews behind number 46, Langley leaped off Fletcher and tied the reins to a ring in an iron post near the door to the stables. Beatrix was perfectly capable of dismounting on her own, but she was strangely reluctant.

Langley turned, grabbed Dorrie's reins and reached up for Beatrix. The burgundy wool of her habit seemed to melt, as if those strong hands on her waist clasped flesh direct. She could feel herself flushing. Thank God his vision at night was not nearly as good as hers. She put her hands on his shoulders. The bulge of muscle under his coat as he lifted her down sent a thrill through the part of her most recently intimate with her saddle. When he set her on her feet, her ankle turned and she fell against him.

"Damn!" she muttered as she peered down. The heel of her boot had broken.

"Easily remedied," he growled, low in his throat. With one arm under her knees he swept her up and, carrying her, walked Dorrie and Fletcher into the stable. She was perfectly able to walk, but suddenly she wanted only to put her arms around his neck. The faint scent of soap filled her nostrils. His hair was dripping from the fog. She was practically breathing into his ear. Indeed, her breast was turned into his chest and pressed against him. His blood beat in the great artery under his jaw. What a strong throat he had . . . The throbbing between her legs ramped up.

The towheaded stable boy appeared, rubbing his eyes and bobbing.

"Take these," Langley muttered. He handed over the horses' reins. "Rub them down well."

"Shall I have the big 'un ready at any special time?" the boy asked.

Langley stared into Beatrix's eyes, almost as though he didn't hear. She should have looked away, but she could not. The longing she saw there was not the simple lust she knew so well. Nor was it the unquestioning adoration she had tired of. What was it?

"Take him round to the livery off Pall Mall as soon as it is light," he said, without looking at the boy. "I'll walk home." He turned and carried her into the house through the rear door.

She laid her head on his shoulder as he carried her upstairs. The servants had gone to bed. No darkness stalked her now; it was reassuring. Still, she was afraid. Tonight she might break an abstention of six hundred years. What was wrong with her? She could lose herself and turn into Asharti if she gave in to her desire. Confusion churned inside her. She had probably forgotten how the thing was done. But she wanted this—wanted it for the first time in centuries. Not for the sex. Lord knew she had proven she could do without that. Then why? Because she felt some kind of kinship with him? Because she wanted . . . connection? She *wanted* to care about him, that was certain. It was almost a hunger. Not like her hunger for blood; it was deeper, more disturbing.

If she made love to him, she must give up his blood. Asharti had taught her that sex and blood don't mix. If she managed that, perhaps she could win through with some shred of herself intact. Could she resist?

"Here," she whispered as they came to her boudoir.

John pushed open the door. A single candle burned on the night table, a fire burned in the grate. It cast a dim, flickering light on rich draperies, a painting of a rounded Venus attended by cherubs, the cut crystal on her dressing table. All were secondary to the great bed with red velvet hangings and brocade coverlets. He was about to make a fool of himself again. The countess did not know the meaning of the word "virtue." She had bedded more men than he counted as acquaintance. Yet she kept a core of herself separate.

The vision of her that had sustained him in the hulks filled him. He was just stupid enough tonight to think that vision and the real woman before him might be one; that his version of her was what she held apart, unknowable by any but him, the part that loved Blake. He *wanted* it to be true with something almost like hunger. His cock swelled against his breeches. She would know the effect she was having on him the instant he put her down. Her breast swelled against his chest, her breath hot on his neck. Ambergris. That was what she had said her elusive scent was. Cinnamon and ambergris. Here they were at the bed and he did lay her upon it, but not with the intent of letting her go for long. Her gaze rose to his. There was such heat, such life there that he felt it like a throb in his spine that passed straight down into his already-swollen cock. How did one begin with a woman who knew everything? Would she think him clumsy?

*Breathe,* he told himself. *Leave it to her. She is a courtesan. She'll set things in motion.*

But she didn't. She looked away and flushed, almost reticent. He had seen the heat in her eyes. She was not unaffected. He swallowed and pulled on his cravat. It was up to him, then. He struggled out of his coat and unbuttoned his waistcoat. She made no move to undress. She meant to watch him. Very well. He cleared his throat, though he had no intention of speaking. He kicked off his shoes and bent to the buckles at his knees. There he was in breeches and shirt. She watched him with quickening breath. Yet she still seemed unsure. He slowed down, unbuttoned his cuffs and pulled his shirt over his head. It dropped to the floor. Nothing she hadn't seen before, but she looked almost fearful.

God! He suddenly realized what she must be seeing. Scars. He could explain those with his reputation for dueling. What would a woman know about slashes instead of bullet holes? But what of the lashes? She would shortly see those. Why had he let himself take off his shirt? He reached for it. "I'm . . . I'm thinner than I'd like at the moment and the scars . . . I'll cover up."

Beatrix felt her tension go with a sigh. She hadn't been sure whether she would let him make love to her or not until this moment. But to see such a strong and willful man so uncertain of himself, so wanting to please her . . . All sparring and jousting for preeminence between them fell away. She would make love to him because she wanted to do it for him, because his desire to please her said he just might care. She must just keep her Companion in check.

"It's all right," she said as she softened into a smile. "I think you are beautiful."

He swallowed, still unsure. "If you would rather . . ."

She rose, still smiling, and took his shirt gently from him. She felt the blood throbbing in his loins as well as her own. "I like making love naked." Was that true? It was now . . .

God help him, if that's what she wanted, that's what she would have. He could keep his back away from her. She need never see the pink new skin. The scabs were gone, were they not? He unbuttoned his breeches and slid them over the fullness of his erection. That at least was well made, he knew. His sex was heavy, so engorged he felt light-headed with desire.

Her smile grew. "Very beautiful." She dropped his shirt to the floor.

He pulled breeches and stockings off in one move for each leg and stood there before her, naked. No woman had ever asked this of him. He firmly put down all thoughts that naked, she would know too much about him. "And you?" he murmured. Her riding habit had frogs and covered buttons down the front in a military style. "Shall I undo your buttons?"

She sat up and he moved in. "Too much trouble. I never liked this habit anyway." She grabbed the bodice with both hands and pulled. There was a rending sound as the frogs parted. John was shocked. What woman would rip such a beautiful garment? She had torn her chemise as well. Her breasts spilled out as she shrugged off the wreckage. Her shoulders were delicate, her breasts heavy, with dusky aureoles around the fine, small nipples. It was not possible to be more aroused, but his balls tightened. His cock quivered in expectation.

She pulled the habit out from under her, kicked off her boots, and tossed the wool on the floor in a burgundy pile. She did not bother to roll her stockings down but slipped them off over the curve of her leg and tossed them after the habit. And all the while her eyes never left John's.

If John could hardly breathe, she seemed to be doing fine. Watching the rise and fall of her breasts was almost torture. She raised her arms, took several pins from her hair and shook it out. It fell in red-black profusion over her shoulders and down her back, glowing with reflected firelight.

John could not stand here resisting the urge to plunge

his cock into the dark thatch between her legs forever. He thought he might burst even now and he wanted this to be a slow pleasure, not some rushed release of fluids. She held out her arms.

Somehow, he only took her hands. She scooted to the center of the huge bed and lay back. He crawled across the richly patterned gold and red brocade and laid himself gently beside her. His cock brushed her thigh. He could feel it pulse against her. She twined her arms around his neck. Her breasts brushed against his chest, the nipples teasing him. His breath hissed in through his mouth. The blood pounding in his genitals was almost painful. He bent to her lips.

The shock of touching her lips almost set him off. How could lips touching lips feel more sensual than the touching of even more intimate body parts? Soft, yielding. Her tongue touched the inside of his mouth, gentle and profound. He spread his hand over her buttocks and pressed her against him as he, in turn, explored her mouth with his tongue. She pushed her thigh between his and his own thigh slid over her hip, capturing her and bringing them even closer together. They were entwined, a single entity where electric need shot between them and around them, engulfing what they had been moments ago. He ran his hands over her shoulders and splayed his palm over her back. The feel of her smooth, fine skin made his own feel coarse by comparison.

Her hands strayed to his hip, smoothed over his buttocks, and then sneaked down between their bodies to cup his balls. She must feel how tight they were with need. She pressed behind them, just at the base, and stroked deep. He gasped. No one had ever touched him just there. It felt as though she were touching the core of his maleness. Then, gently massaging the twin stones in their sac, she came to the base of his cock. Again she pressed deeply to its root and rubbed there. She did not touch the shaft itself, which only made him want her touch the more.

He was busy, too. He bent to her throat and kissed it as his hands rubbed her hip. She bared her neck and moaned in some kind of ecstasy as he suckled there. Then his lips strayed to her breast. He drew on it gently. She arched into him, her nipple hard in his mouth. The pleasure of feeling her nipple on his tongue was only heightened by knowing the pleasure it gave her. When he thought he would burst, she pulled away. Her eyes were serious. What was wrong? She looked so . . . concerned.

"I can't call you Langley."

He nodded, a little puzzled. "John would do. May I call you Bea?"

"No, that is what . . . others call me. I call myself Beatrix."

He smiled. "Beatrix," he breathed into her mouth. He felt her smile in return.

"John."

She did a surprising thing. She pulled away and rolled him over onto his back, her hands upon his shoulders. He raised his brows in inquiry.

"Give yourself over to the moment, John." She straddled his hips and hung over him in the light of the candle, her palms on his shoulders, breasts swaying, dark hair like a curtain. Her head dipped and she licked at his left nipple, then his right. Then she took it gently between her teeth, and sucked hard. Feeling shot through him. She sat up. Arching her back, she moved the moist parts between her legs along his cock until he shivered with sensation. Her eyes closed. Up and back. He could see her breath come faster.

"God, Beatrix. You'll draw me too soon," he warned.

She opened her eyes. Some trick of the candle near the bed made them seem almost to glow with a reddish light. She leaned down and whispered in his ear. "I have faith in you. You have an almost infinite capacity for pleasure. I can tell."

He knew somewhere inside that he was still weak from his experience in the hulks, but that seemed far away. She pressed her breasts against him and licked at his neck. He shivered. The hair on his right arm and leg stood erect. Let her do what she would with him. He gave himself over to his hunger for her. Her heart thumped against his chest. Something sharp dragged along his neck just under his ear. Her teeth? He shuddered again.

Suddenly, she pushed up off his shoulders with something almost like a growl. She closed her eyes and when she opened them the reflected glow from the candle had faded. She managed a crooked smile. "A near thing," she said in that contralto he would cross seas and sands to hear. "But I'll do now." He didn't know what she meant and didn't care. She raised her hips and with one hand slipped him inside her, then spread her thighs and pressed down even as he thrust up.

"Ahhh," they both sighed as he filled her. She was very tight. That was a bit surprising. He held her waist and lifted her. She straightened and ran her hands through her hair as she moved on top of him. It lifted her breasts. And then John felt a pulling at his cock in rhythm to their movement. It was the muscles inside her, caressing him. He made a low sound in his throat.

"You can hold it, I know you can," she said. And he could. He wasn't sure how. He teetered on some brink of ecstasy, trembling on the edge just this side of insanity. Her breath was coming faster now. They went on, moving in unison like horse and rider, one. He adjusted the angle to reach her sweetest spot, far up inside her womb. That made her eyes open.

And then her eyes went unseeing and her moan of pleasure wound up the scale. He could feel her muscles contract around him and that sent him over the edge himself.

His back arched to meet her and he loosed his seed in some never-ending fountain of ecstasy.

Beatrix almost fell onto the bed beside him. He drew her into his arms and cradled her against his side. She had come off safely. A near thing. She had wanted so to taste his sweet blood. Her muscles continued to contract in fading echoes of orgasm. God in heaven! It was six hundred years since she had felt this. Had it ever been like this? Her brain was muddied with the power of her release. Her Companion scratched at her veins in disappointment, but it was a distant distraction. John would have allowed her to feed from him. He might have *welcomed* it he was so consumed in passion. She would have only needed to use a little extra compulsion to induce him to forget her feeding. But she had resisted. Yes. She was safe.

She wanted him to remember her for who she was, not some mistaken dream. It had been a grave risk even to use feather-light compulsion on him to prolong his enjoyment. She might have lost herself and fed. But if she had not he might have wasted himself too early, and she wanted to give him the best possible experience.

It occurred to her that it might have been some time since he had found release as well. Interesting. Especially for a man who had a reputation for bedding women at the drop of a hat.

He distracted her by kissing her hair, gently. He drew the coverlet over her against an imaginary draft in the warm room. "Are you cold?" he murmured with that deep bass rumble. She could hear it in his chest. She snuggled in to him and wrapped her arms around him.

"Surely you jest," she whispered, and spread her palms across his back.

What was this?

She moved her hands up toward his shoulders. "Will you stay the morning with me? You can leave at noon as though you paid a morning call." She said it to distract him. There were two or three scabs still. But she felt the long lines of new scarring as well. He had been whipped, and fairly recently. No wonder he had been shy of his nakedness.

He chuckled. "In satin knee breeches and evening slippers? Why not post a notice in the *Observer*? It will save the gossips the effort of speculation."

Why had this man been whipped? Under what circumstances could a gentleman possibly have come to that? "I shall send my incredibly discreet servant round to your incredibly discreet servant and collect some more discreet clothes, of course." She murmured it almost into his mouth. "You need your sleep after all, since you are recovering from the influenza."

"What makes you think I intend to get any sleep?"

She looked up into his eyes and saw the glow growing there. As impossible as it was, a throb began between her legs. She, who could not bring herself to make love even once in six hundred years, now wanted a repeat performance. Perhaps several. "Are you strong enough?" she murmured. She could make him strong enough. But she wouldn't, not even the whisper of compulsion she had used to give him staying power a few moments ago. Why not? Had she not been using compulsion of one kind or another with men to feed her Companion for seven hundred years? Even if she did not use the power of her Companion, she used her knowledge of men to make them do her bidding, whether they would or no. Only this man had refused her. Only this man came to her freely, because he had the strength to say no to her.

"I shall endeavor to please," he said, with mischief lurking behind his eyes. "Perhaps we could go a little slower this time? Just for my health, of course."

She thought that slower just might kill her, judging from the reaction in her loins.

"Would you mind terribly if I tasted you?" he asked, feigning politeness, though his voice was husky. An Englishman who wanted to use his tongue?

Unheard of. But intriguing. "Be my guest," she whispered.

John woke in the darkened room. Beatrix still lay in his arms. She looked fragile and innocent wrapped in the red brocade of the comforter. It made her skin glow white in the dim room. He had pleasured her with his hand, his mouth, his cock, had brought her, trembling, to some state of perpetual desire. He himself was spent to the point of being raw inside and out. How he had lasted three, no four times to her five, he could not imagine.

He had achieved what he had wanted of her for nearly two months. He half expected that achieving the citadel would give him the welcome protection of indifference. But as he watched her breathe in sleep, he knew he was more entangled than ever.

Who was this woman? And why should she attract him so? Was she not as much a user of men as Angela or Cecilia, Pauline Bonaparte or countless others? For one who had tried so hard and so vainly to find virtue for himself, she was all wrong. She was the opposite of virtuous. Why was he so damned attracted, then? Probably only because she could have ministers, poets, the Prince Regent himself according to some, and yet she had just succumbed to her passion with him.

She probably succumbed to her passions with someone every night. Who was to say that he was special to her in any way? Had he not known women who were addicted to the sexual act? And yet . . . she had seemed so surprised at the rising of her passions again and again in the last hours. She had clung to him as she cried out. True, there had been no clawing of his back, a sure mark of a woman's passion. For that he was, frankly, grateful.

Yet she seemed genuinely transported. He was glad. And she had been clever, gentle, and kind at coaxing his own pleasure, even after he moaned that he could not. For that he could thank her experience, no doubt.

He sighed. This evening he would report to a cutter in the Pool and depart for France. At least he would not make an assignation he could not keep this time. He pressed his lips together. He would have to tell her.

A feeling of futility washed over him. What had he achieved here? He was going away, perhaps for months, perhaps to die. He was all his country had in defense against this mysterious woman, Asharti. That was the life he had chosen. He had made this commitment long ago in his search for some kind of virtue in himself. It was a commitment Barlow and those he stood for counted on John to keep. The choices were hard. He killed. He lied. He betrayed. But never his country. That life was the only island of certainty about himself he possessed.

And that life allowed no room for an ongoing relationship with a woman who had never met virtue, let alone embraced it. He had wanted her, without compunction, without reservation, because of the dreams of her that had sustained him in the hulk. Had he made her in his mind into something she was not? Perhaps even now, she thought to use his desire for her to induce him to tell her his secrets. Secrets which she could betray, if she was a spy.

He would never be sure of a woman's motives again. He lived in a world where everyone's motives were suspect and lies were a way of life. And this woman? She was not pure of heart any more than she was pure of body. This woman, more than any other, could never be part of life for a man like him. In truth, she had asked him nothing. Perhaps she sought to ingratiate herself and the prying would come later. The thought pained him. It didn't matter. He would be gone before she had a chance to compromise him.

He looked down as she stirred in his arms and stretched like a sleepy cat.

"What are you doing awake?" Beatrix muttered, stretching. "Did I not exhaust you?" She had never felt so . . . full. It wasn't just the sated feeling of desire wakened after six hundred years. No. She had had sex without succumbing to Asharti's brand of evil. She had wanted only to bring John pleasure, to bring them both the satisfaction of a union. She hadn't mixed the sex and blood. Was it only sex? She looked up. His dark lashes brushed his cheeks as he closed those intriguing green eyes for a moment. There had been a connection between them, a bond of caring. His caresses, after the first passionate fires had died down to glowing coals, were tender. She felt safe here in his arms for the first time in . . . in a long time.

She blinked once. Was she crazy? This man would despise her if he knew what she was. She sat up. She was who she was. He would call her a monster.

All right. She would use him to interest her for as long as she could to stave off the memories and the darkness. If he could help her, he would have served his purpose. There was no such thing as desire that lasted. That had been proved to her from the very first passion she had conceived for a man. She would not think of that other word. When one resolved not to think about it, yearning for it was all her mind could encompass. Love? Not for the likes of her.

Let not some intrigue and a night of passion contradict centuries of experience. She must gain her balance and the upper hand. She knew to her cost what happened when she did not. She had lost her balance after Stephan . . .

"Beatrix, I must tell you something," he said, breaking into her thoughts. She pushed down the memory of that horrible time and looked up into green eyes like the sea in the late afternoon sunshine with the light behind the waves.

Her throat was full in anticipation of something, she didn't know what.

"I leave tonight." He put it out bluntly, without excuse.

Her heart thumped irregularly in her chest. Repetition cascaded over her, bringing blackness at the edge of her vision. "Oh, really?" she asked, somehow managing a casual tone even though his arms still held her, though her heart was stabbed clear through. What had she expected? How stupid was she to allow herself to be tempted into engaging, so much that she had actually had sex with him? All the hurt from all the years came hurtling down upon her. Mother, Stephan, Asharti . . . How could anything be different? Darkness gathered . . . "Do contact me when you return. We could perhaps arrange another night like this one. I enjoyed it."

His expression shut down over a flash of shock. "It might be some time."

She shrugged as she sat up. "At your convenience, love." She managed to be sure it did not sound like an endearment. "If I am not engaged you can count on an evening of frolic."

He swung out of bed. She saw the pink weals across his back that would shortly be scars. He had forgotten himself, after all his care for so many hours. She turned away, just as he glanced back in horror, realizing his mistake. "Should I send round for your morning clothes?"

"I'll take my chances," he growled, shrugging on his shirt.

Her insides were knotted, her throat full. Damn him! She rolled herself in the heavy coverlet and stood, not wanting him to see her naked anymore. "I take it you won't breakfast?" she asked, attacking in self-defense. He looked daggers. "No. Well, then." She escaped to the dressing room and donned a rose-colored wrapper. She could feel her own flush. As long as she had lived and she still could not prevent her blood rising to her face?

Langley bowed, once, crisply. He was dressed, though his cravat was tied indifferently. "Your servant, Countess," he said stiffly.

"Not at all," she returned. "The pleasure was mine."

He turned. The door closed. He was gone.

She blinked in shock. Darkness lurked in the corners of the room. Before she could resist the memories came pouring over her. Her mother, Stephan . . . and after Stephan she had clung to Asharti as the only way forward. Oh, God in heaven . . .

*CASTLE SINCAI, TRANSYLVANIAN ALPS, 1105*

*After Beatrix had comforted Stephan with love as though his confessions and his betrayal did not matter, she found herself adrift on confusing emotions. She loved Stephan. He needed her. But no matter what he said, he did not love her in return. How could he when he said he loved Asharti, too? She needed someone to tell her what to do. Stephan had been the only one she could turn to for advice when she was confused or in pain. Now he could not help her.*

*Who could possibly understand this? The answer surprised her. Asharti must know Stephan bedded both of them. What did she feel about that? She was older only by a few years, but she had lived in society, whereas Beatrix had existed almost outside the world of men. Could Beatrix bring herself to consult her rival?*

*It was a mark of the turmoil in her breast that she resolved to try. She slipped out of the stable. Stephan slept in the fresh hay under a horse blanket. She edged into the keep by the kitchen door and trudged up a winding stairway to Asharti's chamber in the west tower. Scratching on the heavy timbered door, she pushed in without permission. She was not sure Asharti would want to talk, and she intended to give her no choice.*

*The sight that met her eyes made no sense. The covers*

*of the bed, lit only by the fire in the grate, seemed alive, bulging and poking in several directions at once. A strange double grunting issued from under the counterpane. Then the coverlet fell away to reveal Asharti's supple, naked back, her black hair hanging to her waist as she sat up. She knelt astride a boy propped against the pillows. Beatrix recognized him from the stables. Blood trickled down his neck. The boy lifted Asharti's hips and she ground herself against his loins. Their bodies were covered with a light sheen of sweat, gleaming in the firelight.*

*Beatrix stood transfixed as the momentum increased. Asharti pounded her nether parts against the boy. The base of his erection was alternately revealed and sheathed in her. Asharti's groan of pleasure drew up into a wail. The boy arched his hips in throbbing silence. Still, she raised and lowered herself against his pulsing cock, gasping. A low wail escaped her.*

*Asharti's back relaxed. Flushing, Beatrix retreated. But Asharti caught the movement. Beatrix froze. Asharti waved her in, a sudden gleam in her eye, without a trace of shame.*

*"Come in, sister." She lifted herself off the boy. He seemed dazed. His erection softened. Beatrix was shocked to see the marks of Asharti's canines on the inside of his elbow and his thigh. She had never fed from a human other than at the carotid. This smacked of . . . play.*

*"Shall you partake?" Asharti asked. "I can bring him up again in a moment."*

*Beatrix's flush grew hotter. "I wanted to talk to you. I'll wait." She turned to go.*

*"Nonsense. I am done with him. Up," she ordered. As the boy rose she smacked him on the buttocks with an open hand. "Back to your stable. I will call for you tomorrow night. See that you're clean and ready." She pulled on a heavy velvet robe. The boy hastily dressed from a pile of clothing next to a bath set in front of the fire. "I do so love a bath," Asharti remarked.*

*The boy ducked his head and retreated. Beatrix wanted to do the same. How had she thought that Asharti would understand the emotions swirling in her breast? Beatrix certainly didn't understand what she had just seen. Asharti had sex with that boy only hours after she lay with Stephan. How could she? Had she no respect for Stephan?*

*"You know Stephan forbids feeding among the servants." Beatrix sounded small and petulant to herself.*

*"And do you always obey Stephan?" Asharti asked, raising her brows.*

*Beatrix looked down at her hands. Asharti was so much bolder, more experienced.*

*"Have you come to berate me for taking Stephan from you?" Asharti asked, wrapping her velvet around her and tying the silken cord about her waist. "I did not, you know."*

*"No. I do not blame you," Beatrix murmured, ashamed.*

*"Ahhh," Asharti breathed. "He has told you." She crawled up onto her bed.*

*"What do you mean?" Beatrix was stalling. Asharti knew?*

*"His experiment, of course. I told him it was cruel to let you go on. Your dream of bliss was always doomed." Her laugh had an edge. "He can't love us, not one as old and knowing as he is." She curled like a cat among the quilts, her eyes narrowing. "I never expected that."*

*Asharti knew. And it did not hurt her. Beatrix felt small and naïve all over again. A longing to be as invulnerable and independent as Asharti came over her.*

*Asharti's eyes darkened in anger. "What I do not forgive is that for all his theory, in his heart we are not equal. He favors you because you are born. He is as prejudiced as those he would convince."*

*"He likes you better for your courage and your self-reliance."*

*"Nonsense. Men always like to be in control. He fears*

*my independence. That is different."* Asharti peered at her. *"Your lips are swollen. He tried to make you forget your outrage by swiving you, didn't he?"*

Beatrix lifted her chin. *"No. He thinks we will leave him, and he was so cast down . . . I made love to him to comfort him."* She sounded so gullible!

Asharti snorted. *"Me, I find that even one as experienced as he is cannot satisfy my needs entirely, especially since he must save himself for teaching you, as well. I have a great sexual appetite."* She stretched, almost preening. *"I must supplement the pleasure I take from him."* She seemed invulnerable. Beatrix wished she had Asharti's armor.

*"And will you leave him?"* Beatrix asked.

*"When I have taken everything he has to give."* She shrugged. *"He has taught me much of sex, and how to draw the power, how to control the reappearance when we translocate. I am nearly done with him and his precious experiment. What I want to learn next, he cannot teach me."* She smiled knowingly. *"You, however, will stay with him, and comfort him and do his bidding without thought. You are the perfect experiment."* She snuggled down into the quilts. *"Perhaps he will find another who is made to fill my place in his little exercise."*

The prospect of Stephan filling Ashurti's place confirmed his perfidy. She was ashamed that she had made love to him even when she knew the whole. Anger followed on the heels of shame. *"I will be no experiment,"* she muttered.

Asharti sat up abruptly. Her red velvet gown fell open, revealing the swell of her breasts and one dusky nipple. *"Then let us go tonight."*

Panic surged around Beatrix like the tide around a rock. *"Now?"*

Asharti crawled to the edge of the great bed on hands and knees. *"He doesn't love either of us."* She straightened. *"Perhaps he's right. It is time for us to go."*

*Fear churned in Beatrix's belly. To be on their own . . .
where would they go?*

*But what choice was there? Beatrix could not bear to
stay, letting Stephan make love to her, knowing that to him
she was only an example of a vampire born, as Asharti
was an example of a vampire made. She longed to let the
anger rage inside her until it consumed her pain.*

*Still, Stephan was old and powerful. "He will come af-
ter us." she whispered.*

*Asharti shook her head. "He expects us to leave. He
will be too despondent to pursue us. His little experiment
has failed, after all. I refuse to be displayed to the vampire world like a trained bear. We are free if we have the
courage to open our cell doors." She raised her brows.*

*Beatrix swallowed. Fear and anger and grief all
swirled inside her. Asharti was her only way out. Asharti
was the one who knew how the world really worked.*

*She nodded. "But I won't leave him without telling him."*

*"Go then. Tell him," Asharti said. "But try not to let
his cock lure you into staying."*

*Beatrix started to protest, but she couldn't. Asharti was
right. So she simply turned and started for the stable,
heart thumping in her chest.*

*In the darkness of the barn, with the breathing of the
animals all around, Stephan opened his eyes as she approached. The green smell of new-cut hay mingled with
the scent of horses. As he sat, the blanket fell to his waist,
exposing his chest and shoulders. She stood in the doorway, trying to build a wall against the realization she saw
dawning in his eyes. "We're leaving, Stephan. Both of us.
I just came to let you know." She wanted him to shout that
he would never let her go, that she was the love of his life,
and this experiment nonsense was just a lie.*

*Instead, he nodded. "I understand." He heaved a sigh.
"You will come to hate me before you forgive me. At least
I hope you can forgive me. But be sure to forgive yourself."*

"*She has nothing to forgive herself for.*" *Asharti's sharp voice came from behind them. Beatrix turned sharply. Asharti was dressed and a cloak covered her shoulders.*

"*You didn't trust me to say goodbye?*"

"*I didn't trust him, sister.*" *She motioned to Stephan.* "*Let us go now.*"

"*Be your own person, Bea,*" *Stephan whispered.* "*If you need me, I'll come.*"

"*Bea will not need you,*" *Asharti sneered.* "*I'll teach her what she needs to know.*"

*Beatrix stood, paralyzed, staring at Stephan. Her eyes filled as well as her throat.*

"*Come, sister,*" *Asharti barked. Beatrix turned. Time stopped. Surely Stephan would stop her! Asharti stretched out her hand. Already her eyes were reddening. Beatrix walked to her as though in a dream. Asharti grasped her hand. Beatrix took a long breath and called her Companion. The life that surged up along her veins reminded her that she was still alive. She would go on, in spite of Stephan Sincai. A whirling darkness enveloped the two young women.*

Stephan had not stopped her. What worse could there be than Stephan's betrayal? Giving herself over to Asharti? She slumped on her dressing table. She knew what worse there could be—the repetition of rejection; memories that tortured her, music that wailed off-key and images that ran like watercolors. Blendon. Ponsonby. Prinny. Mirso Monastery.

Darkness.

# Twelve

The cutter darted over the Channel making a crisp thirteen knots, the usual choppy winds replaced by a fair blow on her quarter. John paced the deck, unable to stand confinement in the cabin. His body could bide no more stillness than his emotions could. If only the biting wind that drove the ship plunging forward could blast his heart clean.

It had all meant nothing to her. Had he been so naïve as to think she must somehow feel what he felt in that bed last night? He meant nothing. He was just another in a string of men she used to amuse herself. She had not even protested when he told her he must leave.

He could not let her callous indifference undermine his focus for his mission. Or let false illusions of her invade his dreams as they had on the hulk. His last interview with Barlow made clear how much was at stake here, both for England and for John himself. As he stared out over the spitting sea into the darkness the bow wave of the ship unfolded below him. He forced himself to remember the warm glow of Barlow's study.

John saw himself taking the sheaf of papers with his

instructions, his identity, how to signal for pickup. He heard Barlow clear his throat. "Don't let yourself be taken, boy. I wouldn't trust you not to break under torture." The man was fidgeting with a portfolio of papers.

John stared until Barlow looked away. "You're suggesting I save a bullet for myself?"

"Or I can give you a poison capsule," he said, taking up a penknife to sharpen a quill.

"If I run out of bullets I can always slit my wrists." John made his voice light.

"When an agent knows as much as you do, we should not send him into the enemy's den. We should make you a courier to Scotland, no more." He fidgeted with penknife and quill.

So that was what awaited him; suicide if he failed and being put out to pasture if he succeeded. Very well. But right now he needed the distraction of a mission and England needed him. "How unfortunate, then, that you have not a dozen others to send in my place."

"You're right." Barlow's hands stilled. He looked . . . sad. "Go with God."

John shivered. That was what he had said to the dying Dupré on the hulk. Barlow thought he was sending him to his death? He had nodded to the old man, so vibrantly alive since recovering from his bout of illness. "I'll approach her immediately, do the deed, and get back to Le Havre. If it is going to take longer, I'll send a message no later than the first week of May." He pulled on his gloves. "If you don't hear, then I saved some bullets."

"Remember, it cannot look like an assassination," Barlow warned.

"I understand. They must believe their intelligence is safe."

"And find out what the devil is capable of draining the blood from a body."

John nodded. He had never seen Barlow so agitated.

"The drained bodies—they've shown up in England, haven't they?"

Barlow started. "What do you know about that?"

"Lucky guess," John murmured.

"Dover," Barlow said, his clipped tone brooking no further questions. "Now get to Paris."

John grabbed his hat and let himself out before Barlow changed his mind.

So here he was, an assassin on a fast cutter for Le Havre. He would seek no information, steal no papers, poison no sources. Barlow had told him just to kill her, or her husband if it turned out he was the one. John would not have interrogated her in any case. He had just enough pride left to refuse to torture women. That left assassination.

Not what he had imagined when he thought to serve his country and make something of his life. But assassination was required. He always did what was required. He should concentrate on coming back alive. The damned French seemed to know everything.

His mind returned without his permission to Beatrix Lisse. He still felt stripped by their lovemaking, both physically and emotionally. He could almost feel her lissome body writhing over him, under him. He turned restlessly from the rail just as the cutter came up on the wind, and was thrown against the rigging. He clung with one hand to the ratlines and regained his feet.

It was best to end with her this way. His attachment was to Barlow and Whitehall. His passion must be saved for hating Bonaparte, his attention focused on accomplishing his mission. It might well be his last. He had no time for mooning over some woman he thought was mysterious. Mysterious? Her soul was an open book. She was like every other woman of easy virtue. It had only been his naïve longing for her to be someone special that created the mystery.

Well, he would drown that disappointment in work.
It was only a few hours to Le Havre.

Beatrix popped out into the night from her whirling darkness near the main road through Hounslow Heath. Coaches stopped for a lone woman. Or there might be a single horseman on his way back to London. She was hungry and in no mood to deny herself but she couldn't bear another night of adulation in order to fill her need. The moon was a lopsided sliver, grinning rakishly down at the world. The trees overhanging the graveled road gave her good shadow. She would feed tonight because if she didn't Symington would bring her another young applicant for the position of a footman she didn't need, and because if she mooned over Langley, the bastard would have won. At least here she could be alone. She felt as though she was clinging to some shred of herself, using anger at him to stave off something worse.

She became aware of someone else in the shadows some way down the road. A horse's feet shuffled in the long grass of the verge. There he was; a mounted figure. Ah, a rarity. The patrols had almost banished highwaymen. Almost.

She moved through the night, silently. With a thought, she quieted his horse. By the time he turned, her blood was up, her Companion surging through her veins, her eyes already red. His hand moved to his pistol, but it was too late. His will was hers. She made him dismount without a word and come to her. Then she took him at the neck. She did not allow it to be a sexual experience. God, no! Not after Langley. She was feeding, nothing more. She tried to tell herself that sex and feeding did not intermingle for her anymore. *Then why do you never take females or old men unless you are desperate?* But this highwayman did not seem sexual. No, it was Langley who had lured her to drink from him as they made love. It had taken all she had to resist. Sex and feeding together made her like Asharti . . . and she was *not* like Asharti. Not anymore . . .

NICULA, NORTHERN TRANSYLVANIA, 1112

*"Of course we can handle him,"* Asharti admonished, passing Beatrix the tankard of rough peasant's brew. *"The trick is to cut him out from his fellows. But he will do that himself. Do you want one of your own, or will you share?"*

Beatrix looked at the half-dozen men around the fire of the tiny inn doubtfully. They were far into their cups and the carousing had ramped up to rowdy laughter. Beatrix and Asharti couldn't handle all of them. They had to be careful, even though they were vampires. They traveled with two grooms, paid well for their silence, and had an older woman as a chaperone. But those sops to propriety and safety were left behind. Tonight they were on the hunt. "I'll share."

Asharti rose and swayed her hips as she strolled to the circle. A roar of interest went up from the men. She put her hand on the shoulder of the big blond they had picked out. He wore the mark of the cross, sketched roughly on his jerkin. He had been to the Crusades. Asharti always picked Crusaders. "And what is your name, my fine buck?" she asked, her voice throaty.

"Rolf, you have a live one!"

"Share, you devil. We'll all take a turn . . ."

"Ah, no, gentlemen. Rolf here looks like the jealous type. Aren't you, Rolf?"

Beatrix could hear Asharti's hum ramp up, just enough to put compulsion in her voice.

"To hell with you all," Rolf said, standing. He knocked over the bench he had been sitting on. "Now, darling, what were you saying?"

*"I was inviting you to my room for a drink . . ."* Asharti said, looking him full in the face.

*"Then let us go, before these louts get greedy."*

A jealous roar frosted with laughter raced around the circle. Beatrix faded into the shadows and ran lightly up the stairs to their shared bedroom. Hunger rasped along her veins.

Asharti drew Rolf through the door. *"This is Bea,"* she murmured.

Rolf took on an avaricious look. *"Ho, ho, Bea, is it? Always room for one more."*

Asharti pressed her body along his. He held out his arm for Beatrix. She sidled into him. He leaned from one to another, planting beery kisses. He smelled of sweat and horse and mead.

*"How long since you had a bath, Rolf?"* Asharti whispered.

*"Eh, what's that?"*

*"How long since you bathed?"* Beatrix insisted.

Rolf looked startled. *"I . . . I don't know."*

*"Just so,"* Asharti said. *"Why don't you strip off your clothes? We've had a bath brought up."* She gestured to the halfbarrel on the far side of the bed. Rolf got a mulish expression. Asharti's vibrations ramped up. *"It's not a request, Rolf. Strip."*

Beatrix watched his expression melt. This one would be no trouble. Her help was not even needed. He pulled his shirt over his head. Beatrix worked at his breeches. Asharti unlaced his rough boots. They had him naked in no time. He was well enough. Asharti liked them smooth and lean, though Beatrix did not. But he was tractable, if not exciting. While he bathed they changed into the loose robes they favored for nights of play and feeding.

*"He's strong as an ox,"* Asharti whispered. *"He'll have lots of stamina."* Asharti fed almost every night. For her, feeding was always entwined with sex, and she had an

*insatiable appetite for sex. Beatrix had noticed that the guide they employed had marks on him, though Asharti had promised not to feed on their attendants. Of course she had sex with them. Asharti swived almost everything in sight. But she was not supposed to feed.*

*Beatrix got a towel and handed it to Rolf as he stood. He dried himself then moved to wrap the cloth about his waist.*

*"No, no, my pretty one," Asharti said. "Not allowed." She motioned to the bed.*

*The cloth dropped. He climbed into the bed. His blue eyes glowed and his genitals tightened into an erection. This first one was natural.*

*"Excellent," Asharti murmured. She crawled up onto the bed next to him, even as Beatrix tucked herself against his other side.*

*"I am a lucky man," he growled, "to have two such beautiful wenches to pleasure me." He reached to pull Beatrix's head down to his lips.*

*Beatrix felt her Companion cry for sustenance. She let her eyes go red. Her Companion washed compulsion over him. This was their game, not his. He would be quiet now. He bared his neck to her. The Companion ran out her fangs. Hers would be the first feeding of the night. She pierced his carotid where it pulsed against her lips. The sweet copper tang of blood excited her. She pulled at the twin wounds, even as she ran her hands over his chest. The place between her thighs throbbed. He groaned under her lips. She broke away. She must make him last for Asharti.*

*But Asharti was already at the great artery in his groin. She stroked his erection even as she sucked. It was this which had no doubt extracted the groan. Asharti raised her head. Blood stained her lips. "The first sip is always the sweetest, yes?"*

*Beatrix nodded, smiling lazily. She felt almost drunk on the sensation.*

*"Mouth or cock?" Asharti asked.*

*"Mouth." Beatrix hiked herself up and straddled Rolf's neck. Asharti sat astride his loins behind her. Rolf did his job. He had no choice, in fact. Asharti had him well under her compulsion and soon both women were panting and racing toward their climaxes.*

*When both had finished shuddering, they climbed off the dazed man and nestled against him, letting the gleam of sweat on their three bodies evaporate in the cool night air. Asharti had not allowed him to release his seed. She would want the use of him several times yet. For Beatrix, it was her Companion who was not sated. She had not fed in more than a week. It was she who first called her canines again and began sucking at the vein inside his elbow. Asharti was not loath to follow her lead. Asharti drew a furrow in his shoulder and licked at the cut. That always excited her. She made Rolf harden and offered his cock to Beatrix, who declined.*

*But Beatrix watched as Asharti took him, and she could not help but be excited by it. As she watched, Beatrix allowed her Companion freedom. She answered its demands and rolled Rolf's head to the other side. She pierced his other artery and sucked at his neck as Asharti made small, frantic sounds, impaling herself again and again on Rolf's erect member. The blood, thick and luxurious, coursed down Beatrix's throat. Her Companion thrilled along her veins. She had never felt alive as she did in these moments of blood and sex, she and Asharti and the men who served them. Life sang so in her veins she could hear nothing else, feel nothing else, just the rhythm of Asharti's cries and the joy of sucking the warm copper life.*

*Asharti climaxed in a shriek of ecstasy and Rolf began to shudder. Beatrix never wanted the sensation to end. She pulled harder at his throat. And a sweet, poignant sensation overcame her as he trembled under them. Beatrix had*

*never felt anything like it. It was if something whispered
to her along with the blood, so faint she must strain to
hear. She couldn't hear. And then it was gone. She sucked
at his throat harder, but nothing came.*

*She pulled away, disoriented, disappointed.*

*Asharti stared at her from those kohl-lined, black eyes.
Beatrix felt the rush of the Companion cycle down.
The room looked dirty gray, all color leached away. Her
gaze came back to Asharti's startled face then fell to Rolf.
He lay, eyes wide and staring at the ceiling, incredibly
pale except for the trickle of blood from his wounds. His
flesh seemed shrunken.*

*Beatrix felt distant from herself, and stupid. "What
happened?" she asked slowly.*

*"You . . . you drained him," Asharti whispered. Then,
when Beatrix did not seem to understand, "He's dead."*

*Beatrix jerked back to Rolf. Dead? He was dead? She
had killed him?*

*Asharti crawled up to her on hands and knees until she
was looking directly into Beatrix's eyes, Rolf's body under her. "It felt good, didn't it?"*

*She couldn't answer. The world was coming back and
with it the horrible realization of what that whisper she
couldn't quite hear might have been. "Asharti, what have
I done?"*

*"What you have done a hundred times. Don't make
such a fuss."*

*"But that was before I knew. I never drained one, they
just bled to death. That's different. And I haven't killed—
not since Stephan said—"*

*"Stephan!" Asharti snorted. "Stephan wanted us half-
alive." Beatrix began to tremble as Asharti took her by the
shoulders. "We were born to feed upon them. Does the
lion spare his prey? We were made to kill them by whatever made them, and us."*

*Beatrix touched her lips with her fingertips.*

*"You felt his soul, didn't you?"* Asharti's eyes glowed, not with the red of the Companion, but with excitement. *"Let's go downstairs. I want to feel a soul tonight, too."*

Beatrix jerked away from her highwayman. "You will remember nothing," she muttered as her Companion subsided. She passed a hand over her eyes.

*This one didn't die,* she told herself. *I haven't killed for more than six hundred years.* But her breath was short. The highwayman slumped against a tree. He would wake, a little weak but nothing a good meal wouldn't fix. Beatrix stumbled into the dark.

She had been appalled she killed Rolf that night, and ashamed. She still remembered the Crusader's name after nearly seven hundred years; a man she had known for an hour or two. But he was not the last. Asharti made game of Beatrix for her squeamishness, prodded her into watching as she experimented with taking the last drop. Nothing came to strike Asharti dead. It seemed she paid no price at all for her blasphemy against Stephen's teachings. Soon, Beatrix would start the feeding, and though she let Asharti end it, still she was a willing accomplice to the act. She watched as Asharti learned to magnify the feeling of that last gasp of life over her lips by pairing it with orgasm. Beatrix watched Asharti flutter in breathless ecstasy and then grow even more alive. Though the flying feeling was always followed by irritability and depression, Asharti said the ecstasy was worth it.

One night, something broke inside Beatrix. Why should she deny herself ecstasy when there were no consequences? Asharti sounded so reasonable when she said that sucking the last drop was a symbol of their freedom from Stephan. That night Beatrix sucked a strong young peasant dry in a fresh-mowed field under a harvest moon. It made her shudder even now, with shame, not ecstasy. Beatrix and Asharti took the last drop again and again, looking for the taste of a man's soul as well as his blood. Luscious sex was paired with blood and death. They raged over Europe for almost a hundred years, all boundaries gone, addicted to the rush of a fulfillment to which nothing else would ever compare.

Six hundred years later, on the edge of Hounslow Heath, Beatrix began to run, her night vision more than human, up a boulder-strewn slope as though she could run from what she had become so long ago. Trees gave way to a clearing. She turned her face to the moon and put her back to a gigantic boulder. The stone was rough and cold through her cloak. She sank to the earth, trembling.

She had rejected all that. Blood was not paired with sex anymore for her. She had stopped even making love to them when she fed, in case Asharti's demons lurked inside her. A century late perhaps, but she had found the will to resist the seductive sucking of life. Yet all these memories kept rising to torment her. Why? What were they trying to tell her? Why couldn't she shut them off anymore? She had to find a way out of this. Maybe she had to experience it all before she could be done with it. She forced herself to remember the last time she saw Asharti.

*KRAKOW, MALOPOLSKA, 1221*

*Beatrix raised her head from the young squire's neck and eased herself off his softening member, a feeling of lassitude drenching her. She looked over to where Asharti's English knight bled from half a dozen cuts and bites. He was still erect. Asharti still wanted the use of him. His eyes were glazed, though, and his chest heaving. He would not last much longer. Asharti looked up from where she curled against him upon the Turkey carpet in the castle that reminded Beatrix of Stephan's. "Are you satisfied, Bea?" she asked. "Do you mind if I use both of them?"*

Beatrix shook her head, feeling queasy in a way she couldn't fathom. "He's yours."

She watched as Asharti took control of them both. She lay back on the rug. The firelight gleamed on Asharti's golden, creamy skin. The knight turned in to her. The squire scrambled to her other side. Each bent to suck a nipple. Asharti purred like a cat when it is stroked and arched her back. The knight, older, more experienced of women, was Asharti's choice to finger her wet sex. Beatrix watched, unable to look away, yet repelled in a way she could not explain. What was happening to her? Had she not done the same? She liked being pleasured by two at once. The feeling of subtle horror had been coming on for some time. That she knew.

Asharti brought the young squire's neck up to her teeth and sucked just as she climaxed.

She collapsed, and they with her. "Ahhh, Delightful," she whispered after a moment. She opened her eyes. "What for you, Bea? Mouth? Cock? Or would you like something more exotic?"

Beatrix felt her gorge rise. Asharti had developed some strange proclivities lately. She liked to work the anus of her victims with whatever was to hand: broomsticks, whip handles. Beatrix shook her head and looked away.

"Why not, sister?" Asharti raised herself on one elbow. "Are you sick?"

"I don't know," Beatrix managed. Sick? Yes, she was sick. Sick of the death, the endless repetition of ecstasy and the horrible letdown when it faded. It was a treadmill grinding away at her, and if she did not get off now, she might never escape. It had turned out there were consequences far worse than lightning striking.

Asharti waited. Beatrix knew Asharti could feel that she was becoming distant of late. Beatrix's small seed of independence threatened her. Beatrix wasn't sure why. They both knew Asharti was stronger. Was her strength *because she fed more often, or was it that she took in the power of the souls that shushed past her lips like a whispering breath? She certainly killed more.*

*Beatrix said nothing. Thoughts swirled in her head. She had no mother. No father. No siblings. No Stephan. She was alone in a world that thought her a monster, among beings who could never understand her, let alone accept her. She shivered. Asharti was all she had in the world now. That thought was all that kept her with Asharti these last months.*

*But Beatrix knew there was no choice but to deny all this, even if she was denying who she really was. Asharti's way was tearing at the very fabric of her. Beatrix took a breath. What could she say? Asharti waited, black eyes flat. Perhaps it was already done, and the words were not even needed. "I don't think I can, Asharti."*

*"But you aren't sick." Asharti pronounced it like a sentence.*

*"I think I have been sick," Beatrix said, then rushed forward. "Stephan hurt me, hurt you, no matter what you say. We have been trying to punish him by breaking all his Rules. But he isn't here, Asharti. He isn't hurt by this. Only we are."*

*"Hurt?" Asharti's eyes narrowed. "Us? We are vampire, immortal."*

*"But our souls, sister, our souls are eaten away with every life we take, like rust on iron, like the rot eating the flesh of the leper."*

*Asharti stood and pulled her velvet robe around her. "What nonsense are you talking?"*

*Beatrix pressed her lips together. "Let us not become the monsters they all think us."*

*Asharti laughed. It was brittle. "You never did have the courage to be who you are, Bea. And you were born to it." She pointed to the knight, still gasping on the carpet. "They have no purpose but to slake our thirst. They are small beings. We are large. We have the Companion in our blood, and two are more than one plus one."* An expression of hurt flickered in her eyes. *"Don't be small, like them, Bea."*

Beatrix just tried to breathe. She knew she had little if anything in common with the men on the floor, so close to death, or indeed any being within a hundred miles, or five hundred, other than Asharti. Asharti was her soul mate.

*"Have you been seduced into shame by these Christians?"* Asharti peered at her.

*"No. I know no god who would claim us,"* Beatrix whispered.

*"Then what? Why can you not accept who we are and embrace it?"* Asharti's voice rose. *"We can be anything, Bea. We can rule the world. We can have all the pleasure there is. You like books. We can learn everything there is to learn."* The words had the air of pleading. *"We are gods, Bea."* Something she saw in Beatrix's face made her continue. *"You want to spare these?"* She kicked at the knight. *"We spare them. What is more godlike than that?"*

*"I have to stop this, Asharti."* Beatrix was surprised at how even her voice was. It made her sound more sure than she was inside. *"Come with me. Let us find new ways of living."*

Asharti went still. She straightened. *"I like this."*

*"Too much."*

*"What is too much? How can you like living too much? What is left of life if you hunger for nothing?"* The words tumbled from the too-wide mouth in that faintly accented French.

*"Passion for life is important,"* Beatrix said carefully, trying to tell the truth as she knew it. This was her sister, her friend, the one she had always admired, the only one who understood her. *"But desire must be tempered, like steel, if it is to last."*

*"We are* immortal*!"* Asharti spoke as if to a child. *"What is more lasting than that?"*

"I know. And it frightens me." Beatrix swallowed. "I need a new path. Join me . . ."

"No."

Just what she feared and expected. She glanced down. "I must go. Let them go, too."

"I want the last drop from them," Asharti said, lifting her chin.

Beatrix stared at Asharti for a long moment, not knowing how to convince her that her path was one of self-destruction.

Asharti must have known she was losing Beatrix. Her face contorted in rage. "You think their death matters? Then you don't know how the world works, sister. I was made after the sacking of Jerusalem by the Christians in the first Crusade. I lived through the breaking of the walls. The infidel soldiers like this brute here raged through the streets, hacking at anyone; women, children, old men as well as Allah's warriors. Heads were piled in every square. It was worse if they did not take your head. They hacked away hands and feet, so you crawled, dying, in your own blood." Her face was lit with a ferocious hatred Beatrix had never seen. "I hid near the temple of Solomon. There were twelve hundred Jews inside. And the soldiers locked the doors and burned it down in the name of Christ. The stink of burning flesh, the screams . . ." she trailed off, breasts heaving as she gazed down at the tabard that bore the cross where it lay discarded next to the naked knight. "Robert le Blois made me that night; he who ordered all that carnage in the name of God. He found me being raped by various Christian pigs and took me for himself. He too raped me, infected me, and brought me back to France to serve him. He planned to kill me when he tired of me. Stephan won me in a game of dice instead." She lifted her head, drained. Beatrix saw tears gleaming in her eyes. "That is the way the world *works for those who are not strong. I survived. Now I am the strong one. I will never be a victim again."*

Beatrix was stunned. "I'm sorry, Asharti." It seemed so inadequate. No one had ever cared for either of them, not even Stephan. "You are right. We must make our own way. But there must be other ways than to indulge in the world's brutality. Is your experience what we are doomed to re-create for others?" She asked this of herself as well as Asharti.

"I am not doomed, sister," Asharti sneered. "I choose my fate. We can be the ones who hurt or the ones who are hurt. I know which way I will go."

"I cannot go with you." Beatrix turned toward the doorway.

"You want to take them with you?" She poked the knight with her toe. "You can."

"You would let them go?" Beatrix glanced to the barely conscious men on the floor.

"All you must do is best me. Prove you are the strong one."

Beatrix felt her heart go cold. So this was it. She hesitated. She could just go. Again her eyes strayed to the men on the floor. Their chests heaved. They were still erect. How could she leave them without trying? She took a breath. Companion, come to me. The flash of power rushed up from her heart.

Asharti smiled. Her eyes narrowed, already red. Her power drenched Beatrix.

Companion! Beatrix pleaded. Their power created an electric hum in the air. Beatrix began to tremble. Asharti's grin widened. Beatrix felt her Companion waver.

"Ahhhh!" she groaned. Asharti's power ramped up exponentially.

Beatrix went still. Her Companion shushed back down her veins. "You win," she panted.

*Asharti laughed and raised her arms. A red halo pulsed around her. "My power is fed by my hunger for life," she shouted. "I can do anything!"*

*Beatrix shuddered.*

*Asharti's red glow faded. She lifted her brows.*

*Beatrix glanced, panting, one last time to the men on the floor. They were doomed. Then she whirled and rushed for the door.*

*"You will regret this for the rest of your life," Asharti shouted after her. "Do not think I will take you back after your betrayal."*

That was it. She had never seen Asharti since. She heard things, of course. Asharti had returned to the Levant. She had made a servant, Fedeyah, a eunuch who procured for her. She led a cult of cannibals in darkest Africa. That could not be true, of course. She had thought for a while Stephan would hear of Asharti's antics and stop her somehow. But he did not. Apparently the Elders at Mirso did not care as long as she was not in Europe.

Beatrix got reports of Stephan from time to time. He had lived in Nepal. They called him something outlandish. Dali Lama? Something like that. He met Cortez on the shores of the New World, which of course was not new at all, since the civilization Stephan then ruled as a god had been there for a thousand years. They provided him blood through human sacrifice. She heard from Khalenberg that Stephan was in Amsterdam now. It did not matter. She was alone, as vampires were required to be. One to a city. One, alone, just as the Rules prescribed.

Beatrix put her head in her hands. The cold from the ground and the stone at her back seeped through her. She had rejected Asharti's way more than six hundred years ago. She had tried everything since then to find passion and purpose in her life; art, and causes and literature. She had never since taken the last drop of life. If she killed it was in battle. She had used the money which came so easily to take in orphans after the endless wars in Europe, and start hospitals. What had it gotten her? The good she did was a drop in the ocean of man's inhumanity to man. Power and politics no longer interested her. Even art had paled of late. It couldn't keep the memories at bay. Music faded. Witty conversation wasn't. She would never hold salons in Berkeley Square again. She could not imagine making the effort to speak to His Grace of Devonshire or stave off the attentions of the Prince Regent.

She had no hunger for life.

She had been very near wanting something again. Three weeks ago she had wanted Langley. And he had left her. Casually. Without even regret. Did these memories of Stephan and Asharti haunt her because she had let herself be intrigued by Langley and been betrayed? It was, after all, when Stephan betrayed her that she had run amok with Asharti. Or maybe Langley was the cause of the visions, not the respite from them she had thought. God! She didn't know! She only knew she couldn't lose control again. She would *not* become like Asharti.

There was only one answer for protection from the memories, and the darkness and from becoming like Asharti. Mirso Monastery.

Time to pack.

# Thirteen

John bowed with too much grace over the hand of the Comtesse de Fanueille. She was not what he expected. "How can a poor merchant express his present honor, my lady?"

The woman with the kohl around her eyes was probably the most beautiful creature he had ever seen, including Lady Lente. Even in the large receiving room of the Emperor Bonaparte, among the flower of the French Empire and against a backdrop of lace and silk and gold braid, she put them all to shame with her air of the exotic. She even smelled exotic. It was somehow familiar. Around the room, eyes secretly followed her. She was the toast of Paris, a curiosity, if you will, who had taken the town by storm. He could imagine this woman getting whatever she wanted. But a mastermind of French intelligence? It hardly seemed possible. He wondered if Dupré had left him false information to lead him a merry dance.

"You are too kind." Her smile was brittle. The Comte de Fanueille claimed her as wife, whether or not she actually was. "But I hear you are far from poor, Monsieur Presset."

He bowed his head in acknowledgment. Barlow had chosen his cover well. John was supposed to be patriotic, extremely wealthy, and enamored of young boys; in short, a pigeon with weaknesses, ripe for the plucking. Barlow said Asharti and her comte could always use money. But just because she was greedy, it did not prove she was a mastermind of spies. "There are many kinds of riches," he said. "Beauty, for one."

"You are wise, monsieur, and politic." She surveyed the room. "I know what you want. Let me introduce you to the emperor." John was very glad that he had consorted with the man's sister in Sicily rather than in Paris. Yet it made him uneasy. He hoped Pauline was still in Italy.

The emperor wore heeled shoes that only emphasized the fact that he was extremely short. John could see his scalp through thin hair and he was roughly pear-shaped— altogether unimpressive. It was difficult to imagine this man ruling all of Europe, having risen from obscurity in a backwater like Corsica. Fanueille was the one who looked like an emperor. He glanced at the comte, tall and straight in regimentals overdecorated with gold and medals. He had very fine mustachios, but seemed . . . staid, workmanlike, probably pliable; just the man "the comtesse" needed to front her ambitions. Not the center of an intelligence operation.

"Monsieur Presset has been supplying cloth from England in his ships for our soldiers' uniforms. Isn't that brave of him?" Asharti asked rhetorically.

"But yes," the emperor said, sipping champagne.

John's heart contracted, in spite of his best intentions. Beatrix always drank champagne. He forced his attention to the emperor and a vacuous smile to his face. "The least I can do," he deprecated. "You must tell me when I can do more." That should give them the opening they needed. But Asharti was smart enough not to jump upon the first opportunity.

"I had a report today from Champollion. He is almost done with translating that stone they found in Rashid, or Rosetta as the English call it," she remarked to her emperor.

"So you will be able to read that strange picture writing so in evidence in North Africa, my dear." Bonaparte patted her hand. It was not quite avuncular. "Though what you expect to gain from knowing what all those people long dead were saying to each other, I cannot hope to guess. Probably bills from their tailors."

"Perhaps." The woman's eyes became hooded. There was something more she wanted from reading those stones. "I have sent Fedeyah on ahead to scout likely locations."

"And you will be pestering me for louis by the cartload for expeditions, I expect."

Ah, this was an innocuous opportunity. "I might have an interest in funding such expeditions. Ancient treasures are all the rage. That could be lucrative."

There were secrets in her eyes as she said, "Oh, yes."

"Then perhaps my lady could spare some time to fill me in on the details?" He raised a glass of champagne to his lips, held with three fingers only.

She looked him over. The tiniest hint of amusement lurked in her eyes. Did she enjoy his impudence, or had she smoked out his ruse? His cover was carefully designed so that if she sensed he was dissembling she would first imagine that his reputation as one who liked his own sex best was the deception and that his purpose was to invade her bed under the noses of her comte and the emperor. "Delighted. Shall we say at sunset tomorrow? Twenty-seven Rue Bonaparte."

He nodded seriously. He had his private meeting with her.

The emperor smirked. "You have saved my treasury for the war effort," he remarked. "I cannot seem to tell that woman no. Beware, Presset."

Oh, he was very likely to beware.

He escaped to his hotel. He lay in his bed, hearing the small sounds of night in a hotel wind down. What a shame to kill such a creature! He must do it himself, of course. He had to know it was done. And it would take two deaths. He would arrange it to look like Fanueille found her in bed with a lover—some ready groom or footman. An innocent, in fact. She would lose her life, the innocent would be slaughtered, Fanueille would be imprisoned, and Boney's intelligence would have lost its mastermind without anyone knowing that England engineered it.

If he did not escape, he must take Barlow's way out. He knew far too much. God forbid he should give them Barlow's name. What could the French not do with Barlow's knowledge? He liked to think he would stand firm under any circumstance, no matter how dire. But he feared in his soul that Barlow was right. He might break.

He had no illusion his country would thank him, even if he brought this off. He would be lucky if they did not murder him in his bed as a preventive measure. Barlow might regret it, but Barlow was a practical man. He lay listening to the staccato rain on the windows of his room. Paris in the spring. A longing for a simpler time came over him. Nothing was clean anymore, not Barlow, not himself, not his country. All he could cling to was that men, virtuous or not, deserved the right to be free. England was free and he would do his soiled best to keep her so.

*She* would never know if he died here. What would Barlow say about his death? Put it about that he had gone to the Continent to avoid debtors, renounced the title? The estate would go to his second cousin, Grinley, who would find it in better form than he expected. But Beatrix would never know. God, couldn't he get her out of his mind? She cared nothing for him. Wasn't that enough to cauterize his wounded heart?

Apparently not. He glanced to the window. The sky had grown perceptibly lighter. He would hide here in his lair until his appointment with the comtesse. And put Beatrix Lisse out of his thoughts. This very evening he would kill a woman and an innocent, and ensure that another man stood trial for it. Oh, the glory of serving one's country.

"So, my patriotic merchant," Asharti, Comtesse de Fanueille, purred as she lounged on a delicate Louis XIV chaise upholstered in red brocade. "You are come to make me a proposition."

They were alone in her boudoir of red and cream and gold at Twenty-seven Rue Bonaparte. John had counted on her receiving him in private, in her boudoir. It confirmed what she might suspect of his role. It would also make hiding what he was about to do easier. A fresh-faced young man with doe eyes had led him to the boudoir and now stood ready outside to answer the bell pull. He looked to be a secretary. How convenient. The only one who had seen him enter the house would be first into the room at the sound of a shot and would be the second victim. Was the young man really a secretary? He seemed slightly too . . . self-satisfied somehow. John pressed his lips together. It did not matter what he was. He would be dead shortly.

The comtesse looked . . . dangerous. Her eyes snapped beneath the feigned languor. Her supple limbs were disposed in careful disarray. She was dressed in old gold and Brussels lace, her breasts pale with a faint olive undertone in the square-cut neckline. It was cut so low her nipples might show their aureoles at any moment. Her eyes were not so dramatically lined with black tonight, but the eyelids were smudged with it and her lashes darkened, too. Her nails were longer than was fashionable and painted with gilt. She looked the picture of an exotic lioness, all tawny strength and cunning. For the first time, John believed she was the first of spies.

"Or hear a proposition," he said, sitting negligently in a dainty chair next to her. Over the mantel a water clock chimed eight. He had a small pistol tucked into the band of his trousers underneath his coat. It had only two shots, but that would be enough. One for the comtesse and one for the secretary. "I would know more of your expeditions. Do you expect to bring home treasures like the Elgin marbles?"

"I expect to find treasure beyond belief," she said, pouring a brandy for him and one for herself. She drank like a man. "A legend of my people tells of a temple with a fountain made all of jewels. And that is not the real treasure, only a signal of the true riches within."

"And you know where this treasure is?" He let himself sound skeptical.

"No. That is why we need the stone of Rosetta. I have hired scholars to translate the ancient texts and search out the location of the temple."

"That could take years."

"But as we search, we will find more than enough to fill one of your ships with ancient trinkets to sell to the idle upper classes for unconscionable sums."

"Ahhh." He flashed an expression of avarice, then frowned. "But we must take precautions. There is a disease abroad that has apparently afflicted several ships' crews in the British Navy. The symptoms are quite disturbing." He leaned forward confidentially. "Not to disturb your sensibilities, but you should know what we are up against. Drained blood."

The comtesse's smile turned into chuckles.

"You may laugh, my lady, but we will have trouble crewing ships when this leaks out." John managed indignation.

"I think I can guarantee that any ships we use will not be so afflicted." She still could not suppress a smile. "I will provide the ship's crew myself."

So she knew what it was. "But the loss of a ship . . . the cost . . . Without knowing what is causing the phenomenon, how could we possibly . . . ?"

She considered. "Actually, I know what causes the drained blood. It is no threat to us."

He put on the skeptical look again.

"Curious? Curiosity killed the cat, you know."

Dangerous ground. She suspected his motives. But what did it matter? She would be dead soon. She either told him what it was or she didn't. He plunged ahead, drawing himself up with some hauteur. "I am a man of business, Comtesse, who risks his fortune in the service of our emperor. Have I not earned the right to a certain amount of confidence?"

She gave him a measuring look. "Vampires."

"What?" The word jerked from his lips.

"The drained blood is caused by vampires, let loose upon the crew to suck their blood."

Was she serious? "You mean the South American bat?"

"I mean men who have drunk the blood of a vampire and must drink blood themselves to survive. They have other unusual qualities, quite useful in our cause."

She told him a fairy tale to make him angry. He couldn't let his anger show. Time to cut his losses and complete his main mission. "Very well." He rose and approached her. The butt of the pistol tapped against his side. He gathered himself. Now was the time. She lay back, contemplating him through half-closed, mocking eyes.

John pulled out the pistol in one smooth movement, aimed and shot her, straight through her lovely left breast and into her heart. The report was deafening in the boudoir. Her eyes went wide. A burgundy flower bloomed on the old gold of her dress. Acrid smoke hung in the air. She blinked where she lay on the chaise. The door crashed open and the young secretary stumbled in crying out, "My lady!" John turned the gun on him. The secretary crumpled. John turned to the comtesse, or Asharti—whoever she was. He must get her to the bed, arrange her limbs (and the secretary's too) in a tableau of interrupted passion and make his escape before the rest of the household rushed in.

She was still aware as he reached for her arm to pull her over his shoulder. He dared not hesitate, even for decency's sake. The moment he pulled her up, he knew something was wrong. She was not limp at all. She stood, set her feet, and with incredible, startling strength, she pulled his arm, turned him about, and clasped both his hands behind his back in a grip that was more binding than the shackles of the hulk. He tried to twist away. A roar of anger filled the room and he felt a blow across the back of his head that blurred his vision. He staggered.

"Quintoc," she called sharply. "Pull down that bell rope."

John's sight swam back toward normal, and he saw the pink-cheeked secretary stagger up, though his olive-colored coat sported a dark and spreading stain. How was this happening?

"Mistress," Quintoc acknowledged, ducking his head, and grinning in a way that was very unlike a secretary. He jerked the bell pull from the wall with a single snap. John saw what was coming. He struggled against the grip that held both wrists again now. Could he not break free from a mere woman?

They bound his wrists so tightly he would lose feeling shortly in his hands.

"I have friends, madam," he gasped. His senses reeled. "You cannot hold me." Asharti pushed him to his knees. A servant peeked into the room, looked about, and then withdrew. Had not the man seen John, tied and kneeling? Did he not see the blood everywhere?

"Go change, Quintoc, and order up the barouche," she barked. "I think we will take this one up to Chantilly."

The secretary bowed and exited as though John had not shot him through the heart at point-blank range. She turned back to him. "Brave words, but pointless," she sneered at John. "I am very powerful. No, my fine assassin, you will bend to my will now."

John was stunned, not only by the blow to the head, but by the fact that he had been disposed of so easily. He refused to think how that had happened. Escape. He must focus on escape. With hands securely tied he would be reduced to head-butting his captress or kicking her. The door was closed and he had no hands to open it. He must wait for his chance. In the street. When they were bundling him into the carriage, perhaps he could wrench away.

He lifted his head. She stood there, hands on hips, the front of her gold dress and her Brussels lace soaked in blood, glaring at him. Then her face dissolved in a grim smile. "I thought you were concealing something. Not an intent quite so lethal, of course." She raised her brows. "And now I come to think on it, I believe you are not Presset at all." She tapped a finger to her lips. "In fact, I think you are Langley." She looked sideways at him and switched to English. "I had thought to eliminate you in London, but you outwitted my poor tools. I should have recognized you immediately. But your French is excellent, and although I did not believe your fey predilection for a moment—you exude a manly essence, you know— still I thought you might only be feigning to get into my boudoir. What a bold move you have made to come directly after me! How did you know it was me and not my dear, stupid Fanueille?"

John closed his mouth. He would give her nothing. Whatever she was. What was she?

"Ahhh. Of course, Dupré. He must have told you before he died. We should have disposed of him more quickly."

"You paid the guard to shoot him?"

"Clumsy, I acknowledge, but effective in the end, I understand."

During this speech, John's shame at being taken so easily had been rising. Was he some amateur that she could see through him? But there was worse to come if he did not extricate himself from her grasp. Women could be more cruel than any man when it came to torture. His gun was useless. He had no knife and no capsule from Barlow. A tiny tendril of fear wound round his belly. How was she so strong? And how not dead?

"Now," she said, hands on her hips again. "I must change for the journey." He watched as she slipped her gown off her shoulders and let it pool on the floor. She shrugged out of her shift and kicked off her slippers until she walked, back straight, wearing only her stockings and garters, to her dressing room. Sounds of rummaging came from inside. John staggered to his feet. Could he open the door by backing up to it and get down the stairs before Quintoc reappeared? He was halfway to the door when he heard her voice behind him.

"Which one, do you think?"

At the door, he turned, fumbling at the knob. He glanced up and saw her, her heavy breasts perfectly formed, the hair dark at her groin. She held up two dresses, unconcerned at his attempt to escape. *Turn, knob,* he thought. *Damn you! Turn.*

She stood quite still, holding the dresses up. As he watched, scrabbling at the door handle, he saw something he could not credit. Her eyes went red, bloodred, a color no eyes were. She seemed to exude a halo of darkness around her form.

He stopped groping at the knob. Slowly he straightened. Without willing his legs to move, he found himself drawn toward her. Then he was standing before her, looking down into the bloodred eyes. Before he could stop himself he had knelt before her and bowed his head. He wanted to rise. He hated her for the fact that he had knelt.

"I have no time for this." He felt a stunning blow to the head. Darkness sparkled up from the edge of his vision. He was falling, falling into red eyes, and blackness all around.

"Stack the trunks in the hall, Symington," Beatrix said, not bothering to look up from her pen scratching its way across the heavy rag paper of the note card. A packet left for Amsterdam on Thursday. Then up the Rhine to Vienna, across to Budapest, and so into the Carpathian Mountains to Mirso Monastery. An uncomfortable journey, but it would be her last.

Why did she bother writing apologies to her regulars? She would never see any of them again. Perhaps it was closure. She was shutting down her life here. She had given her art collection to the Prince Regent for the use of the British people. The artists, poets, and musicians she sponsored would want for nothing. She endowed the orphanages and the hospitals. And she provided for her servants. It had been a busy week. She purchased annuities from her surprised bankers at Hoare's with sacks of gold coins engraved with Viking ships or the stamp of the Holy Roman Empire. Symington would see to everything. And then it was time he retired. He had given her a full life of service. Now, she had provided him enough to support himself and his sister and indulge every want.

Her pen scratched across the note to the Duke of Devonshire explaining that she was called to the Continent by a family emergency. Regrets. Gratitude for the acquaintance. Hope for a future meeting. Meaningless.

"Your ladyship?"

Ink blotted the card. She looked up to see Symington hovering, his face creased in worry. He had been fussing ever since she announced her departure, even though it meant a life of ease for him. The old just couldn't stand change. "What is it?"

He closed the door. "I thought your ladyship would like to know."

She raised her brows.

He cleared his throat. "Admiral Strickland's man mentioned that a ghost ship was brought in to Portsmouth last week."

"A ghost ship? What do you mean?" Something disturbing nibbled at her brain.

"The crew was drained of blood off the coast of France." Even Symington could not keep his impassivity. His voice was tight.

Two hundred men, five hundred if it was a ship of the line! Shock shivered down her spine. It meant a rogue vampire. Or many. "Have they . . . have they caught the perpetrators?" She didn't need to tell Symington what this meant. It might mean the end of the world as he knew it. Vampires were not obeying the Rules. And the Rules were what preserved the balance.

"They have not. The admiral dispatched his staff immediately with several notes to convene an urgent conference on the matter. His man Darby was entrusted with requesting an interview at the Admiralty with . . . the Earl of Langley."

"What?" Beatrix blinked, then stared down at her note. The ink blot had spread outward unevenly. Her brain did not register the ruination of her effort. The Admiralty sought out a notorious rake on this emergency?

Ahh, no. It all fell into place.

He disappeared for a month at a time. The mill was a pretense. Would he be whipped so brutally at a mill in Petersfield?

"The admiral was quite distraught that he was out of town," Symington noted.

She sat up. Was she so preoccupied with her own past that she thought of nothing but his abandoning her? Langley led a double life, a life that led an admiral to believe he could depend upon him in a dire emergency. They wanted him to be involved with this death ship? They wouldn't know vampires were behind the disaster. John would not even know the horrible danger he was in. She must warn him away. "They haven't found him, yet, have they?"

"I don't know, my lady."

Then she must. She stood and began to pace. She might be angry at him, but she had no wish to see him drained of blood. He had been so purposeful about leaving. He might be on some kind of mission. Pray it had nothing to do with vampires and she was not too late. She wouldn't think of that. Where would he be? He may actually have gone to Petersfield for that month, though she wagered it was not to see a mill. Symington would know. "You're sure he went to Petersfield when last he went out of town?"

"My sources are infallible on that point, my lady," Symington said. "At least that is where his initial destination was."

Was that where he was now? Did the current trail start in the same place? Would there be those in Petersfield who knew what he was, and where? She tossed the Duke of Devonshire's card into the wicker Indian basket beside the escritoire. "Order the carriage. Pack your things. I will have need of you. Oh, and send in Betty."

"Yes, your ladyship. And, uh . . . for how long should we pack?"

"A week, I think." She tapped the quill on the inlaid burl wood of the escritoire. She could spare a week to be sure John did not involve himself in anything to do with vampires.

# Fourteen

John swam in and out of consciousness. It was dark. Jolting hurt his head. He wanted it to stop, but he knew it never would. At one point his stomach rebelled against the pain in his head and he vomited. Someone cursed him. A woman.

Later he woke more surely. He was in a carriage. Lavender water as well as something else, fainter, made his gorge rise again. He controlled it this time. Cinnamon? Beatrix. A glow suffused him. Beatrix.

He opened his eyes. Asharti stared at him from the corner of the coach.

"If you vomit again, I will punish you," she said, and turned her head to look out the window. Her profile was bathed in moonlight. He was Asharti's prisoner. He licked dry lips with a dry tongue. He had shot her dead, but she was not dead and neither was Quintoc. She had subdued him casually, without effort, though she was only a woman. He would say he had dreamed it. But here he was bound in a coach with a broken head, the woman who should be dead staring at him. Her eyes . . . her eyes had gone red. Surely *that* was a dream. Eyes weren't red!

His breath came shallowly. He couldn't think about that. Escape. He must focus on escape. He tried to move his hands, expecting numbness. But they responded with a clank.

Shackles. He moved his feet and heard another clank. Glancing down, he saw his chains were fastened to a ringbolt in the wall of the coach. The coach was moving fast over good roads. How could he escape when he was shackled hand and foot in strange country? Even if he tore himself away they would hunt him down. A tendril of despair wound round him. He gathered his slender strength. The coach slowed and turned onto a rougher lane.

After what seemed an eternity the carriage stopped. The door was opened. Asharti rose. God, she was bringing him to a place where he could not escape!

She stepped out. Rough hands reached in for him. "Here is the key," he heard her say. They slid the clanking chain through the bolt and pulled him from the carriage. His legs would not support him. Two massive brutes, one on either arm, carried him bodily up through crunching gravel to the massive doors of a sixteenth-century chateau, all stone gables and rounded Renaissance turrets pushing into the dark.

He mustered his senses and looked around. They had come across a causeway over a lake like a moat. The water was clogged with a tangle of plants, the causeway overgrown with weeds. He glanced up toward the chateau again and saw dark tongues of soot in the slit stone windows of the upper stories from a fire now some years distant. He shook his head to clear it. He knew this place. Chateau de Chantilly, once the seat of the grand Condé, head of the Bourbon-Condé dynasty, looted and brought to ruin by the mob in the first violent rush of the Revolution. He had thought it deserted. It wasn't. A spider had moved in and made her nest.

"Get him down to the dungeons," Asharti said over her

shoulder as she waved a languid hand and moved through massive wooden doors opened by an exceedingly pale, black-clad servant. Inside, the first efforts at restoration had begun. The front hall was reasonably intact, if several of the rooms beyond looked desolate still. Asharti ascended one of two graceful curling staircases, the banisters still bare wood in places where they had been repaired. He was hauled through a heavy wooden door to the right of the great entryway, down some steps and then another stair into the bowels of the earth. The chateau had been used as a prison several times in its long life. The passages here were lined with torches that provided flickering, nightmare lighting. Through open arches he saw the small stacked tiles of hypocausts. Between the towers of tile bubbled steaming hot springs that would heat the rooms above. The air smelled of sulfur. The chateau was built over a Roman ruin.

All this registered in some part of a mind still filled with cotton. The two brutes hauled him into a darkened cell. He had the impression of rough stone. They bolted his shackles onto chains that fell from rings in the ceiling. He half hung there, the metal biting into his wrists, his legs too weak to bear him up. The place was hot and dank, filled with the smell of mold over the sulfur. The door clanged shut and he was left in darkness to contemplate just what Asharti might do with a man who had information she wanted, with a man who, to all intents and purposes except the final result, had killed her. If he was a praying man, he would beg for courage.

John was wakened from a semiconscious state not rightly sleep by the shriek of the hinges on the metal door. He was sweating in his broadcloth coat and waistcoat. The flickering light from the corridor silhouetted a sinuous figure surrounded by a gauzy haze of fabric. With an effort, he grasped the chains above his shackles and hauled himself up. He would meet his fate standing. The movement made his head swim. He breathed through his mouth to keep the nausea at bay. *Barlow, I should have taken your offer of a capsule,* he thought.

Quintoc entered behind her, carrying a torch, his rosy, open countenance marred by a self-satisfied smirk. In his other hand, he carried a large, curved knife.

Asharti was wearing almost nothing. A gathering of semitransparent silk in olive green that passed over her shoulders in two swathes covered her breasts, was cinched at the waist with a belt that looked as if it was made of copper coins, and fell in frothy pools to the floor. Her hips were revealed and the side curve of her breasts. Her nails were now painted with copper instead of gilt. She had what looked like amulet bracelets on her upper arms. A beaten-copper necklace lay between her breasts. Her skin glowed with a light sheen of perspiration. Still, she looked at ease in the stifling atmosphere. As she walked into the room it seemed to come to life.

"Now," she said, "we may indulge in some truly private conversations. Many in fact. We have all the time in the world." She spoke English, her accent flavored with the Eastern Mediterranean. She nodded to Quintoc who put his torch in a metal holder set against the stone wall. John eyed his knife, trying to keep fear out of his eyes. The man with the innocent face stalked over and ran the knife tip along the line of John's jaw. It was almost a caress.

"All the time in the world," he whispered.

"Get to it," Asharti snapped.

Quintoc grinned and popped the buttons one by one off John's cream-colored waistcoat. He pulled the end of John's cravat, unwound it and threw it to the ground as Asharti stalked around them, watching. Then, systematically, Quintoc cut off John's coat, waistcoat, trousers, and stockings. Several times, John felt the prick of the blade on his body as Quintoc was careless with the point. Shoes were pulled off, shirt and smallclothes ripped away, until John stood naked in his chains. Quintoc stepped back, twirling the knife in one hand.

"There, that's better," Asharti observed, pausing in front of him. "I like my men naked." She looked him up and down. "Especially men built as well as you are." She smiled. "You are strong. Your scars say you have borne wounds and pain before. You'll last a long time." She swept one finger along a cut. It came back coated in blood. She brought it to her mouth and licked, slowly, sensually. Her dark pupils sparked red again. He was not dreaming now.

John gritted his teeth. Horror washed over him. What *was* she? He felt so vulnerable. That's how she wanted him to feel. He pressed down the panic. She had better get used to disappointment. "You might as well kill me. I'll be no use to you," he growled.

"Use?" she tittered. "If you mean you won't tell me everything I want to know, you lie. You'll whisper all your secrets eagerly, like sweet nothings in my ear." She cocked her head and studied him. "But that is only one use I have for you."

Behind her, Quintoc chuckled. It sounded avaricious.

Asharti whirled on him. "He is for my use alone, until I say otherwise," she hissed.

John saw a flash of fear in Quintoc's eyes. "Of course, mistress," he muttered, cowed.

"Leave the key to his chains when you go."

John watched as a large metal key clanked upon a table whose heavy wood was scarred with age and use. Did she mean to free him from his chains? His mind skittered over possible escape. Could the table be used as a shield? Could he smash it against the wall? A leg might serve as a club. Or the torch . . . he could lunge for the torch. Quintoc did not bother to shut the door on his way out. Hope flickered in John's heart.

When he glanced back to Asharti, there was a look of amusement in her eyes. "We are about to have our first lesson, I think." Her voice was low and throaty.

John blinked and tried to breathe as she bent and unlocked the shackles on his ankles, then reached for the locks at his wrists. She was a tall woman, but still it was a stretch. Her breasts brushed his bare chest. She was going to unlock him! He must be wary. She was strong.

She looked straight into his eyes as his hand came free. He must wait—wait until she unlocked the last chain. Would she really be so foolish as to set him free with a door open and weapons, even crude ones, to hand? He stared at her, defiant. She would expect that.

And then her eyes went red. The feel of her nipples raking his chest through the translucent cloth made his loins feel heavy. Her eyes, red but fascinating, promised pleasures the likes of which he had never known. He would like to know them. She thrust her hips against him. The cool clink of the coins that dangled from her belt sent a shudder through him, but not of cold. He felt his cock rise. How could his body betray him thus when all he should be thinking about was escape? But he could not hold those thoughts. The scrape of fabric across his belly, the swell of her breasts, the throbbing in his genitals, filled all the corners of his mind.

She reached a hand behind his neck and drew his head down to her lips. Something scraped across the flesh at his throat. Goose bumps shot down his right arm and his leg as she whispered, "Come. Let us wash the stink of travel from our bodies before we play."

She turned, and walked through the open door.

God help him, he followed. He passed the table, the torch, without taking action and followed her through the stone passage. Every detail stood out as it does in a dream. The light of flaming brands in holders flickered over her form. Her dark hair swung, loose to her waist over the olive-green gauze. The leather of her sandals was worked in copper thread. He looked down and saw his own erection, stiff and throbbing. He was sweating. The walls were sweating. All was heat and desire.

The passage opened onto a stone room lit by torches all around. The air was heavy with moisture. They crossed a little stone bridge over water that steamed. Ahead, on a raised dais, was a round stone rim with tiny nudes cavorting among grapes and leaves, the figures sharp once but now rounded with age. From inside the rim steam rose. Set against the right-hand wall was a wide marble bench similarly decorated and laid with red and purple cushions.

Just over the little bridge, Asharti stopped and turned. She gestured to steps that led down into the steaming water. Next to the steps were some rough towels, much-used soap, and a terra-cotta bowl of leaves. He knew what she wanted. She did not speak. But he knew.

He stepped slowly down into the water. It was hot, but not hotter than the blood that boiled in him. Slowly he knelt, submerging his erection in the heat, until the dark waters were up to the middle of his chest. He looked up slowly at Asharti. She smiled in satisfaction. Then she bent and tossed him the soap. He splashed water over his shoulders, ducked his head then stood, the water up to his thighs. As she watched, he lathered his body. He ran his hands over his shoulders and down his arms. He rubbed his chest and his belly. That's what she wanted. Then in answer to her unspoken command he slid his fingers between his buttocks and lathered his anus, blushing in shame at the look of satisfaction on her face. He soaped his genitals, heavy with desire for her. He slid his foaming hands up and down the length of his cock until he was almost in pain with the need for release. But, on the edge of coming, he did not. He could not look at her, but he knew what was required anyway. He ducked again in the water and rinsed. When he stood, water sluicing off him, she allowed him to ascend the steps. He dried himself with the coarse cloth she offered. He could feel her approval of his body. Then she held out the bowl. He took some leaves and put them in his mouth. Mint. He chewed and finally spit into the bowl.

"Now my turn," she said, low in her throat. She went to the edge of the carved stone rim. John followed and knelt beside her, fear and shame mingling in his breast. It was a great stone bath. Various bottles of colored glass were set nearby on a heavy silver tray. Wine bottles sweated in terra-cotta canisters filled with melting ice. Rich towels far softer than the ones he had used were stacked near the bench.

Asharti unbuckled her belt and pushed the olive fabric from her shoulders. Naked except for her armbands, she wound her hair up and fastened it with two great wooden pins John handed her from the tray. The gesture made her breasts rise. John was afraid his loins would burst.

"Not yet, my pet," she admonished, as though she knew how close he was, and stepped into the bath. There was a kind of circular stone bench around the inside. She settled herself and then beckoned with one copper-nailed finger, to John. "Bathe me," she ordered.

John stepped in after her. The waters were as hot as the springs under the bridge below, but slick with scented oils. As in a dream, John laved it over her shoulders as she leaned back and closed her eyes in sensual absorption. He selected a soap and lathered his hands. Then, kneeling in the water beside her, he rubbed the suds over her shoulders, her breasts. Her nipples hardened under his hands. She sat upright, and he soaped her back and arms, alternately lathering his hands and caressing her skin with the slickness. She stood, and he, still kneeling in the water, soaped the roundness of her buttocks, and slid his hands down her thighs. Dread welled in him as he realized that he was to bathe her private parts as well. The soapy slickness on his fingers met inner folds already slick with desire. He felt her pleasure point, swollen and eager, and slid two fingers along it until she was breathing fast and shallowly.

Then he was standing. She wanted him to apply the soap to his cock, and he did. God, he was going to do anything she wanted! He lifted her so she could straddle his waist, her arms round his neck. His hands on her buttocks lowered her onto his soapy cock. He groaned, and she breathed out as he filled her. Her hands moved over the muscles bunching in his shoulders as he raised and lowered her. She arched back and locked her ankles behind him. Then she bent forward with something like a growl. He felt her breath against his throat and then two stabbing pains. She sucked, rhythmically, as she impaled herself again and again on his member. He felt far away from himself, the sucking at his throat and the stimulation of his cock swirling together into a haze of ecstasy. He teetered on the edge of coming—that pleasure so intense it was more like pain—but somehow he never did.

Asharti did, however. She pulled back from his throat with a shuddering cry. He could feel her contractions around his cock. She went limp over his shoulders and he slowly lowered her into the water. She disengaged herself and lay back as he rinsed her. Where was his will? One part of him was anything but pliable. He could hardly think for the ache in his loins and his erection showed no signs of subsiding. She had sucked his blood! Under the dream he was horrified, even as he knew he let her do it and would do so again.

When he had finished rinsing her body, Asharti bade him get out of the bath, though she used no words. He stood dripping, holding a huge, luxurious-feeling towel for her as she rose. He wrapped her in the soft folds and gently dried her. She touched his neck and her finger came back bloody. She licked the tip. "So, you have been whipped recently," she remarked, pulling the towel around her and reclining upon the cushions on the stone bench.

He knelt beside her, still dripping on the stone floor. The damp heat meant his perspiration mingled with the bathwater. "Knees wider. You will always kneel that way to me." To his shame, he complied. "Now where and by whom were you whipped?"

He did not want to answer her, but the words came tumbling out. "Portsmouth. The commander of the prison hulk ordered me lashed."

Asharti propped her head upon one elbow. "Well, it looks as though making it off the hulks alive was a near thing. I personally thought you would die there. I cannot say I am sorry, though. If you had died, I would have missed this lovely interlude at Chantilly." She lifted his chin with one finger. "Who were you there to see?"

This was the beginning of her questions, but it would not be the end. John knew he must refuse to answer if he was to come away with his honor. He clenched his teeth around a guttural sound that swelled in his throat. But he found his gaze being pulled up to her face. He strained to jerk away. He closed his eyes, but they would not stay closed, and there they were, her red eyes. He gasped, and the words were torn from him. "Dupré," he grunted, so low it must be unintelligible.

But she heard. "Ah yes, Dupré," she said. "You were supposed to kill him. But you didn't."

"No," John croaked. But she knew that already. She had him killed herself. She was toying with him. John shuddered. She would ask him everything, and God help him, he would answer.

"You're doing well." She reached out and ran her hand over his shoulder, touching the scars. "You have had a busy life. And to think they all believe you are a worthless rake. You have caused havoc for my dear little emperor, you and your rebellious diminutive island. While you have that navy he is not safe, though he wins battle after battle by land. He wants the world. I want it through him. But first we must pull out this English thorn."

She cradled his jaw and ran her thumb over the muscle he clenched there. "My agent almost had you several times in London." She said it like a caress. Her hand stroked the arteries that beat with the flutter of his heart in his throat. She held his neck between fingers and thumb, lightly. "But you have come to me instead. How delightful. How many secrets you must know!"

She must have seen the fear, the horror rise in his eyes. "Delightful," she whispered. "But we will save that for future conversations. I find your resistance . . . stimulating. Futile, of course, but that is part of the attraction." She threw aside her towel, revealing her lithe body, and John crawled up onto the cushions and lay, wet, beside her. "I believe I am still hungry for you."

Part of him despaired even as he throbbed against her and bent to kiss her nipple.

Beatrix paced the snug coffee room of the Crowned Head in Petersfield. Langley had been here all right. He put up at this very inn the night before the prizefight. His name was in the ledger. He had driven out the next morning. Everyone at the inn assumed he had gone to the mill. Beatrix was willing to lay odds he had not. Neither had he gone to imaginary friends in Hampshire. But how to trace him? Livery stable. "Symington," she called.

A few hours later they were bowling along toward the first posting house on the road to Portsmouth. He had not gone to the mill. The groom at the livery said he had driven toward Portsmouth. She was betting he had gone all the way to Portsmouth, but she had to be sure. Now came the tedious part. If he was really bent on some innocent visit he would have stopped at the big coaching houses for refreshment, and so would be easily traced. However, a man with secrets would not continue in that so-identifiable carriage with the Langley crest on the doors. That man would stash the carriage in a byway, and continue, whether to Portsmouth or a some other destination, in a more circumspect vehicle. To trace him she had to find the place where he had changed his livery. The possibilities were daunting.

The first step was to inquire at the major posting houses. Though it was six weeks ago, Symington's guineas provoked real effort at memory. So Beatrix knew Langley had driven his own phaeton through Weston, Horndean, and Purbrook, stopping to water his horses and take a glass of negus or porter at the major coaching stops. Now they started checking smaller houses, too, being very close to Portsmouth.

She was impatient and snapped at Symington twice. If Langley were even now being called back from whatever mission he was on, to be set upon the trail of whatever rogue cult had drained the blood of a whole ship, she might be too late to save him. It had been some time since she had wakened in the evening with anything like anticipation in her breast.

They had checked six smaller inns before, on the third day, they found the one where he had left his own carriage. The inn lay at the crossroads of the way to Southbourne and Fareham. Beatrix alighted in the evening and drew up her skirts over the dirty floor of the taproom. The Plow and Angel was far from angelic. Several characters eyed her earrings with open avarice. She sat at the table next to the fire where she could see the entire room.

Symington ordered sherry for her and laid a gold coin on the bar, drawing every eye in the place. "Can you tell me whether a carriage with an earl's crest on the door came through here the second week in April? The owner might have bespoken another carriage."

Silence in the room. The landlord looked at the guinea and chewed his lips. "Crest." He glanced to a man in the corner.

Beatrix saw the tiny shrug out of the corner of her eye. Her Companion felt her excitement and began to throb at her. They knew something here.

"I remembers it now, I do," the landlord said, pocketing the coin. "Stopped for dinner. My rib does a right fine beefsteak, if you and the lady would like to partake."

He was trying to change the subject. Beatrix sighed. "By all means, let us have some dinner, Symington. I fairly faint with hunger."

Symington nodded. "Very well, your ladyship. A private parlor . . ."

"No, I should like to eat here. I swear I could not stir another step."

Symington made his face go blank. "As you wish, your ladyship. Do you have a menu, my good man? I shall select a repast."

The landlord looked nonplussed. "My rib'll scare up whatever we have. Carrots, maybe, and spring peas with the beefsteak . . ." He trailed off.

"That will be fine," Beatrix said firmly. "While we wait, landlord, a round for the room?"

"Yes, your grace, I mean your ladyship. Poll, Poll there, get drinks." He hurried off, leaving a slatternly girl to pour beer and porter and brandy and carry them round on a tray. Glasses were lifted to her amid cries of "Here, here," from various disreputable characters. The man in the corner who had exchanged looks with the landlord now examined her closely. Good.

"Symington, why don't you see to the horses?" she whispered. Symington was the soul of discretion, but she did not want his sharp eyes to intimidate her prey.

She waited, sure of her quarry. It was not five minutes before the man rose and brought his drink to stand above her. The other patrons had gone back to checkers or noisy drinking.

"Frederick Younger, if I may be so bold," he said. "Thanks to your ladyship."

He was educated. She did not introduce herself. "You look like a better sort of person. Do sit down while I wait for my meal." She had no idea what he would reveal, which was exciting in itself. But he might lead her to John, which was even better.

"Your ladyship is generous." He sat. "Less high-and-mighty than most in your position."

"When in Rome," Beatrix said, looking at him closely. He was perhaps thirty, but pox had marked him early, and though his features were regular enough, he could not be called handsome. "Now, Mr. Younger, what is your trade?"

"I work for the Transport Office."

"Forgive me. I have not been long in your country. What is this 'transport office'?"

"We are officers of the law," he said, trying to muster pride. She realized he was studying her in return. "We arrange for criminals to be shipped to the penal colonies in Botany Bay, or if there ain't room on a transport, to be shut up in the prison hulks floating in Portsmouth Harbor."

"Prison hulks! Dear me. What are these things?" She sipped her sherry and looked interested, which she was. This man knew what had become of John.

"Dismasted ships, beyond repair. Still float, though. You can get five hundred prisoners aboard a dismasted frigate, not to say a ship of the line."

"It sounds . . . crowded."

"Oh, they ain't a bed o' roses," he laughed. "But it's only criminals after all, or prisoners of war." He took a long gulp of the brandy, and threw out a calculating look. "Couldn't help overhearing you was looking for the Earl of Langley's coach."

Not a good secret-keeper, she thought. She had never

said Langley. And a man like him would not ordinarily recognize the Langley crest. "One doesn't like to be displaced in a man's affections, Mr. Younger. A woman scorned, et cetera."

He relaxed visibly. "Oh, well, that's just the way of the world, your ladyship. The way of the world." He took another gulp of his brandy.

Now, when he was relaxed, was the time. She coaxed up just a bit of her Companion. Anyone looking would think it was reflected firelight in her eyes. "But you know where Langley went, don't you, Mr. Younger?" she asked softly.

He nodded, suddenly vague about the eyes, mouth slack.

"Tell me." Her voice was so low he wouldn't normally be able to hear it over the noise in the taproom. But he heard it all right, so deep in his soul he could not refuse her.

"I picked him up and took him down to the hulks. Paid right well for it, too. I drew up the papers, all legal, and clapped the irons on him myself."

"As a prisoner?" Beatrix was shocked. "Why would he do that?"

"Don't know. I sure as hell wouldn't want to be there. No provision for getting him out, either. That was part of the deal. For all I know, he could be there yet. Or dead."

But he wasn't. He had been in her bed, thinner than usual and with recent scars from a lashing, little more than a week ago. Beatrix was thinking fast now. There were things she must know if she was to trace him further. "So you sent his carriage back to London?"

The man nodded.

"What name did he use, and what ship was he imprisoned on?"

"St. Siens, Jean, on the *Vengeance*."

He was posing as a French prisoner of war. John was certainly a spy. "And who paid you?" This was crucial.

They might know where John was now.

"Don't know, your ladyship. A packet, with instructions and the money."

"But you've done work like this before . . ."

"Yes. Oh, yes. And since. Got orders to arrange parole in Fareham for two French prisoners just this week. Reynard and Garneray from *Vengeance*."

There was no more to get out of him. And yet . . . "Is there a ship in Portsmouth Harbor brought in because all aboard had died?" That might be where John was now . . . investigating.

"That one was burned. Plague ship, so I hear."

*One avenue closed.* Her resolution was not diminished, however. Someone on this prison hulk might know what John was doing there, who gave him his orders. Or what he found out there may have sent him on his current mission. "You will not remember our little conversation," she whispered. She let her blood subside and watched him come to himself. "Good brandy, yes?"

He stared at his much-diminished glass and raised his brows.

Beatrix rose as the landlord reappeared. "So sorry," she murmured. "I find I cannot stay to eat. But here is recompense for your trouble." She placed another sovereign on the bar and hurried out, leaving astonished looks behind.

"Portsmouth, Symington," she said to the phlegmatic servant. "We will bespeak a fair dinner at the Blackfriars Hotel in Pembroke Street. Then I am for the *Vengeance*."

# Fifteen

John swam up through blackness, haunted by red, evil eyes. His own eyes jerked open upon more blackness. His breath heaved in his chest and he was shaking even in the heat. Sweat coursed down his body. He was curled in a corner, naked, on the stone floor. It took a moment for him to come to himself. The nightmare was as much a reality waking as asleep. Hopelessness washed over him. The smell of sulfur made the atmosphere of this hell complete.

The bitch demon wasn't human. And she could make him do anything. He flushed to think she had forced an erection on him somehow, that she held him in thrall, from driving him mad with lust, even to the point of stopping his ejaculation. And she drank his blood. Not enough to kill him—that was the tragedy.

What was she? His brain wouldn't think. It was muddled by the loss of blood, or loss of will, or simple emotional exhaustion. She wasn't human. That was all he could think about. Strong. Bloodsucking. Mind-controlling. God help him, she would make him betray everything he and Barlow had worked for. Of course she was the mastermind of French intelligence. She could know anything she wanted to know, force men to do anything she wanted them to do.

Escape. His dull brain turned over the possibilities. He moved his body, aching from hours of unconsciousness on the hard stone. He was chained at the wrists. He followed the chain and came to a heavy iron ring in the wall. He scooted up, braced his feet, and pulled until he thought the muscles in his thighs and shoulders would burst. The ring was anchored solidly. He collapsed, panting. Damnation! Nothing sharp or hard he could use to dig at the masonry lay to hand. He tried to think. She would unlock him again, he was sure of it. But never without controlling him. Quintoc—would he be more careless?

Misery crept up from his belly into his throat. If Quintoc was careless it would have to be soon. At any moment, Asharti could force him to reveal everything.

The only sure way to prevent that was to kill himself right here, right now. Lord, but he wished he had taken Barlow's capsule! Realistically, though, he might not have taken it soon enough to have prevented this. How could he have known the woman could overpower him, or that she would not even notice a bullet in her chest?

*Focus,* he commanded himself, shaking his head. He had to find a way. Not enough chain to hang himself. He ran a finger around the inside of his shackles. They were rough enough to rub his wrists raw, but not sharp enough to saw through flesh to artery. His eyes, grown accustomed to the darkness, now perceived a faint light from the hallway leaking through the base of the cell door. It was not enough to lighten the room, but enough to show the deeper pool of blackness that would be the wooden table in the corner. A splinter perhaps. But it was out of reach. Bang his head against the stones? Uncertain result.

He was still casting about when darkness eclipsed the faint glow emanating from under the door. He stared into a whirl of black, more black than even the darkness in the cell. The whirling stopped. The line of weak light reappeared under the doorway. The air vibrated. A smell of cinnamon wafted over him, and Asharti walked forward.

John gasped.

"Dear me, I just cannot seem to stay away from you," Asharti said, in that throaty voice. She loomed over him. John pressed himself against the rough stone wall that sweated just as he did in the heat. "I drained two inmates of the local workhouse this day, and still I am not sated."

Fear beat at him. "What are you?" John said, through clenched teeth.

"I am your better, human man. That is all you need to know." She knelt in front of him. John felt his loins begin to tighten. "And soon I will have the world arranged to my satisfaction. Vampires will live openly, as many to a city as I want. No more Rules. Humans will be what they were meant to be. Cattle. Slaves."

John let out a low moan as he felt his member rise. He could not see her in the dark, but he was fairly certain if he could, her eyes would be red. Her scent drenched him, spicy and sweet. She leaned in until her breasts brushed across his chest, and cupped his balls with one long-nailed hand. "What shall I indulge in first? Blood, sex . . . information?" She squeezed him. He knew she was strong enough to unman him in a single wrenching movement. "Should I take you to the bath, or have you right here?" she whispered. The darkness was palpable.

She obviously made her choice, for he knew she wanted him to open his hips to her. He fought the desire to obey her, but he wanted to do it more than anything he had ever wanted. He spread his legs. She pulled herself up to kneel between them and bent to him. Her long hair brushed his erection. Her canines scraped his skin just at the joining of his hip and thigh. He felt his blood pumping in the great artery there. He knew the sharp pain would follow, but she toyed with him, licking his skin until his flesh crawled and he wanted to scream. But he didn't. He couldn't, because she did not want him to scream. The piercing, when it came, made him shudder. He throbbed as she drew at his groin and his hips moved in counterpoint to her sucking. A strange light-headedness came over him. The stone digging into his back receded. He knew only heat and lust. He wanted her to take his blood. He wanted to give her whatever she desired.

When she finally tore herself away, someone grunted, low. It might have been him. She straddled his loins where the blood still welled and eased herself onto his cock. They moved in counterpoint, sweating. He could barely make out her body arched above him, moaning. His own body reached that point of painful pleasure that would result at any other time in his release.

"Perhaps later," she said, as if she knew his state. "As a reward for all the lovely secrets you tell me." Then she renewed her efforts. He thrust his hips with fierce intensity. She slid frantically along his cock, until she shuddered, moaning, and then collapsed upon his heaving chest. He could feel her waning contractions. She allowed him no respite, however. He was still hard inside her.

After some time this way she laid her head upon his shoulder where she could whisper into his ear. "Most satisfactory. Better than any in a long time. I wonder why?" she murmured. "Perhaps because your will is strong. Perhaps because, underneath, you hate it so. Most like it, right up to the end." She stroked his cheek. "Now for something you will hate even more."

John might be drained of energy, if not of lust, but his small store of wits was returning. If he could have ensured his own death in the next seconds by will alone, he would have done it.

"A name," she whispered. "And an address, in London, I presume."

He tried to wrench away from her, groaning. The clank of his chains tore at his mind.

"No, no, my sweet young suckling, you have no choices here." She turned his head back toward her in the darkness. "You know the name I want, the name of the man who sets you your tasks, who sets all the tasks of men like you for England." She smiled seductively.

John could not get his breath. His chest heaved against her weight. A low crying sounded in his throat and he could not control it. He arched his body against the pressure to fulfill her every desire, even this last most vile demand. And then the dam burst.

"B . . . Barlow," he stuttered. "Thomas Barlow."

Asharti ran her fingers through his hair, chuckling. "Good little suckling. Address?"

"Sixteen Albemarle Street."

He collapsed against the stones. Betrayed! He had betrayed Barlow, and thus England.

Asharti, in the darkness, kissed his shoulder. "There, there," she murmured. "I know how much that cost you. Delightful." He felt the scrape of teeth. They pierced the flesh of his shoulder, but he did not jerk away from the pain. He almost relished it. What did he not deserve in retribution for his treachery? This time she dragged a furrow across his shoulder and licked at the wound. That excited her again, and she began to move her hips once more over his cock. He grunted with effort as he heaved his hips up off the stone. This time she made no effort to control his ejaculation. He spent himself in her in some twisted mixture of induced desire and despair, even as she writhed above him in her own release.

His orgasm subsided. Her throaty laugh echoed against the stone, filling the cell. "There, did I not promise you a little reward for your cooperation?" She pulled herself up. "I so enjoyed myself," she murmured, standing. "We will talk again soon."

John could not be sure whether the whirling blackness was inside his head or outside, but all consciousness deserted him.

Beatrix stared across the water in the growing gloom. The sharp winds off the channel between Portsmouth and the Isle of Wight pulled at the heavy curls of her hair where they were pinned on top of her head. It took the strands once coiled in careful disarray at her temples and made their escape from order real. She was wearing black tonight, the better to blend into the night. A Norwich shawl covered her shoulders and was thrown across her breast to keep its pale skin from gleaming, as well as to shield her from the night wind.

The water lapping at the transport dock was overlaid with the oily filth of a port. The clean and fecund smell of the sea mingled with tar and the rotting smell of all the things tossed overboard as ships' excrement. Across the harbor, under scudding clouds, the deformed silhouettes of the dismasted hulks rocked in the swell, menacing and melancholy. Once they were proud fighting frigates or ships of the line. Now through age or injury their fighting days were done, and they spent their last days in shameful employ.

"Which one is *Vengeance*?" Beatrix asked the small boy at her side. His father served as a guard on one of the frigates, and he had been to many and many of them, so he said.

"That 'un, there." The urchin pointed. It was the one anchored farthest away. "Don't nobody want Frenchies escaping," he explained. Four miles perhaps. Too far for translocation without a middle stop and she didn't want the attention a woman drawing alongside in a boat would provoke. What were her options?

"Certainly not," she said. He was perhaps eight or nine, dressed respectably in nankeen breeches and a flaxen shirt with a bandana round his neck. He wasn't clean, but then boys his age so seldom were. His mother would want him home for dinner soon. "Has anyone ever escaped from *Vengeance*?"

"No one didn't never escape until last month," he confided. "The TO don't want it about, even still."

"That someone escaped?" Beatrix felt a strange thrill of excitement.

He nodded vigorously. "It were only that bugger Rose that let it happen, says m'father. He's a disgrace on the TO."

"The captain of the *Vengeance*?"

"Lootenant. Ain't no more, though. Got picked up fer counterfeitin'. Run out 'o the service." The boy nodded in agreement with the verdict for that bugger Rose.

Interesting. A prisoner escapes from *Vengeance*, its captain is taken up for counterfeiting shortly afterward, and two prisoners are paroled. "Tell me, young man," she said, still staring out to sea, "since you are so familiar with all the workings of the Transport Office. Is it usual for prisoners from *Vengeance* to be paroled?"

"No, in course," he said, marveling at her ignorance. "Parole is for officers. The Frenchies on *Vengeance* ain't officers."

Beatrix felt in her reticule and brought out a shilling. Any more would excite too much comment, though she felt like showering guineas over the boy. "Thank you, child. You've been most enlightening. Run along to your dinner."

His retreating footsteps thunked hollowly on the worn timbers of the quay. She glanced after him. Lights were on in the town. Men still strode along the quayside road called the Hard, but the hivelike atmosphere of a port was subsiding for the night.

She picked out a ship halfway to *Vengeance*. Then she settled down to wait behind a heap of barrels where she was shielded from the Hard, wondering whether she was only wasting her time, and if there was any other way to find John. Around midnight she reached out to her Companion and brought its power up along her veins. The whirling life engulfed her, bringing that familiar rush of vitality. Mentally, she grabbed at that energy, calling for more, then drawing it up around her like a cloak. The energy came shrieking up the scale until the moment she popped out of space in a wrenching, ecstatic moment of pain. She reappeared upon the deck of her chosen ship, rocking in the growing night.

Gaping shock registered on the faces of two uniformed men on the deck. One was self-possessed enough to call out. She waited only to master herself, then drew up the power of her Companion again. The sailors disappeared in the whirling black. The excruciating ecstasy came again and she was standing next to the quarterdeck on *Vengeance* as the spinning blackness melted away from her. She gasped for air as the pain receded. The deck was empty except for a guard pacing the forecastle and one the quarterdeck behind her, though boisterous laughter and a voice crying, "Polton, Polton there, the bottle stands by you," sounded from the cabin. Countless voices murmured under her feet. The shabby ship was battened down for the night. Still she could smell the stench of unwashed men wafting up from below and the making tide had not yet washed away the effluvia from the heads at the forecastle.

Why had she come? John had been here. She was certain he escaped, the only one ever to manage that. What she wanted to know was *why* he had arranged to be manacled and imprisoned on this terrible hulk. Did it have something to do with the mission he was on at this moment? He had stayed only a day in London before he was off again. Would the officers know? She didn't think so.

They were not in on his secret, or he would never have been punished so.

She looked down at her feet, knowing that five hundred prisoners, some perhaps murderous, all desirous of escape, were down there. Some of them must have known John, or St. Siens as he called himself. Maybe one of them knew why. She took a breath. She was stronger than they were. She could see in the total darkness down there in the holds. They wouldn't know how to kill her. She could make sure they thought her presence just a dream. But she had to admit that going down into that teaming mass of angry and frustrated men gave her pause.

She smiled. When had anything last given her pause? Nothing since the battle of Agincourt. All those thousands of French knights coming down on them screaming . . . She remembered the release of hacking about yourself with a sword, dressed in chain mail like a man. She had distinguished herself that day with strength that was more than a man's. How long had it been since she lost herself in a purpose? She wanted something now. She wanted to know the whereabouts of John Staunton.

The guards were turning and pacing toward her. Now or never. She brought the darkness up, and popped out of space, into the teeming darkness below.

She stumbled and fell to her knees, provoking several growls and a cry of "Watch yourself, you goddamn sodomite," in French. She scrambled to her feet. The stench almost overwhelmed her. Unwashed bodies, vomit, urine, tar, and underneath all the slightly sweet smell of sickness and approaching death. She breathed through her mouth and pinched her nose with one hand. The prisoners slept on top of each other on the floor and hanging in hammocks like rows of some kind of chrysalis, swinging with the swell.

Beatrix mastered herself, leaning against the ladder,

and drew just enough of her Companion to shower compulsion on a figure she could see through darkness which would be absolute to one not of her kind. "Tell me about St. Siens," she whispered.

"Don't know him," he moaned, cracking an eyelid. "Like to know you, though."

She tried another. "Merchant," he whispered.

So the night went. Toward dawn she was down in the orlop deck. Time was running out. She knew much about John's stay here. Combing about among the sleepy prisoners and whispering her compelling questions to their dreams, she heard he took the blame for a friend's act of defiance and paid with a flogging and time spent in someplace called the Hole. She heard about singing "La Marseillaise" and the fever that nearly killed him. No wonder he lost weight. She heard his plan to have a painter named Garneray engrave banknotes to set the prisoners up again when the lieutenant threw their belongings overboard. She felt the prisoners' immense satisfaction when Rose was arrested right on board the ship for counterfeiting. They were sure John had arranged it. She did not doubt it. She heard of his escape, naked, in an empty provisions cask with a bribed boatman. Some thought the boatman had betrayed him, some that he had been thrown into freezing sea and drowned or that he had been picked up by the Transport Office, naked as he was. They were afraid to believe he had actually made it. At the same time they wanted him to know their current state; that the new captain did not allow the guards to take a cut of what the prisoners earned, that the Hole had been sealed up and floggings were banned, that things were better, however bad they might still be.

She realized he had given them hope, a sense that they could affect their destiny. She squirmed her way among the prisoners, beginning to stir then stopped. She woke one and whispered, "You heard from a guard that St. Siens made it back to France. He escaped." The sailor would embellish it and tell the others. It was a small enough gift.

She sighed. She must go. Though she knew much more of John, she had not found anyone who knew why he had imprisoned himself in this dreadful place, or where he was now. He would not have engineered an escape without completing his purpose, not if he was the man she was beginning to believe he was.

But what was his purpose? Had completing it sent him on another mission? Where? Another night of questioning seemed pointless. Where to turn? Wait. Many prisoners mentioned that the men who had been paroled, Garneray and Reynard, were John's closest associates. Might they not know his purpose? And Younger had paroled them, and so knew where they might be found.

She needed a bath, and some sleep. Then it was time to visit Mr. Younger again.


Beatrix slid through the streets of Fareham in the darkness, dressed again in black. Down the High toward the east side of Portsmouth Bay, then left into a small court. Reynard had been paroled to live with an older couple whose neat house lay at the end of the tiny circle, according to Mr. Younger. In return for their promise not to try to escape or aid the enemy, officers were allowed to live among the populace until the end of the war or until they were exchanged. The small, whitewashed building with the flower boxes was quite a contrast with the hulks.

No lights offered from the house. She drew the darkness and reappeared just inside the red wooden door to the street. It was harder this time, the sixth time tonight. She was exhausted. Translocating took its toll. As the whirling black dissipated around her she saw that she was in a tiny front hall. She tiptoed up the creaky wooden stairs to the bedrooms above. The first door she opened held a snoring man and a heavy woman in nightcaps. Beatrix closed the door quietly. The next door held an ancient crone, no doubt the mother of one of the couple. Finally, in a tiny room at the back of the house under the eaves, a man sat up in bed looking straight at her.

"Who are you?" he whispered. "What do you want?"

"A friend of St. Siens'," she said and drew her Companion up. Best get this over quickly and be gone. She felt her eyes go red as she stepped forward. "I have questions." She seated herself on the edge of the bed near the foot, out of his reach. Though his name was synonymous with the fox, he was a bear of a man. His nightshirt collar lay open, revealing a chest full of matted black hair. His eyes went vague in the darkness.

Now that she was here she hardly knew how to begin. "You knew St. Siens on the hulks?"

"Yes." He whispered just as she did.

"Who was he?"

"A merchant and, I think, a spy for the emperor," the big man said.

That was new. But if John was a spy, it wasn't for Bonaparte. She tapped her finger to her lips. "Was there another reason he was there?"

Reynard frowned, thinking. "Not that I know of."

Dead end. Perhaps this man knew nothing. Or perhaps she just wasn't asking the right question. Should she start with the end? "Why did he need to escape so badly?"

"He had important information for the emperor's cause." The man talked in a monotone, as if reciting. "Dupré knew who it should be delivered to. Neither trusted the other enough to share their secrets. They agreed to escape, each with their piece of knowledge. But Dupré was sick. They had to escape before he got worse."

Dupré? She had heard nothing about any Dupré in her questioning of prisoners last night. And only one prisoner escaped, according to the boy. "Did they make it?"

Reynard shook his head, sadly. "Dupré was killed by a guard."

Here. It was here somewhere. "Then . . . then how could St. Siens deliver the information?"

"Dupré told him, just before he died, the true head of Napoleon's intelligence network."

Beatrix saw it all. John wanted the name. He had come to the hulks at great personal cost to get that name. And now he was no doubt secretly pursuing whoever headed Bonaparte's own ring of spies. She needed the name as much as John did, if she was to find him. Reynard knew the exchange of information had been made. Did he know more? "And did you overhear the conversation between St. Siens and Dupré?" she whispered.

The big man nodded slowly.

Beatrix leaned forward in the darkness. "Who is the head of Napoleon's spies?"

"A woman," Reynard said, a little wondering.

"What is her name?" Beatrix let her impatience be felt.

"Something strange." He hesitated. "Asharti. Her name is Asharti, the Comtesse de Fanueille."

Beatrix sat back with a gasp. Asharti? She leapt to her feet, her mind chaotic. Asharti directing spies for Bonaparte? Of course, she would be wonderful at extracting information, even as Beatrix was doing now. Only Asharti would not take such care that her subjects survived the process. Bonaparte was the most powerful man in the world at the moment. Asharti would like that. Was Asharti controlling Bonaparte? She could. Lord knew Beatrix had attached dozens of kings and emperors during the centuries when she had an interest in power. And Asharti must be behind the English ship full of men being drained of blood . . .

John was going after Asharti! A lightning flash of horror lit her soul. He didn't know what he was up against. He couldn't. Asharti would . . .

Oh, God.

Everything changed in a single instant. The rush and magnitude of change nearly robbed her of her senses. How much she had to lose! Beatrix drew the darkness without even leaving Reynard some convenient dream. He slumped back into sleep as she reached the bursting point and disappeared. In a split second she had acquired a purpose. But she had lost the freedom to choose her course. She was for Paris. She couldn't let John face Asharti alone.

# Sixteen

Three interminable nights she had waited for the official "unofficial" cartel to enemy shores to depart. The cartel passed back and forth between Dover and Le Havre carrying diplomats, scientists, and even more secret passengers. The smuggler would have saved her a night, but they were too likely to be taken. Though every delay was torture, failure entire would doom John. The cartel was sure. She was bound for Dover tonight. It would leave in the morning. Four days from the time she had heard Asharti's name from Reynard's lips!

Of course Asharti chose France. No other vampire went anywhere near France since the Revolution became infatuated with the guillotine. The very thought of that instrument of decapitation made her Companion shudder in revolt and cling to life all the harder. Decapitation was the only sure way to kill a vampire. So no vampire would even know Asharti had left Africa. But where in France? Could Beatrix take the chance that it was Paris? And if in Paris, where? She did not have the luxury of an extended search.

Beatrix had gone over and over how long John had been absent from London and what might have happened in that time. Nearly three weeks. If he had found Asharti, could he have survived this long? She knew what Asharti did to men. And if he was dead? What?

She paced the drawing room that once would have been full at midnight. Damn Asharti! Stephan should have killed her when he knew what she had become. He could have done it. Beatrix couldn't have, not even six hundred years ago. Asharti thought the depth of her dark passions fueled her strength. She might have grown stronger at a faster rate than Beatrix. How could Beatrix stop her now?

This was what came of making vampires! Beatrix's anger bubbled over in a growl. Suddenly she collapsed into a burgundy-striped brocade chair. Asharti had probably already killed the only person standing between Beatrix and Mirso Monastery.

John would have betrayed everything and everyone he believed in by now. Asharti would have them all killed. She would not only have taken John from Beatrix, but perhaps ensured that England would fall to Bonaparte. John would be devastated. Even if she could not save him the pain of his betrayal, she could try to prevent Asharti from winning. Beatrix stood, wavering. Beatrix might not be stronger than Asharti, but she could warn those in danger. Someone had sent John to the hulks. It was possible that person could protect himself and the other English agents. Another thought struck her. John's director might also know just where he had gone to find Asharti. That would quicken her search. But how to find this shadowy man? She knew nothing of John's contacts.

But she knew one who might.

She rang for the footman and called for the carriage. There was yet time. She need not leave for Dover for hours. She dismissed her dresser, Betty.

A woman could not go openly to bachelor's apartments like Albany House. But she had other means. She thought carefully about how far it was from Berkeley Square, just where in the dark corners of the court she wanted to be. Out of the light from the streetlight on Piccadilly . . .

Then she called to her Companion.

In moments, she lurked in the shadows of Albany Court gazing up at the lighted windows of Number Six. The night was positively balmy. May was giving way to June and promising summer. There! A shadow moved across the windows. Yes . . . She drew the power again and blinked out of space, reappearing in the darkened foyer of Number Six.

The rooms smelled faintly of cigarillos, furniture polish, and shaving cream. Under those aromas was the scent of John Staunton, Earl of Langley, and someone else. It was the someone else she wanted. She heard him moving about in the small room in the back. Keeping the power of her Companion ready, she moved silently in that direction.

No one in society understood why such a moralistic valet would serve a rake for years. Beatrix understood. John Staunton was as moralistic as his valet was in his way. Withering was an old man but not decrepit by any means. He sat in a wing chair reading a newspaper by the light of a lamp on a nearby desk, wearing a brocade dressing jacket and slippers on his feet. The only other contents of the tiny room were a narrow bed, a crowded bookshelf, and a rather handsome oak wardrobe. He had the look of a well-to-do squire, or in other words, of a perfect valet. At her entrance, he glanced up, his surprise turning to disapproval.

She let the red come up into her eyes, and saw the disapproving look evaporate.

"What is your name?" she asked gently, sitting on the edge of the bed.

"Withering." His voice was perfectly modulated. He had probably trained all his life to be the consummate valet to an earl. In her experience, even if one tried to keep secrets from valets and dressers, they always knew virtually everything about one. She hoped it was true in this case. In fact, she should have started here, in Albany Court, instead of chasing off to Petersfield. She had panicked. Perhaps Withering knew exactly where his master was.

"I have questions, Withering. Where is your master?"

"I don't know, your ladyship."

He knew who she was. "Did he go to France?"

"I don't know, your ladyship."

She wanted to cry out in frustration. Well, but at least she knew her chase to the hulks was not in vain. "What is the name of the man who gives Langley his instructions?"

"I'm sorry, my lady. I couldn't tell you."

He didn't know what she wanted to know. A sigh escaped her. Perhaps valets didn't know everything after all.

But maybe he didn't know he knew. She chewed her lip. "You know what Langley is?"

"Yes, my lady."

"Well, what is he? And don't tell me he's a rake."

"He does work for the government, your ladyship. Without payment, of course."

Interesting. Of course a man like John wouldn't take pay. "Do you know what he was doing in Portsmouth?"

"No, your ladyship."

Beatrix paced the tiny bedroom. "But you must have known he had been lashed."

"Yes. I cared for him upon his return. His lordship often requires medical attention."

"Damn it, man! You have no idea who gives him his orders?"

"I do, my lady. Someone who lives at Sixteen Albemarle Street. All his instructions come from that address." It was said matter-of-factly, of course. Beatrix sucked in a breath and let it out with a half-chuckle. She had asked for the name, and he didn't know the name. To think she had almost despaired! Now to repair the damage

John would cause under Asharti's compulsion, if it was not too late, and to find out exactly where he went, before she made a dash for Dover.

She stood. "You will remember nothing of my presence," she whispered softly to the old valet. She would have Symington pay him off so handsomely he could retire in style if it came to that. No use for him to wait here forever for a master who might not return. She blinked several times, absorbing that, and took a deep breath. She didn't know for sure. And she would hold back despair until she did.

She had much to do. And she would *not* miss the cartel that sailed with tomorrow's tide.

John woke in darkness, as always. Pain from the cuts on his body throbbed at him from far away. He lay on the hot, sweating stones. A small sound escaped as he dragged himself into a sitting position. The darkness around him swirled with his own dizziness and he nearly fainted again. He heaved himself over to the wall, chains clanking.

He would die soon. He must. He could not take much more of her opening veins, making wounds, all to suck his blood. Or he might die of heartbreak or shame. He had betrayed a dozen men. She had used him for her pleasure against his will times without count. Each time he fought against her. Every time he lost. He had bathed her, licked her, penetrated her, begged her. And she had penetrated him. He . . . he would not think about that. It *must* end soon.

Or perhaps it would go on forever. Perhaps she could will him not to die. She would draw out his death by taking his blood so sparingly that he would go on forever in this twilight life of shame and misery. Or at least until he had no more names to give. How many names were left? He put his head into his hands and tried to master his emotions.

How long had he been in that almost-unconscious state that passed for sleeping these days? How long would he have before she came again? When the door opened, leaking painful light, they brought food he was required to eat, or exchanged the chamber pot just reachable from his chains. If the door did not open at all, it was her . . .

He breathed deep and closed his eyes.

He saw in his mind's eye a chandelier, cascading light over a drawing room. Beatrix was there. Her auburn hair glowed in the light. Light refracted through the champagne in her glass even as her laugh broke over him. Beatrix. Sophisticated, strong, vulnerable in ways she did not want others to know. She did not want him. He knew that. But thinking of her had saved him in the hulks and now she was the antidote to Asharti. Asharti was dark, evil. He ripped his mind from Asharti and thought about the light in Beatrix's eyes when she had talked of Turner, or of Blake's second innocence.

They were wrong to believe in Blake. Second innocence! Dangerous drivel, nothing more. There were some things so horrendous one could never recover from them. No one could believe in goodness once they had experienced Asharti.

He jerked his thoughts back to Beatrix and blessed light, then shook his head as despair washed over him again. Beatrix was *not* goodness. She was a courtesan—an intelligent, beautiful courtesan somehow damaged, but a courtesan nonetheless, a courtesan who did not want him.

Footsteps echoed outside the wooden door. Two pair. A key clanked in the lock. He straightened. He would not let them see him crouching, afraid. The door creaked open. He raised one shackled hand against the light. Quintoc held a brand aloft and lit the single torch.

She strode in, her gown drifting around her. John felt his breath come shallowly. She was dressed not in one of her diaphanous scraps of chiffon, but in a traveling cloak over a rich, laced fabric. She bent over him, placing her thumb and fingers around his throat to feel the pulse.

"He will last until I return. I'll be gone only a few days."

"I could get names out of him in your absence, mistress." There was a leering anticipation in his deceptively innocent face.

"Not necessary." Here her voice grew sharp. "You may have him only twice, Quintoc, before I return on Saturday. No blood."

"No blood?" Quintoc cried.

"Quench your need from the workhouses or the prisons." She smoothed John's hair back from his forehead. John was past shuddering at her touch and he was still reeling at what her instructions to Quintoc might imply. "He is quite sweet. He hates it so. And yet he gives quite expertly. I have not had one I enjoyed so much in centuries." She turned her head, and gazed steadfastly at Quintoc. "If you take blood, I will know it."

Quintoc met her gaze for only a moment before he looked down. "Yes, mistress."

"You are young, Quintoc, and his will is strong. He may prove difficult. It will be an excellent training exercise for you. Perhaps," she continued, almost airily, "I will allow you to show me how you have coaxed him to perform when I return. That could be . . . stimulating.

"And you," she purred to John. "Gain strength. I must go to Paris, to set certain matters in train through Fanueille. But I shall want you when I return." She spun on her delicate kid slippers and made for the door. At the last instant, she turned. "Barlow is lost to your cause. The others will die if they are not dead already. You have been most satisfactory on all fronts."

John shrank inside, suffused with horror. He had betrayed his country, his friend, himself.

Quintoc smirked at him as he said, "Mistress, may I call the carriage?"

The door closed. The lock snicked shut. Their voices and their footsteps faded down the hall outside the door.

John should have been relieved that Asharti could not be at him for a few days. But relief was far away. He was almost more afraid of Quintoc.

Beatrix stood outside Sixteen Albemarle Street, blinking. As she came to herself, she realized that something was wrong in the still, narrow street.

Vibrations cascaded over her. She squeezed her eyes shut. There was a vampire in that house. The vibrations were only a murmur. The creature was newly made, not strong. The implications poured over Beatrix. Had John betrayed his mentor to Asharti, who made him vampire instead of killing him? If Asharti had made him vampire . . . he must serve her.

And if Beatrix could feel him, he could feel her. She should depart immediately. Another thought intruded. Either Asharti had come to London and managed to avoid Beatrix feeling her very powerful vibrations, or Asharti had sent another vampire to make the one inside.

A man presumably high up in England's confidence, in thrall to Asharti—the consequences of that . . . There was but one way to prevent the damage this one could do. What was her obligation here? She had never stooped to killing another of her kind . . .

Beatrix drew her power, dread of what she might do suffusing her. She could not let her courage fail. Asharti could *not* prevail.

She trembled into space in front of an old man, warming his hands by the fire. It was him. He started in surprise. "Who are you?" she asked. She did not use compulsion. Yet.

"Sir Thomas Barlow," he answered, wary. "What do you want here?"

"I am from her," Beatrix lied.

Barlow relaxed. "We are well positioned. The agents are all dead, or soon will be. I have information on Wellington's plans in the Peninsula. Bonaparte can have Portugal for the asking if he sends Soult's forces to support Masséna. Here is an outline of Wellington's weaknesses." He moved to his desk.

"I am curious." Beatrix tried to breathe evenly. "How did she turn a lifelong servant of the British crown? I would follow her lead." She needed to know this.

The man's great eyebrows rose. "The nephew of my housekeeper. He brought me to her in Dover. We talked. Then he turned me and gave me his blood while I was sick." He glanced at Beatrix. Those eyes had seen all of man's dirty soul in a single lifetime.

Suddenly Beatrix had to know one more thing. "How long ago did you turn?"

"Last quarter day." He said it casually. But it showered relief over Beatrix. Two months. It was not John who had betrayed this man to Asharti. Light dawned. The footpads, the night there had been a shot outside her house just as John left . . . the reverse was true! Barlow had been trying to have John killed. Not directly, and he used none of his vampire powers . . . he must have been trying to be discreet. But Beatrix was sure he had tried to kill John. Even sending John to the hulks could have been an effort to kill him. Had he killed Dupré, too? But he hadn't killed John. So perhaps he had sent John to Asharti so she could dispose of him.

But why would he do this? "She can't control you when you are in London and she in Paris, so she must have your sympathies." Would she need to force him? She could. He was new.

He shrugged, and she knew compulsion wasn't necessary. "One gets tired of the stupidity of government officials. Endless arguing, recriminations even when the path is clear. They don't do what they must. That means Bonaparte will prevail." Barlow stared at the brandy swirling in his glass as though he could read the future there. "He is a military genius on land. His navy is rebuilding at a frantic pace. Our ships are aging, worn to death by blockade duty. We starve our sailors and our new-built ships crumble because our suppliers are corrupt. It is only a matter of time until the French break the blockades and invade England. Especially now that we can invade a ship, drain the crew and render it harmless. The experiment breaking the blockade at Brest was only the first." He looked up at her.

"So you wanted to be on the winning side." Beatrix put an iron clamp over her anger. He had betrayed John for avarice and greed for power. She had only seen it a thousand times.

"You despise me, I see." He smiled, as though indulging her. "But you follow her, too. Her vision of a new society for our kind is powerful. She is direct. She takes action. None of this dithering or ambiguity. She will transform the world. I am an old man. The grave was going to remove my ability to affect anything in a few years. For me the chance to live forever and change the world was . . . attractive."

"So you betrayed your country?" She managed not to shriek at him for betraying John.

His eyes flashed. "My prince and my parliament betrayed my country. The suppliers who shortchange the navy betray their country. England was already doomed. I have moved on to shape what will be the next empire. We will start fresh." His expression grew wary. "You do not serve her, do you?"

Beatrix felt her eyes fill as the inevitability of what

must happen here suffused her. She let her eyes go red. He struggled. His own eyes glowed. But she was older. She had him firmly before she answered. "I did once." She must be sure before she acted. "Did you betray Langley?"

The sharp eyes went dull. "I sent agents against him in France. They wounded him, but he prevailed. I tried twice in England. Then he was supposed to die on the hulks with Dupré. Sending him to Asharti was the last resort. She can deal with him."

Beatrix shuddered. As she had guessed. There was no cure for what this man had become. There was no leaving him in place to continue undermining all John worked for and believed in. Her breath came shallowly. "And Asharti—where is she?"

"Paris. Rue Bonaparte."

There was only one more thing to ask. "What is the nephew's name and direction?"

"Jerry," Barlow croaked. "Jerry Williams. He lives in Woolcomber Street in Dover."

Beatrix closed her eyes. There was one last way out. When she opened them, Barlow had his will back. "You are helping evil take the world, man. I have known Asharti for seven hundred years. She is twisted, perhaps by experience, perhaps by being made, but hers is not the way. Give it up. Together we can serve her out."

Slyness flashed through his eyes for an instant, before he said, "Perhaps you are right."

The slyness was her answer. There was no more excuse to delay. There was no alternative. She had never done this. She gasped and let her eyes go red. *Companion! More power* . . . She advanced on Barlow.

"Old man, you've had your run." She watched his eyes widen as she caressed his temples. "I hope the service you rendered most of your life outweighs your betrayals in your maker's eyes. May he forgive you, for I cannot."

She took a breath, looking into Barlow's eyes as a

penance for what she was about to do. Then she squeezed. And twisted.

Blood sprayed the walls, her face, her dress. She was holding Barlow's head. It gaped at her as his body toppled. With a shriek, she dropped it. She bent over, sobbing, gasping for breath as her Companion deserted her. The head rolled to the hearth and stopped, face up, eyes staring, blood pooling on the carpet.

A knock sounded on the door. "Sir Thomas?" The housekeeper.

Beatrix stumbled to the window, called her Companion, weakly. The housekeeper's scream echoed through the blackness that enveloped her, before the room melted from view.

Beatrix stared out of the carriage window as it bowled briskly along behind its four matched grays. She felt numb. The moon drifted through diaphanous clouds. Asharti was making new vampires to do her bidding. She was bent on creating a new world. What kind of world would someone like Asharti create? The possibility was unthinkable.

The cartel was to sail from Dover. Where Jerry Williams lived. The horror she had just committed had to be repeated. Her breath caught in her throat. Had she not begun life ripping throats from those she fed on? Had she not drained the last drop with Asharti, or killed in battle as only one of her strength could?

But she had not killed in cold blood in six hundred years. She had sworn it was behind her. She let her mind skitter on past that. France. She was going to the land of the guillotine to beard Asharti in her den, and find out from evil's own lips what she had done to John. He was dead, no doubt. Beatrix couldn't stop Asharti. The whole exercise was probably pointless. It would end in her own death at Asharti's hands, in the same way she had just killed Barlow.

But it couldn't be avoided. She couldn't just abandon John the way she had abandoned that knight and his squire, the way Stephan and Rubius had abandoned whole continents to Asharti as though they didn't matter. Anger coiled in her belly. Foolish, really, but she wanted the confrontation. Her fingers squeezed the squabs of the upholstered seat. Asharti couldn't win.

Maybe her death was meant to be. She was going to find out.

The unkempt town of Dover sprang up around the carriage. She leaned out of the window into the air now tinged with the fecund smell of the sea. "Woolcomber Street, at the base of the castle," she called to the coachman. Even from here she could see the cliffs with the Roman lighthouse silhouetted against the bright moon. She told the groom to wait at the bottom of the hill and slipped out into the night. It was still an hour until the dawn tide. Plenty of time.

She drew her Companion and shimmered into the front bedroom of the little house that clung to the hill in back of its tiny, bedraggled garden. He was awake there, in the dark. She could feel his vibrations just as he felt hers.

"What . . . what do you w-want?" Her night vision told her he was a skinny youth, spotted, with large ears set away from his head. And he was afraid of her. As he should be.

She made herself hard, refusing to think, refusing to feel. "Not out foraging?" she asked softly. "Or are you hiding here in this house with your mother? What kind of vampire are you?"

"One as done what he were told." The voice had a definite quaver.

"Did Asharti not tell you about trespassing on another vampire's territory?"

"No. But I'm gone for good tomorrow night," he whined.

"You are gone for good tonight."

"Please," he almost wailed. "I just done what I were told. I don't know this Asharti person, you're a-talkin' of. I swears I don't."

"Who made you vampire?" she snapped. "Are you telling me it was not Asharti?"

"LeFèvre," he gasped. "LeFèvre made me drink his blood. I never wanted it, I swears."

"Where is the one who made you now?"

She saw his eyes fill. "He went back to France, miss. And how will I go on without him to tell me what to do?"

She growled and shoved Jerry back onto the bed. The one that made him was out of her reach. But this one wasn't. She knelt on Jerry's chest and took his neck in both hands. *Numb,* she thought, panting. *Be numb. No choice.* She squeezed, closed her eyes, and prepared to twist.

"It warn't my fault. He woulda killed me and worse!" he sobbed. Beatrix tried to breathe as Jerry heaved with tears under her.

And she couldn't do it.

She pushed herself off him and stood, panting. God, what was she about? He was made, and by one of Asharti's tools. He had to die. She could still do it. She would.

But this one did not hold a position where he could change England's destiny.

"Thank you, ma'am," Jerry panted. "I swears you ain't never going to regret this."

Beatrix pressed her lips together, shamefaced. Asharti would not have hesitated. She sighed and looked at the acne-scarred young vampire. "Come on," she growled, and jerked the thin man up. "We sail for France. If you prove useful, I may even let you live."

New fear welled in his eyes and washed over his countenance. "France? But *she's* there."

"So you do know Asharti."

"Not personal. LeFèvre talked about her all the time I was sick."

"Perhaps I shall introduce you." Beatrix set her mouth. "We are for France and Asharti."

It had been two days. Or at least a plate of food had been brought in four times and he was made to eat by one named LeFèvre, a heavy brute. He could compel John, but not as easily as Asharti did. Still John ate the food with little urging. Asharti thought there was a possibility he could withstand Quintoc's compulsion and he wanted every advantage. He was weak from loss of blood. His body bore the wounds, some healing, of Asharti's attentions.

During the long darkness, he clung to his image of Beatrix. He knew she had rejected him; that he meant nothing to her. But he reconstructed their last words into commitment, and he envisioned her as a virtuous widow, sought by all but possessed by none but him. He did not allow himself to imagine their lovemaking, but in the heat and darkness he could feel her kiss on his lips, his neck, her lovely hands running through his hair. She loved him. That was what he wanted from that dream. Love, light, freedom.

He was in the middle of one of these dream-visions, when the door creaked open on a silhouette. Beatrix's haunted eyes dissolved. Quintoc swaggered in, holding a torch. LeFèvre was right behind him, glowering. John swept his courage into a heap, hoping it would bolster him.

"Good Lord!" Quintoc wrinkled his small, straight nose, and gestured toward the chamber pot. "Remove his soil, LeFèvre." He eyed John. "And you . . . you are foul with sweat. Perhaps I shall take a page from Asharti's book and bathe you."

LeFèvre took out the chamber pot. John shuddered. He must not give in to fear. He could feel that underneath

Quintoc's bravado, he was not sure of controlling John as Asharti did.

"Sounds like a good idea," John whispered.

Quintoc stepped forward quickly and gave John a back-handed cuff that sent his head snapping to the side. "Don't think you can disrespect me, English dog. I will take you like a dog tonight, and you will whimper under me."

John deliberately licked the blood from a split lip and glared up at Quintoc's baby face. Quintoc's eyes began to glow. The blood excited him. LeFèvre stalked back into the room.

"Unlock him, LeFèvre," Quintoc ordered. "First the bath, and then I want to take him out of this heat to somewhere more comfortable."

"What about the servants?" Resentment echoed in LeFèvre's voice. John wondered why.

"Did you see any servants?" Quintoc snapped. "I dismissed them for the evening."

John tried not to let his exultation show. They were going to take him upstairs. There were no servants—only these two. Escape . . .

LeFèvre unlocked John's chain and prodded him to his feet with the toe of a boot. "Can't see why she tolerates someone of your warped tastes, Quintoc."

"You're still angry," Quintoc sneered. "All you had to say was 'No, thank you, Quintoc,' and I would not have misunderstood you."

"You thought I *wanted* your advances?" LeFèvre almost shouted.

Quintoc shrugged and turned his back on the bigger man. "Langley here will want my advances. Shall I tell you all the delicious things I intend to do to you?" Quintoc purred, his face beginning to flush. "Or shall I surprise you? You shan't sit for a week. And your cock will stand at attention throughout, I assure you."

John pressed down his fear. He couldn't afford fear.

LeFèvre dragged him from the room, muttering. Quintoc followed with the torch. The thing was not done yet, John told himself.

The room with the underground hot springs had become familiar. LeFèvre lit torches. Quintoc ordered John into the water almost too hot to bear. Under the eyes of the two men, John soaped himself, his chains still clanking. At least Quintoc was not forcing his erection. Not yet. Perhaps he did not want to waste his strength. Good sign.

"Be sure to wash your anus well," Quintoc ordered. His eyes flashed red in threat. John recoiled. Not that Asharti had not required the same of him. But it held new meaning now. John mastered himself. It would not do to rebel here, so far underground. He lathered his hands and slipped one between his buttocks. Quintoc grinned and motioned John to duck himself.

Dripping, John stepped out from the pool and toweled himself dry. A small smile hovered around Quintoc's mouth. He approached and laid a lock of wet hair behind John's ear. John stiffened, but made no move to resist.

"Now you are ready for me. Come, let us go up."

John stumbled along behind LeFèvre, trying to memorize the turnings of the passage. Three flights of stone stairs. Heavy door at the top. Marbled foyer. Huge. Dim. The door to the outside was so near! Pushed, he stumbled. Dragged up another set of stairs to the first floor. A door, closed red draperies, brocades and silks, a great bed covered with leopard skins. Asharti's boudoir! Her scent was everywhere. The same scent Beatrix wore. She couldn't know how that tortured him. He had an impression of odd furniture, very old wood peeking through gilt. He could swear some was inlaid with lapis lazuli.

"I shall take it from here, LeFèvre," Quintoc muttered. His voice was low with lust.

"Can you handle him?" LeFèvre asked bluntly.

"I intend to handle him quite roughly." Quintoc shoved

John forward onto the bed. His chains clanked. Would they leave his chains on? He might use them to strangle Quintoc if he could keep his will his own. But LeFèvre unbolted the heavy wristbands and hefted the chains.

"Sing out if you need help," he said. "I'll be downstairs."

"You wouldn't like to watch?" Quintoc asked with a sly smile.

LeFèvre only stalked out and closed the door, glowering.

Quintoc turned to John. John swallowed. Quintoc's eyes went red in earnest. Now was the moment. Asharti thought Quintoc would have trouble with him. It was enough to give him hope. John stared into those eyes and pushed back at the red. He let all his hatred of this weasel and his mistress strike out in a thrust against Quintoc's will.

"Damn you!" Quintoc breathed.

John felt the tightening in his loins. Revulsion swept through him. He lashed out with his mind. He was *not* going to be raped by this fair-cheeked devil. Not while there was breath in his body. He'd been raped by Asharti because he couldn't resist her. But he was bloody well going to resist Quintoc. Quintoc towered over John, implacable. John began to tremble, but he could see a sheen of sweat on Quintoc's brow. And then the throbbing in John's loins subsided.

He managed a slow grin. Quintoc's red faded and he let out a shriek of frustration. John realized he had only a split second to act. He lunged off the bed and past Quintoc for the door. He had caught the creature by surprise. Two strides, three—he was there. He heard Quintoc behind him. John pulled at the knob. A hand on his arm. He twisted through the door. Down the stairs three at a time. He was gasping. Would his strength last? Across the marble tiles. Quintoc thundering behind him. He fell, brought down from behind. He kicked Quintoc in the face and scrambled for the door. He pulled on the great doors, two men high. The light of gloaming softened the shallow stairs, the gravel drive, the lake beyond. Quintoc shrieked behind him. He stumbled down the stairs of the portico. The air still smelled of sun-warmed grass and some kind of flower. Roses. Heavy footsteps. Where to go?

The blow caught him full on the temple and felled him instantly. He was being dragged across the gravel. The world faded at the edges. He heard the thunk of closing doors.

A huge boulder of a man sat on his chest, crushing the breath from him. LeFèvre. He shook his head to clear it. He had to keep his wits about him. A coil of fear around his spine said he would not be able to stave off Quintoc again.

"Takc him back upstairs," Quintoc ordered. One cheek was scraped.

The big man didn't move. "You ain't up to it. And I ain't watching you bugger him, neither. Which lets out me helping you control him, by the way."

"You . . . you'll do as you're told!"

"I'll sing to herself if he gets away."

John blinked up at them. LeFèvre got up off him and grinned down. "A little sip of English blood might not go amiss, though."

"She said not to take his blood," Quintoc pouted.

"You think she'll know?" LeFèvre snorted. "She just said that to frighten you. He's got a few days to gain strength. We'll use the places she used already."

Quintoc brightened. "If we weaken him, it will be easier to have my way with him." Together, they dragged John up, and pushed him, still reeling, down the steps into the heat.

LeFèvre shackled John's wrists behind his back, then dragged him over to the familiar chain set in the stones of the wall. LeFèvre pushed him to his knees and they were at him from behind, their teeth puncturing the arteries in his throat on each side. He struggled for a moment, but the will of two together was too much. His senses shrank to the throb of his blood and the slurping pull at his neck. His vision dimmed. He began to drift.

One jerked away. "Enough," he heard LeFèvre say. "If he's drained, then herself *will* know what we've been at." Quintoc pulled his fangs out. John swayed and collapsed.

"I could take him now . . ." That was Quintoc. John heard him from a distance.

"You had your chance."

"Bully!"

"Goddamn sodomite!"

The door creaked shut. Voices and footsteps receded. The darkness invaded John's head.

# Seventeen

The carriage blinds were pulled tight against the daylight, so Beatrix could not see the passing of the French countryside. The jolting of her vital organs must provide the sense of swiftness she craved. She pretended to sleep, though she was aware constantly of the other occupant of the coach; the cowardly Jerry. The last hours had been ones of constant movement—tossing on the sea inside her cabin all day and another night with contrary winds, hurrying through Calais in the hour before dawn to find a carriage for hire, and now racing in the day toward Paris. Too long. It had all taken too long.

She sighed. Through her lashes she watched Jerry chewing his lip in the corner. Unprepossessing. Perhaps all he needed was someone to help him to go on. God, now she was sounding like Stephan! And look where that had led. She did not have time for Jerry. She must find out what had happened to John. She dared not hope John was alive. Even if Asharti used him for her pleasure for a while, he could not have lasted this long, could he? But if there was any chance, she had to try. And she had begun to think that she should not just brave Asharti in her den on the Rue Bonaparte. Once she revealed herself to her old enemy, they would be locked in a death struggle—and what of John in that case? No, she had to find out where John was being held without Asharti knowing she was in Paris looking for him. If he was alive, she had to get him to safety before she took on Asharti.

Her eyes turned back to Jerry. He was shivering.

"Are you cold?" she asked. "Or do you need to feed?"

"Just cold, I guess." He broke a frightened silence he had kept all across the Channel and huddled into the corner. "I fed pretty good recently."

She didn't want to know if he had killed his victim. She tossed him her lap rug. He looked at her, speculating. His fear of her had been subsiding as he realized she didn't mean to kill him. "Thankee." He wrapped the rug around his shoulders. "Why're you going after 'er?"

Beatrix set her lips. "She has something of mine. I want him back."

Jerry's eyes grew big. "If you don't mind, I'd rather not be around when you find her."

She nodded, and gave a little mobile smile. "Fair enough. After I'm done with her, I'll help you learn how to go on."

The carriage slowed. She chanced a look out of the window with eyes slitted against the fading sun. The outskirts of Paris. It would still be several hours until they could ensconce themselves in a hotel. Now, how to find John? Perhaps the best place to find out where prisoners were held for interrogation would be in the Rue Villar, the heart of the French intelligence agency. She only hoped Asharti was not there.

Jerry was gone. He had slipped away while Beatrix was doing her night's work. Beatrix looked round the little room at the Hotel du Soleil, feeling she was failing at every turn. What else had she expected from Jerry? She was so distracted she could not keep track of him. She would just have to take care of him later.

Her visit to the Rue Villar had been most enlightening. She had waited until late, though it hurt her to delay. She knew some functionaries would still be working at the nerve center of French intelligence, and Asharti would not be anywhere near somewhere so mundane at that time of night. She slipped inside, and questioned each man she found bent over a desk by lamplight, until she found one who knew where the most valuable prisoners were taken for questioning. She had thought the answer would be some local prison like the Conciergerie. It was not.

Very special prisoners were taken to the Comte de Fanueille's villa just outside Chantilly. Of course, she had wanted to run off immediately to Chantilly. But she had caught herself in time. First she must know whether Asharti was there. She went instead to Madame Robillard's small house in the Rue d'Armenac. Madame knew everything about everyone. Beatrix had met her in Vienna . . . oh, thirty years ago. Normally she would not chance seeing anyone she hadn't seen in thirty years. Madame would have grown older. Beatrix would not. But this was different. Beatrix wore a veil, and let on that she had had a disfiguring accident. She firmly squelched Madame's curiosity for "just a peek" and spent a frustrating hour reminiscing, and leading the conversation round to Asharti and her whereabouts.

It was not good news. Asharti was heading back to Chantilly tomorrow.

The porter collected her valises. She rolled the map she had sent the boots to purchase and stuffed it into her reticule. Would anyone who had known her in Amsterdam or London ever believe she could travel with so little baggage? But no one in those cities knew she had crossed the Carpathian Mountains with a Romany caravan, or trekked overland through India, either. She ran down the stairs to the waiting carriage, shedding louis to pay for the room. She was dressed for travel in a gown of dark blue cut low over her bosom and a pelisse of navy. A sapphire solitaire hung on a chain at her throat and sapphires dangled from her ears. The sweep of white bosom would be covered by her pelisse.

"See that the shades are pulled in the carriage. Tight, mind you," she ordered the groom who stood near the front door as she drew on her gloves and pulled the same heavy veil she had worn to Madame Robillard's over her fashionable dark blue felt hat, studded with a spray of blue-black feathers. There was not a moment to be lost. She took a breath and made a dash for the carriage. The sun made her eyes burn and her skin prickle, even covered as she was.

The doors were clapped to. "Chantilly," the groom yelled up to the driver, "and her ladyship says as how there's a handsome tip if you spring 'em." The driver gave his mettlesome grays the office to start. They surged forward.

Beatrix found herself leaning forward on her seat as though that would make the carriage go faster. It was not fifty miles to Chantilly, but the congestion of Paris must be navigated before they could make anything like good time. She pulled out her map and studied the area around Chantilly carefully, to take her mind off her impatience. Between the journey to Paris, Madame Robillard, and Rue Villar, another night had gone since she arrived from Dover. Could John possibly survive Asharti's brand of attention for as long as he might have been imprisoned in Chantilly? She wouldn't think. She just willed the carriage on through the burning sun.

John lost track of time. The dark, the constant heat, the dank, sweating stones, the smell of minerals in the water all combined to assault his senses and his sanity. Quintoc had not been back, but that wouldn't last. He had a feeling he had been unconscious off and on for some time right after both had fed from him. So he did not know when to expect Asharti. All he knew was that Quintoc would be back before Asharti reappeared. And he wasn't sure he was up to fending him off again. LeFèvre brought him food and took away the chamber pot to replace it with a fresh one, but the brute was taciturn and never spoke. John's hands were still shackled behind his back, so LeFèvre forced him to eat like a dog from the plate. It was humiliating, but John put his pride aside and ate to keep up his strength. It seemed the whole was happening to someone else.

It was with no surprise that he saw a slighter form than LeFèvre's silhouetted in the opening door. He caught his breath as Quintoc walked into the cell. The knife in his hand glinted in the torchlight.

Quintoc placed the torch in the holder and turned to John, grinning. "So, shall we try again? I think we will dispense with the bath. I'm feeling a bit bestial tonight. I'll take you in all your dirt." He ran his thumb over the knife edge. A drop of blood oozed from the cut. He put his thumb to his mouth and sucked. His flushed features looked demonic in the torchlight.

"Cuts might be conspicuous," John said with more bravado than he felt.

"Not if I open wounds she already made," he said. "She'll just think you're healing poorly. LeFèvre put me in mind of that strategy." His eyes glazed with red film.

John felt the compulsion shower over him. It made him gasp. He tried to gather himself as he had before. His will fluttered at the edge of the pounding compulsion. A gleam in Quintoc's eyes said he knew John was no match for him now. He stalked forward.

John felt the telltale rising of his cock. Damn the devil! He pushed out with his mind as hard as he could, groping for purchase against the compulsion, but it was no use. He was definitely weaker. Quintoc knelt before him as before an altar and used his knife to open a long, half-healed slash Asharti's teeth had made across John's breast. He held John still with a mental grip that felt like steel while he licked at the welling blood. A feeling of revulsion engulfed John, but it did not matter. He could feel his hips moving, his cock now hard. *God in heaven, help me,* he thought. *I can't bear this. I know I can't bear this.*

Quintoc slit open a cut on his thigh and suckled there as John trembled violently. Quintoc's hands moved over John's body. He shifted his attention to John's hip. The pain of the knife was lost in the horror of what would happen next. Quintoc suckled at his hip, the hand with the knife brushing lightly over John's erection. John fought against the compulsion, breathing hard now. But he was too weak. Quintoc would have his way.

He turned John over, stroking his buttocks. The pain of the knife. The drawing of Quintoc's lips. John thought he could feel his mind going. *No!* he shouted silently. He couldn't bear this, but he couldn't let it drive him insane, either. He would think of Beatrix, the revisionist Beatrix, the one who loved him. He would not think about this monster who was about to rape him, or the demon's mistress who would return and make him betray his country once again while she too raped him and fed on him. He wouldn't think. John's mind grasped at Beatrix before it slipped away to somewhere else. As from a distance, he saw Quintoc unbutton his breeches . . .

The coach clattered over the bridge across the moat-lake of the chateau at Chantilly. Beatrix glanced out to the woods that coated the undulating hills. Far away the lights of the town of Chantilly twinkled, and beyond was the Forest of Givenchy. That would serve her purpose. She turned back to the chateau. The slitted windows that faced the drive were dark. They looked like empty eyes. She dreaded what she might find here. Incipient anger turned her stomach sour.

Beatrix leapt out and tossed too much money to the coachman. *"Merci, mon homme très gentil,"* she said. "Please take my bags to that inn we passed, the Grapes." He touched his cap and drove on. If she needed to escape quickly, with, God willing, someone else in tow, a coach would never keep ahead of the kind of pursuers she might acquire.

She stalked up to the great wooden doors, under the staring eyes of those blank stone slots. Inside there were vampires, she could not say how many. But their vibrations were slow and new. Asharti was not here. She must hurry, before they sensed her own presence. She drew her Companion. Once inside, she saw her way quite clearly without a lamp. The house was warm. Asharti had always craved warmth. Her heightened sense of smell picked out the scent of new wood, the soot of lamps recently lit, and underneath . . . sulfur? Strange . . .

She tripped lightly up the stairs to the first floor. No gleam of light along the corridors. She was looking for a servant, someone who might know where unwilling guests were kept. She trotted up the back stairs. Voices came to her faintly. Servants; not vampire.

But no. Vibrations shuddered along her senses behind her. Slowly, she turned . . .

The hulk of a man came round the corner, drawn, no doubt, by her own vibrations. He stalked forward, silent, glowering. He was Jerry's description of his maker, exactly.

"LeFèvre," she said. "I might have expected you." That drew him up short.

"How do you know my name? Who are you?" he growled.

His consternation gave her time to draw her Companion. The hum of power up her veins gave her confidence. This one was no match for one born to the blood during the Crusades. "I am your master, LeFèvre," she said, and let her power shimmer out through her eyes.

He struggled only for a moment, swaying on his feet. Then his eyes glazed over.

"I would know if you have an English prisoner here, John Staunton, Earl of Langley." All depended on his answer. Beatrix held her breath.

"Yes, he is here."

Beatrix's heart fluttered. Oh, God! "Alive?" she breathed.

"Yes. The mistress wants him alive when she returns." His voice was flat.

"Where?" she hissed.

"In the cells, down in the hypocausts."

Beatrix's mind raced. Hypocausts—of course—to feed Asharti's love of warmth. "Show me." She motioned down the stairs.

In the great entry hall, he pointed to a heavy wooden door. "There."

Beatrix hesitated. "Is he alone?" She felt other vibrations, but she couldn't locate them.

"Quintoc is there. Quintoc wants use of him before herself returns."

Beatrix's heart went cold. She whirled away, dragging LeFèvre with her, and threw open the heavy wooden door with a single jerk. Her throat swelled as she ran down the steps, LeFèvre stumbling after her. Damp heat, passageways everywhere, a glimpsed maze of hypocausts with tiny towers of stacked tiles. No burning coals, but pools of hot water between the tiles. Chantilly was heated by hot springs. The smell of sulfur suffused the air now.

"Which way?" she hissed to LeFèvre. He resisted for long moments then finally pointed. She pulled him after her. To her right through another door she saw a river of steaming water under a little bridge. How far to the cells? Had LeFèvre misdirected her? She blocked out LeFèvre's heavy steps behind her and used her senses. Under the sulfur, under the faintly mineral smell of the water, what was that? Blood. One of her kind could always smell blood. Blood and groaning. Quick breathing.

She did not need LeFèvre's slow directions anymore. She turned left through a low passage, following the sounds and the smell of blood. She burst into an intersecting corridor. Her anger rose and her Companion coursed along her veins. Three cells, but she had attention only for the center one, with the door open and the smell of blood oozing out. A low moan from the cell wrenched a cry from her own throat.

She pulled the door open. Its metal hinges creaked and broke. It swung at a crazy angle. She let go of LeFèvre and darted inside. The sight that met her eyes checked her. John lay, almost insensible, turned on one hip, and chained to a ring set into the stone. He was naked, pale and sweating, bleeding in a dozen places. He had an erection. His buttocks and back were covered by a young man, fully dressed, who stopped the thrusting of his hips and looked up with startled eyes. Beatrix felt his vibrations and smelled the stink of his particular version of cinnamon and ambergris. An animal growl issued from her throat as she lunged forward. She pulled the man off John and threw him against the wall. His gaping breeches revealed his own erection. His head thunked sickeningly against the stone. But he was vampire. He merely shook his head and lunged up at her. Behind her, LeFèvre joined the attack.

She swung round and LeFèvre thrust a pike at her. Where had that come from? She ducked to the side, but it caught her in the shoulder. Her midnight-blue dress ripped away. Quintoc grabbed her other shoulder and tore her away from the point of the pike. His hands groped for her neck. She knew he meant to tear her head off. LeFèvre's pike found her side. She groaned. *Companion!* The single thought was desperate enough to bring her partner surging up with its last bit of strength. She pulled away from the pike and Quintoc's grip and lunged at LeFèvre, her fingers cupped upward.

LeFèvre's eyes bulged as her nails cut the skin of his throat like butter. Blood spurted everywhere. She gripped, and ripped at flesh. LeFèvre staggered back, gurgling and clutching his throat. But Quintoc was on her from behind with a shriek of fury. She twisted round and thrust the heel of her right hand at his chin. She could feel the snap of his neck. He fell back.

Even a broken neck would be healed by the Companion within minutes. Her earlier compunction about killing was drowned in the surge of her fury. She hardly thought, but gripped Quintoc's head in both hands and, with a wail rising up the scale, twisted. A spatter of blood and she was holding a bulging-eyed head, its baby lips still moving in a fading protest.

She tossed the head aside and rounded on LeFèvre. He held out one hand in defense, shaking his head as blood welled through his throat. Beatrix felt her Companion slide back down her veins. The killing urgency went with it.

"Go!" she hissed. "Tell her Beatrix Lisse has taken back what was mine."

LeFèvre scrambled backward until he could turn and stumble heavily up the stairs.

John's comforting distance from himself vanished. Beatrix. It was Beatrix standing there over Quintoc's headless body. He blinked as though to dispel a dream, but she remained, her breast heaving, eyes glowing red, blood soaking her dress at shoulder and side. Her face was spattered with it. Quintoc's blood. She had torn his head from his body with her bare hands.

He took a shuddering breath. She was strong . . . like them? Beatrix was a monster like them! It took all his strength to pull himself up to sit. She stood like a statue of vengeance over him while the red slowly faded from her eyes. He became aware of his nakedness. His erection was subsiding, but she had seen it. Shame filled him. She had seen it all. And she was like them.

She must have seen the horror in his eyes, for she made small, soothing sounds and stepped forward, her hand out as to a wounded animal. He shrank away. Would she suck his blood? Would she force him . . . ? He had gone to bed with her when she was like Asharti!

She lowered her hand, but her voice still soothed as she approached. That she moved at all with such bloody rents in her body only served to underline her alien nature. She knelt beside him. He trembled as she touched his face, but he was too weak to escape.

Her eyes filled. "My poor John," Then with some of her former ferocity, "I will never forgive what she has done to you." She put her fingers to the pulse in his neck. "We must get you away. There are others in the house and Asharti might return at any moment."

He wanted to leave this hellish place more than anything. But that was not possible. He moved to let his chains clank in illustration. She calmly took hold of the iron ring with both hands and jerked. With a squeal of stone against metal and a puff of dust, the ring came free. John stared at the hole in the stone with widening eyes, then glanced up to her in fear.

She sat back on her heels and looked seriously at him. The dreadful wound in her shoulder did not seem to be bleeding so much. Somewhere he heard running feet. "Now, John Staunton, they are coming, and there is only one way out of here. You must trust me." She sidled in to sit next to him, her body pressed against his. Even in his weakened state, he felt her warmth, the thrumming, vibrating life that always seemed to surround her, the cinnamon scent. A brief flash of fear shot through him as he realized why she smelled like Asharti, and even, in some

twisted way, Quintoc. It wasn't that they used the same
perfume.

"No, no," she shushed, as she felt him stiffen. "Let me
hold you, thus." She pulled him close, held his body
against her bleeding shoulder. He felt her blood, hot, min-
gle with his own. "There will be a little pain as we leave,"
she murmured.

He relaxed against her, he was not quite sure why. The
vibrations that seemed to surround her cycled up some
scale. The cell was filmed with a red haze. He saw Quintoc's headless body and the head staring in blind shock
from the corner. There was the familiar torch, now bloodred, the heavy table. Then the red film grew darker. The
vibrations became almost unbearable. Through the doorway with its dangling door burst LeFèvre and three others. How could the man live with his throat torn so? The
room went almost black. The vibrations shuddered into
some realm almost beyond consciousness. A stabbing
pain flooded his body. He cried out. It was if he was
turned inside out. And all sense left him.

Beatrix and her burden reappeared in the Forest de
Givenchy a mile, perhaps even two, from the chateau. A
stiff breeze ruffled the treetops of the oaks and the birches
above, but below all was quiet with the soft, rotting damp
of last autumn's leaves to cushion them.

Beatrix looked down to where John lay in her arms. He
had lost consciousness. Just as well, for she must draw the
power again and again to get him away from here. She did
not worry about outwitting LeFèvre, but Asharti might return at any time, and she knew only too well what a wily
and relentless adversary Asharti could be. All thought of
confronting Asharti was banished. Beatrix must get John
somewhere he was safe from her.

Now she must think what to do with a naked, bleeding
man in the middle of a country where her adversary held

political as well as personal power. Her thoughts were a little muddy with the pain of her wounds. A country inn, a tavern; one with a stable perhaps, out of the way but not too far. The Companion would heal her wounds shortly. But her strength for translocating was limited now, especially with John as a burden. She pictured the map around Chantilly in her head. Neuilly-en-Theille? Not the least likely refuge, but not the most likely, either. Neuilly-en-Theille, then. Find an inn, leave John in the stable. Then translocate with John into the room she was given. Clothes. He would need clothing, even if it was rough or simple. She would have to steal or coax it out of the landlord or a likely-sized guest.

She realized she was slowly rocking the unconscious man. His breath was shallow against her breast. She must get his chains off. Chains would rouse suspicion and they were one more burden on her translocation. She laid him back on the spongy forest bed. She heard the rustle of a hare and farther away a stealthy fox. The leaves overhead cut out all moonlight. Still she could see his body clearly. It had been long since she had witnessed Asharti's handiwork. Shame washed over her to think she had participated in the squalid romps that were precursors to this horror. John's sweat had dried but his gashes still drooled and he was deadly pale. Twin marks of incisors dotted his neck, the inside of his elbows, the big veins that wound from groin to thighs. Slashes on hips, chest and shoulders, thighs, stood out black against his flesh.

She couldn't let him die. She'd tend his wounds as soon as she got him to safety. The wounds to his mind from this experience were beyond her control, however. How would a man like John Staunton react to torture, humiliation, violation? That gave her pause. At least she could take away the shame of having betrayed his country. It was he who had been betrayed.

For the first time, she thought beyond getting him away from Asharti. He had seen her kill Quintoc and rip

LeFèvre's throat. She did not regret her actions. But John now knew about her. He would be disgusted. They always were. So, in saving him, she had given up any hope of . . . of what? She blinked. There was never hope for anything except stolen moments of pleasure, and that only as long as he was ignorant of what she was. It startled her to realize she had been hungering for more . . . Foolish woman! After all these years to be trapped by hope?

She was muddled by the loss of blood. She glanced to her shoulder. The wound was drawing together. In a few minutes her flesh would be virgin, unscarred.

As she took hold of his chains and gathered strength, her thoughts turned to Asharti. Asharti was making vampires, lots of vampires, and she was bent on controlling Bonaparte, or dictating his successor when he had served his purpose as a military genius. She would change the balance of the world between vampire and human. The rules of vampire society, honed over centuries to preserve the status quo, would be washed away in a flood of chaos. Humans would become livestock, and war between the species was inevitable. What would Rubius say? He and the other Elders had established the Rules to preserve the precarious balance. Asharti's world would have no rules at all. Could Pandora's box be closed? She must send to Rubius for help.

She grabbed one of John's shackles in her left hand and held the chain in her right. With a quick snap, the chain came free. She freed the other hand and tossed the length of chain and the heavy ring into the underbrush. She gathered him into her arms again and called on her Companion. Neuilly was ten miles at least tonight.

John's nightmare was filled with Asharti and Quintoc. They took turns at him. He struggled, but he couldn't get away and then he didn't struggle and then Asharti told him he would come to like it and he lifted his lips to hers and begged her to use him, his blood and his cock and his mouth, and God help him, his anus. She laughed and gave him to Quintoc.

With a cry, he woke to a darkened room. All was in shadows. He flailed, trying to escape, but something held him down. A dark silhouette hurried over to loom above him.

"Shush," the silhouette breathed. He recognized her scent and struggled all the harder.

She sat on the bed and held him. He thrashed his head from side to side. "You're all right." Her voice more soothing than any he had ever heard. "She does not have you now."

He relaxed in spite of himself. The sheets and quilts were what pinned him.

"A nightmare," the rich contralto voice whispered. "No more." It was Beatrix.

He was sweating. An itching along his veins tore at his nerves. She turned up a lamp that only partially banished the shadows with a soft glow. Then she took a cloth from a basin at the side of his bed and mopped his brow, his face, his neck and shoulders. "Let me cool your body." She pulled down the covers. Her voice was so soothing, so sure, that he did not struggle even though he remembered what she had done to Quintoc and LeFèvre. She was like them.

But she was gentle as she washed him. "I stitched you up with some button thread I got from the landlady." John looked down and saw the tidy stitches. How did a woman who lived in Berkeley Square know how to stitch up wounds? He looked up at her questioningly. "One learns surprising things in a long life," she murmured. "I have clothes for you. We must go soon. The landlord has a gig that will take us to the posting station at Chambly. We'll hire a closed carriage there." The cool cloth moved over his belly, his private parts, his thighs.

"How long have I been here?" he croaked.

"Only since last night."

He tried to sit up but she pushed him back firmly but gently into the pillows. His teeth chattered. She pulled the quilts up, examining him closely.

"I have a question," she said calmly in spite of the intensity in her expression. "Think back. Did you ever come into contact with their blood? Asharti's blood? Quintoc's?"

"Blood," he muttered. "There was s-so much blood. But it was mine . . ."

"Think," she insisted.

He was shuddering now. "N-n-no," he managed. "My blood." He rolled his head to look at her. "Quintoc's." He thought of the splatter, but she had been in the way. "Yours?"

Her look of shock told him he was right. She glanced down at her shoulder then ran her fingertips over the gashes in his shoulder, his chest, swollen red flesh held by black knots like caterpillars winding over his body. "Oh, God," she murmured. "I held you to my breast . . ." Her glance darted about the room, until she returned to his face and stared. She took a breath, as though she required all her courage. "You have been infected with the Companion."

"What?" What was she saying?

She swallowed. "That which runs in our blood now runs in yours. You are vampire."

Vampire? Vampire! *Sucking blood. Feeding on humans.* Was that what they all were? Was that what *he* was now? "T-take it away," he stuttered, horrified. "I won't be like you!"

"There is no cure." She retreated somewhere behind a mask. "You will die a lingering, horribly painful death if you do not drink a vampire's blood to give you immunity."

He could not speak. His mind raced. Was he to be a monster, too? The last weeks had been so full of horror, this final, ghastly truth was not hard to believe. Despair sat on his chest as he heaved for breath. "Then there is a cure," he rasped. "The cure is death."

She rose suddenly and began to pace the room, pulling first at a curl that had escaped the heavy knot of hair gathered at her nape, then at the ribbon just below her breasts. She wore burgundy with a wide square neck. *Bloodred,* he thought. As she paced back to him, he saw her shoulder where the pike had wounded her. It was new and whole. He had been longing for death rather than betray his country. How small that longing seemed. Now he needed death as he had never needed anything. "Kill me now," he whispered. "Spare me the lingering death."

One more turn, and when she faced him, her face contorted. Her breath came heavily, making her breasts heave with emotion. She shut her eyes tight and swayed her head back and forth. "I should," she wailed. Then her voice sank to a whisper. "I should."

He pushed himself up, shuddering and sweating at once. He could almost feel some alien force coursing through his veins, pumping with his heartbeat. "Do it. I forgive you. God forgives you. I cannot live like that."

She approached his bed, her dark eyes big, her skin luminous. A red film came over her eyes. Now she would do it. Tear his throat like LeFèvre's, rend him limb from limb . . .

The red faded. "I can't." She said it like a sentence, on herself, on him.

"You must, damn you! You got me into this, now release me," he said hoarsely.

Her face was sad, resigned. She made the decision against her will, but she had decided.

"Bitch," he said through clenched teeth. "If you don't kill me, I'll kill myself."

She sighed. "No you won't, John. Once the Companion takes hold in you, it has such a will to life it is almost impossible to try. And it's very hard to kill one of us. You saw the only way I could kill Quintoc. Unless the head is entirely severed, death is impossible."

He clutched his sides, drenched in his own sweat. "You are . . . immortal?"

"Immortal," she mused. "What does that mean? Quintoc was not immortal. But I have lived seven hundred and thirty-odd years, and I am one of the youngest born to my kind."

"You . . . You have sucked blood for centuries? What kind of monster are you?"

"I told you. I am vampire. So are you."

"I choose the painful death." He almost hissed it.

She came to kneel beside him, eyes filled with pain. He shrank away. The room wavered around her. "I take it upon my head. Letting you die is killing you, and I cannot kill you. You will grow used to your new state. We are not all evil." Her eyes shaded into red.

He felt acceptance wash over him, though he fought against it. He would submit, just as he had submitted to Asharti, to Quintoc. He knew he could not withstand her and he hated himself for it. She leaned close and kissed his forehead, smoothing a damp strand of hair away. Then she lifted her wrist to her mouth. Incisors flashed. Blood welled. She held it to his lips. "Suck, John," she commanded. "The blood is the life."

God help him, he did. The copper thickness filled his mouth with indescribable ecstasy. He pulled at her wrist even as Asharti had suckled at his throat or his thighs. He groaned, whether in protest or in fulfillment he could not tell. Peace welled up through his bowels and his belly to suffuse his heart and mind.

"That's right." She lay next to him as he sucked at her wrist. The shaking subsided.

The last thing he heard was her whisper. "The blood is the life."

# Eighteen

Beatrix watched John Staunton shiver and sweat, racked with the fever brought on by the Companion. Her gaze dwelt upon the girdle of muscle that rode over his hips and cradled his genitals. It brought back memories of their night together. She shook herself out of her abstraction and sat down beside him with a damp cloth. He was so weak he might not survive the invasion of the Companion long enough to absorb the immunity her blood could give him.

She wiped his body, careful not to tear his stitches. The wounds were not fresh. She hoped the stitches would hold. His body would be marked forever with the scars from any wounds healed before his reaction to the Companion subsided. If he lived long enough to achieve peace with his Companion, the others would heal quickly and leave no trace. The flesh against her fingers was hot with fever. She took some salve she got from a crone in the village of Neuilly and gently spread it over his wounds. He quieted under her touch. She turned him to treat the twin furrows on his buttocks, his shoulders. Asharti had always loved symmetry.

All the while she worked, Beatrix was thinking. The best place to hide from Asharti was Paris. Beatrix could conceal her vibrations in the surge of unruly life, unless Asharti came near enough to detect her. She must get John to Paris.

How could she plan calmly when she had just made him vampire? Had she not sworn never to make a vampire? It went against everything she believed since Asharti.

She turned to the window. A smiling moon floated among the fluttering leaves of an alder tree. She'd killed Quintoc in a rage at what he was doing to John, without a qualm. She'd killed Barlow because he refused redemption. Her hands were soiled with blood. Why couldn't she kill Jerry? Because he seemed a victim and he might still be redeemed? And what of John? He had begged her for death. He was a made vampire, and the Rules said he should be killed.

Would John turn into a monster like Asharti because he was made? Would he make others, would he torture his victims and drain the last drop? His dark lashes brushed his cheeks. How little she knew of him! What made a man spy for his country? It was a dirty life that exacted a price that chilled the soul. He didn't do it for money. For honor? What honor?

She took a breath and resolved to tell herself the truth. She refused to kill John because of how she felt about him. The truth was that John Staunton had crawled under her skin as no man had since . . . well, since Stephan. He had secrets like she did. He had been hurt by his life, as she had. But he had a core of goodness in him. A man who loved Blake and Turner could not be like Asharti. He struggled to serve his country, in spite of all he knew of men. Almost second innocence. She could not face a world that did not have the possibilities John represented in it. She might be wrong. God knows she had been wrong about Stephan and Asharti. But she decided to believe in John.

Perhaps this was the real test of Stephan's theory. Did being made vampire change your nature? Or was the effect of the Companion merely an attenuation of your natural tendencies? She was about to find out and so was John. He would not thank her for what she had done. Despise her for a monster and himself into the bargain, more like. But it was done. There would have to be more of her blood, even though she would have to compel him to take it.

But first they had to get out of Neuilly. Some clothes for John, a gig from the landlord, and they were for Paris, because Asharti would not be far behind.

Beatrix held John up to drink, though he was almost insensible. The small sordid room in a Marais garret was not a place she thought Asharti would look for them. Asharti would assume Beatrix demanded the rarefied atmosphere of a fine hotel or apartment. The Marais had lovely old homes, but the rich had gone elsewhere in the last century, leaving this part of the city to decay, subject to the inroads of the industrial impulse. Now it was filled with crumbling mansions turned into rooms or warehouses.

"John," she called sharply, with compulsion. His eyes swam up through fog to the pain. He sucked in breath convulsively and bit back a small sound in his throat. "Drink," she commanded. He gulped the water from her mug. She had never seen the making of a vampire. She had certainly never made one. Stephan told her that the process was horrible. He was right. It was humbling to see how much pain she had caused. John had been suffering for days now.

She bit her lip and laid John down. He sank immediately into a state not far from comatose. She wrung out a cloth in a bowl of water next to his pallet and pulled back his coverlet. Wiping his body with a cool cloth had become her own torture. Twice each day she had to hold herself in check as she ran her hands over the strong column of his neck, his shoulders, bulky with muscle, the soft nipples, the ribbed belly, and then lower, following the vee of hair; hips, genitals, God forbid, and thighs. It was a feeling she thought she had lost forever. He possessed just the type of body she liked, masculine to a fault, mature. But it wasn't just that. No, she was attracted to the courage he took for granted, his despair at being made. It was her memory of eyes that laughed at her in spite of all her worldly sophistication, and the fact that she did not know what he would do. Would he accept his vampire nature? And how would his experience at Asharti's hands scar him? Could he survive the self-hatred he would feel? She felt she knew him better than she knew almost anyone, yet he was still a mystery.

She pinned her hopes on his courage.

He woke again, in a dim and squalid room. It must be some kind of garret, for the ceiling was sloped at the edges with the peak of a roof. He smelled the tar that sealed the roof tiles, along with dust, mold, and the smell of burning coal. There was a grate with small, licking flames. The pain that was torture worthy of Asharti had receded to bearable, though it lurked there still. The pain of sorrow, regret, shame lurked inside as well, but they had been joined by a tiny thrill of . . . life. He was alive, very alive.

He rolled his head. Beatrix sat near the grate with a single candle on a tiny table next to her. She was in her shift, reading in an upholstered chair of a color between brown and gray whose stuffing protruded in several places. It was the only furniture in the room apart from the pallet he lay on, a narrow bed, and a rickety table by a great window filled with impenetrable darkness. The soft, buttery light of the candle made her pale skin glow. The thin white fabric of her shift hardly concealed her form. How could a woman so beautiful be a monster?

Her dark lashes swept her cheeks as she read. He realized with a start that she was pale because he had drunk her blood. Revulsion overcame him. He had been totally dependant upon her in these last days of indescribable pain. How many? He didn't know. Each time he woke she forced him to take her blood. Horrible, and yet . . . She had rescued him from Quintoc and Asharti. How had she appeared in France? And why? She had rescued him at the cost of dreadful wounds, stitched him, cared for his squalid needs. According to her story about this infection, she had saved his life with her blood. He contracted. She had made him a monster.

She lifted her head and stared at him with dark eyes made enormous by her pallor. A small smile touched her lips. "I felt you waken," she said. "You have your own vibrations now." She rose and came to kneel beside his pallet. "That may mean the worst is over."

"Are you . . . well? You were . . . wounded, I know." His voice was a harsh rasp.

"I am fine." She reached for a pitcher and mug sitting on the bare floor next to a small iron caldron. He saw the outline of her breast and nipple through her shift as she poured. "Do you remember me telling you that the Companion in your blood gives you the power to heal?" She lifted his head and dragged another pillow under it. He was damnably weak, in spite of the thrill of life along his veins and arteries. The water felt like heaven as it coursed down his throat, almost as good as her blood . . . He took a breath. He wouldn't think of that.

"What is this . . . this companion?" he asked to redirect his thoughts.

"An organism, in scientific terms," she said as she laid his head back on the rough canvas ticking of a pillow without a case. "When our blood is infected with it, we become one. Symbiotic, if you wish. More than we could ever be alone. In fact, you will never be alone again." She set the mug down. "I want to tell you about it. You only know about the blood. That is the hardest part for those not born to the Companion. Will you listen then, while I feed you?"

His eyes grew round.

"Soup, you ninny! Just soup. The body still requires food and water."

He felt a little sheepish. "Tell me, then."

She pulled the caldron closer and took up a battered spoon. "The Companion shares our blood. I was born to it. My mother was vampire. But children are rare. I may have been the last. We live, one to a city, so as not to call attention to ourselves, except at Mirso Monastery. There are many there." She lifted his head and spooned soup into his mouth. It was barley with some vegetables and perhaps a little beef. Where had she gotten the ingredients? Had she cooked it over the fire? "Mirso is the last refuge of our kind. It is in the Carpathian Mountains, through the Iron Gate of the Danube at Tirgu Korva. You may need it one day." Her eyes bored into his.

Why did she tell him this first? He swallowed the soup. "What about the blood? How can I avoid drinking human blood?" This was what he had to know.

"You cannot. And if you resist, the urge that comes upon you might lead you to take too much. It is forbidden to drain your donors. You must have it every two weeks at the least, but I advise you to take it even before the first signs of hunger come on you, a little from each."

"What signs?"

"An itching along your veins, a longing. You will know."

He looked inside himself. He knew it already. A tingling, itchy feeling. Panic set in.

"You feel it now," she said, reading his thoughts. "For a while, you will need it often."

He nodded, trying to master his revulsion. "*Why?* Why must I drink blood?"

She sighed. "Assuming your question is not metaphysical, it is because the Companion is the true vampire. It feeds on red blood cells, and they must be replenished."

"Animal blood—would that do?" He knew he sounded desperate, but he couldn't drink human blood. He wouldn't. Suicide flashed through his brain again, but at the very thought of it, the throbbing life that itched along his veins ramped up in protest.

"No," she said quietly. "I'm sorry." She moved on. "You will be sensitive to light, especially at first. For a while, you will be able to be abroad only at night. Later, by covering your skin, and using blue or green tinted glasses, you may withstand a brief time in the sun. I will show you how to translocate when you are better."

"What do you mean?"

She sat back and looked at him steadily. "The Companion gives us power in return for hosting it. The power can be used. You saw the strength. You felt the translocation when we escaped from the cell. You know the compulsion we can exert. All that is from our partner."

He felt the blush rising as he thought of Asharti, of Quintoc, and the compulsion he had felt. Insufferable shame . . . he could not even muster anger. He glanced away. Beatrix too had compelled him. She laid a hand along his cheek. He pulled away.

"Not your fault," she whispered. "Theirs. Remember that. Be outraged, be angry, but never ashamed. Quintoc has paid." Her eyes darkened. "Asharti will pay, too."

He wanted to be angry. But all he could do was let his head sag away from her. Her hand dropped to his bare shoulder. He realized he was naked under the quilt. It sent a thrill along his spine and into his loins. That frightened him. He suppressed the feeling ruthlessly.

"So. Translocation. We draw the power of the Companion until the field is so intense it collapses in on itself and we pop out of space. Our reflections in mirrors disappear, because no light escapes the field. We can direct the reappearance with a fair amount of accuracy. A mile or two, three at a stretch. Walls are no barrier."

His curiosity got the better of him. "What prevents you from reappearing in the middle of a tree or a mountain?"

She raised her brows. "I am not sure, frankly. Perhaps the solid mass resists us more than air. I have landed in water and got my feet wet, but never anything more solid than mud."

"What about garlic and wolf's bane and crosses?"

She drew her delicate brows together. "Myths. And we do not turn into bats. I think bats are a metaphor to explain our ability to relocate and our love of darkness." She offered more soup and he shook his head. She pushed the caldron away. Then she turned deliberately back to him. "But let us deal with your real question. You want to know if we are evil. I can touch a cross. I have prayed both in churches and in military trenches over the years." A shadow of pain crossed her face. "And if I am no longer sure the divine presence takes a personal delight in every sparrow, I do not believe our kind is born to evil, either. Some of us even do great good." She turned her head away. "I have been sinful in my time. More sinful than most people can imagine. I have killed, along with Asharti. My guilt is never-ending. But I do not do those things anymore. I try to find a way in life that harms no one. I do not forgive myself, you understand. I am not sure God forgives me. But I go on."

He searched her face. She believed she harmed no one, in spite of the fact that she drank human blood? Her expression said she did. There was humanity in her face.

Pain, surely, but humanity without question. "What about Asharti?" he croaked.

Her expression hardened. "Every race has its failures. I would agree that she's evil."

He wanted to know more of Asharti. Yet another question burned. "Why did you save me from them? And how did you know where I was?"

"You left a trail for one who knows how to look. I saw Reynard and heard the name Asharti. I knew your danger then. I saw your man, Withering. I saw Barlow." She started at her mistake. He knew by her expression what had happened.

He contracted inside. "Dead?"

She took a breath as though for courage. "Yes. I killed him."

He clenched his eyes and swallowed. "God in heaven," he whispered, more to suppress the tears that clogged his throat than in supplication. He turned away when she reached for him.

"You did not betray him," she said flatly. "When I saw him, he had been vampire for perhaps three months. He served Asharti long before you returned to London. He betrayed you to her, and your government, as well."

John jerked his head back toward her. "You lie! Barlow would never betray—"

"Think," she insisted. "Was he sick for a while, like you are now? And were there not attempts on your life? Who knew where you were the night of the footpads . . . ?"

John's brows drew together. The footpads attacked as he came away from meeting Barlow, the bullet in Berkeley Square . . . and what about the hulks? No Faraday. He had been transferred. Dupré was killed. Was it because he knew about Asharti? Would the guard have killed John that last day if the prisoners had not saved him? Barlow had been surprised to see him back . . . It was possible. "Not Barlow . . ." he murmured.

"He told me he had tired of serving so irresolute and corrupt a government. He was at the end of life. She offered him eternity, and a chance to carve a new reality. He would not renounce her . . . I had to . . ." She hesitated, then changed the subject. "Will you take blood?"

He shook his head, too vehemently. She would force him now. A lead weight anchored itself in his belly.

But she didn't. She pulled the quilt up. "Sleep if you can." She sat back on her heels.

He grabbed her hand and held her. "How do you live with it?"

She did not ask him what he meant. "I was born to it."

"Your mother taught you from the cradle . . ." He shook his head, rejecting the idea.

"My mother taught me nothing." Her voice held an echo of bitterness from long ago. "She abandoned me. My father I never knew. I was left to fend for myself when the need for blood came on me at thirteen or fourteen. I got what I needed on the back streets of Amsterdam in the eleventh century by ripping the throats of men who wanted to use me and got more than they asked, if not more than they deserved."

He let go her hand. The thought of a beautiful young girl of fourteen forced to make her way in the back streets of Amsterdam was horrible. He tried not to think about the eleventh century. "Was there no one to help you?" he asked quietly.

She smiled, her eyes far away. "Stephan. Stephan Sincai. He rescued me." She came back to the room in spirit, and looked at him seriously. "Asharti, too."

John's brows drew together. She had known Asharti all her life?

"Yes," she answered the unspoken question. "We were like sisters once, only I was born vampire and Asharti was made, like you. Stephan saved us both. It was forbidden to make vampires. It still is. They were killed on sight, since they often went mad. Stephan wanted to prove to the Elders at Mirso Monastery that born and made vampires were not different once the made vampire assimilated to his new condition, if they were nurtured equally, given love."

"He loved you?" There was a prickle of something like irritation around John's heart.

"I don't know." She said it calmly. At one time, he would wager she had not been calm. She had loved this monster. Perhaps she still did. "I'm not sure I know what love is. After we left him, he wandered the world. He was hurt somehow. Does that mean he loved us? I think not."

"Looks as though his experiment failed, if Asharti is any mark."

She looked away. "Perhaps"—her gaze roved over the room—"perhaps she always had this seed of evil in her. Perhaps he just picked the wrong person to prove his point." She took a breath. "I learned, centuries later, that he talked the Elders out of killing Asharti. Maybe he did love her. He took full responsibility. But he has never called her to heel."

"Could he?"

"He is very old. That means he is powerful."

"How old?" What did a woman who had lived seven hundred years consider old?

"Oh, thousands of years. I do not know exactly. Not so old as Rubius, the Eldest. Some say *he* goes back six thousand years to when men hunted with sticks and gathered berries."

John took a breath, trying to digest that. All he could think of was that this Stephan could control Asharti, but he did not. "So this man, or whatever he is, simply lets Asharti bring down governments and create . . . vampires right and left?"

"By the time he returned to Europe, Asharti had gone to ground somewhere in Africa, no one knew where. I heard her name for the first time in four hundred years from Reynard."

An itching along John's veins made it difficult to think. "Where is this Stephan Sincai now? She must be stopped. She will change Europe . . . no, the world . . ."

"I hear he took over Amsterdam after I left," she said, her voice tight with constraint. "He lives on the Herengracht. He would like it there. I lived at number Three-eighty for many years."

John was more sure than ever Beatrix still held feelings for this man who had first loved her in her youth. She knew where he lived even now. His heart sank.

"He does not care for the world anymore," she continued. "He will not stop her and I cannot." She stood. "Rubius could. I shall send to him. But the Carpathian Mountains are far away. Discretion is the better part of valor, now. I will get you back to England. You can recover your strength and learn how to be vampire. Then you must find a city of your own." Her big, dark eyes stared at him with an expression he could not read. "There is only one of us allowed to a city, so our presence does not manifest itself to humans. Perhaps the New World? Or the Far East. But you will have time to decide."

*How lonely,* he thought. *To alienate yourself from the only ones who can understand you.* There was nothing to be said. He was overwhelmed by what she had told him. No, there was one more thing he must know. "Can she find us?"

She knew who he meant. "Yes. By our vibrations, if she can get close enough."

He opened his eyes in surprise. "That humming feel of life in any room you occupy?"

She nodded. "And the scent. Cinnamon and ambergris, some version of it. So sleep now, and gain strength. We must away as soon as ever we can."

She stirred the coals and drew heavy draperies over the

window that looked out on a paling sky, then laid herself out on the counterpane on the bed.

Weakness overcame him. He closed his eyes but it was long until he slept. Barlow had told Asharti everything, long before she compelled John. She let him think he betrayed his country, why? For amusement? And did it lessen his shame that there was no consequence to his betrayal? Shame . . . there was more than enough of that to go around. Asharti . . . Quintoc! His mind skittered over that to what he had become. No, there was plenty to shame him.

Beatrix sat in the darkness in the overstuffed chair and watched John sleep. He had slept all day. It was nearly midnight now. He would live. Her copy of *Tom Jones* lay abandoned by the grate, now glowing with coals alone. After all the blood she had given him, she was light-headed, but that might be convenient. Her vibrations would be lowered with her weakness. That would make it harder for Asharti to find them.

Beatrix had no illusions about what had happened at Chantilly when Asharti returned. Beatrix wondered if LèFevre would survive telling her the bad news. Her prey had been stolen from her, her majordomo killed, all by the woman she once considered her protégée, the woman who had rejected her in Krakow six hundred years ago. She and who knew how many minions would be combing Paris for them.

John had asked questions about his state with some degree of focus. He did not look as though he was going mad, but it was early days. She clenched her eyes shut. It was she who might be going mad. She had to acknowledge a tendril of hope that if he accepted his state, he might . . . they might . . . They might break the Rule of one to a city.

What could be more mad than that? She was going sentimental over a man? He had interested her enough that she had tracked him over most of the south of England and even into France, into Asharti's very lair. That spoke to a fair amount of interest. But it wasn't love. Even when she was interested, as she was with Henry or da Vinci, love was impossible. They were from different species and they grew old and died. Vampires? Not likely. Perhaps her capacity for love died when she left Stephan.

Her gaze strayed to John. John shared her secret. And he would never grow old.

She got up and paced the room in front of the dying coals. It was wrong to hope. But neither would she abandon him or let him go mad. He *must* accept being vampire. She watched him toss again in some nightmare. His Companion, now that the immunity was taking hold, demanded blood. She would have to bring John to feed on his own. If he could do that, perhaps he could accept his fate. He was too weak for hunting. And she did not want his first experience to be a whore in the streets of the Marais. She wanted to make certain he did not get one who would struggle because John was inexperienced at compulsion. Struggling would horrify him.

There was one answer. The demands of the Companion in his blood might make it possible. She slipped her shift from her shoulders. She wanted to do it for him. The prospect of lying naked next to his hot flesh and baring her neck to him excited her. The wet between her legs had been there off and on for days. It pressed at her now, demanding satisfaction. But the thrill of desire mixed with the taking of blood wouldn't be dangerous when it was not her who did the taking. Would it? Her shift pooled on the ground. Naked, she stood above him in the predawn chill where he tossed on his pallet.

# Nineteen

John dreamt of Beatrix. It was a hot summer's day in Gibraltar where he had laid the agent Jean Michel by the heels in '08. They were lying on a secluded beach and Beatrix was gloriously naked. He noticed with surprise that he was naked, too. They were both covered with a light sheen of perspiration. Her lips against the throbbing veins in his throat were softer than he could imagine. She put her arms round his neck and whispered endearments in his ear. She loved him. He wanted to make love to her more than he had ever wanted anything. "Beatrix," he murmured. The soft brush of her nipples against the hair on his chest as she raised herself to kiss him sent thrills straight to his core. His loins swelled with desire, hot and urgent.

The heat began to prickle. It seemed to soak into his veins; an itching that distracted him from Beatrix. "No," he muttered, as the itching ratcheted up almost to pain.

"Shush," said Beatrix, kissing his throat. "You can make the pain go away."

He nuzzled her throat, then her breasts. It was almost enough to distract him from the pain. He ran his hands down over her buttocks, pressing her to him. "Beatrix," he moaned.

"Call your Companion, dear John," she whispered.

He blinked. "What?" The dingy room flashed in around him and replaced the beach in Gibraltar. Except Beatrix was naked and he was naked, too, and sweating. She had her arms around his neck and her lips moved over his throat, kissing softly. Her breasts were pressed against his chest. His loins were heavy, throbbing. "Beatrix." But then there was the pain, itching inside him. He sucked in a breath and let out a little moan. Need ramped up along his veins.

"Call, my dear, just call," she whispered. "For me, just try."

"Stop it," he said. "Can you stop it?" He didn't mean to stop the kissing. He wanted her to make the pain stop. But she seemed to know.

"Call. Just say to yourself, *Companion*. It will know how to stop the pain."

*Companion,* he thought.

Life rushed up along his veins, exuberance. His eyes closed, all focus internal. He had never felt anything so joyous. A long breath. Yes! But still there was an aching need. He had never needed as he needed now. But what? What did he need?

"Yesssss," she breathed. "Now again. *Companion, come.*"

*Companion, come!* And the rush of life and needing was intensified. God, how could he stand so much exhilaration? He opened his eyes. A red film covered everything; the seedy room, the glowing coals, Beatrix's expectant face turned upward, baring her throat. He bent and kissed her, the need inside him making him urgent with her. He pressed her against his cock, fully erect now. She pulled away a little and examined his face tenderly. Her eyes glowed red, too, like burgundy-colored coals, even through the wash of red.

"This does not have to be sexual, you know . . ." she whispered.

"I want you, Beatrix Lisse. Is that so hard to understand?" He almost growled the question. His answer lay in her dilated eyes, her breasts rising and falling against his chest, in the wet he felt against his thigh. It had been long since he had wanted a woman like he wanted Beatrix. He knew what she was. Evil, probably. But the life coursing through him made everything else unimportant. He wanted her anyway.

"No. And perhaps that will make it easier." What did she mean? She kissed him, as roughly as he had kissed her. He rolled her onto her back on the pallet and she spread her thighs to him. She wanted no caresses. She wanted him. And he obliged. He slid his member into her slick folds as she arched up into him. She was tight around him. He thrust slowly home, in order not to hurt her, but she curled her legs over his back and pulled him down until he was fully sheathed in her. He was groaning, so was she. Slowly, he began to move, in and out, as she adjusted the angle for her maximum pleasure. The pulsing life he felt in her matched the thrill along his own veins. He had never felt such sensation! Every fiber of him was alive with it. Her skin, her breath, the silk of her hair . . . She banged her hips against his, urging him on. He held himself above her, thrusting inside her. She threw her head back, baring her throat. Then, as though drawing herself back from some brink of ecstasy, she pulled him down to her, kissing his neck, his jawline, all the while they thrust in counterpoint. He kissed her, sharing his rasping breath with hers. His teeth scraped his own lips. He tasted blood. The excitement in his veins ramped up some scale he had not known existed into frantic fibrillation. This was something more than sexual. He was confused and the insistent throbbing in his cock, in his veins, would not let him think. He needed, that was all he knew, a red need that required satisfaction in the next seconds or he would burst into flame.

She quickened the pace, sliding his cock in and out of her. Again she arched her neck. He could feel her blood throbbing in arteries just under her jaw like a pair of drums that shattered his body with their insistent booming. "Here, my love, is what you need. I give it freely."

In one awful moment, he saw it; what he needed, what she gave, what his body and soul shrieked at him to do. He opened his mouth, knowing somewhere that his canines had elongated even as Asharti's did, Quintoc's did. Yet, horrific or not, he could not stop himself. The need shrieked at him. Her blood called and he buried his fangs in the throbbing artery in her throat even as he thrust deep inside her.

She gave a little gasp, no more, and then the blood was flowing; thick ecstasy. His body moved against hers in a rhythm with his sucking as he drew at her. She moaned, but it was not a moan of pain. She must feel the ecstasy that suffused him. He never wanted it to end. He drew at her throat even as he felt an explosion gathering in his loins, in his brain. Red went almost black. She shrieked, a long ululating cry as her muscles contracted around his cock, squeezing it at last into the threatened explosion. Blackness pulsed at him as he came and came, hunching into her, and sucking.

She drew away with a cry.

He stared at her, his breath coming fast and short. The pain in his veins was gone. He felt strong and sure. His orgasm was so strong it nearly rent him in two, but he was still hard inside her. Life surged not only in his veins, but in his loins, as though he could take her again this very moment. The room around them slowly faded from red to dingy gray. Her eyes were big, but they held no accusation. Even as he watched, the twin wounds in her neck disappeared.

"The blood is the life," she whispered. "But that is all I have to give."

He opened his mouth and ran his tongue over his teeth. The canines retracted. He gasped, and withdrew from her. His cock was still embarrassingly erect. "What have I done?"

"You called your Companion and fed for the first time." She drew a hand tenderly over his brow. Then, as she examined his expression, "From someone who wanted to give. You cannot say it was horrible."

He had enjoyed the blood. He had wanted it. It had satisfied him. He was vampire. "No, and that is the most horrible part."

"Hold me, that we may sleep together with the coming dawn."

Her voice held no command. It was a woman's supplication for at least the appearance of affection. "I'm sure you do this often," he accused, and pulled up the sheet to cover the fact that he wanted her again, even now.

Her face contracted, and he felt ashamed at lashing out at her. "No, not like this."

He might be damned, but he loved her. He could not remember a time when he had not loved her. The realization was an anticlimax. Something else, far more consequential than love, had intervened. He pulled the coverlet over both of them, leaving the sheet between his throbbing cock and her milk-white hip. He gathered her in his arms and held her head against his chest, so she would not speak, nor ask him to speak. He was too confused, too horrified by what he had done, and how wonderful it was, to bear any more questions. She went to sleep almost immediately, and he realized that with all the blood she had given him, she was weak.

He might have killed her if she had not pulled away. The wild ecstasy of blood and sex was . . . shattering. He had no control. He would have taken all the blood she had, willing the orgasm of blood and sex to go on forever. But no, he could not have killed her. She was immortal, except for decapitation apparently. And so was he.

As he held her in his arms, the reality of his new nature washed over him.

Love? Such as they were did not deserve love. All his life he had looked for a way to live with honor. He had resisted loving a courtesan, since by definition they were strangers to virtue. A courtesan was pure as virgin snow compared to what Beatrix actually was—what he was, now. Honor and virtue were banished from his life forever.

He could judge her, but he could not blame her for turning him. If she had been infected with this cursed parasite, he would have given every drop of his blood to save her. She had saved him, by her lights. She might even care for him.

If he stayed she would seduce him to her way of life, just as she had seduced him to drink her blood. He imagined existence stretching on into eternity, sucking human blood, being the stuff of nightmares. He closed his eyes. The joyous feeling in his body was Satan's lure. He was a monster now, like Asharti. He had drunk blood as she did. He felt his insides go cold. Thoughts tumbled through his mind in dark chaos. What should he do? What *could* he do now? He had to think, think without the lure of loving Beatrix poisoning his reason.

He disentangled himself from her arms and slid out from under the coverlet. He stalked over to where his clothes were hung upon a peg. His cock had softened, finally. That was good. If he stayed with Beatrix, he would accept his condition. He would suck the blood of innocents. He did not know what other choices there were, but he would never make them if he stayed.

He had to go now, before the thrill of life along his veins became the most important thing in the world to him—more than human life. Before he went mad, or became like Asharti. He heard a dog on the prowl in the street below and the late step of a streetwalker. He pulled on trousers, a shirt, its ruffle open at the collar. He had no money, no way to live. He glanced at Beatrix's delicate bead reticule lying on the rickety table.

No. He would not take her money. Some part of him gave a cruel laugh. He would take her blood but not her money? He turned to look at her, sleeping peacefully under the quilt, her auburn hair spread over the pillow. It was not right that she should look so innocent.

He turned to the door. He dared not look longer at her. Time to go, before he stayed forever.

Beatrix stretched. She was stiff from sleeping for what must have been hours on the pallet. John. She smiled and put out her arm, wanting to feel his flesh under her hands.

Her eyes snapped open. No John. She scanned the room even as she sat up. Had he gone down the hall in some misplaced fit of modesty rather than use the chamber pot? But she sensed no vibrations near. She pulled on her muslin night shift and pattered barefoot down the hall in spite of the light making its determined way through the grime on the windows. Jerking open the door to the necessary room, she provoked a yelp from the fat baker's boy relieving himself. But no John. She flung herself back to the darkened room. Only a whisper of smoke said the coals had ever burned. She went to the window and peered out, eyes squinting against the painful day. It was raining and gray. But John could not be out in daylight, new as he was.

She pulled herself from the window. He was gone. She had thought . . . after the blood . . . Perhaps the exhilaration was too much for him. Damnation! She should have forced him. Then he could have hidden his joy from himself until he had time to get used to it. Beatrix paced in front of the dead coals. She had rubbed his nose in what he was.

How would he survive on his own? He was new and weak. She put a hand to her mouth. If he got desperate enough to feed he might kill inadvertently and hate himself the more. And the daylight . . . had he found a place to go to ground? She hefted her reticule and felt its weight. He had no money. She looked around wildly. She must find him, bring him back . . .

Beatrix darted to the bare pole and pulled one of her only two dresses off its hanger.

The hum of power behind her made her go still. She clutched the dress to her breast.

Enough power to cause an audible hum meant there was more than one of them. They would materialize before she could dash through them, before she herself could translocate. So it would be a fight. She turned slowly.

There were six, including Asharti. The men stood around her once-sister in a semicircle, some smug, some wary. They were not strong in themselves, but all had called their Companions, and they used their power to augment Asharti, who fairly buzzed in the center.

A heavy cloak of red wool swirled over a cream-colored kerseymere dress embroidered with spider delicacy in matching red. The borders of the cloak were worked in gold pictographs. Her eyes were venomous black slits in her face. "I warned you once you would not be welcome back in my life," she said, and her voice echoed in the room with the power of her five minions added to her own. "Now you have stolen what belongs to me."

Beatrix swallowed. The hum of power hemmed her round. Only a vampire much older than she was or several setting their power together could pinion Beatrix. It had never happened to her. With one vampire to a city, there was little possibility of combining powers. Beatrix lifted her chin. "Actually, you told me I would regret leaving you. I have not. And he was mine." It sounded petulant but it was the best she could do.

"Then what was he doing in Paris? He was fair game," Asharti hissed. Her figure seemed to grow larger in the darkened room. "Where is he? Thierry said he sensed two vibrations, so you must have made him." She sneered at Beatrix. "Hardly your style."

"He has gone."

"He left you twice?" Asharti laughed. "You are sunk quite low in the world, Bea."

"He was . . . upset. You of any know how unsettling your first days as one of us can be."

"We will find him, never fear."

Beatrix did fear it. *I hope you have run far and fast, dear John.*

Asharti began to fidget. Her gaze darted about the room. "Do not think that just because he has escaped you that I forgive your betrayal. You hamper me at every turn. How can I be what I am destined to be, with you always looking over my shoulder?"

What? She hadn't even seen the woman in six hundred years. "And what are you destined to be?" she asked, just to say something.

"I was made by Robert le Blois, as you recall," she said, drawing herself up. "In the way of our kind, I am his descendant. That means France belongs to me . . ."

"France belongs to the French people, little though Bonaparte likes to own to that." Beatrix realized Asharti must be teetering on madness.

Asharti snorted. "I suppose you supported the Republic, with all its bloodletting. Almost as bad as the first Crusade, I assure you. Not that I cared. I am after something more important than a human empire."

What was Asharti up to? Beatrix felt a thrill of fear move up her spine.

"You always thought you were better than I am," Asharti raced on, her voice ascending the scale. "Even *Stephan* thought you were better. Well, I am going to prove just who is better." She began to pace inside her circle of consorts. "What have you done with your life, Beatrix? Even when you fought wars, they were human wars, wars of their conscience or struggles for their freedom. Wasted effort. And now I hear you love only art and music. Silly."

Beatrix was stung enough to retort, "Is that any different than supporting Bonaparte?"

"Controlling all of Europe and Africa is just the means to an end. We vampires will feed as we choose, live as we choose. Humans will take their rightful place as the cattle we raise for our use. I will set our kind free."

"An unusual concept of utopia," Beatrix said tightly. "I assume you mean you and the vampires you make. By the way, if everyone makes vampires, there is an end to it."

"A case of the pot calling the kettle black if ever I heard one," Asharti sneered.

"Rubius and the other Elders will not allow it."

"*Allow* it? Even now, through Bonaparte, *I* control the mountains that hold Mirso Monastery. Rubius exists upon my sufferance." Her voice shook. "His time is past. His Rules keep us from any kind of life. One to a city!" This last was said with such a maniacal gleam in her eye, Beatrix realized that hatred must have been brewing in Asharti ever since they parted. Had she ever been sane? Or was she driven mad by that horrific experience in the first Crusade?

"I will not stop you," Beatrix murmured. "I acknowledge your power." There was no use in antagonizing her. If Beatrix could get away she could go to Mirso, warn Rubius. No matter what Asharti thought, Rubius and the other Elders could stop Asharti's mad career. But what about the others? How many vampires had Asharti made?

"I think you know where your precious Langley is," Asharti hissed, and the sibilance coruscated back from the walls of the dingy room. "You can't hide him from me."

A shudder went through Beatrix she hoped Asharti missed. "I swear I do not."

A slow smile spread over Asharti's face. "He had begun to respond to my training, you know. He needs a strong hand." She raised her arms and the power of the lesser vampires behind her seemed to focus even more intently upon Beatrix. "Now he is vampire, he will be stronger. I can draw out his service even longer. But first, my sister, I must deal with you."

The power of the six combined made it difficult to breathe. Beatrix must find a way out of this. The others' forms were shrouded in darkness. Only Asharti seemed to draw the light of the flickering candle on the table. "What have such as you to fear from me?"

"You came to Paris. You stole your Englishman from me. You killed Quintoc!" Her voice lowered. "I deal with challenges most directly."

"Then call your Companion and fight me for control right now," Beatrix gasped. She knew she could not win, but she could think of nothing else.

Asharti's throaty chuckle echoed around the room. "No. Even though I bested you in Krakow, who knows what has happened in the intervening years? I like inevitability. No, dear Bea, Napoleon says the French mob needs periodic lessons in passionate devotion to the cause." She paused, and the red of her eyes grew even deeper. "Traitors get a very public execution and by means most fatal to our kind. I shall introduce you to Madame Guillotine."

Beatrix sucked in breath as her Companion rebelled in protest of giving up its grip on life. She felt it as a wave of nausea. "You'll . . . you'll never get me to put my head on the block." But she glanced to the phalanx of vampires who held her motionless and knew they could do whatever they wished if they worked together.

Asharti's eyes narrowed and her smile grew unctuous. "I see you realize your words are mere bravado. Gentlemen? Let us help our sister to the coach. I think a little time in the Conciergerie will help her reflect on her sins."

The shadowy phalanx closed in around Beatrix. She had to do something. *Come to me, Companion!* she thought. Life surged up along her veins. But against her will she took a step toward the door. She had never been stronger than Asharti and now she was weakened by loss of blood. Asharti grabbed Beatrix's cloak and reticule and stood aside. It was now or never. *Come now!* A red veil dropped over the room. Darkness whirled about her feet, pushing up toward her knees, her hips. A moment and she would be free!

"Stop!" Asharti commanded. It came to Beatrix as from a distance. Asharti pushed through the circle. The other vampires turned. The blackness sank.

*Come, Companion mine!* she pleaded. The blackness pulsed upward. Everything seemed to slow. Asharti's red eyes gleamed, even redder than the red haze. Beatrix could not get her breath. The others pushed at her. Asharti pushed at her. Beatrix gasped for air, her hands clasped to her breasts, wringing the last bit of power from her Companion.

All at once the blackness dissipated. Air surged into her lungs. The red film faded.

Asharti grabbed Beatrix's jaw in one hand and turned her face, so she could not escape staring into Asharti's red eyes. "You see?" she hissed, their noses almost touching. "You are not better than I am." She pushed Beatrix away. "You never were."

Beatrix half fell. Several hands gripped her elbows and propelled her to the door. Asharti stalked after her. She could do nothing. She was at Asharti's mercy.

The night was wet as John stumbled down the narrow Rue Montmorency. Around him he heard the whispered propositions of the prostitutes, the crisp steps of gendarmes, revelers' drunken calls, the clatter of wheels on stone, and the clop of horses' hooves. Cats yowled, doors banged; the night was alive with sound. And sound was only half of it. The city reeked with competing smells: the rot of vegetables, pungent horse manure, cooking cabbage, unwashed men, and early summer rain. John was almost overwhelmed by the evidence of his senses. His hair was dripping, his clothing plastered to his body. The hollow feeling in his center had nothing to do with hunger or thirst. In fact, he felt strong and dangerously alive. It was a heart-sickness that could not be cured. He would deal with that later. He must get out of Paris, as quickly as possible. Asharti was here. And Beatrix.

He would not think of either of them, or of himself, or of the horror they all had in common. He needed a horse or a coach and he had not a sou to his name. He walked north toward prosperity.

After a time he leaned against the corner of a small house half-timbered from a former century. Boxes filled with geraniums clung to the windowsills. He glanced up. He could hear the snoring even behind closed windows on the first floor. It was a well-to-do house. Perhaps a merchant lived here. He glanced to the door. Might as well try the latch. He glanced up and down the street, then took hold of the knob and twisted slowly. There was a little resistance, but it opened with a snap. He slid inside.

He hadn't remembered a moon, but there must be one, because he could see inside the house quite well with

only the light from windows that looked out upon the
night. He avoided the front parlor and made his way to
the library. He could smell the leather and the paper
of the books. The desk drawers had keyholes. He thought
they would be locked, but they opened easily. The third
drawer had bills, and gold. This was too easy. He stuffed
his pockets, then took ink and quill and scratched the address of the house on a scrap of paper. Then he wrote a
note. "I regret the necessity of borrowing your monetary
resources. I shall return them with interest." He glanced
up and saw a cloak laid across a chair by the cold fireplace. "And the cloak." The pen hovered over the paper. It
seemed too churlish to leave it unsigned. Then he
shrugged. If he was captured by Asharti and her minions,
this petty thievery would not matter, and if he was not,
they would have their stake returned and more. "Langley," he wrote with a flourish.

   Then he swung the cloak about his shoulders and let
himself out into the street. Three streets over was a tavern. He could hear the laughter, both male and female,
even from here. Good. In a neighborhood like this there
might be some high play.

John left the tavern a few hours later, his pockets jingling,
a coat slung over his arm. He had cleaned his opponent's
pockets at piquet with two septièmes and a rare huitème.
He had played in the end for M. Leveret's coat, since that
looked to be the closest fit. It was almost dawn. The din
of the night had changed. Early vendors called. Servants
hurried to work in the dark. Heavy carts rumbled through
the streets. He remembered Beatrix's warning about sunlight. He must get to a place of safety. So he hastened toward the Seine. He wanted to be close to the docks to find
a ship going out to Le Havre and across the Channel to
England. If only he could get home, he might be able to
think again about what he was to do with himself.

He found an inn along the quay suffused with the reek of the Seine, a bit rundown, but it boasted shutters that looked as though they could be tightly shut. He roused the house. The landlord was a round little man, cranky at being got up at that hour, but glad to have the louis John dispensed. John could smell the fish being delivered at the rear for today's bouillabaisse.

John asked for wrapping paper and a string, hurried up to his room. He pulled the shutters to and drew the curtains. Then he wrapped the cloak and the money he had borrowed in the paper, wrote the direction on the outside, and tied it with string. He would send it back by the landlord's boy.

He felt the sun rise. It wasn't painful. No light leaked through the windows. It was just that he knew that somewhere the sun was rising.

A terrible tristesse came over him. He sat heavily on the bed. It creaked under his weight. He had been so busy tonight he had hardly noticed how different everything was, how different *he* was. Slumping there, he replayed the last hours. The evidence chunked into place. He could see in the dark. He could hear things he shouldn't be able to hear. He had opened doors and drawers he now suspected had been locked after all. He closed his eyes and felt the roar of life along his veins. It was impossible that he should feel so . . . complete, when he had become a monster. He could well believe that newly made vampires went mad. He clenched his eyes shut. To be condemned to such a life of horror, to be reviled as evil . . . to drink human blood! And worst of all, to feel so whole and alive in spite of it—*because* of it.

How he longed for that simple disillusionment he had felt a month ago! Then he had found his occupation required small acts of sordid dishonor, and all men—and women, he could not forget women!—were disappointing creatures comprised of equal parts selfishness and smallness of soul. Lord, even Barlow . . .

Barlow. Dead now. Deservedly so. The others . . . dead. Barlow had betrayed them. John too betrayed them. They were doubly dishonored. But no, they had died without deserving it, what honor they had intact. He on the other hand . . . Asharti had used him, but his cock had been only too eager to service her. He flushed in shame. And Quintoc . . .

He buried his face in his hands. He drew the line at Quintoc. He could not, would not, think about that. But he could not draw any lines anymore and the final humiliation with Quintoc drenched him. Beatrix had seen it, she must have. God in heaven, he had consorted with Satan's spawn, and done their bidding. And Beatrix was no better.

Beatrix. He loved her. God help him, he still loved her, in spite of what she was, or what she had made him. His soul would no doubt be forfeit now in any case, he might as well admit he loved the devil himself. Or herself.

He raised his head. Across the room, his reflection in the mirror of a small dressing table stared back at him like some strange wraith. His face was pale, his eyes a haunted green with purple smudges under them almost like bruises. The John Staunton he had been was erased by Asharti and Quintoc, and drowned in dark waters of Beatrix's cursed blood.

He jerked around, looking for some weapon. Why had he not stolen a pistol or a knife? His eyes came to rest on the flickering candle. He went calm inside. Slowly he held out his hand to the flame. He half expected his strength would wipe out pain. So he was pleasantly surprised by the searing flash of agony. Trembling, he forced himself to leave his hand in the flame. He saw it blacken, smelled the burning flesh. It was only when he realized that if he was trying to kill himself it was a ridiculous way to do it, that he jerked his hand back. He just wanted to hurt the creature he had become. He turned his hand over. The palm was charred and blackened. Pain shot up his arm. The throbbing anguish made his head swim. Then he focused again. To his surprise the pain receded. The ragged black circle shrank.

"No," he murmured. His damnation was being laid before his eyes. The black faded to red. "No," he said, his voice rising. The red faded. The palm was whole. Life and strength flooded through him in deranged joy. He was powerless to change his state. The dread thing in his blood coveted life. "God, no," he choked, clenching his fist to his heaving chest.

He *must* find a way to kill himself. It was the only way to avoid being a monster now. Beatrix said it was hard to kill yourself. The damned thing in your blood wouldn't let you. Well, maybe it didn't get a choice. He must do it before that wonderful feeling of being strong and alive seduced him permanently. What had Beatrix said? Decapitation.

He laughed and the laugh circled up into some animal sound he couldn't control. Tears filled his eyes. His sides shook. He mustn't run home to England too soon. The French were experts at decapitation.

# Twenty

Beatrix marched under the twin conical towers, Tour d'Argent and Tour de César, of the most sinister building in France. The troop of vampires had walked across the Seine on the bridge, the long front of the Conciergerie rising into the night in Gothic menace. Asharti had gone ahead to prepare the way, after making certain the five remaining could hold Beatrix. They could. They trooped through the fourteenth-century arches of the guard room, empty now except for an old man with a great set of iron keys on a ring. Prisoners now were held in the dungeons. The group headed toward the cells at the back of the first floor, the old man tottering after them.

Beatrix knew the building well. She had intrigued with Hugh Capet, who built it as a palace, and started the long reign of the Capetuan kings. Frenchmen now stood in awe of this building because it was the last stop for victims of the Revolution as diverse as Marie Antoinette and Robespierre himself. They had suffered nothing compared to Ravaillac, who had murdered Henri IV in 1610. His screams still seemed to echo from the stone.

They stopped in front of a cell. Black bars from floor to

ceiling ensured the prisoner had no privacy. The old man fumbled at the lock. The door protested with a scream of metal, and one of Asharti's minions pushed her in. She stumbled through the straw to the bare stone bench.

"This cell will not hold me . . ." she said, trying to believe her threat.

"No," said the oldest-looking of the vampires. His hair was shot with gray. Not Asharti's usual type. "But we will." The door screeched shut with a clang. The old human man locked it and hurried away. "There will never be less than five of us here at a time."

Beatrix's heart sank. "You cannot keep me here forever."

The oldest one smirked. "Not required. Madame Guillotine entertains on Sunday."

"At least I'll have your fine company," Beatrix observed as though she was lighthearted.

Asharti appeared out of the shadows. "They are forbidden to speak to you, or look into your eyes." She glanced around at the men she had made vampire. "Is that understood?"

They murmured agreement, cowed. That was the effect Asharti had on all her victims, and these were victims no less than the ones she drained. Beatrix still might be able to subvert one. Surely some at least were uncertain, afraid, even unstable if they were newly made.

"Now, position yourselves in the cells on either side and here in front." She turned to Beatrix. "Well, my sister. It is a bit harder to look down your nose at me now, is it not?" Her expression grew almost avaricious. "How I shall love seeing you lay your head in that semicircle of wood with that great gleaming diagonal blade hanging above you. Will you cry, or even—dare I hope—beg for your life? Your Companion will be thrumming in your veins, trying to avoid the death. But there is no avoiding it. No, your head will tumble into the basket with your eyes still blinking in protest, your lips mouthing words you have no throat to utter." Asharti shuddered in delight. "I shall arrange a special nighttime execution, just to make sure my . . . associates feel comfortable as they escort you." She grasped the black iron bars with both hands. "How I wish Stephan could see it!"

Beatrix gazed into eyes transformed by the ecstasy of anticipation into something alien and felt not only fear, but pity. "Then what, Asharti? After I am dead, what then?"

Asharti let a slow smile transform her face. "Then I will make a world where vampires are everywhere. *I* will reign. And I will set us free from Rules and hiding."

"You will destroy the balance!" Beatrix hissed. "When you have made so many vampires and they make vampires, where will it stop? We will spread like an infection until there is not enough blood to sustain us. Then we all die." She made her voice as calm as she could. "Every species must live in balance with its fellows, Asharti, or they do not live at all. Even us."

"We will stop making vampires when there are enough," she said lightly.

"When made vampires often go mad, drunk with the power the Companion gives them? You will control nothing."

"You are a small thinker, Beatrix. But I cannot stay to enlighten you. Fanueille is called to the emperor, which means the emperor in reality calls for me. I am the fulcrum upon which the world teeters. I must dispose of business before I can look for your Englishman."

She whirled and was gone. Asharti's followers took up their posts. Their will descended like a curtain. It was effective. Could they keep it up if they changed out watch by watch?

Beatrix felt the sun rise, somewhere. She held out little hope for herself. She only hoped John was away to England. He would not survive the world Asharti was planning for long, though. No one would, not even the vampires.

· · ·

John slipped out into the shadows, determination roiling in his belly. The sun was setting behind the buildings around him. He had not wanted to wait until night, fearing his resolve would dissipate, but he was unable to even peer out the window in the daylight.

How strange! He had always imagined those poor souls who wanted to end their lives as being so empty they drifted into self-murder. In truth, it took a terrible intensity of will. Or perhaps that was only because the impulse to life inside him was so strong, it took an equal, if opposite, urge toward death to withstand it. He was not certain he would be able to do the deed in the end. Perhaps the thing in his blood would win out at the last moment. That was why the guillotine was perfect. Once the blade descended there was no going back.

It was a long way to where the guillotine had been erected in the Place du Trône. The din of the city was a roar in his head, the competing smells almost crushing. He stumbled down the Rue de Rivoli, one of the streets renamed by Bonaparte for a victory. People stared and whispered as he passed. He glanced down. His neck cloth was askew, his shirt wrinkled, his coat creased and ill fitting. He must look wild-eyed. He took a deep breath. *Slow down. Where is your control?* He twitched his cravat into some semblance of order and slowed his step.

The Place de la Bastille rose round him, the hub of half a dozen streets. The guillotine had once stood here. The ruins of the old prison still poked through the new construction. Napoleon was re-creating Paris as a capital fitting for the emperor of the world. He was really creating it for Asharti, whether he knew it or not. She was going to win out. That slowed his steps in earnest. An ache echoed in his belly. He would be dead and she would win.

He shook his head, as if to clear it. Who could stop her? Beatrix said she could not. Only someone named Stephan

Sincai in Amsterdam, and he would not. Or someone named Rubius who was locked in some monastery in the Carpathian Mountains. No, Asharti would win.

He suppressed the wave of rebellion that rose up through his throat. No helping that. His job was to avoid becoming what she was, drinking blood, victimizing . . .

On through the Rue de Faubourg, between the new stone houses rising on each side of the wide boulevard. The cacophony of noise about him banged at his senses. What would he do when he got there? Surely there would be guards. But he was strong now. He could take care of guards. The Place du Trône opened ahead. The rectangular maw of the guillotine outlined itself against the new streetlights. Sere relief first drenched John then forced a gasp as his Companion surged along his veins, protesting. But what was this? Hammers pounded. A crowd had gathered around the perimeter, murmuring. This was bad. How would he achieve his purpose in this crush of humanity? The diagonal blade gleamed above them in a wicked slash.

What was going on here? John drew into the twilight gloom under one of the trees surrounding the great circle of grass. Inside the ring of onlookers, uniformed soldiers were stationed around the huge device, but men in working clothes swarmed over it. Ropes hung from the heavy top rail that held the blade.

"Let the blade go!" one called.

"Stand away, fools!" another yelled. The crowd hushed in anticipation.

The blade sliced down with a metallic swoosh of finality and was secured at the bottom by other workers. John sidled into the crowd of unwashed bodies. The ropes hanging from the top rail tightened as a line of workers prepared to haul.

"What is happening?" John whispered to his neighbor, a stout man who smelled of garlic.

The man's eyes were riveted upon the tightening ropes, but he said, "They are removing Madame la Guillotine to the Place des Grèves."

The huge machine tipped to one side. "Out of the way, there!" a man who must be a foreman called. "Gendarme! Keep those people back." The guillotine was being laid onto a platform set with huge wheels. Sturdy Percherons in harness stood ready to haul it.

The crowd held its breath. The wood creaked in protest. Ropes from the opposite side now tightened as men took the weight of the giant machine and let it down slowly.

"Why?" John asked as he watched all his hopes for tonight tilt toward despair.

"Fanueille is having some woman executed on Sunday. We have not had a woman executed since the emperor took control from the Committee."

Fanueille? A woman? "What woman?" John asked sharply. It couldn't be. It wouldn't.

"Some red-haired foreigner, I heard," John's neighbor to his left said knowingly. He wore an apron that smelled of fish. "A spy for England."

John's stomach dropped to his feet. He did not need to run through all the agents he knew who spied for England. There was no red haired woman among them. "Where . . . where is she being held?" he finally croaked.

"The Conciergerie," the garlic man said as the guillotine was eased onto the wheeled platform. It came to rest with a thud that shook the ground itself. A cheer rose from the crowd.

"They haven't moved Madame for an execution since . . . since the king, I think, when she stood over in the Place de la Révolution. This one must be important." Men began to lever the huge timbers of the guillotine onto the cart, while others pulled on the ropes from the other end.

"I hear they don't want to bring her all the way here from the Conciergerie. She's so beautiful, they're afraid the crowds will rush the tumbrel."

"Then why not move her closer?" the fishmonger asked.

John stayed to hear no more. He whirled into the fringes of the crowd now gathering behind him to follow the progress of the instrument down the Rue du Trône.

Beatrix was locked in the Conciergerie. And Asharti was going to execute her Sunday.

John slid across the Pont au Change toward the Conciergerie on the Île de la Cité. Below him the river Seine rolled in massive unconcern. There were few abroad now. The great clock in the Tour de l'Horloge ahead struck one. God-fearing people were asleep, if not the idle rich. The smell of tar and refuse where the water slapped the quay was almost sickening. Above him, the stone of the Conciergerie loomed, impenetrable. How was he to get in?

Get in he must. He had put away his terrible resolve. He could afford the luxury of killing himself at some later date. For now, he could spare nothing of the adamantine will he needed to free Beatrix. Her centuries-old connection with Asharti had not spared her Asharti's wrath. His mouth was dry, knowing Asharti could be somewhere near. Fear churned in his belly. He had been in dire situations before and his courage had never yet failed him. He prayed it did not fail him now. He could not leave Beatrix to her fate, no matter the cost.

So, dry mouth and queasy belly or no, he turned right down the Quai de l'Horloge. Guards stalked in front of the arched gates. He drifted past. What he could not make out was how Asharti was holding Beatrix. Why did Beatrix not—what did she call it?—translocate? There must be something else to this . . . what was it, magic? Skill?

Whatever it was, he did not understand it. That was obvious. Unless Beatrix was hurt, and that was why she could not draw the darkness. His stomach heaved. What could hurt one who could heal like that? Yet something was wrong. Beatrix was imprisoned. Could it be she was weak because she had given him blood? The breath he sucked in was almost painful with guilt.

All right. She might be imprisoned because she was weak. And that might be his fault. It must only harden his resolve. Now how to find her in the midst of all this stone? The bureaucrats of Bonaparte's regime held sway behind the grand façade that faced the Seine, silent with night above him. Would she be in the dungeons? That's where most prisoners were held. But Marie Antoinette had gone to her death from a cell that looked out on a little courtyard. Rumor had it the queen still walked there. Some said you could hear her screams. Beatrix could be there as well. How could he find her? He turned into Rue de l'Harlay their left onto Quai des Orefevres.

The street was quiet. No guards here. There were some high window arches several stories up, but the windows themselves were hatched with metal bars. Even if he could reach them and use his new strength to wrench out the bars, the endeavor was likely to be noisy.

He glanced down the endless stone wall, and peered again up into the night to where the gray rock disappeared against the black sky. Very well. There was one way inside that would attract no attention at all. He took a breath and blew it out.

He bowed his head. *Companion!* The surge of power along his veins startled him. Was it called so easily? It was almost as though he was speaking to himself. He remembered Beatrix saying that two were one, that he would never be alone again. Perhaps he *was* speaking to himself. He steeled himself against that thought. Beatrix needed him. *Companion, come to me.* A red film oozed over his vision. He tried not to panic. *Bring enough power for the darkness.* The vibration of life inside him grew. He began to throb all over, until the throb was almost pain. Darkness whirled around him until even the stone of the Conciergerie wall was enveloped in black. A keening sounded somewhere as the vibrations shrieked up the scale. It was coming from his throat. A stab of pain thrust through him. It was as though he was turning inside out.

Then it was gone, pain, vibrations, shrieking, everything. Darkness washed from him like a rain shower, until it was a shrinking puddle on the floor . . . of where? He looked around, disoriented. He was in a small, dark room. The smell of blood almost gagged him. Dark amorphous shapes swayed in the darkness around him. Heart in his mouth, he put out a hand to the nearest shape, and met cool slickness. It swung away with the creak of a chain. For a single moment he could not imagine what horror he might be touching. Then he realized. It was a carcass. He was in a meat locker. He took a breath. A meat locker to feed the prisoners, or the bureaucrats, or both. That was all.

Now to find Beatrix. He heard voices somewhere. A slit of dim light at floor level showed him the door. The lock on the outside was no match for his strength. The metal gave a single shriek and yielded. He stopped still and waited, but the voices carried on.

He slipped into a hall with other wooden doors along it. Root cellars, dairy room, a curing room by the smells. At the far end of the hall was an archway. He slid down the corridor, back pressed against the side. He peered through the arch down another corridor. At the end another arch spilled brighter light. The voices beyond were clear now.

"Baking bread in the middle of the night!" a voice like a raven's caw said with disgust. "What is this world coming to?"

Another laughed with a croak that dissolved in coughing. She hacked and then continued. "Who cares? They pay well for us to be here at this hour."

"They better pay, for me to go up there, with all them red eyes glowing from dark corners. Eyes o' the dead, is what I says." This from the one who cackled like a bird.

"It's your turn to go, Leesi." The coughing one sputtered. "I took up water earlier."

An idea began to take shape in John's mind. These women knew where Beatrix was. They were allowed to see her, if only to give her food and water.

"I feel sorry for her, so beautiful and so sad." This from a gentle female voice. "What could she have done that she should have her head cut off for it?"

"Me, I thought we put that nonsense behind us, killin' everything what moved."

"You two are squeamish old maids. Now, how about a nice fish pie for the second remove? At least the minister of justice appreciates a body's effort."

"That pig . . ."

Three women who had access to Beatrix. Two at least were souls hardened to working in a prison. Would they help? But he had always trusted to his luck and used the material at hand. And how else would he find her?

He stepped through the lighted doorway into a huge stone kitchen of the medieval kind, with gaping hearths as tall as a man and wooden tables on which rising loaves sat in neat rows. The room was filled with the smell of yeast and salt, lard, and smoke from the fire.

Three women gasped. One grabbed for a butcher knife. "Who are you?" the stout old woman with the voice like a crow screeched. Her jowls jiggled as she waved the knife.

"How did you get in here?" the young girl echoed, frightened.

"Whoa," John said, palms out, as the third woman, a

grizzled crone with a thin, corded neck and veins like ropes over her knobby hands rose from a table where she had been scratching a list onto rough sheets of paper. "I mean you no harm." He backed against the wall by the door. He knew he looked disheveled and probably wild-eyed, but that might work to his advantage. "I come on an errand of love."

Three sets of brows drew together. "Love," the stout one jeered.

"My betrothed, Beatrix, has red hair."

"Oh," the young one gasped. "Her!"

"You cain't do no good here, boy," the old woman with the pen said, kind under her rough tone. "Her head's in the basket Sunday."

"You'll never get her out, if that's what's in your mind," the stout one rasped.

"Is it so hopeless?" He let his shoulders sag as he examined their faces.

The stout one harrumphed. "They got five o' them creatures guarding her anytime."

Five of Asharti's vampires? Did they keep Beatrix imprisoned with sheer numbers? That's what they meant by red eyes in every corner.

"Ghosts, I says. You cain't fight ghosts." The crone punctuated her point with her quill.

Real hopelessness closed in around his soul. He couldn't afford that. If only he could talk to Beatrix, she might be able to tell him how he could help her. He glanced up at the three faces. Two held pity, one contempt. "Then all I ask is to be able to declare my love for her one last time. Perhaps it will give her strength in her final . . ." He let his eyes fill. It wasn't hard.

"You don't guess they'll just let you walk up to the cell and start recitin' poetry nor nothing, do you?" The stout one chuffed her disdain. As John watched she slipped a floured wooden paddle under two loaves of bread and swung round to slide them into a narrow, arched oven. She stirred the coals underneath with a poker until they emitted angry sparks.

He looked around, desperate. It was an act, but in his belly it was strangely real. "Let me write my love with your paper and quill, and . . . and you can bake it into the bread you take her."

"I guess as how not!" the stout one barked. "You want to get us in trouble?"

But the other two were wavering. It was just the kind of gesture that would appeal to whatever romantic sentiment working in a place like this hadn't ground out of them. "Whoever takes it up, say, 'Pay special attention to the bread, my lady, it was baked with love.' That's all you have to do. She'll know. She'll be discreet. You won't be caught."

"I'll take it up," the young one blurted. "I'll say that."

The old woman tapped her lips with one finger. The stout one turned. "You'll take my turn tonight, Marie? And the next?"

The young girl swallowed and nodded.

"I don't go again until . . ." The stout one counted on her fingers. "I don't go up again at all." A gap-toothed grin spread across her face. "I'll bake your bread." She hustled over to John. "You just sit down, young man, and write out your poetry pretty. Give him your pen, Jeaunty."

"She can write back to me on the reverse."

"You're not baking my quill inside a loaf," the old woman protested.

"I think someone would notice a quill," the young girl offered, hesitant.

John glanced around. A huge bowl of fruit sat on one table, and a bunch of grapes on a battered tin plate along with a wedge of cheese. "Are you taking her that plate?"

The young girl nodded.

"Why don't you give her one of those pomegranates?"

"Ink, like. I see. But what will she write with?" the old crone asked, uncertainly.

"With a fingernail of course . . ." John said as he mended the quill with a paring knife. "And you will show me to the yard below her cell, and she will let it flutter down to me." He looked up at the stone ceiling darkened with soot. "It may be the last I will have of her." God, he hoped this tenuous scheme would work. It all depended upon Beatrix.

The young girl let out a sob.

"My first was hanged," the old crone muttered. "I wisht I had some last word from him. I'll take you to the yard." Then she blew her nose in her apron.

Now, please Lord, let Asharti not be guarding her. He was putting himself in Asharti's way again. And the thought made him tremble.

# Twenty-One

Beatrix huddled in a corner as far from the window to the courtyard as she could get. It was dark now but all day the light through the window had tortured her. True, she had her blue spectacles from the reticule and her cloak. And she crouched in a corner out of the direct sunlight. But the general brightness sent prickles of pain along her skin. That was bearable for the short forays into sunlight sometimes necessary in normal times, but after long hours it became almost insupportable.

Her captors stayed well out of the light, lurking in the darkened cells adjacent or in the corridor. Faceless and silent, they only added to the unreality of her situation. She tried periodically to draw her power, testing the limits of her captors. But even the attempt alerted them and their eyes glowed brighter and her power wouldn't come.

She had been unable to sleep, of course. She had refused all food, not from fear of poison, but from lack of appetite. As her fate became more real and more inevitable, she came to think that perhaps it held an answer to her long struggle against a final journey to Mirso. Asharti was not killing her, but setting her free.

For the first time in centuries she wondered whether there was an afterlife, or whether she believed in some kind of God. They were not the same. Afterlife was an odd concept to one who might well be immortal. The last time she had this conversation with herself, she concluded that no one could know whether there was a God, or an afterlife, so one could only live as if there was. She believed one should do good if one could, or at least not do evil. She did not kill anymore. She left fond or exciting memories in return for the blood she took. She made sure those influences that transformed men into the best they could be, art and music and literature, flourished where her money or her influence could sustain them. She indulged in bouts of charity, though the orphanages and hospitals hardly scratched the surface of misery in the world.

Should she have gone to Mirso earlier? Was a life of contemplation more worthy than a life lived in the world? Perhaps the world was right, and God, if He existed, could never love a vampire. She did not feel a spawn of Satan, though she certainly sympathized with him. The world hated him too much for all that hatred to be earned.

In the end, her carousel of thought was as useless as ever. One muddled along doing the best one could until it ended. It was about to end for her. Was there not relief in that? She had been rejected by her mother. Her father had not stayed to see her born. Stephan had rejected her. John thought her a monster. Abandonment so often must mean she was worthless. Maybe that's what the memories had been trying to tell her. Death had been knocking, and only the Companion had barred the door. Asharti would let it bar the door no longer.

She hoped John escaped. Perhaps he would do better with eternal life than she had. He did not see the Companion as a gift. But perhaps he would, and perhaps he would use his power to change the world for the better.

A noise in the corridor. It was one of the women with the food she would not touch. She could feel their fear. The guards stepped back into the darkness.

Beatrix glanced up. It was the youngest, holding a trembling lamp high, and glancing about her fearfully. She pushed the metal plate through the narrow slot at the base of the bars. It slithered across the stone.

"Here, my lady." Her voice quavered, then steadied. "Pay special attention to this one. The bread was made with love." The girl nodded with a piercing stare then whirled and ran.

Made with love? Beatrix laid her head back against the wall, exhaustion washing over her. Made with love! Those women did not love her. No one loved her.

She glanced at the bread. A thread of curiosity wound through her. It couldn't be. Still she sat up. The dented metal dish had a stubby loaf, a wedge of cheese, and . . . a pomegranate on it. A little flutter in her middle pushed her to her feet. Not the old trick with the pomegranate . . . She took a breath to steady herself. She collected the plate and sat back on her stone bench, glancing furtively about. One of her silent jailors leaned against the opposite wall in the corridor, combing a very fine set of mustachios. His eyes were red but he paid no attention to her.

She broke the bread and heard the crackle of the paper. She slipped it out and hid it in the folds of her dress, then went on calmly eating bread and cheese while her heart banged. She broke open the pomegranate, tested a pit with her nail, and saw the bloodred juice dye her bread. The guard changed. Red eyes were replaced with red eyes. The new one stood a little to the side. She scooted over and opened the paper on the bench beside her thigh, where he couldn't see.

*Tell me how I can help you escape, my love. I am
yours to command. Drop your instructions into
the yard.*

*John*

The first tears since she was captured dripped on the
sheet. He may not have forgiven her for making him, but
he had not abandoned her. That touched her and frightened her. She was frightened for him. There was no helping her. He must away.

She popped a pomegranate pip into her mouth. With
her thumb, she popped another, and scratched her nail
upon the paper. It took a long time to write her answer.
When she was done, she twisted the paper into a tight
screw and went to stand at the barred window, her reticule
hanging on her wrist. Immediately, he stepped out from
under the single tree in the tiny yard below. Her heart
stuttered. Too much risk! How dare he come here? His
dear face, staring up at her, handsome and worried, made
her tremble inside as Asharti and the vampire guards had
not. She leaned her head against the bars and dropped her
screw of paper, followed by her reticule.

She saw him glance around himself, pick them up and
step back under the tree. She knew what he would be
reading, writ in bright red juice with her thumbnail.

*Nothing to do. All for the best. Take this. Be safe
in England.*

*Beatrix*

He looked up and shook his head, his expression
frightened.

She smiled, tenderly. Did he care for her? "My love."
That's what the note said. She would take solace in that.

She shook her head, deliberately, then stretched her hand out the bars, once, in salute. And then she turned from the window and returned to sit in her corner. She mustn't let Asharti's tools see her sob. She clasped her cloak around her and bit back the sound.

John watched Beatrix disappear from the window, frantic. Nothing? Nothing to be done? He would not believe it. He would not go from here until she told him what to do to get her out. He picked up the reticule and sheltered under the courtyard tree again. But after almost an hour of willing her to come back to the window with the real note he began to despair. He realized he still clutched the delicate bead reticule she had dropped to him. Perhaps there was another note inside. He forced himself to pull it open gently, lest his newfound strength rip it. Inside he found notes against a bank in Paris for what amounted to a fortune. What did he care for money? There were two rolls of gold louis as well and a pair of spectacles made of some glass so dark as to be almost black. He drew his brows together. She meant him to use the money to leave France. He clutched the tiny bag with enough force that his nails dug into the palm of his hand. He could smell the blood he raised.

Above him, he heard an all-too-familiar voice. An involuntary shudder shook him.

"Well, my sister, how did you like your first full day in a sunny cell?"

"I've had better accommodations." Beatrix's voice was defiant. He loved her for that.

"We shall have to take that cloak from you. Ah, you have been crying . . . how sad. And you told me you were resigned. I see something changed your mind."

Silence. Then Asharti came to the window, eyes full red. John slipped behind the trunk of the tree. He could see the hateful visage clearly in the darkness. "I feel a vibration out there," Asharti said as she surveyed the courtyard.

He had to go. Capture now would be disaster for Beatrix. He took a breath. *Companion, come to me. And quickly.*

The darkness whirled up around him. He imagined the street underneath the clock tower. The pain cycled up rapidly this time to some kind of a rending screech, and he staggered against a lamppost on the Quai de l'Horloge, just as the great clock struck four. The river and the cobbled street wavered once and stabilized. Pain subsided. He took off at a run for the Pont Neuf.

He could have run forever, he felt so strong, but he did not know where to run. Once across the Seine he stopped beside what used to be the church of St. Jacques la Boucherie. That a butcher's guild could build so beautiful a church always seemed an affirmation of the common man. It was the common man, however, who had pulled it down during the Revolution. Now only the flamboyantly Gothic tower was left. He gazed up at it, panting, desolated. Perhaps a republic could not bear something uncommon. Still, the tower stood as a courageous outpost of flamboyance.

Beatrix was going to be killed and there was nothing he could do about it. He, strong as he felt, was not strong enough to break Asharti's hold. He wanted to beat his breast and scream that the world dared not lose something so precious and flamboyant as Beatrix.

But what world did he mean? The daylight world of millions? The human world? That was not his world any longer. He stilled himself, looking up at that lonely tower. He needed someone stronger than Asharti. Someone who would come to save Beatrix from her.

Stephan Sincai.

Beatrix said Sincai could stop Asharti if he would. And did he not bear some responsibility for her current reign of terror? He had nurtured both of them. He must have known what Asharti was. How could a mentor *not* have known? Beatrix still loved him. Sincai was of her kind. He had taught her to be what she was, taught her to love.

Who else would she love? He steeled his heart against the pang that caused. What mattered was Beatrix. If she loved this Sincai, then he might come to rescue her.

His brain began to dart this way and that. Sincai was in Amsterdam. Three hundred and fifty miles, even four hundred, and four hundred back. Beatrix was going to be executed on Sunday. It was Wednesday, nearly dawn. The roads were good. Riding day and night, changing horses every twenty-five or thirty miles . . . it was just doable. The best horses only. That would be an expensive proposition. But between his huitième in piquet and the notes in Beatrix's reticule, he was well provided. Could someone ride day and night for that long? Perhaps someone as strong as he was could. He would find out.

Ah, but riding day and night. How was that to be? He could not even look out a window. If he traveled at night only, he would never make it back in time. Not fair! He could not lose her only chance. Could he send a message? But what if Sincai would not come? John must be there in person. He would not *let* the brute refuse. It must be John. And he must ride in daylight as well as at night. He looked down at the reticule he still held in his hand, the last he had of Beatrix. Darkened glass spectacles . . . Very well. He swallowed. Gloves. A cloak with a hood he could bring up over his head. Muffle the lower part of his face.

He whirled and set off at a run. There was a livery at the Place Gervais.

Beatrix was growing fuddled. Long days in the light dressed only in her fine linen night shift and snatched sleep in the darkness were taking their toll. The brightness in the cell hurt her eyes, and sent shooting needles against her skin. She needed blood. She had drained herself for John, and now with Asharti allowing no feeding, she was weak and in pain.

She spent the days huddled on the floor in the corner,

holding her hands over her eyes. She tried to think about John wending his way to safety, to take her mind off her hungry Companion that scratched insistently at her veins, and the pain of the light. Where was he now? Le Havre? Could he get a packet immediately for Dover or Portsmouth with some smuggler? Would he have to wait? Asharti might send her vampires to Le Havre. She hoped he had been wise enough to head north to Calais and cross from there . . .

He would wear the blue spectacles. He would cover himself—he was resourceful. The Companion would insist on feeding, and sooner or later he would not refuse. She wished she could be there to make his way easier, but she could not. He would manage.

He had come to try to free her. She smiled to think of it. Fortunes had been thrown at her feet, duels fought, crowns abdicated, armies engaged to win her. But never had someone who knew what she was sacrificed so much for her. He had come in spite of how afraid he must be of Asharti. She knew what that had cost him. She would take the gift of his sacrifice to her grave. Still, it made her uneasy. How could someone like her deserve that commitment?

In some ways she was sorry for his gift. She had come to welcome the guillotine—a solution more final even than Mirso Monastery. But now, to have that gift, so tantalizing, right when there was no hope of finding out just what he meant by it, seemed a final cruelty.

A clatter at the door said her guards were changing. They could apparently keep up their concentration for only two hours at a time. The next round shuffled in to take their posts, ramping up their Companions' power before the old crew let theirs slide down.

Beatrix glanced away, sighing. Then she turned back. Was it . . . ? "Jerry!"

The glow faded in his eyes and he looked shamefaced. "Countess," he muttered.

"Why did you return to her?" Beatrix breathed.

"And where else was I to go?" he asked, peevish. "Where else is there for one like me?"

"You could have gone back to England . . ."

"Didn't have no money."

Beatrix rolled her eyes. "My God, man! We can always get money!"

Jerry lifted his chin. "Maybe you can, Countess. Besides, I have mates here, coves what understands a body's needs."

Beatrix glanced to the other vampires, who had drifted to their posts. "I know. It's nice to have someone you know nearby. I'm glad you're here."

"Don't start your honeyed words, Countess. I know what side my bread is buttered on. I'm here to guard you same as them, and she don't want us talkin' to you."

His eyes went red. He stepped back into the shadows.

"Jerry . . . Jerry, listen to me. You don't have to be here. I'll show you how to get money . . ." But she had lost him, and the others were listening.

She took a breath. "You've made a mistake, Jerry, but it's not past rectifying." Then she sat on her stone bench and tried to slow her pulse. John. She would think of John.

John had been riding for two days without sleep, stopping only to wolf a sandwich he did not care to eat, or to change horses. He had been through nine horses. Daylight was the worst. It sapped his strength. The spectacles allowed him to avoid being blinded if he squinted, but everything was surrounded by a corona of light. He had wrapped a knitted comforter about his lower face and over his nose like some highwayman even in the heat of June, but if his hood slipped back he could feel the upper half of his face burn immediately. And always there was the needle-sharp prickling of his skin, even under his clothing.

The first night was one of unremitting rain. Splashed

with mud and wet to the skin, he had to go more slowly to avoid slipping in the heavy going of a rutted road. It was maddening.

Everywhere he went he engendered fear, looking so much like a Spanish bandito and muffled head to foot. He always muttered something about a disease, and that, coupled with monetary largesse, bought a semblance of service if not good will.

He unwound his comforter and took off his cloak at sunset on the outskirts of Amsterdam. The beast he rode was all but dead, and he was little better. He picked his way slowly through the old streets and along the canals. Herengracht had been dug in the seventeenth century. Called the "gentlemen's canal," the largest and most elaborate houses were built along it. He had been thinking about how to find Stephan Sincai most quickly. Beatrix said she had lived at number 380. He had a hunch that Sincai was not as immune to Beatrix as she believed. John decided to start with number 380 and see just how sentimental Stephan Sincai was.

John plodded along the narrow street that lined the Herengracht. The canals smelled of fecund green. Number 380 was an ornate copy of a Loire chateau in solid Dutch stone. Reclining figures embellished its main gable and the bay window was surrounded by cherubs, acanthus leaves, and mythical monsters. How appropriate. When he dismounted, his knees gave out under him. He held to the stirrup leathers until his head stopped swimming. Then he dragged himself up the five steps to the portico and rapped with the knocker, shaped like a golden bat, wings outspread. He might have the right house. And Sincai had a streak of whimsy in him.

The dour servant dressed in green livery who opened the door frowned down at him. "Tradesmen to the back door," he said in high Dutch. He was about to close the door, when he added, "No beggars allowed."

John realized he was bareheaded, wearing the same ill-fitting coat he had won at piquet, covered with the dust and mud of three countries and without a bath since Beatrix had wiped the sweat from his body in a tenement in the Marais.

He pushed open the door with a strength the old servant could never match. "I am here to see Stephan Sincai," he said, mustering his best Dutch. It might not match his French, but it was serviceable. He was surprised to find his voice was hardly more than a croak. How long since he had taken water?

"Mijanheer Sincai does not entertain anyone, let alone riffraff or down-on-their-luck tradesmen. Be off with you."

Again the door began to close. But now John knew his hunch was right.

"Tell him I come for Beatrix Lisse. He will see me. He must." John tried not to let his desperation show. That would not encourage the old servant to let him in.

"Go away, or I will call a watchman," the old man warned, his voice rising. "Mijanheer Sincai will give you no alms. Get to a workhouse!"

"Let the man in, Mechlin," a deep voice sounded from somewhere inside.

Instantly, the servant's face went blank. "Yes, Mijanheer Sincai."

John stepped past him into a foyer bathed in light from a chandelier with a thousand crystals. The floor was laid in black and white marble squares. An elegant staircase curved up on the right to the first floor above. There, leaning on the rail, was a man clad elegantly in a black coat that fitted his broad shoulders exactly, a frothing neck cloth intricately tied, and close-fitting knee breeches. He was dressed for the most formal occasion or for another time. A diamond winked in the folds of his cravat and a gold signet with a cabochon ruby weighed on his right hand. His hair was dark and worn long about his shoulders, his cheekbones imposing, his lips full, though at the moment he pressed them together most severely. It was his eyes that captured your attention, though. They were dark pools of . . . emptiness. You could not call it sorrow. They held everything and nothing.

They stood looking at each other. Vibrations showered down on John. They were almost a curtain of solid . . . energy. John closed his mouth forcibly. He had a sense of incredible power.

John took a breath, swallowed, and nodded. "Thank you."

"Take the man's cloak and gloves, Mechlin."

John put them into the old man's arms, noting the distaste with which he took them.

"And send some brandy to the library?" Sincai motioned John up the stairs.

John went over what he had been rehearsing in his mind for two nights and days. He trudged up the stairs, trying to muster his wits. Sincai motioned to a chair by the fire, silently.

"I . . . would not accost you without introduction except under extreme provocation," John began, but he did not sit. "I dared not stay my importunity even until you fulfilled your social obligation tonight. Time is of the essence."

"You mistake. I do not go out these days, but I like to dress for dinner." Sincai's voice came from deep in his chest cavity, sonorous. The weight of ages hung on each syllable. He had a languor about him John found vaguely familiar. Before he could say more, brandy was delivered on a tray by a suddenly very correct Mechlin. Sincai poured from the cut-glass decanter as Mechlin bowed himself out. He handed the glass to John. "From your accent you might be more comfortable speaking French, or . . ." Here he paused, as if listening. "English?"

John was disconcerted. The man had a good ear. He realized he had not even introduced himself "English, if it is my choice. I am John Staunton, Earl of Langley." There was no point in subterfuge. He could not afford any perception of insincerity.

"Perhaps," Sincai said in perfect English, "we should begin with you telling me why I should not wrench your head from your body in the next minute."

John blinked. Whatever he had expected it was not this. "Because then you would not know why I came or how I know of you, or what Beatrix Lisse has to do with any of this."

"I know it must be Bea who made you. I thought she had more self-control."

"How did you know I was made?" he could not help but ask.

"Your vibrations are slow—those of one quite young. It is impossible to hide. I would guess . . . days . . . a week at most. Now I ask again, why should I not kill you?"

John bowed his head, cursing himself. Of course this man would hate him for being one of the made after his failure with Asharti. Sincai might despise Beatrix for making him. Would he refuse to help her? John felt himself in deep water. All he had been thinking about was the overwhelming need to get here and to save Beatrix. He had not realized there would be such a formidable adversary between him and his goal. This man was filled with distrust. He had retreated from the world. What was in John's way here? The languor! It was a much more pronounced version of the disinterest that had emanated from Beatrix when he first met her. John gathered himself. He wouldn't answer Sincai's question. Not directly. "Do not blame Beatrix. We were both . . . wounded. Her blood mingled with mine. She did not make me willingly."

"We all have choices. She could have let you die."

"Perhaps she is tenderhearted."

"Bea?" Sincai snorted.

"You do not know her as well as you think," John

observed. Sincai examined him in surprise. Good. Keep the old sinner off balance. Perhaps that would break through his lethargy.

"Did Bea send you here?" Sincai snapped.

"In a way. She said you were the only one who could call Asharti to heel."

"Why do you bring this tale of woe to my door? I have no interest in either of them anymore." Sincai downed his brandy and poured another.

*You lie,* thought John. *I can feel your agitation.* Now he could play his trump card. "Because Asharti has Beatrix imprisoned and means to have her guillotined on Sunday."

Sincai paused, his expression frozen, glass halfway to his lips. Then he tossed off the brandy. "Nonsense. They were peas in a pod, a very twisted pod. I was right in that at least."

"You mean because made and born are the same?" He stared at Sincai defiantly. "You hurt her when she found out she was part of some experiment."

"I know." The eyes did not show emotion. He blinked once. "But I'm sure she came to properly hate me, as did Asharti. They left me easily enough, and spurned my . . . care for them."

"I know Beatrix followed Asharti away from you, in her pain. But they are not the same."

"I believe I know them better than you," Sincai said bitterly, waving a dismissive hand.

"I have just spent a month as Asharti's . . . guest. I have known Beatrix for the last three. How long has it been since you have been in contact with either one of them?" He waited for that to sink in. "You do not know what Asharti has become, or what she means to do."

Sincai lost all pretense of composure. His eyes snapped to red, then back to brown-black pools. He set the glass down. Tension vibrated in the room. Sincai took a breath, and the vibrations scaled back a notch. His expression flashed something that might have been regret, then hardened, as though he steeled himself. "Very well. Tell me what Asharti has become."

John swallowed, suddenly tongue-tied. Could he tell this man, or this more-than-man about Asharti? He started as the glass shattered in his grip and brandy spilled upon the Turkey carpet. His palm was deeply lacerated. The seeping blood seemed a metaphor for what Sincai was asking him to do. As John stared the cut began to close. He clenched his hand, not wanting to see the healing, clear evidence of his changed state. He looked away, breathing hard.

"Sit." It was a curt command. John managed to glance up. For the second time tonight, Sincai motioned him to the chair. John mastered himself. This was what was required of him. He must spill his soul and somehow tell Sincai about Asharti. John sat. Sincai turned to pour another brandy. John stole a glance at his palm. The cut turned to a pink line then disappeared entirely.

Sincai held out the brandy sternly. John pressed his lips together and took the glass. Now it was his turn to gulp what he hoped was liquid courage. He looked up with as much steadiness as he could muster. "She plots to control Bonaparte, and replace him or rule through him once he rules all Europe. She is making vampires. Many vampires. She wants to start a world where humans are raised for slavery and as a food supply, and she rules." He swallowed hard. "I suppose you might think that kind of world desirable."

"Of course I wouldn't," Sincai snapped. "Order would be lost. So many made vampires would make others. There would be no respect for the Rules. Soon there would be too many and not enough blood. The balance would be shattered. I might have objected once to killing them if they were made accidentally, but I did not want them made at the drop of a hat."

John nodded. What Sincai didn't hate was the idea of human cattle. What could John expect? "Asharti made wounds on my body that became infected with Beatrix's blood."

Sincai waited.

"I came to kill Asharti, not knowing what she was." John snorted a laugh that broke in the middle. His voice lowered to a murmur. "She has . . . ways of extracting information and . . . and making one do . . . other things, as well." John looked up, plastering defiance over his shame. "I betrayed my country to her, and myself."

"And how did Bea's blood get into your wounds?" Sincai's voice softened to a rumble.

John sipped convulsively from the glass Sincai refilled. The room smelled of spilled brandy. Shards of glass still winked in the light of the chandelier. "Beatrix followed me to France when she discovered my mission. Foolish of her. Asharti's vampires wounded her. She . . ." Here he swallowed hard. "She held me while she transported us both out of Asharti's reach."

"I see." Sincai backed up to the fire, a pensive look on his face. "In short, she saved you. And now you want to return the favor."

John stood. All the urgency of his mission washed over him, wiping out the shame he felt over succumbing to Asharti. "Asharti has a phalanx of newly made vampires holding Beatrix. You are strong enough to best them. We have just enough time to reach Paris before Sunday."

Sincai threw back the last of the brandy. "I do not go out. I can save no one," he rasped.

"You are responsible!" John accused. "You know what Asharti is, and yet you have done nothing. You *must* save Beatrix." He could feel the man's vibrations in the air. Sincai was stronger by thousands of years than he was. John could not force him to do anything.

"Responsibility? Oh, yes." Sincai's tone held an infinite

sadness. "I am responsible for both of them, feral kittens that they are. They are both killers. Yet I did not kill them. I should have. Just as I should kill you."

John chose to ignore the threat to his own person. "Beatrix is not a killer. She left Asharti. She lives a difficult life as best she can. She is world-weary almost unto death, like you are. She thinks Asharti killing her is for the best. But she has much to live for if she only gets the chance."

"She *was* born, not made," Sincai mused. "Perhaps Rubius is right. There is a difference."

"Bloody hell! You have been wrong on every count," John swore. The man had to be startled out of his complacence or he would never go after Beatrix. "Born or made, people are individuals. We play the hand we are dealt. Beatrix may have been led astray by Asharti, but she was young. She played her hand. She righted herself and she tries to go on. Asharti did not right herself, not because she was made, but because she was always wrong inside." He drew himself up. "Now it is your turn to right yourself, Sincai."

"You see the world so simply, you who have lived but a single lifetime." Sincai's eyes filled. "I cannot kill either of them."

"And yet you will let Asharti kill Beatrix?" John almost shouted. "What kind of a man are you? Beatrix loved you! I know she did. She still loves you!"

Sincai looked stunned for a moment. Then he examined John's face and finally looked down into his glass. He swirled the rich amber liquid lazily. "Oh, I think not. Not anymore."

John was growing desperate. "Then don't kill Asharti. Just use your strength to get Beatrix away from her. Bestir yourself, for God's sake, on behalf of one you brought out of barbarity, one who loved you." John drew himself up. "You can kill me after I have seen Beatrix to safety. Rid the world of a made vampire. According to her, that may be the only way I can die. You would be doing me a favor, as well as the world at large."

"I wonder." Sincai looked pensive again.

John clenched his teeth around the impulse to punch the man in the jaw. "How easy to wonder! Harder to act." He glanced around the elegant room wildly. "If it is me that bothers you, give me your word you will save her and kill me now. I'll tell you where she is . . . where to go . . ." He trailed off. Sincai had gotten a faraway, empty look in his eyes. What leverage did he have to make this man . . . *move* from this house this minute and go after Beatrix? John followed Sincai's gaze and turned to see what he was staring at. He got a shock, indeed. There was a tiny portrait, no more than a foot square, of a woman who was unmistakably Beatrix, done in the flat style typical of Byzantine painting. She wore a red dress with stylized folds and a square neckline. Around her head was a gilt halo. Beatrix as a saint, or the Madonna.

"A besotted artist painted that in thirteen twelve. Religious art was the only kind allowed back then. I made him a rich man." Sincai's voice held more sadness than John had ever heard.

John held his breath. The man loved her. Would that not be enough to counteract the torpor that seemed to shimmer around him?

Slowly, Sincai set his glass and the decanter upon a tiny table. "Sunday did you say?"

John nodded.

Sincai rose and strode to the door. "Then there is not a moment to lose." Energy spilled over the room in almost painful abundance. "Can you keep up? If not, stay here and await my return."

John's Companion charged up through his veins as relief sluiced over him. "I'll keep up."

# Twenty-Two

Sincai showered Mechlin with orders. Two horses called for by name, sandwiches ordered to take with them, and his valet was to provide John with soap and hot water and a change of clothing. At that, John protested.

"I'll not ride with a scarecrow," Sincai said with finality, "and one who smells into the bargain. It will take a few minutes to prepare our departure."

John opened his mouth and shut it. He was alive. Sincai was going to save Beatrix. And truth be told, he was exhausted. Perhaps ten minutes to wipe his body with a steaming towel would help keep his senses about him. The journey back would be long. "As you wish."

An austere and disapproving gentleman's gentleman led John up one flight to a luxurious bedroom done in rich browns and gold. A fire crackled in a grate. A hip bath stood next to the hearth. In trooped a whole line of servants, men, girls, and boys, each carrying a pail of steaming water. John's jaw dropped. "When . . . how did you . . . ?"

The servants plashed their buckets into the bath. "Mijanheer Sincai likes to have water ready whenever he may call for a bath," the valet announced, eyeing John sharply. "Yes. I think so." He inclined his head an inch only. "I shall return with suitable clothing."

The last servant was a girl in a mobcap and white apron. She ducked her head and laid soap and two large towels near the bath. She was still closing the door when John hastily stripped off his clothes. The bath was hot enough to send shivers up his spine. He soaped and scrubbed ruthlessly, aiming for speed, ducked and washed the dirt of travel from his hair. He stood, dripping, but feeling somewhat more alive.

A knock at the door was followed immediately by Sincai, dressed for travel. In one hand he carried gleaming Hessian boots, a pile of clothing over his arm, and in the other a silver-chased goblet. John could smell the blood in it. Sincai glanced briefly at John, laid the clothing on the bed, and set the goblet on the night table. John hastily stepped from the bath, coloring, and turned his back on Sincai. His heart throbbed in his chest and a dreadful neediness crawled up his veins. He could hardly get his breath. Sincai brought him blood! Revulsion made his stomach turn. *Think, man!* He shook his head. *Do you imagine you can save her in the state you're in? Very well, then,* he answered himself. *Blood it shall be.*

"Do I delay you?" John's voice barely shook. He reached for the towel and dried himself brusquely. Looking down, he realized Sincai had seen his scars front and back, even those Asharti made on his groin and his buttocks. He pushed down the desire to stride to the table and gulp the contents of the goblet, and wrapped the towel around his waist.

"No, my groom is just bringing the horses round from the mews. You have time."

John turned. Sincai sat on the bed, next to the clothes. The man's eyes moved slowly over his body. John lifted his chin, trying not to hear the call of the goblet. "The scars are not from Beatrix, if that is what you're wondering. They belong to Asharti," he said stiffly. "These were already healed when I was infected."

"You seem to have quite a variety of scars, actually," Sincai remarked, throwing him the freshly ironed shirt. It smelled of the soap used to wash it. John pulled it over his head.

"I'm familiar with various kinds of steel." John reached for the trousers, hand shaking. He did not mention the lash. Sincai would have seen those scars as well.

"It had occurred to me that you might be drawing me into some sort of trap. Those two cannot have any love for me."

Was the man backing out? John cast about. Anything he said proved Sincai's point if looked at through another lens. He stared at the floor, trying to think in spite of the itching in his veins. The screw of paper he had carried next to his heart in the inside pocket of the snuff-colored coat lay on the carpet. He had unfolded that little screw of paper and read it at every stop for water or food, however brief. He leaned to pick it up and tossed it to Sincai.

Stephen Sincai looked at the screw of paper warily, then smoothed its worn folds and read. "It might not be her hand," he whispered, doubt turning his mouth down and drawing his brows together. "I can't remember."

"You would not recognize it. It was written in pomegranate juice with her fingernail. Asharti did not care to loan her a quill."

Sincai took a breath. He looked up at John, inclined his head and rose. "Ring the bell if you can't get into the coat. I used to wear it hunting, when I hunted, so it fits me a little loosely. Talmere thought you might get those shoulders of yours into it." At the door, he turned. "You know, if my Companion was as hungry as yours is I would have downed that goblet the instant it was set upon the table. Are you perhaps trying to resist your needs? If so, you're a fool. You were weak when Bea made you and you're only a few days out from the rejection sickness. You may be a liability."

"You have my permission to leave me if I can't keep up," John said, his voice tight.

"I don't need your permission," Sincai reminded softly.

John pulled on the trousers over the smalls and stood. "Then we understand each other."

"Drink my small offering," Sincai drawled. "You'll find it beneficial."

John pulled on the boots, refusing to look at the goblet. "And what innocent suffered to produce it?"

The ghost of a smile drifted across Sincai's lips. "Oh, surely not innocent. It's my blood."

John looked up sharply. "Why?"

Sincai shrugged. John could not read his eyes. "Beatrix may have use of you. The blood of one as old as I will give you strength," he said as he slipped into the corridor. The door closed.

John stared at the goblet. Sincai's blood. He would give that to John? He must truly still love Beatrix. John sighed. He had to drink the stuff, of course. That was the new reality. And what would he not do for Beatrix? He must be strong for her. Closing his eyes, he took a breath, preparing for the gagging ordeal ahead. No use delaying. He strode to the tiny table and clutched the goblet. The vibrations in his core ramped up until they seemed a kind of song. His blood was singing at him, urging him to drink. His chest heaved as he raised the heavy silver cup with a hunting scene of stags and slavering dogs. Where had he seen that tableau before? The scent of blood filled his nostrils. The song inside became an operatic chorus. He was trembling as he brought the goblet to his lips. *Let me not vomit it up,* he thought. He gulped the thick liquid. Copper! Viscous life! It coursed down his throat. He gulped convulsively. Far from vomiting, he wanted to keep drinking forever. The song was now a thousand voices strong, making him feel so alive he thought he would burst.

Then the blood was gone. He licked the rim of the goblet, and set it down. His hand no longer shook. The song died away, but it was not quite gone. It had turned into a hum that made his center vibrate with life. He breathed. The feel of air in his lungs tasted like cool water to a parched man. He turned into the room. There was the bath, steam still faintly rising from it. The fire cackled and flapped in coruscating colors. The lamps cast a soft glow over the reds of the draperies and bed hangings. God, but he loved the color red!

He felt alive, so damned alive! "Damned" might be the prescient word. He might be damned. But he was strong. And he was going to save Beatrix.

He ran down the stairs to the foyer, grabbed the cloak Mechlin handed him, and pushed out the door into the night of the tree-lined canal. Sincai was just swinging up onto a black gelding, seventeen hands if he was an inch. A groom held a prancing, big-boned chestnut mare.

"Sandwiches in the saddlebags," a generously proportioned woman in a mobcap called from the doorway in Dutch. "And four bottles of hock."

John swung up on the spirited mare. She was more than up to his weight. Leave it to a man like Sincai to have two such fine pieces of horseflesh in his stable.

"Pick the horses up at the Gronigen Inn in Rotterdam," Sincai shouted to his groom.

They were off. A light rain began to fall. The horses were a handful in the streets of Amsterdam as they made their way across the concentric rings of the canals. John hunched his shoulders against the drizzle, glad Sincai knew the city. It would be a long way to Paris. The glow inside John said that he might be strong enough to make it now. And if he was cursed he was glad. He might lose Beatrix to Sincai. In fact, he was sure of it. But she had a chance to live.

Beatrix sat in the twilight, trembling. The day had been long. The evening brought no comfort, though. For that was when Asharti came to gloat. Even as Beatrix thought about her, her throaty laugh could be heard in the corridor. Beatrix's stomach knotted in anticipation.

"Well, my little conspirator, Friday evening. Only two nights left." Asharti spoke in the old language, the language of Transylvania in the eleventh century. She was dressed for the evening in an empire-style gown of cream brocade with large figured stripes worked in gilt thread. The gold and diamonds at her breast were worth a fortune. Her dark hair was swept up and pulled severely off her face, accentuating her cheekbones and her almond eyes.

Beatrix was silent. She would not give her enemy the satisfaction of a reply.

Asharti smiled slyly. "You have grown so silent. There were times when all you wanted to do was talk, talk about what we could do with the world at our feet, plan utopias and new societies." She seemed to have a thought. "Now it is I who plan for the world's future, not you."

Beatrix looked up at her with tired eyes. Her clothes were dirty. She was past the need to eat, but she could no longer stand without wavering. So she sat, staring dumbly at her adversary.

"Ramon tells me you accept your fate. You are ready to die."

"How does Ramon know anything?" Beatrix was prodded into speaking.

"You talk in your sleep." Asharti smiled. It was not an attractive smile. "You know your problem?" Asharti remarked, pacing back and forth in front of the bars. "You simply aren't interested in life anymore. You have no desire. You don't *hunger* for anything." She stopped and turned. "I want everything. It keeps me interested in life. It keeps me strong."

"If you think that makes you superior, you're wrong," she muttered.

"So it's true!" Asharti practically crowed. "Why, I'll wager you were on the brink of retiring to Mirso."

Beatrix was thankful she was probably too pale and worn to flush. She wanted more than anything to wipe that smirk off Asharti's face. "On the contrary, I was involved in solving a little problem that *interested* me."

Asharti raised her brows. "Oh. You mean you were trailing your Englishman here to France." She chuckled. "Oh, my. We were interested in a man, and that gave us purpose in life. How small of you."

"Believing in love isn't small." Her own voice sounded small in her ears as she said it.

"It is the smallest, dear sister, the smallest thing to believe in at all."

"Only if you've never been in love." There.

"I'll wager you've been in love a thousand times," Asharti sneered. "That would be just like you. Naïve."

Beatrix looked up at that proud, sneering face, and everything came clear. "No," she said slowly. "I have not been in love since Stephan. I lost the courage for it." Asharti started to interrupt and Beatrix held up a hand. Something in her manner or her face must have made Asharti pause. "No, no, I have just realized this. You are right. It *is* naïve to believe in love after you have seen all the permutations of love gone wrong, love marred by death, love withered with age, love sapped of vitality by petty irritations or boredom. Even if I told myself it was not for me, still I saw it all in others. But there is courage in that kind of naïveté. I . . . I think it may be second innocence." She stared up at Asharti, not seeing her, but seeing William Blake's childlike drawings of stars and suns and animals, hearing his wonder at the symmetry of tigers.

Asharti looked taken aback. Then her eyes flashed hatred, transforming her features into a mask that bore almost no resemblance to the young woman Beatrix had known seven hundred years ago. "Well, you'll have to find another lover. But I forgot—you'll have no time. I suppose I understand your fascination. The Englishman is skilled and well built. Last night I had him licking me until I shrieked. And he struggles so against the compulsion. Most satisfying."

Beatrix fought not to fling herself against the bars. "You don't have him."

"I've had him for two days," she spat. "I wanted to wait to tell you until you were there on the platform, with the blade gleaming above you. I wanted you to see him, naked, perhaps, or wearing only a cloth about his loins, kneeling beside me under the basket. How delicious your rage and your defeat would have been." She spoke with relish and total conviction. She did have John! "His blood is even sweeter flooded with the Companion. I'll have to kill him when his strength becomes a problem, but still, compelling another vampire is even more delightful than when he was merely human. And he heals now, so I can do what I wish to him."

Beatrix felt her heart flutter against her rib cage. The cell wavered. "Bitch," she breathed.

Asharti laughed. "Well, I'll leave you with that thought. I must to the Maison Marillac. The emperor awaits. And then home, to a night of sweet sexual attention and a little blood from an English earl. He has such a fine cock, and it stands to attention at the slightest encouragement."

Beatrix lunged at the bars and hung there, watching Asharti's retreating form.

"Love," Asharti chuckled, shaking her head as she disappeared.

Three of the vampires guarding Beatrix surged forward. Red power washed over her.

*John,* she thought. *God help you, for I cannot.*

The run south was a silent affair. The two men spoke only to point out a place to change horses, or to give orders for food or ale. Though the horrible feast had given him strength, still John grew a little dazed with the passing miles. At one point he looked around himself and did not recognize a single landmark. "Sincai," he called hoarsely to the man cantering ahead of him.

The chestnut Sincai was now riding broke to a trot, and John's gray gelding came up with them. "Is this the way to Paris?" The rain had stopped and the night was bright; the three-quarter moon peeked through shredded clouds as it set. Sincai could not have gotten lost. Sincai pulled up his horse and turned to face John.

"We go through Ghent, around Brussels. I want to come into Paris by way of Reims."

"That is . . . thirty miles out of our way, fifty!" Panic rose in John's breast. They had lost time, and needed to get back on the main road . . . "For God's sake, man, she's going to be executed Sunday night. It's nearly dawn on Saturday. What are you thinking?"

"I'm thinking I might not be enough."

John stilled. Not enough?

"You said many. How many vampires are there?"

"I don't know." John ran his hand through his hair. His gelding sidled nervously. "Only two or three at Chantilly. They could have joined Asharti in Paris, though. The cooks saw five at a time guarding Beatrix. They must change out."

"So there could be as many as a score."

"Yes."

"Then I might not be enough. And you are new and exhausted, in spite of my blood. So, we must take time to go to Reims." He turned his horse's head southwest again, toward Brussels. The horses were blowing. Sincai asked only for a trot.

"What is in Reims?" John asked, following suit.

"Khalenberg, I hope. He controls the Austrian delegation to Bonaparte's court from behind the scenes. They gather in Reims before entering Paris."

"I hope he's strong." John muttered, low.

But of course, Sincai heard him plainly. "I only hope he is willing to help us."

Asharti had found a new way to torture Beatrix. The bitch told long tales of what she did to John. The blood, the abasement, the forced sex with her and others; it went on and on. Asharti would go away for a few hours, only to come back with new tales, repeated breathlessly in front of the guards. They both knew John could last a long time now that his wounds healed almost instantly. Indeed, it was only Asharti's saliva that kept them from healing before she could suck. By the time she killed him he would probably be insane, one way or another. Asharti thought he would come to love his treatment at her hands. It happened. Surely that was one form of insanity.

The thought of John suffering almost indefinitely at Asharti's hand drove Beatrix wild. The thought that he might come to like it was even worse. She covered her ears, but of course she heard anyway. She paced or sobbed, she banged her head against the stone of the cell wall hoping pain would distract her from Asharti's endless horror stories. It did not.

When she realized that her reactions made Asharti relish the telling even more, she went quiet. She just sat, looking at her hands, letting all the emotions churn inside her with not a scrap of outward sign. If she found herself rocking, forward and back, forward and back, she stopped. If she found herself clenching her jaw she forced it to relax.

But the effort took its toll. She was so exhausted from the sunlight, so weak from feeding John, from lack of food, from the struggle not to concede Asharti any further emotion that finally she just went away. Her body might sit in a cell in the Conciergerie in Paris, but her mind was elsewhere. Her thoughts drifted to the night she had ridden in Hyde Park with John. They wafted over the night they made love, without blood, with only caring between them. He had returned for her, but that was because he hadn't fully compassed what she had made him. And now what she had made him simply drew his torture out. Sometimes she thought about second innocence, so pointless now. She would never know whether she could muster the courage for naïveté. She and John were both in hell. She would be released on Sunday. He would not.

Asharti told her she would see John again at her execution. A final torture. Still, she longed to see his dear face again before the blade came down. That was selfish. She knew it. But it would be one last sweet pain before she was released.

John and Sincai pulled up their horses in front of a grand hotel in the Rue Voltaire not far from the cathedral where all French kings had been crowned since Louis the Pious in 815, in the daylight of Sunday afternoon. They had heard bells pealing out in cascades across the countryside, calling the faithful from miles away. Now the streets were alive with social callers and workers on their single day of leisure. Two men in hooded cloaks provoked stares, but John was too tired to care. They placed their horses in the care of waiting ostlers. Once inside the dim luxury of the hotel, they threw back their hoods. John unwound his muffled face. Sincai had no need of mufflers, and seemed little affected by the sun. John wondered if it had to do with his age and his strength and tried vainly to remember if Beatrix had told him about that.

Sincai did not accost the grand personage who sat behind a small but ornate escritoire. He did not ask any of the myriad porters for assistance. He did not even mention the name of this Khalenberg they had come all this weary way to see. He simply stood. To John, he said, "Do not speak. You may anger him. He has no love for me and will have less for you."

John swallowed. Sincai seemed too concerned. Was he afraid? Hotel staff all stared at them, but no one dared approach. John was sure Sincai had lost his mind when from the first-floor balcony above them, a stern voice barked, "Well, you had better come up, Sincai."

John looked up to see a hawk-faced man with two iron-gray streaks at his temples in a head of black hair. His eyes were gray steel. The energy that cascaded down over the room said he was old. He frowned at John. "Bring your abomination with you."

Sincai nodded curtly and took the stairs lightly. John trudged up behind him. Khalenberg led the way past a large room full of expostulating men. John recognized Metternich. Khalenberg kept high political company. He opened the door on a small library. A single fierce look sent two portly gentlemen with cigars scurrying for another place to smoke.

Khalenberg turned on them. "What are you doing here, Sincai? And why do you think I will tolerate a made vampire?"

"Shall we say, the lesser of two evils?" Sincai asked calmly as he sat in a leather wing chair by the fire and motioned Khalenberg to the other. Neither offered John a chair, so he stood.

"Come to the point," Khalenberg snapped. "I have little time."

"Nor do we." Sincai paused as if to gather himself. John could not imagine what had possessed Sincai to think this hard man would help them. "I realize," Sincai continued, "that we once disagreed quite violently about allowing those made vampire to live."

"You are soft, Sincai. You always were." Khalenberg glanced to John with a sneer.

"Perhaps. I came round to your view in time."

"After that chit you found in the Levant went wild. I would have taken her head off myself if she hadn't gone to ground."

"She is back. And she is making many others about eighty miles from here."

Khalenberg went quite still. He glanced again to John. "Did she make that one?"

John flushed. " 'That one' is accidental." Sincai looked daggers at him for speaking.

Khalenberg snorted. "No such thing as accident."

Sincai interceded. "Beatrix's blood got into wounds Asharti made on him. Beatrix gave him the gift to save his life." Khalenberg scowled. He obviously did not care about the reason. "It was he who came to tell me Asharti has made a score or more of vampires. She is supporting Bonaparte that he might conquer Europe. She will make enough vampires to overpower us older ones, then take control from Bonaparte."

At that Khalenberg went white. "You mean by treating with Bonaparte, we are actually enabling this creature to her end?"

"And destabilizing our carefully constructed society," Sincai agreed.

"She must be stopped." Khalenberg's voice hardened even further.

"So Langley, here, thought," Sincai agreed. "He also thought I could do it alone, but in spite of his confidence, I am afraid there may be too many for me at this point."

"So you expect me to ally myself with this creature who is the epitome of everything I abhor?" Khalenberg did not deign to look at John.

"He has offered his head, before or after our little mission. Apparently he did not exactly covet Beatrix's gift. I chose to let him keep it for the nonce, since he may prove useful."

John was shocked to hear himself disposed of thus casually. But he clenched his fists and stayed silent. If Sincai thought they needed this man, then any way they got him to go along was fine, if only Sincai would not be so goddamned slow about it!

"Well," Khalenberg chuffed. He got a thoughtful look. "We should send to Rubius. He will gather the forces."

Sincai cleared his throat. "There is some little urgency to this matter. Asharti is using her newly made disciples to keep Beatrix in prison. She's going to have Beatrix guillotined."

Khalenberg paled, then flushed. John too felt his Companion rise in protest of this, the one sure way to death. Beatrix said the Companion spent its being fighting the death of its host. Khalenberg examined Sincai, then nodded. "Soft," he said almost to himself. "But she is one of us. We can't allow a made one to start killing the born." He took a breath. "When?"

"Tonight, I'm afraid."

"In Paris?" Khalenberg's bushy brows drew together over that hawk nose. "Too far to transport if we are to have any strength left for action when we get there."

"I would suggest fresh horses, and a certain amount of alacrity," Sincai remarked. John was ready to crack their heads if they did not get up this instant.

Khalenberg was mentally making the calculation John had made a thousand times in the last hours. "We can make it if they do the thing at midnight."

And if Asharti did it just after sundown, they would not.

Khalenberg looked for the first time at John. "He's exhausted."

John flushed, but brought his chin up to face the scrutiny.

Sincai sighed. "Unfortunate. Apparently Asharti was at him for a while before he got the gift. He was less than a week past the rejection sickness when he arrived in Amsterdam."

Khalenberg scowled. "In that case, he should be . . . wait! His vibrations are faster than one made so recently." Khalenberg turned on Sincai.

Sincai shrugged. "He knows where Beatrix is. That will save time. I gave him my blood."

"You shared your Companion with him?" Khalenberg sneered. "You *are* soft."

"A little old blood ensures we don't lose his knowledge. We can always remedy the situation later."

So Sincai did intend to kill him. Well, he wasn't sorry. And certainly Khalenberg wouldn't weep at his grave. Would Beatrix? She wouldn't have a chance unless they saved her.

"Very well. It is you and I then, Sincai." Khalenberg stood.

"Can we get going?" John asked, exasperated.

Khalenberg turned to him disdainfully, about to remark.

John cut him short. "And bring as much gold currency as you can muster."

"What?" Sincai and Khalenberg asked, both at once.

"If we get there too late to take her out of the prison, there will be a crowd. Unless you want everyone in Paris to see what you are, we will need a distraction." He turned on his heel and went to order fresh horses, leaving them to ponder that.

Shadows lengthened into twilight and Beatrix came back from the place away where she had been. She blinked, and looked around the familiar cell, wondering how she would bear Asharti's twisted stories one more time.

But the twilight deepened into night. No Asharti. Only the red eyes of her anonymous guards as they changed themselves with whispered words. What were they saying?

Ahhh. Tonight was the night. She had forgotten. The blade would at last silence Asharti's taunts. She imagined a jeering throng of thousands. They came to speculate whether the head held high knew what had happened to it, and to shudder as they realized there was only one way they could ever know for sure. Would Asharti bring John? Would it be a torture or a comfort to her? If she saw him, somehow she must let him know how much she loved him, how sorry she was that she had made him into something he had no wish to be.

Her eyes filled. Was she sorry she was about to die? She had lived so many, many years. She was sorry that in all that time, there had been only fleeting moments with John. If she could have made him love her . . . if he had not known what she was . . . if he had not gone after Asharti, or been infected with the Companion. He had come to save her out of his innate sense of honor, even though she had made him into a monster, not because he loved her. You could not make someone love you, at least she couldn't. She had not made her mother love her or Stephan. She had learned to be fascinating. But love? You could not coerce true love. You had to be worth it.

"Are you ready to meet your maker?"

Asharti's sneering contralto shocked Beatrix into the present. Asharti stood in the doorway to the cell block, dressed in old gold brocade, high-waisted with a heavy train that fell from the shoulders. Her sandals revealed gilt-painted toenails. She carried a fan, black swirling figures picked out with gilt. She clicked it shut and moved into the light. She had not brought John. Beatrix was half devastated, half relieved. She stared into Asharti's smug smile and said, "As ready as I can be," in a voice that was steadier than she felt.

"Into the tumbrel with you." Asharti motioned to a vampire who unlocked the bars.

Asharti was taking no chances. She added her power to the five pairs of red eyes around her. One of them was Jerry, but he had never spoken to Beatrix after that first night of his return. Beatrix felt herself go numb under the onslaught of power. That was good. They bound her hands with heavy rope, as though that was necessary, and Jerry looped a loose circle of rough hemp around her neck, by which she could be led. In a dream, she moved forward because they wanted her to move forward. She could not feel her bare feet on the stone. The walls wavered around her. Somewhere, Beatrix heard a dull roar of sound. As they wound through the prison the noise grew louder. Now they glided through the Gothic archways of the great hall, and the roar resolved itself into the shouting of a crowd. Asharti's minions threw the hoods of their cloaks up over their heads. They meant to conceal their red eyes from the crowd, Beatrix thought calmly, from a great distance away. Huge wooden doors swung open on pandemonium.

Lunging faces shouted for her head, or called out that she should be whipped, or made other, more provocative suggestions. Men and women, some with babes in arms, children and doddering old crones, humanity in all its ugly diversity, surged against a thin line of gendarmes and soldiers. The press of smell was overpowering; unwashed bodies, onions and garlic, the acid of urine, the smoke from torches dotting the crowd, all overlaid by the faint sweet scent of rain from the shower that had moved through sometime recently. In the center of this chaos stood a rough cart rocking behind a plunging horse. The boy at his head shouted at him to whoa with an opposite effect. It was a nightmare of violent emotion and flickering light.

A breeze from somewhere made the flame of the torches flap. Beatrix shivered. She wore only her fine gauze night shift. Some of the men's calls grew more generally lewd. Asharti was going to give them all a show, that was sure. Asharti turned her attention briefly to the chubby Percheron between the traces of the cart. The animal quieted immediately.

One of the vampires leapt into the cart and tugged at her rope. She pulled herself up by grasping the sides. Her rope was tied off to the back of the driver's bench seat. The vampires ranged themselves around the sides. Asharti walked in front, looking like a queen, as indeed she was in all but name. A drummer with a huge bass drum and a piper struck up a dirge hardly audible over the roar of excitement the crowd let out as the cart moved forward.

# Twenty-Three

John could no longer deny the twilight as they cantered through the village of Bagnolet. It must be close on nine o'clock. The clouds were streaked with that molten lava color no one believed in a painting. His mouth was set in a grim line. They had changed horses twice, but still their beasts were lathered. They had done the miles from Meaux at a gallop until the frequency of villages slowed them. Now the outskirts of Paris were before them. The tower of Notre Dame was a black outline against the streaked pink and orange clouds that made the sky seem green.

Pray to God the execution was not scheduled until midnight.

He was well aware that he was probably arranging a reunion of two lovers. He knew Sincai still cared for Beatrix. The Byzantine portrait was certain proof, even if the fact that he was living in her house was not. He was fairly certain Beatrix still loved Sincai. Oh, the man had hurt her. So she hurt him in return. All this talk of an experiment had blinded her to his true feelings for her. But they had been made for each other for seven hundred years.

He would grant fate that Sincai and Beatrix were made for each other. But he would not grant fate her death. When she was free, then he would stand back, and she would rediscover the feelings for Sincai she had been denying all these years. And he, John, would go his way alone, unless Sincai killed him. At that point it would not matter. It all seemed so clear, so inevitable.

John had been trying to keep his strength up for the last hour. Thank God for Sincai's blood or he would never have made it. The sun had been relentless. Though he had doused his head in a watering trough when they had changed horses at Chateau Thierry, still he was bone-weary. Sincai and Khalenberg seemed tireless. A trail of late laborers wending home crowded the entrance to the Pont de Bagnolet. One swung round to talk to his neighbor. John's attention had wandered and the laborer's hoe scraped the shoulder of John's horse. The creature shrieked and sidled.

"Come on," Sincai yelled over his shoulder. He and Khalenberg surged over the bridge.

John straightened in his saddle and kicked his horse forward. The beast leapt onto the stone bridge. The horse still had strength. The problem was John. He had to be there when they reached Beatrix. Sincai and Khalenberg might be so intent on killing made vampires they would miss the chance to save her. And they might be old, but he had spent his life in surreptitious action. He swallowed and decided. *Companion, give me enough strength to do what must be done,* he thought. Instantly a thrill of power glowed along his veins. The outlines of the small neat houses of Bagnolet lining the lane sharpened. He could smell the green and the rot of the huge cemetery of Père Lachaise off to his right, his own sweat, the leather of the saddle, the hot animal scent of horse. Dinners were being made in the houses around him. Onions and garlic cooked in butter. He took a long breath, feeling the strength come back to his aching body. Then the aches themselves faded. *Thank you,* he sighed internally. *Thank you for your gift.*

They galloped into the outskirts of Paris on the Rue de Bagnolet. The infernal carts and drays that had blocked their way turned to carriages. There were too many people on the streets for the hour. Everyone was hurrying, on foot, in carts and carriages, toward central Paris.

Sincai drew up. Khalenberg wheeled and came back when he saw Sincai drop behind.

"What do you think, Langley?" If Khalenberg was surprised that Sincai left it to John, he didn't show it. "Do we make for the Place du Trône?"

"She is being held in the Conciergerie," John panted. "But they moved the guillotine to the Place des Grèves. If we go straight down Rue Charonne through the Place de la Bastille we can hit the Place des Grèves before we reach the Conciergerie. That way we are sure."

Sincai nodded. "Remember, no display of power in front of the crowd. After it's over, we rendezvous at the north transept of Notre Dame, under the rose window." He turned his horse and spurred forward. John followed and Khalenberg brought up the rear.

The cart's progress was necessarily slow, since the soldiers in their bright red uniforms had to clear a way through the crowd. Was it so long since they had had an execution that everyone in the city must line the streets to see her go by? Peasants from the countryside and laborers, tradesmen and their women, trollops and thieves, but also gentlemen and ladies safely in their carriages, all made their way over the Pont au Change. Beatrix could hardly imagine the throng that must be crowding the square that held the guillotine.

She wavered in the jolting cart, staring ahead at Asharti's back, shutting out the shouts and taunts of the crowd. It was lonely here, standing straight in the cart, in spite of all the people around her. She should be used to that. The cart turned slowly onto the Quai des Gesvres. The Seine lapped at the stones to the right. The crowd surged ahead now, those on the riverside afraid of being pushed into the water. The cart made faster progress.

They turned left into a great square.

Beatrix jolted into awareness. The giant silhouette of the great machine in the center of the press of people rose like a tower, its diagonal blade gleaming in the light of a thousand torches.

They had moved Madame Guillotine to the Place des Grèves. A roar went up as the crowd spotted the tumbrel. The blood lust in the air was palpable. Elegant façades of buildings from previous centuries rose around the square. But the scene was dominated, not by the coarse crowd or the buildings, but by the wickedly simple elegance of Antoine Guillotine's invention.

Beatrix tried to breathe. Her neck prickled in anticipation. Her Companion stirred in protest, but it was weak. She beat it down.

The crowd made way for the tumbrel. Time seemed to race ahead. Beatrix had eyes only for the scene on the platform that held the end to a long, long run of years. A brawny man stood ready to pull the lanyard. Behind him a man in a uniform must be the lord high executioner. A wizened man in a severe blue coat held a large scissors with which to cut her hair. MM. Guillotine had touted his invention as the only humane way to execute a human being. A slither of metal as the heavy blade was released, one quick whack and it was over. The eyes might blink as the head was held high. The lips might move. But still, in the scheme of things it was only an instant, then nothing. She hoped it was nothing. She did not want to feel again, ever, even in an afterlife. Her wish might not be granted. She could burn in hell for what she had done with

Asharti. Whatever happened after death, she was about to find out.

The cart stopped at the base of the platform. The tall frame of the guillotine held its blade poised, high above her. Asharti stood right in front, gloating, her face inhuman in the flickering light. Beatrix didn't see John anywhere. Smoke from the torches wafted over the crowd. Their roar resolved itself into a chant. Beatrix could not make out the words.

Asharti motioned to the others. It was Jerry who cut Beatrix's rope and led her to the back of the tumbrel. She was lifted from the cart and set on her feet. Her knees were curiously weak. Jerry and another gripped her elbows and dragged her up the stairs. She jerked away.

"I am capable of walking to my death," she murmured, and hoped it was true. The power grew around her, as they thought she might attempt escape at the last moment. The executioner motioned to her to face the crowd. Asharti was front and center, her eyes gone red to ensure that Beatrix remained obedient. The man behind her twisted her hair in one hand. She could feel the scissors hacking through it. Was John being brought up perhaps from within the crowd? She scanned the throng. But no. He was not in evidence. She should be relieved. The sight of him enslaved by Asharti would have been unbearable. Why did she want to see him? Perhaps because she still didn't know why he had come back for her at the Conciergerie. Unless she saw his face, she would never know. Perhaps all she would see in his eyes was an accusation that she was abandoning him to Asharti through her death. But he was not here.

It was too late for anything.

"*Mademoiselle, ici.*" The executioner pointed to the place she should kneel.

She knelt. "Be certain of your stroke, sir," she managed with a fair amount of sangfroid.

"Your neck is delicate, mademoiselle," he said, with a professional assessment. "My blade will cut it like butter." He looked sorry, though. Perhaps he was no longer used to hacking off the heads of women who at least seemed young and innocent. She turned to face the crowd. Asharti stood smirking right below her. She could feel Jerry and the other vampire behind her.

The crowd hushed. In the corner of the square there was some commotion. Shouts. A woman yelled, *"Regardez-moi!"* Screams and the clatter of hooves.

The executioner stopped pushing her head down into the groove that waited for her neck and turned. *"Qu'est-ce que c'est?"* he asked no one in particular.

John spurred his horse straight into the milling crowd. There she was, kneeling at the guillotine! "Go for the vampires holding her," he shouted to the others. "I'll create a diversion!"

The executioner pushed her head down. The blade seemed to tremble in the torchlight, eager to descend. "No!" John yelled. The crowd swirled around him. He kicked at the nearest heads and shoved his way forward. His horse reared in fright. The crowd scattered in front of the flailing hooves. Even as the horse came down, he drove it forward into the gap and reached for the saddle-bag. He ripped it open and flung its contents up to his right. A fountain of gold glittered in the torchlight. The crowd gave an avaricious howl and lunged for the coins. Sincai shot through the gap they made. John drove forward. He flung the contents of the other bag into the air. Khalenberg pushed after Sincai. John had eyes only for the platform. He saw the executioner pause, glance toward the hubbub. Around him the crowd had descended into a snarling mass, tearing at each other to get the coins.

Sincai and Khalenberg pushed toward the platform, their figures surging above the crowd. John spurred his horse until it squealed and leaped forward, frothing in fright. Beatrix, so fragile and pale in her fluttering white shift, glanced toward him. Did she see him? He thought her mouth formed a silent "John." He raised his hand. "I'm coming," he shouted.

The press of the crowd around him grew more specific. Hands pulled at his boots.

*"Plus de louis,"* someone shouted, and they all took up the chant.

John glanced down. Hands scrabbled at him. The horse was going down on its knees. He threw the saddlebags themselves into the crowd. Those nearest him turned to watch the arc. The horse scrambled up. He pushed it on.

As he jerked his gaze back up to the platform, he saw the executioner push Beatrix down again. His shout nearly burst his throat. But it was lost in the roar of the crowd. He drove his spurs into the horse's flanks.

But now the crowd, angered that they were too far from the saddlebags to benefit, descended on him in earnest. The horse stumbled. Hands tore at him. As he fell into the seething mass, he saw that Khalenberg and Sincai were still too far to stop the executioner. To hell with showing the crowd their power, they should transport to the platform and kill the son of a bitch. Burned into his brain was an image of the lord high executioner reaching for the lanyard. The crowd closed over him, kicking him, tearing his clothes. Women scratched him, shrieking.

"Companion!" he shouted aloud. "For pity's sake . . ."

He did not complete the thought, for power came rushing down his veins. He surged up, flinging a burly man and two women away. He pushed through the crowd, growling. A red film descended on the scene. They gave way like the red sea. He could see the platform now. Beatrix laid her neck down, but she held her head up, searching the crowd. The executioner held the lanyard. The blade looked too heavy, too sharp, too inevitable to be real.

A voice from his nightmares shrieked, "Do it, you fools!"

There was Asharti, pointing at the executioner. For the first time he noticed that two vampires stood just behind Beatrix, with the man who held two feet of gleaming auburn hair. Khalenberg had a vampire by the neck at the base of the platform. Sincai lunged for Asharti.

John began to run, as in the slowness of a dream. He would never make it. *Companion!* The darkness whirled up. He tried to concentrate on the place just next to the executioner.

Through the blackness he saw the lord high executioner jerk the lanyard.

The great blade hissed down.

Too late!

John! It was John on the horse in the middle of the keening mob. Asharti did not have him! He had come for her! Not abandoned!

"John!" she called, but her voice was lost in the roar.

The lord high executioner pushed her head down. She felt the compulsion shower over her. She laid her neck in the notch on the block. But she didn't want to die. Not anymore. She called to her Companion. *One last time, my friend.*

There was no time to think more. She knew she was weak. She knew it was impossible, with Asharti's vampires damping her power. But she had to try. The surge along her veins said her Companion heard the urgency. *I am old,* she thought. *Older than any here but Asharti, I can do this.* She pulled her head up and searched the crowd for John.

That was when she felt the others. The vibrations of ones even older than she. She concentrated on drawing up the darkness. Inch by inch she pulled it from her veins. The scene before her went slowly red. She saw John go down in the crowd. *Distance yourself. You have your job.* Stephan appeared in the crowd below her, lunging for Asharti.

"Do it, you fool!" Asharti screamed, pointing at the lord high executioner.

She pulled against the power that had been dampening her life force for days.

Above her she heard a clunk as the executioner jerked his rope with a grunt.

A hiss.

*No! Companion!*

The curtain of power that held her slacked.

She jerked her head up.

The great blade thunked into its slot in the block, an inch from her nose. Its passing wafted a four-inch lock of auburn hair onto the breeze. Beatrix breathed in little convulsive gasps. The wall of sound beyond the blade held screams and terrible animal sounds, but they were all distant. Everything seemed to go on quite slowly. John appeared from nowhere, and pushed the lord high executioner off the platform into the crowd. Jerry stepped forward. She looked up at him, curiously. His eyes were not red. They were that pale blue she had seen in Dover. But they were no longer indecisive. They gave off a fierce glow. He had decided to let her go, in spite of Asharti, in spite of his own best interests. She was quite sure of that.

He smiled.

John threw himself down on his knees beside her and took her in his arms. She could hardly breathe, but it felt good not to breathe. His heart was beating wildly in his breast. He was saying something incoherent into her ear. "Yes," she soothed. "Yes."

A man with a hawk face ran up the stairs to the platform. Why, it was Khalenberg. He was covered in blood. Where was the other vampire who had stood behind her? Oh, there was his body. And his head? Yes, over there.

Khalenberg pulled Jerry around to face him. He grasped Jerry's head in both hands and simply twisted it off. Blood splattered her. Khalenberg tossed Jerry's head beside the other.

The crowd's noise rushed in on Beatrix. "You beast!" she screamed at Khalenberg, pulling out of John's embrace. "He saved my life."

"He was made," Khalenberg barked, and grabbed her arm. "Time to go."

She shook her head and pulled away. "John," she said. "John."

"Yes, yes. Come along, Englishman." Khalenberg's hand gripped her upper arm. Darkness whirled up. The stab of pain passed through her and the Place des Grèves disappeared.

John sputtered as the pain receded. The dim space of Notre Dame de Paris stretched around him. Above, the great rose window of the north transept was lifeless with night. Khalenberg and Beatrix stood in the center of the transept, getting their bearings. A second blackness rolled up directly under the window and resolved into Asharti and Sincai.

"Why do you bring her here, Sincai?" Khalenberg barked, as Sincai shook his head. Asharti tried to wrench away, spitting like a cat.

"Because she is my responsibility," Sincai answered calmly.

"Then dispatch her and be done with it." Khalenberg's voice held not a scrap of doubt.

"I'll see you both in hell first," Asharti hissed. She let her eyes go red.

"My dear, you aren't going anywhere." Sincai's eyes flashed and hers faded. "Not even hell, for the moment." Asharti went still, as she realized struggle was useless.

Sincai let go of her wrist. "Better and better. You are not beyond an intelligent assessment of the situation."

"She of any must be killed," Khalenberg said. His face was chiseled stone.

"It must be difficult to have no belief in redemption, old friend." Sincai still studied Asharti. "Beatrix? You know her better than any of us. Shall she die?"

John saw Beatrix go still. If it had been up to him he would have turned his thumb down and walked away without a backward glance while they tore Asharti's head from her body. Beatrix had just felt the effects of Asharti's evil. Why did she hesitate?

"I cannot judge her," Beatrix whispered. "As you say, she is your responsibility."

"I made a bad job of it, didn't I?" Sincai's clipped tone hid pain.

Beatrix looked at each of them in turn. Asharti's eyes were still defiant. "None of you cared what she went through as a human," Beatrix murmured. "She saw incredible atrocities. She was raped, hurt. She understood the suffering of the powerless. She couldn't bear the possibility that it could ever happen again. So the need for power consumed her. Is that so hard to understand?" She searched for answers in their eyes. "Is there no such thing as redemption?"

Asharti said nothing, gave her no help, made no defense. She stood erect and proud.

Beatrix took a breath. "So I say she lives."

Khalenberg turned away in disgust.

John felt a strange combination of emotion circle in his heart. Asharti would live and that made him afraid, but he was proud that Beatrix had the courage for mercy. In some ways, she was the most honorable, virtuous woman he had ever met. She took responsibility for him, when she had infected him with her blood. She took responsibility for

releasing Asharti. How strange to think that of a courtesan, a vampire who sucked human blood.

"So be it," Sincai intoned. "Perhaps she shall be redeemed, kitten. But I think a period of contemplation is
required." Sincai turned to Asharti. His voice grew implacable. "You will not be allowed to make vampires.
There will be no political machinations. I suggest forty
days and nights in the desert to start, or perhaps forty
years. I shall escort you, personally."

"Do . . . do you need help?" Beatrix asked, in a small
voice, flushing.

John steeled himself. He had known it would happen.
His job was to keep still.

Stephan came to stand over Beatrix. He pushed a lock
of hair, rudely chopped, from her forehead. "We must
talk." He glanced to Khalenberg. "Could I perhaps get
you to supervise our would-be empress?" he asked softly,
his eyes back on Beatrix.

Khalenberg made his lips into a thin line. But he didn't
protest.

Sincai didn't notice. "Come, kitten." He took her hand.

Beatrix looked up at him and followed him into the
darkness.

John swallowed and watched them go. There it was.
His die was cast. He would be left alone with his damnation. He took a breath. There was always the guillotine.
But at the mere thought of the sharp blade, his Companion surged inside him in protest. He shuddered in revulsion and knew he could never do the deed. Perhaps
Sincai's older blood had robbed him of the will to suicide
even as it gave him enough strength to reach the Place des
Grèves. Fair trade, on the whole; an eternity of damnation
for Beatrix's life.

# Twenty-Four

Beatrix followed Stephan down the nave of the church. Impossible weights of stone balanced on the arched tracery above them in the darkness. Churches were supposed to be places of contemplation, where you viewed your soul from a distance and knew what to do. She had never known less what to do, and there was nothing like calm in her soul.

What had happened? She had found the strength to resist death. John had come for her. Were the two linked? Jerry had died even though he saved her and she couldn't stop it. And Stephan, Stephan was here after all these centuries. John had brought him, but he had come. His dear face was somehow different than the one that lived in her memory, but now she had seen him she couldn't say how. Her thoughts caromed in her head. She loved him. He had thought her an experiment. She hated him for that. She didn't hate him now. How did she feel? Turning in the darkness, she saw John standing with his hands in his pockets, staring after her. If in the next minute Stephan said, "Come with me, kitten, it has always been you," what would she do?

She shook her head. Stephan wouldn't say that. And John didn't want a monster. He had come for her out of a sense of obligation, because she had rescued him from Asharti. If naïveté required strength, it also required opportunity.

"Bea . . ."

She turned at the sound of Stephan's voice. A smile trembled on her lips. Damn! She didn't want to tremble. "Stephan?" It was all she could manage.

"There are things that must be said."

She let out the breath she held. "What can need to be said after all this time?"

"You thought I didn't love you. But I did."

She started at the past tense. Vindication and regret mingled into something she could not absorb or understand. But she held her tongue.

"The hell of it was I wanted to love Asharti. I felt obliged to love her. But I didn't love her. Not the way I loved you. She knew it. That's why she hated me. That's why she had to take you from me. I realized that in time. I made her what she was. The fact that I didn't love her embittered her and turned her into the path she walks today."

Beatrix frowned. "You think *you* made her what she is? You are responsible for today only because you did not kill her. But her experience and her own tortured soul made her."

"She was damaged, I agree. But love could have healed her. I . . . couldn't, that's all."

She could feel his emotion strangling him. "That's why you never tracked her down."

"That's why I never tracked you down."

"What?"

"Because to love you was a betrayal of all I intended. I wanted to save her, and my love for you damned her." He took a ragged breath. "And my love for you was never fair or right."

"What do you mean?" If Stephan loved her it must have been right, mustn't it?

"You were young. I was very old. You fell in love with my experience. You would have outgrown me, Bea. In some ways Asharti did you a disservice. If you had come to it naturally we could have parted friends. You would not have spent the years wondering."

"Let's not go back to that whole thing about it being inevitable that I leave you."

"Was it not inevitable?"

*Was it not?* She stared at him. It was. He was her first love. But he was right. She was so young. Was that why he loved her? Would he have loved her when she was experienced, when she challenged him, when she came into her own? Could she have loved someone who did not?

He smiled in the darkness. The cathedral smelled like stone and dust. Somewhere water tinkled into the baptismal font.

"We can't come round to love again?" Her mouth said it before she thought the words.

He moved into her and put his arm around her shoulders. She leaned into him and he stroked her hair. Surprisingly, the feel of Stephan's body was warm, comforting. But it wasn't . . . electric. Not like John's. "Let us rather come round to the point we should have reached without Asharti," he said. "Let us be friends. You have your own love now . . ."

She glanced over her shoulder to John, standing, so dejected, under the rose window in front of Khalenberg and Asharti. She squinched her eyes shut. "He will never love a monster. Especially one who made him a monster, too."

"Nonsense. He's wild for you," Stephan said. "He was ready to brave the den of the devil himself, in this case, me, in order to save you. Hell, he mastered his revulsion enough to drink a cup of my blood, just to be sure he didn't fail you. He volunteered his life, if I required he give it up in order to go after you. Don't tell me that isn't love."

She was so confused. She had always loved Stephan, hated Stephan, loved Stephan. But she didn't anymore. She had outgrown him. "John isn't you. He's just . . ."

"Just the man you made vampire. He is the first, isn't he?"

She nodded into his shoulder.

"Surely you know why you made him." Stephan's voice was gentle.

She glanced up, remembering how she could not imagine a world without John in it. Stephan was staring at the cathedral's vaulted arches. She couldn't see his eyes. "Do you believe in love, Stephan? I mean, that it can really last for us?"

"Absolutely, kitten. I believe in love." She could hear his sincerity. He meant it with all his soul. "Now, go and make yourselves happy. The poor devil is looking quite forlorn." He let her go and gave her a gentle push.

She turned to him, still uncertain.

"Take the leap of faith, kitten. You'll see." There was an expression in his eyes she couldn't read, and she thought she had seen every expression in the world.

She smiled. "Thank you, Stephan. You are still the wise one." She reached up and kissed him on the cheek.

And then she turned and walked toward John.


John watched Beatrix come toward him, Sincai trailing behind her. What had he seen? Sharp as his hearing was, he could not make out their words. The immense emptiness seemed to eat them. Beatrix was smiling. She fairly glowed, though she was incredibly pale. She was like a bride who had just taken her vows. His heart clenched.

"I trust you are now ready to shoulder your responsibility, Sincai, or do you need me to play nursemaid a little longer?" Khalenberg's voice rasped out behind John.

"I am," Sincai said. He had the strangest expression on his face. John had never seen another like it. Regret, courage, incredible will, all mingled there in a complex mélange. How different from the emptiness John had first seen in his eyes. Did he regret leaving Beatrix to discharge his duty? Of course. But had they cemented their commitment to return to each other? Beatrix's expression said she had been fulfilled somehow. She was . . . sure.

"What about your other obligation?" Khalenberg jerked a head in John's direction.

Sincai turned his old, full eyes on John. "Langley is not my responsibility but Bea's. She will decide his fate."

Khalenberg threw up his hands. "Soft! All of you."

Sincai moved back to Asharti and put his arm around her shoulders like an iron clamp. A blackness began to grow around them. "Eradicate her leavings, Khalenberg."

Khalenberg's lips thinned, his disapproval of the fact that Beatrix would obviously not kill John writ large across his face. He nodded curtly to Sincai. "The blood is the life."

"The blood is the life," Sincai echoed from the whirling black around him and Asharti.

"Nooooo," Asharti wailed. "I won't be exiled." But the echo back from the stone in the dark immensity of the cathedral was the only thing left of them.

Khalenberg nodded crisply to John. "I will be watching you." The darkness swirled around him and he was gone.

John stared at Beatrix, standing in her bare feet and a night shift in the cavernous dark of the cathedral. Her pale skin glowed. Her auburn hair reminded him of banked coals. It stood out about her head in soft disarray like the corona in the picture Sincai had kept for all those centuries. She stared at him with big dark eyes, so vulnerable, so uncertain. The shell of the experienced courtesan lay broken around her, and what was left was a woman who had the courage to free her nemesis and his, who had come within a handbreadth of death when death was something foreign to her, not her destiny, who had seen her first love disappear from her life a second time in a whirl of blackness. She must be devastated at the separation, even if it was temporary. But . . . she looked so sure. She was strong now, with Sincai's love.

His entrails shrank within him. But he had to say something. He cast about and steeled his features. "I . . . assume congratulations are in order? It must be distressing to be separated from him just when you have been reunited."

Suddenly all her sureness dissolved. She examined his face like an ancient soothsayer must have examined a sheep's liver. For a long moment she said nothing. Then she wet her lips and took a breath. "She told me she had you captive, you know," she whispered. "She told me endless stories of what she had done to you. I thought I would lose my mind."

John's heart stuttered. He too licked his lips. He mustered his courage. And then he couldn't say it. "You . . . you were honorable to let Sincai take her away instead of killing her."

"She lived through the taking of Jerusalem in the First Crusade. I think . . . she was not the same after that. Atrocities seemed unimportant, even demanded by the world of the strong."

"It is you who were strong." His hands clenched at his sides, nails biting into his palms.

Tears welled into her eyes as she stood there, swaying on her feet. She shook her head convulsively, her mouth mobile, whether in smile or sob he not tell. "No. No. I was weak enough to want the blade for a while . . ." She put a hand to her forehead. "Strength," she muttered. She looked up. "I must know . . . why?" The word seemed torn from her.

"Why?" Panic beat at him. What did she mean?

"Why did you come for me?"

It was all here in one roll of the dice. Let his legendary luck not desert him now. He could not admit what he wanted from her. He could only confess his own naïveté. "Because I love you." He ground his teeth together against the tears that welled in his own eyes. "I know it's stupid of me. Crass. I should not speak of it when you have just rediscovered your own love."

He stopped, not knowing how to go on, the emotional pitch between them so intense it seemed to fill the empty, echoing space of the cathedral.

She reached a hand across the space that separated them. Then to his shock, she wavered and folded in on herself. Her head hit the stone hiding countless crypts in the cathedral floor.

John lunged forward. "Beatrix!" He skidded to his knees beside her and reached for her throat. Her pulse beat back at him. She had fainted. As well she might. She had nearly been decapitated. He had distressed her pointlessly with his confession. He gathered her into his arms and carried her through the stone tracery of the decorated choir. There, under the Gothic arches, were ornately carved wooden benches, set with pillows embroidered, no doubt, by local widows. It felt familiar, somehow, as though he had dreamed it somewhere before. He laid her out and slipped his arm under her head. "Beatrix," he whispered, willing her to consciousness. "Beatrix."

She stirred in his arms, gasping for breath, and he held her tenderly. "You are fine. You're safe now. It's over."

"So stupid of me. It's only that I haven't fed. And I was weakened . . ." She trailed off.

He knew why she was weak. She had not fed since she had given him blood. Bloody hell! "We can remedy that here and now," he said, loosening his cravat.

"No," she protested. "I can't take from you . . ."

"Who better?" he whispered, kissing her cheek softly.

"Share and share alike. I have Sincai's blood. It's very strong. I'm more than able to give a little." She was so needy, she might well drain him. It didn't matter. He would be glad to be drained by her.

She moaned a little. He knew she felt the blood throbbing in his arteries and her Companion demanded of her. He tossed his neck cloth to one side, and pulled open his collar. He held her head to his throat, counting on her Companion to make sure she could not resist. He swallowed. She breathed a weak protest as her canines, distinctly sharp, scraped his neck over his carotid. "It's all right," he murmured.

"No," she protested distinctly, then he felt the pain of penetration and she was sucking at him.

"The blood is the life," he whispered. He cradled her body against his own, feeling her breasts free and pressed against his chest, his palm cupping her buttocks. His loins tightened and his member rose. God in heaven, but he wanted her, even though she loved another! He gritted his teeth, ashamed for his body's response when she was weak and needed blood.

Beatrix felt his blood revive her. The sweet satisfaction of pulling at his strong throat translated itself into wetness between her legs. Feeding from John felt sexual. She could feed without having sex, unlike Asharti. She knew that now. She had done it for six hundred years. But with John it was different. Everything with John felt sexual, alive, as her Companion demanded life. And that did not seem wrong. Was she lying to herself?

His blood, his selfless offering, the feel of him against her, all settled in her throbbing core. He told her he loved her. He had not abandoned her. Beatrix was acutely aware of the thick flow of life in her throat, John's hand on her buttocks and cradling her head. Against her thigh a rising hardness said he felt the pull of life as well. Her Companion surged up, showering vibrant power over her. She pushed her hips against John's thigh and his erection, all the while sucking rhythmically. This was not like Asharti. She opened her eyes. John's head was thrown back to bare his throat to her, his own eyes closed in an ecstasy of giving.

She gasped once, twice, as she tried to get control. She must not take so much! He was new, even though he had Stephan's blood. She pulled her teeth from his flesh with a little cry. Two tracks of red wound down his neck from the wounds she had made. She licked them away and watched the circles close. She glanced up and saw him looking down at her. His eyes were liquid heat. His blood revived her. And with returning strength she felt her other need grow.

"Beatrix," he breathed, and brushed her forehead with his lips. It sent shivers down her spine and directly into that point of pleasure now infused with the Companion. The Companion ever strove toward life. And what more final proof of life than sexual congress? She had been wrong about what made Asharti who she was, and what made her different.

Swallowing, John pulled himself away and laid her on the cushioned bench. A broken smile touched his lips. "Apologies, Countess. I was carried away." He turned away in shame.

She reached to touch his face. "I'm not sure you understand. Stephan doesn't love me anymore. He set me free." She smiled. "And I haven't loved him for a long time. I might not have known it, but it was true. Tonight I choose you, John Staunton." It felt wonderful. It felt naïve. She chose to love him. She drew his hand to the place where her arteries throbbed in her neck. Blood. The blood is the life. She could feel his urgency ranged against his reluctance. He was afraid to believe.

But the dam broke. He took her in his arms. The hips that moved so slightly against her thigh, pressing hardness against her, said he wanted this as much as she did.

He was kissing her, and she opened her mouth to his searching tongue. She reached for the buttons over the bulge in his trousers. He kissed her neck and breasts as he lifted her shift above her hips.

She arched into him, signaling her approval of the feel of his lips on her nipples under the gauze. He pulled at her left nipple softly. She pushed his trousers down over his hips and reveled in the silken skin of his cock against her thigh. Yes. That was what she wanted. She ran her palms over both buttocks, feeling the muscles bunch under her hands. The mystery of John Staunton, Earl of Langley, was how she could stand the next few moments until he put that cock inside her. Her Compánion demanded it, and so did his. Good. The Companion's need would wipe out any lingering taint of Asharti for them both. He needed to get back the positive energy that lovemaking was meant to impart. Giving and taking in balance. She slid one hand between them and gently stroked his cock. She felt him shudder. Then she moved down to the root, cupped his balls and rubbed right where the two joined.

"God in heaven, Beatrix," he gasped.

"We are in the right place for that," she murmured, glancing at the mingled gargoyles and cherubim carved above them. It struck her that those figures represented the mix of life; good was mixed with . . . not evil, but at least imperfection. She was imperfect. So was he. So would their love be. Could it be any other way?

His chest heaved. "Is this blasphemy?"

Her hands continued their massage. "I think this is the primal urge toward life," she murmured as he groaned. "God made the world in seven days. He must have felt it."

He bent to her lips, his tongue probing. She ran her thumb over the tip of his cock and slid the moisture there over it. He pulled himself out of her hands. He must be close to coming. She let him slow the pace, if one could call it slow. He slipped his hand between her legs and slid his fingers through her wetness over her point of pleasure. She lifted his shirt and pressed herself against his bare chest. He seemed to know the instant when she could stand it no longer. He touched her knees. She opened. He lay between them and slipped inside her.

The rhythm of their movement was like feeding at his throat. It crescendoed into a single ritual that embodied life itself. Beatrix hurtled over the edge into some contraction or expansion of the soul that approached nirvana. Somewhere she felt John pulsing inside her as she contracted around him. The cathedral was filled with small moaning, grunting sounds that existed before the world was born and would exist after it was a burned-out coal.

They lay there on the choir bench, in disarray. Beatrix wasn't sure how long. The quiet of the church was far from the earlier roaring crowds. The horror of the blade receded.

"Beatrix," John breathed against her breast. "Thank you."

"Thank you?" She smiled lazily. "I should thank you."

He shook his head, ever so slightly, and then, unable to resist, licked her nipple where her shift had torn. "You, who have had a thousand men, must think me poor sport." He raised his head, struck, and she saw him pull back. He sat up. "I mean, well, I suppose for one who was taught by Stephen Sincai, and who has been famous for . . . for her skills . . . I . . . I am sorry that it did not work out between you. I realize I am your responsibility. However, I hope your duty will not be too onerous. I'll find a city. And I will never presume upon your . . . kind impulse here tonight. After Sincai has settled Asharti—"

She sat up and touched a finger to his lips. How could he doubt her? But she had not actually told him that she loved him. She had said she chose him. He might think it was only for the moment. His confusion was comforting. It said more clearly than any bald statement could exactly why he had come for her at the Conciergerie, and again at the Place des Grèves. For the first time in a long time, she was glad of her experience of men. "Do you know how long it has been since I made love to a man, John, before you? Not feeding, but making love?"

There was the most delightful crease of worry between his brows as he shook his head.

"Six hundred years."

She waited to let that sink in. Then she pressed on, more boldly. "You said you loved me. For some men that is only a way to sexual pleasure. Do you want me for more than intercourse?"

He flushed, then went pale. "If I can amuse one of your experience for a few years, I . . ." He actually looked down. "I would be grateful."

She took a breath and closed her eyes, tears filling them for the second or third time tonight. In truth, it might be no more than he suggested, a few years in a long life. She might not be worth loving for very long. She could lie to him and promise him forever. Or she could devastate him by telling him the truth. But what was truth? Was it true that they couldn't make it last? Stephan thought they could. And she would not fail to try even if she felt the pain of all her abandonment telling her she wasn't worth it.

But in truth, Stephan had loved her. It was she who abandoned him. He told her so tonight. Should she feel guilty, or was that a single permutation of the many possibilities there had been for their love? And Asharti? She walked out on Asharti in the end. That should have been the beginning of healing for a wound first made by her mother and her mother alone. Maybe it was. It had only taken six hundred years. That first abandonment might have colored her vision for centuries. It might have brought the darkness. Everything she had believed was upside down.

All she could do now was vow to have the courage to be naïve.

Her breath came shallowly. Could she say it? Could she not? "I guess I'll hazard my chance with Blake," she whispered, "and say I love you, John, for however long it lasts."

"Second innocence?" he asked, his expression saying he almost feared to believe her.

She nodded. "Will you hazard with me?"

He let out a breath and relaxed as though it was an effort. His eyes softened. A tiny smile touched the edge of his lips. "I'm devilish lucky."

She smiled. A sureness glowed inside her. "So am I."

"So that's it, then?" He swallowed and took her in his arms. She felt his heart throbbing in his breast, his blood coursing through his veins laden with the Companion who would give them forever whether they could pluck the fruit together or not. The risk felt good.

She took his shoulders, sat back and angled her head. "England?"

He shook his head. She realized there was still too much pain there for him. His former life was no longer possible. She saw him gather himself. He lifted his chin. "Khalenberg pulls the strings in Austria. Perhaps he can convince Boney an invasion of Russia is a good idea."

She smiled tenderly at him. His idealism in the face of all he had seen was one of the things she loved about him. "You mean to give Europe back to the people, I see. Tricky business. And I shall have to put up with politics, won't I?"

"One has to try." He said it quietly, and it meant so much about how they would live their lives together, and what they would try to do in the world.

"You have a hunger in you, John Staunton, which I find admirable. So second innocence it is," she agreed. "Anything is possible."

He wrapped his arm around her and they walked under the choir screen and out into the transept. "Reims and Khalenberg first, then, and after that, who knows?"

# Coming in April 2006

*New York Times* bestselling author of
*The Hunger*
## Susan Squires

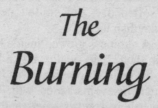

*The*
# Burning

There is a world that comes alive at night and thrives on our darkest secrets and longings. In this world, a young woman finds a man who satisfies her every desire. He can save her or destroy her—but he will nourish her as no one has before...

"Susan Squires has a fascinating, unique voice; she is a rare talent."

—Christine Feehan

"A darkly compelling vampire romance...the plot keeps the reader turning the pages long into the night."

—*Affaire de Coeur* on *The Companion*

From St. Martin's Paperbacks

ISBN: 0-312-99855-4

Visit www.susansquires.com

# Carnival Pride℠
## April 2 - 9, 2006.

## 7 Day Exotic Mexican Riviera Itinerary

| DAY | PORT | ARRIVE | DEPART |
|-----|------|--------|--------|
| Sun | Los Angeles/Long Beach, CA | | 4:00 P.M. |
| Mon | "Book Lover's" Day at Sea | | |
| Tue | "Book Lover's" Day at Sea | | |
| Wed | Puerto Vallarta, Mexico | 8:00 A.M. | 10:00 P.M. |
| Thu | Mazatlan, Mexico | 9:00 A.M. | 6:00 P.M. |
| Fri | Cabo San Lucas, Mexico | 7:00 A.M. | 4:00 P.M. |
| Sat | "Book Lover's" Day at Sea | | |
| Sun | Los Angeles/Long Beach, CA | 9:00 A.M. | |

*ports of call subject to weather conditions*

---

## TERMS AND CONDITIONS

**PAYMENT SCHEDULE:**
50% due upon booking
Full and final payment due by February 10, 2006

Acceptable forms of payment are Visa, MasterCard, American Express, Discover and checks. The cardholder must be one of the passengers traveling. A fee of $25 will apply for all returned checks. Check payments must be made payable to **Advantage International, LLC** and sent to: **Advantage International, LLC, 195 North Harbor Drive, Suite 4206, Chicago, IL 60601**

**CHANGE/CANCELLATION:**
Notice of change/cancellation must be made in writing to Advantage International, LLC.

**Change:**
Changes in cabin category may be requested and can result in increased rate and penalties. A name change is permitted 60 days or more prior to departure and will incur a penalty of $50 per name change. Deviation from the group schedule and package is a cancellation.

**Cancellation:**

| | |
|---|---|
| 181 days or more prior to departure | $250 per person |
| 121 - 180 days prior to departure | 50% of the package price |
| 120 - 61 days prior to departure | 75% of the package price |
| 60 days or less prior to departure | 100% of the package price (nonrefundable) |

**US and Canadian citizens are required to present a valid passport or the original birth certificate and state issued photo ID (drivers license). All other nationalities must contact the consulate the various ports that are visited for verification of documentation.**

<u>**We strongly recommend trip cancellation insurance!**</u>

**For complete details call 1-877-ADV-NTGE or visit www.AuthorsAtSea.com**

---

## This coupon does not constitute an offer from St. Martin's Press LLC

For booking form and complete information
go to <u>www.AuthorsAtSea.com</u> or call 1-877-ADV-NTGE

Complete coupon and booking form and mail both to:
**Advantage International, LLC,**
**195 North Harbor Drive, Suite 4206, Chicago, IL 60601**